THE BOY
WITH PERFECT HANDS

Titles by Sheldon Rusch

FOR EDGAR
THE BOY WITH PERFECT HANDS

THE Boy WITH Perfect Hands

SHELDON RUSCH

BERKLEY PRIME CRIME, NEW YORK

THE BERKLEY PUBLISHING GROUP
Published by the Penguin Group
Penguin Group (USA) Inc.
375 Hudson Street, New York, New York 10014, USA
Penguin Group (Canada), 90 Eglinton Avenue East, Suite 700, Toronto, Ontario M4P 2Y3, Canada
(a division of Pearson Penguin Canada Inc.)
Penguin Books Ltd., 80 Strand, London WC2R 0RL, England
Penguin Group Ireland, 25 St. Stephen's Green, Dublin 2, Ireland (a division of Penguin Books Ltd.)
Penguin Group (Australia), 250 Camberwell Road, Camberwell, Victoria 3124, Australia
(a division of Pearson Australia Group Pty. Ltd.)
Penguin Books India Pvt. Ltd., 11 Community Centre, Panchsheel Park, New Delhi—110 017,
India
Penguin Group (NZ), Cnr. Airborne and Rosedale Roads, Albany, Auckland 1310, New Zealand
(a division of Pearson New Zealand Ltd.)
Penguin Books (South Africa) (Pty.) Ltd., 24 Sturdee Avenue, Rosebank, Johannesburg 2196,
South Africa

Penguin Books Ltd., Registered Offices: 80 Strand, London WC2R 0RL, England

This is an original publication of The Berkley Publishing Group.

This is a work of fiction. Names, characters, places, and incidents either are the product of the author's imagination or are used fictitiously, and any resemblance to actual persons, living or dead, business establishments, events, or locales is entirely coincidental. The publisher does not have any control over and does not assume any responsibility for author or third-party websites or their content.

First edition: September 2006

Library of Congress Cataloging-in-Publication Data

Rusch, Sheldon.
    The boy with perfect hands / by Sheldon Rusch.
        p. cm.
    ISBN 0-425-21172-X
    1. Policewomen—Illinois—Fiction.   2. Serial murder investigation—Fiction.   I. Title.

PS3618.U74B69   2006
813'.6—dc22

                                                                2006011544

PRINTED IN THE UNITED STATES OF AMERICA

10   9   8   7   6   5   4   3   2   1

CHAPTER 1

HAVING a June birthday usually meant you could sleep with the windows open on the night of your special day. At least in the part of the world Elizabeth Taylor Hewitt called home. There were exceptions, of course, on the nineteenth of June. Early season air conditioner days, when the whole of the Midwest would submit to the sun's early summer heat without the saving grace of the northwesterly airflow that brought cool Canadian breezes to their lawns, their front porches, their closed eyelids as they slept.

Hewitt's eyes were open. She rolled her face a quarter-turn to the clock-radio on the night stand. It was 1:54. Her special day had been over for nearly two hours. Having been an evening baby, however, her true birthday—the twenty-four hours of it—wouldn't be over until 6:42 P.M. Almost another seventeen hours. But who the hell was counting? Who the hell would keep track of such personal almanac details other than a very bored or obsessive-compulsive God?

Well, for starters, birthday girls who were still a little too wound up to sleep.

Having a man in bed with her wasn't exactly helping. Her queen-sized mattress was less than a year old. At the time of the purchase, she had decided to keep her old box spring. To save a few bucks. Problem was it had started to creak. And pretty badly. Which was kind of a carnal kick when you were using the bed for recreational purposes. But a metallic pain in the ass when you and your guest entered the tossing and turning hippodrome of actual sleep.

Brady Richter didn't seem to be bothered by the box spring noise. He was out cold, on his back, breathing heavily but not quite qualifying as snoring. Not yet. Hewitt knew she could still wake him up if she had to. But once he drove his somnambular pickup truck into Snoresville, there wouldn't be much she could do with him.

Except, maybe, *decorate* him. Moments earlier she had theorized that she could do something like—*go so far as*—tying a piece of red birthday ribbon around his joystick without Brady Richter ever missing a beat of deep-breathing slumber. To prove a point. To herself, first. Maybe to him later. The point? That she was still a wild, fun-loving woman who was capable of doing almost anything. Even at thirty-eight. *Especially* at thirty-eight.

It was certainly doable. She had access. Brady was lying right next to her, face-up. She had motive. Sort of. And she had the ribbon right there on the floor, with the box and the wrapping paper and the tissue paper and the gift itself, the present from Brady which she first thought of as goofy, but which she now held as dear to her as she'd held Brady's ass in her hands an hour earlier.

Somewhere in some old attic, in some forgotten trunk or toy box, some rummage sale archaeologist had stumbled upon a vintage Elizabeth Taylor paper doll and clothing ensemble. A digital picture here, a scan there, and the deluxe set of it all had made its way to eBay. And one Detective Brady Richter of Wilmette, Illinois, had been the lucky high bidder.

Hewitt rolled onto her side, reached to the floor, felt the box, the tissue paper. The back of her hand brushed the red ribbon. She poked inside the box, found the flat plastic sleeve in which the doll and its outfits had been catalogued. She lifted the sleeve and its contents from the box, rustling the paper, but Brady didn't stir. Nor did the creaks from the box spring appear to nudge his consciousness as Hewitt settled back into the bed and reached for the reading light on the nightstand.

The light was the kind you could clamp on the back cover of a book and adjust to direct the spray of light wherever you needed. Hewitt took the light and set it on the mattress, midpoint between herself and the sleeping body beside her. She positioned the tiny lamp to illuminate the space just above her chest before she reached into the plastic bag and extracted the curvy figure of Elizabeth Taylor.

Hewitt held Little Liz up in the light. All seven or so inches of her, looking radiant in a surprisingly racy one-piece undergarment, periwinkle blue, with a yellow braid pattern down the sides. With yellow and blue slippers to match. Given the year of the doll's production, 1957, the undergarment was especially racy. All those years Little Liz had been waiting for someone who would truly love her, not for the sexy way she looked in her underwear, but for who she really was. A paper doll with an attitude.

Hewitt's dad had fallen in love with the real Liz when he'd seen her in *Cleopatra*. And that had been enough to convince him, years later, to brand his daughter as part of the franchise. But *Elizabeth Taylor Hewitt* did have a certain flair to it. Even after thirty-eight years.

Nearly four decades of water under that bridge. And from her view from the top of the bridge and her frequent dives into the water below, she had seen almost everything, every kind of effluent Old Man River had been able to serve up. The sweet waters of her early childhood. The river of tears that came with the death of each parent. The murky, bloody tea the universe served up with every homicide that came calling on her for, if not a perfect answer, at least the right morally outraged questions.

Hewitt tightened her fingers on the thin waist of Little Liz, felt an utterly inane urge to hug the paper doll in the cold, shuddering vacuum created by the last of her thoughts. But you couldn't really do that, could you? You couldn't really hug a paper doll.

Well, fuck it. She had something to hug now. For the first time in a long time she had something to hug that would hug her back without stipulations and, more importantly, without any hint of desperation. Fully grown people clinging to each other was never a good idea, was always the telltale indicator of the craziness to come.

It was what children did. Clinging to a parent. If they were lucky, two. But parents had a way of exiting in the first or second act of the play. What did you have to cling to then? A lover here or there. And when lovers were gone, you were left to snuggle up with the inflatable doll of a career.

Part of her career was lying next to her in the bed. Brady Richter was a real cop. Or at least more of a real cop than she would ever be again. But he was younger. He hadn't seen some of the shit she had. He hadn't gone inside and taken up residence in the shit like she had.

Maybe that's why he could sleep like this, while she was lying there next to him, clinging to a paper doll.

Brady had crossed the line now. He was deep in the center of the Snoring Zone. She would have to execute the little rollover push to get him to sleep on his side. But not for another minute or two.

Hewitt relaxed her grip on Little Liz, let her hand find the edge of the bed. She lowered the paper doll into the trappings of the box, her nervous system once again informing her of the tactile details of each element.

With her body parts all firmly returned to the bed, she used her hands to direct the beam of the reading light to her bunkmate. His big sleeping face on the pillow. His closed eyes peaceful as a baby's. His jaw square and a little too tight. The stubble of his beard already in serious need of a morning shave.

She adjusted the light, ran the beam down the shape of him beneath the sheet, this little searchlight in the prison yard of creme cotton.

CHAPTER 2

MUSIC didn't play in his house. Not at this time of night. And definitely not music like this.

It was piano. *Piano*. Coming from downstairs.

Del Rasmussen sat up in bed, sat up faster than the two herniated disks in his low back had allowed him to sit up in years. A shot of adrenaline through the bloodstream could do that. Music in his house in the middle of the night could do that.

His shoulders relaxed a little then and his lumbar became a few degrees less rigid. He sighed. His *Ah, shit* sigh.

Maggie. This was her doing. When she'd been over that afternoon, he'd seen his four-year-old granddaughter futzing around with the boom box in the living room. The one Maggie's mom had given him for his birthday, with the Chicago Bears helmet sticker she'd put on to personalize it. She'd even pretuned it to the AM station its DJs referred to as *The Home of the Bears*.

Little Maggie had done this. She'd futzed with the buttons and somehow programmed the Goddamn wake-up alarm that was built into the thing for a reason he never quite got. And somehow in the futzing, she'd set it to a different station. A station that played this kind of music. Classical music.

The Home of the Beethovens, he said in his head.

As part of the futzing, Maggie had also jacked up the volume. Enough to have jacked his bad back up from bed.

Del Rasmussen made his way to the hallway, a great big bear in underwear, walking on the carpet that led to the staircase. *To turn off the Goddamn radio. To turn off the Goddamn piano.*

Ah, what the hell. It was Maggie. Hard to be mad at a four-year-old kid. Hard to be mad at her. With Claire gone now, the little girl was one of the things that kept his world warm. So maybe it was okay. Maybe it was good. On a cool June night, with the windows open and just one body in the big bed upstairs, maybe this piano music made possible by his granddaughter was some kind of blessing he would understand only at the end of his life.

In the downstairs hallway, the bones of his feet making their little muffled cracking sounds against the wood floor. The music pretty damn loud now. The piano pretty damn loud. Loud enough that the thought struck him that if he turned into the living room and saw someone in the middle of the room playing a piano, it would've been crazy only for the fact that he and Claire had never owned one. But as he entered the living room, there was, of course, no such thing. Just the big room asleep in the dark. Except for the little green and red lights of the boom box. And the piano coming from its speakers.

Moody piano. A piece, at first, he thought he'd never heard before. But now, right here with it in the living room, sounding more familiar. Either way, it was the middle of the night, time to turn the damn thing off. And that's exactly what he would have done if he hadn't felt the nest of hairs on the back of his neck ruffle, prickle, as if some ice-cold insect had just run across that part of him.

Instinct turned him in the direction of what that same instinct had already told him was the presence of another living creature in the room. In the fraction of a second that passed before fear flooded his brain, two thoughts flashed against the dark screen of his mind. The first, that the green and red lights from the boom box were enough to illuminate a young woman sitting in his rocking chair. The second, that she was asleep. And as the rivers of dread met at his heart, his mind flashed another bulletin.

She was sleeping with her eyes open.

CHAPTER 3

HEWITT ignored the first three rings of the call. But since it was the line responsible for wake-up and other calls of intercession from ISP headquarters, and being that HQ would be calling only if something calamitous had gone down while Hewitt was asleep, she picked up on four. As she lifted the cell phone to her sleep-numb face, Brady Richter began to fumble and kick his way out of sleep—like some newborn calf trying to stand for the first time.

The sound of anything on this line other than Captain Ed Spangler's voice was something Hewitt was still adjusting to. The fact that the voice belonged to Captain Richard Lattimore made the adjustment all the more of a scramble. Where Spangler had been the surrogate father, Lattimore was showing every dark sign of the classic evil stepfather.

"Another young woman's turned up at a wayside, Hewitt. In Du Page County."

From a crackle of intercom in the background, she could tell he was in his office. At 7:04. On a Friday morning. Couldn't wait to get the hell out of his dysfunctional house and into the more controllable chaos of ISP Homicide.

"MO's like the first one. The picnic table. The display. But now it's two different counties. So it's our jurisdiction. It's *your* jurisdiction."

Hewitt ran down the case file in her mind, saw the photographs of the first victim. Jenna Neuheisel. Doe-eyed dishwater blonde with straight teeth and a slightly asymmetrical mouth.

Next to Hewitt, the baby calf had gotten his legs under him. Brady was awake, and with that would come some information to his own hotline, information that would get his own head cooking.

"Do you have a description of the victim?" Hewitt heard her morning voice query.

"Yeah," Lattimore said. "Hits all the same buttons as the first victim. Definitely part of the glee club."

Kind of a prickly way to put it, Hewitt thought. But that was all part of the stepfather matrix. And on that subject—prickly—Brady was waking up to the reality of something he'd never experienced before. At least she hoped he hadn't.

In her ear, Lattimore was giving her the details of the location of the wayside in Du Page where a crime scene unit was already in full exploratory mode. While she wrote down the coordinates, she could see Brady was in full exploratory mode too.

"What the hell, Hewitt?" his morning voice croaked.

Hewitt pushed the meat of her thumb over the receiver grill on the phone, in time. She didn't need her stepfather to have a sleepover thing to add to her dossier.

She shushed Brady with a finger-to-mouth gesture and a little elbow to the side ribs. He managed to get in another *What the hell?* before Hewitt released her thumb-mute from the phone and signed off with Lattimore. By that time, Detective Richter had already thrown back the sheet.

"What the hell is this, Hewitt?" her birthday buddy demanded, the evidence now in full view.

Without the wake-up call from Lattimore, Hewitt would have been laughing. But the call, its contents, its predictive power over her future had closed the door on her birthday party and its priapic aftermath. It had closed it so tight, she doubted she would think about her birthday for at least another 364 days.

"YOU just don't tie a ribbon around a guy's thing."

They were in the Mazda, Hewitt driving, Brady waiting for a response, watching her from the passenger seat in a way that suggested he would be watching her more closely from now on.

"You're right," Hewitt said. "You don't."

"Then why did you?"

"Maybe I didn't."

"Well, I guess that scenario hadn't occurred to me," Brady said, the sardonic tone of his voice as clear as the fact that he had left her place without having had time to shower.

"What makes you think it's such a slam dunk?" Hewitt proffered.

"Opportunity, for starters."

"Opportunity I'll buy. What about motive?"

She had reached down to turn on the radio to the morning jazz station. Her ears filled instantly with a velvet fog. Mel Tormé. "'I'm Glad There Is You.'"

"Motive?" Brady said, in the Luke Skywalker voice that penetrated the velvet fog but didn't quite harmonize with it. "There you're going to have to help me, Hewitt. Because I'm not sure I want to crawl that deep into the mind of the perp. But since you're apparently immune to any such fear, why don't you serve up your best conjecture."

It was a beautiful day on the cusp of the summer solstice. And the angle of the sun, with the presence of an armada of cumulus clouds escorted by the warm front, was the kind of thing Illinois residents dreamed about during the blizzards of winter.

Hewitt pulled herself back from the atmospheric getaway. "If I was going anywhere but a Du Page County wayside to see a dead twenty-four-year-old girl, this would have all the makings of a perfect summer day."

Her statement had the effect of finally getting Brady to stop staring her down. He joined her in turning his focus to the road ahead—traffic-infested, the faces of the drivers as metallic as the skins of their vehicles.

Brady went to his pocket, took out his sunglasses case, popped it open.

"Ah, shit," he sniffed.

"Problem?"

"I left my shades at your place. On the kitchen table."

Hewitt had her hand in the side pocket of her black blazer. "I grabbed 'em on the way out."

She handed him the ultraviolet-protection olive branch. He took it as if it were that, put the sunglasses on, adjusted them until he was satisfied with their position on the bridge of his nose.

"You just don't do that," he said. "You don't mess with it. You don't . . . *accessorize*."

CHAPTER 4

VEHICLES with kids who drank too much juice or with older men whose prostates had grown a little too big for their surroundings would have the squirmiest time passing the Du Page County wayside that morning. But they wouldn't have a choice. And the people in the official vehicles that were permitted to enter the wayside crime scene would have their own reasons to squirm.

Hewitt flashed her credentials to the state trooper at the checkpoint, but he already knew her. His reaction to the recognition followed what had become a disconcerting pattern for Hewitt. Initially his face lit up in an accommodating, almost friendly way. But in the brief interval it took for a human brain to access a preconceived opinion, the trooper's face had gone dark, and the suggestion of a smile had folded in upon itself.

"Okay, Agent Hewitt. You're good," he said in the tone she knew he used with motorists after ticketing them. "But I need to see something from the gentleman."

A mosquito had entered through the open window and was making a pass at Hewitt's face.

"And an hour ago I could have really shown you something," Brady Richter said, but only loud enough for Hewitt's benefit.

Hewitt swung at the mosquito. At first she thought she'd gotten it, but the damn thing fluttered down into the darkness beneath the dashboard.

"He's a colleague from the Wilmette PD," Hewitt told the trooper.

"I'm her birthday present from the governor," Brady Richter said as he spilled his ID for the trooper's eyes.

The trooper stepped back, waved them through with his chin.

"Have a good day. And if you figure out how to do that after what happened here, let me know."

Hewitt's foot barely had time to reconnect with the accelerator when the first visual hit her. The words flashed in her mind then, words she knew would accompany the sketch she would make in her notebook. *Sleeping Beauty Picnic*. Barely moving as it was, Hewitt let the car slow even more. She felt a little sting at the side of her neck.

"'Pavane for a Dead Princess,'" she heard Brady's voice say at the same time she felt his fingers strike the side of her neck.

"Ravel," he added, as if that were the name he was giving the dead mosquito he pulled from her. He flicked it out his window.

Hewitt parked the Mazda and the two of them got out and approached the other busy courtesans around the princess's body. If it hadn't been for the hair, the whole Sleeping Beauty/Princess thing wouldn't have been so self-evident. But it was the top of the head of this victim, as it had been with the first, that took things into that fairy-tale realm.

Eleven days earlier, when the first victim, Jenna Neuheisel, had turned up at a wayside in McHenry County, Hewitt had been attending an FBI seminar in Quantico, Virginia. So all she had seen of Victim One was the crime scene photos, which she now knew hadn't done justice to the actual scene, its setting, its gestalt, its choreography. But as she paused to stand on the perimeter of the activity, the impact of this display was overwhelming.

The hair. All that lovely hair. The only thing missing was the tiara. Yet even then, there was the sense that the dome of the head, the shimmering, ruffled coif, was a crown in its own right. The face, mottled by the passage of time since the stoppage of the victim's heart, still retained a patina of loveliness. And Hewitt was kicking herself now that she'd decided to go to Quantico for the damn seminar that had shown her a couple of new profiling wrinkles, but nothing that would do any significant rewiring of her brain. Her unavailability had rendered her, she now knew, incapable of feeling the true impact of the taking of the first victim. And subsequently, it had perverted her ability to feel the full bloom of outrage at the perpetration of this, the second act.

The rest of the victim's body was covered by the State of Illinois—

issue plastic sheet. Yet even this supported the princess persona. The royal blue of the sheet, covering everything but the head and hair, seemed, in the warming sun, like a funeral cloak dropped over the fallen princess by some traveling prince who, exhausted in his attempts to kiss new life into her, had stood up from his genuflection, remounted his horse and moved on.

"He likes 'em pretty, doesn't he?" a voice said from the other side of the castle wall. A voice that wasn't Brady's.

Hewitt turned, saw the face that had produced the sound. The newspaper filing system in her brain instantly pulled up the microfilm. *Trooper John Davidoff.* Burned like hell as the result of a high-speed chase that ended with his vehicle on its side and his face in a pool of fiery fuel. Hewitt had encountered him once on a case before the accident. He was as good-looking a cop as she'd ever seen. He'd flirted with her. She'd returned the compliment. They hadn't dated. Primarily because he was married.

Well, he wasn't married anymore. One of the daily papers had gone out of its way to document that. The wife who didn't stand by her horribly scarred man.

"So far," Hewitt said. "So far he likes them quite pretty."

"I see your partner does too," Davidoff said, through lips that looked more like they belonged on a turtle than a man.

"Brady Richter," the partner in question said, extending his hand. Davidoff took it, shook it with his perfectly normal hand.

John Davidoff identified himself, knowing, as Hewitt did, that he didn't need to. He smiled. And if a turtle had teeth . . .

"I was the first responder," Davidoff told them, his neck pulling into the collar of his blue shirt in a way Hewitt couldn't have missed either. "Victim's name is Cassandra Langford. Twenty-four-year-old resident of Arlington Heights. She lives with a female roommate—*lived*—who didn't report her missing even though she never came home from work last night. She had a boyfriend. According to the roommate, she slept at his place routinely."

"Guy's not exactly shy," Brady Richter offered. "The perp. Picnic table at a rest stop. Second time. I mean that's pretty Goddamn brazen."

"Middle of the night, these places aren't exactly a hotbed of activity," Davidoff offered back.

"Who found her?" Hewitt asked.

"Trucker," Davidoff answered. "Guy with a refrigerated trailer full of hog parts."

"He see anything?"—from Hewitt.

"Place was quiet when he pulled in. A little after four-thirty. He went in to buy an Almond Joy. Ate the first half inside. He was walking back to his truck when he saw her. As far as I know, he never got to the second half."

"Makes you wonder how he could have missed her on the walk in," Hewitt interjected.

"It was dark," Davidoff said. "He was craving something sweet."

Hewitt understood the chocolate craving thing. Liquid version. She was looking hard at the blue lips of the victim, wondering what kind of sweets she had craved, what favorite sensory confections she would never taste again.

Cassandra Langford. *Cassandra.* Even the name worked into the whole princess matrix. Hewitt flashed the memory of how she felt when she heard the news about Princess Diana. How the world seemed so suddenly and utterly diminished. That's how it was now. How it would always be. When the world lost a princess, it was a very dark day, and an even darker night.

CHAPTER 5

BRADY Richter worked the weekend shift. Actually, Saturday through Wednesday. So Thursdays and Fridays were his weekend. And being a Friday morning, this was his Sunday brunch time. Despite that, he volunteered to hang with Hewitt for the day to support, assist, anything he could do to help, short of supplying the icon of his malehood for further artistic interpretation.

Hewitt knew detectives craved their time off as much as they craved the variety of brown liquids they could pour into their bodies when they were working. And besides, Detective Richter was still an employee of the Wilmette Police Department. With this being a case that crossed municipal and county jurisdictional lines, Brady had no just cause to be a part of it.

So Hewitt had dropped him off at his place, although some of his male energy had managed to stow away inside her car even after his body had exited. And that was probably a good thing. Because Hewitt's next engagement was with Cassandra Langford's boyfriend.

Calls to Jeromy Edwards's home and cell phone had gone unanswered. His employer, Illinois Energy, had informed Hewitt that Thursday was a day off for him as well. Who knew? In another world of social arranging, he and Brady could have gotten together for a best-of-five game of squash. Hell, maybe Hewitt would've been able to rearrange her schedule to join them in doubles. Since it was never a good idea to partner in sports competition with a significant other, Hewitt would have needed someone else to complete her tandem. And she knew, if she really wanted to win, she would've picked John Davidoff as her squash partner. The way Brady had struggled to keep from staring at the brisket that now passed for Trooper Davidoff's face, he would have had a hell of a time keeping his focus on the little rubber ball.

On the ride back to his apartment, Brady had checked his own face in the visor mirror a couple of times before he'd pinched off the question. "When you looked at him, talked to him, you did it without even flinching. But more than that, without making it seem at all like you were trying to be nonchalant about it."

"So?" had been Hewitt's efficient rejoinder.

"So how the hell did you do that?"

"Remember the *Twilight Zone* episode? The one where the woman is in the hospital bed with the bandaged face. And she's scared to death of what she'll look like when the bandages are removed. And all the while, the nurses are there and talking to her and reassuring her and seeming and sounding all normal?"

Brady was nodding. He'd seen it.

"But the scenes were shot in such a way," Hewitt continued, "that you never got a good look at the other people's faces. And when the bandages came off, the woman looked beautiful. But the doctors and nurses all gasped. And that's when we finally got a good look at them."

"They all had pig faces," Brady said.

"That's right. And so I always try to keep in mind that from some contrary perspective, some other way of perceiving the world, the one who I think is hideous could be normal. And I could be the pig face."

THERE was nothing pig-faced about Cassandra Langford's boyfriend from any perspective. Confirming Hewitt's hunch, he was home at his apartment, sleeping off a boys' night out, not picking up his phones, even when they were ringing an inordinate number of times. He did, however, answer his doorbell after multiple rings, wearing old gym shorts and an even older T-shirt. Hewitt's first thought upon seeing him was that he had one of the most vulnerably handsome faces she'd ever seen. Her second thought was that he had absolutely no inkling that his girlfriend was dead. And her next thought was that it was going to be a human tragedy to have to destroy that face with the news she had.

Hewitt hated that more than anything in the world. Being the delivery person. Being the reluctant associate to the acts. The grim reaper's conscripted lieutenant. It hit the young man like a suicide bomb. And Hewitt had to actually step back from the first explosion of expectorated emotion. Right then she would have rather been hit by flying blood and bone. The cleanup would've been a lot easier.

Advisable or not, she was still a cop with a beating heart. So she had no choice but to step forward and help Jeromy Edwards hold on to some familiar aspect of the world that would keep him from being swallowed alive. And for better or worse, that aspect was her thirty-eight-year-old body.

So she let him have it. Her body, herself. For whatever it was for him, whatever his free-falling mind could grab on to, whatever he could turn her into for the purpose of survival. Mommy. Universal mother. A temporary stand-in for the lost princess. Or all of them bundled into one. In the form of an almost-forty, lady-in-waiting homicide detective.

Training said you were okay to comfort with words. But physical comforting, while not entirely controllable or enforceable, had to be limited for obvious reasons. As Hewitt held up Jeromy Edwards, those reasons became more obvious than ever. Because when boy met girl, even when boy's real girl had just been found dead and displayed on a wayside picnic table, well, human pheromones didn't come with an on-off spigot.

Hewitt didn't go anywhere near that. Because she was a pro. And because, having left the condo with just a face and armpit wash, Brady's chemistry was still all over her.

"I know," Hewitt said in her mom/universal mother voice. Not because it sounded like the right thing to say, but because it was true. "I know."

She led him back inside his apartment, sat him down on a kitchen chair, held him there by the shoulders when it appeared he was going to get up for another emotional scrum with her. Her action had an effect. His eyes cleared a little, the first glimpse Hewitt was looking for that, at the end of the world, there was still some small piece of earth left.

"What?" he managed.

Just the one word. So Hewitt told him, softening it only with the tone of her voice. The details of the wayside scene. The ways in which it mirrored an earlier homicide. He was aware of that killing, just as any Chicago-area citizen with a TV, a radio or a pulse would have been.

"How?" he half-whispered then, his lungs sticking to his heart. "How did she . . . How did Cassie die?"

Toxicology tests on the first victim had taken several days to process and analyze. The State Medical Examiner, Carlton Zoeller, had voiced his internal opinion only within the last forty-eight hours. He was still waiting for final confirmation. So nothing had been disseminated to the public. But Hewitt knew it was a done deal. So she decided to release the information to one member of the public, now.

"The first victim died from a lethal injection. There were no physical signs of trauma with Cassandra. So I can't say with certainty, but I have a strong feeling that's what happened here too."

"Someone injected her?"

"Again, I can't say conclusively. There are tests they'll do to determine that."

The full weight of his bones was pressing against the kitchen chair, his muscles having let go of any reason to pretend they were strong. As if he had received an injection himself.

"Like the death penalty," he said, his throat thickened by his male reflex to suppress tears. "Like she was sentenced to death."

CHAPTER 6

THE little girl is running up the sidewalk, her face broad with the smile she saves for one man on earth. And because she wishes to show her smile to the man as soon as possible, she is running too fast. Behind her, barely out of the gravitational pull of the giant white SUV, her mother calls to her, cautioning against exactly this.

The girl hears her mother's voice, hears not so much the words as the warning tone. Like a fledgling bird reacting to its mother's cry. She turns her upper body in the direction of the warning call. But her lower body, her legs don't slow down. And when her little tennis shoe hits the deep pock in the sidewalk, she is down instantly, her bare right knee absorbing the impact.

Her mother knows she can gauge the degree to which her daughter has been hurt by the delay between the first cry and, after the furious, labored sucking of air, the second. And for a moment, as she hurries across the sidewalk herself, she wonders if the second cry will ever come. It does. And it is a beauty.

On the angel's wings she never knew she had until she had a child, the mother swoops in, scoops up the little girl. The knee is already a bright red mess. And for just an instant, the mother surprises herself with the thought that blood, fully exposed in the light of the June sun, is a pretty color.

Then she is moving up the walk, taking the steps to her father's porch, opening the door.

"Dad!" she calls through the house. "Can you get me a wet washcloth? And the Neosporin. Maggie had a little boom-boom."

The crying from the little boom-boom is at full bore. So when she doesn't hear a report back from her father right away, there's nothing to think. She moves through the foyer and through the hall to the kitchen, sits her daughter on a chair, and hurries to the sink.

The application of the cold washcloth sets off a higher pitch of crying, closer to yelping. But within a minute, the sting eases and the crying quiets.

It is in this small respite that Megan Charlton tastes the first secretion of concern.

"Dad?" she calls, *her* voice now the loudest thing in the house. "*Dad?*"

"*Mommy,*" her daughter moans. But it is subdued, muffled. To the child, the sound of her mother's voice has become an even more frightening thing than her bloody knee.

Maybe he went for a walk. For groceries. To put gas in the car. Maybe his sweet tooth acted up and he went to Krispy Kreme.

The potential explanations stream against the backs of her eyes.

But the front door was open. And Delbert Rasmussen was an obsessive door-locker.

Megan Charlton picks up her daughter, in a protective posture, and moves through the kitchen, to the hallway, to the back door. And it is there that her life changes forever. Because the back door is open. *Forced open.*

Her skin runs cold, falling, it feels, to the temperature of the washcloth she drops to the floor.

Hurt child on her hip, Megan Charlton pauses to listen to the house. Her daughter has stopped crying. But she continues to breathe, in a pronounced, heavy pattern, as if the crying could resume at any time.

Other than the two of them breathing, and the hum of the refrigerator motor, the house is quiet.

Footsteps on the kitchen floor, then. Her own.

To the hallway, the foyer, crossing to the living room.

Years later she will still remember her failure to shield her child's eyes, to turn her daughter's face away from the impossible thing she sees at the far end of the living room floor.

CHAPTER 7

THE odds of investigating two distinct fetish homicides in one day were extremely improbable. But not, as Hewitt was now brutally aware, impossible.

The day's second victim and, based on the evidence she had seen at the woeful crime scene in Libertyville, the second in its own serial line, was lying in state on the steel table of the Lake County Morgue. Hewitt had her notebook open, was doodling her sketch of the one body part on Delbert Rasmussen that called out to her as loudly as if the victim had reanimated and cried *I'm Alive*!

Visored and gowned, the tallish man with the forward sloping shoulders could have been any number of middle-aged forensic physicians. But the way his eyes twitched periodically, and the way his too-white teeth gleamed through the plastic mask as he observed the work of the young female tech with him, eliminated all other possibilities.

"You ever going to show me any of that artwork, Hewitt?" the State Medical Examiner asked through the visor.

"Last time I checked with Lattimore, he was very amenable to hosting a gallery night and barbecue at HQ. I'll make sure you get an invitation."

"Of all your nuances, that's the one I admire least," Dr. Carlton Zoeller replied, with a couple of glints off his canines.

"My penchant for barbecues?"

"Your penchant for hoarding evidence."

The tech was working the victim's neck now, that area where the murder weapon had been found, the pair of nylon stockings.

"I can look you in the eye," Hewitt offered, "and tell you I've never hoarded evidence in my life."

"Okay," Zoeller said as Hewitt continued to stare, lifting his visor to enhance the eye contact. "Maybe not direct evidence per se. But your *in my own little corner, in my own little chair* approach. The way you sit on things."

"Any good hen knows the proper amount of time to sit her eggs," Hewitt said, drawing an oral shimmer from Zoeller and a glance from the tech.

"In the animal kingdom, I don't think I'd ever put you in with the hens. You're definitely more of the feline type."

Hewitt knew where that was intended to go. And she wasn't just going to sit back while Zoeller played with her.

"You said *feline*. But you meant *pussy*."

The muscles in Zoeller's jaw pulled together to seal his mouth.

The tech looked up again, this time a little longer, made eye contact with Hewitt, approving eye contact.

"And since we're on the subject of straightforwardness," Hewitt said, turning again to Zoeller, "I'll be happy to share my observations with you."

Hewitt traced a few more wild hairs above the eyes of Delbert Rasmussen and closed the notebook.

"Three things jump out at me," she said. "As I'm sure they have to you. First, the fetishistic nature of the murder. Second is the similar age of the victims. Terrence McCullough was fifty-eight. Delbert Rasmussen, sixty-one. And third, the general body morph of the two victims."

"Well, that makes us both three for three," Zoeller said, still not completely recovered from Hewitt's feline comeback.

"But there's a fourth element I find very interesting," Hewitt continued. "Actually a fourth and fifth."

Everything about Zoeller paused to listen, even his teeth.

"Leonid Brezhnev," Hewitt said. And from the reaction of the other two professionals in the room, she might as well have said *Let's all get naked.*

"The eyebrows," Hewitt specified. "He has Brezhnev eyebrows."

Zoeller's face darkened and puckered into the look of all those dark, puckered men standing at the Kremlin wall in photos from Hewitt's mental history book. She turned, picked up her attaché bag from the floor and removed the case file for what was now the *first* nylon asphyxiation victim, Terrence McCullough. She pulled out the head shot, held it up for Zoeller.

"The first victim, Terrence McCullough," she said. "Brezhnev Brows."

She could see Zoeller wasn't exactly buying.

"Hewitt, I'm a man who's comfortably into his fifties," he said in his lecturing voice. "And I have to tell you, from about age forty-five on, a man's eyebrows begin to have a life of their own. And the more you trim them, the more they resist any attempt at control."

"So you're saying if you didn't trim or have yours trimmed, you'd be a candidate for the old Politburo too."

"I'd prefer not to find that out."

"And I'd prefer to have more with the other facial features," Hewitt said. "But as it stands I have age, body morph, cause of death and eyebrows."

"Your ability to connect the dots has always had my utmost respect," Zoeller offered. "And in this case, if you manage to connect all those little bristles into something meaningful, I'll call my florist and tell him to put together something really nice for you."

Hewitt's thoughts rattled forward to images of the daughter and granddaughter at the graveside of the latest victim. Zoeller's flowers had triggered it. Megan and Maggie Charlton had been the first to find Delbert Rasmussen in that hideous fiasco of a crime scene. In a few days, no doubt, they would be the last to leave the florid tableau of the burial scene. Maybe they wouldn't be the last ones to leave physically. The deep mourners were typically spirited away at the end of the service, under the wings of well-meaning, close family members. The more peripheral mourners, distant family and friends, would actually be the last ones to mill about the site, like some cloaked sentries assigned to stand wait.

"Thinking of your favorite flower?" she heard Zoeller's voice inquire.

Hewitt looked up, saw the tech preparing the saw to open the sternum.

"I was thinking about flowers," Hewitt said. "But not the kind I want anytime soon."

CHAPTER 8

KELLY Gratchen heard the story all day. About the girl in Du Page County. The girl on the picnic table. The girl who was put there by what the radio stations were calling *The Wayside Killer*. There was the other story too. The one about the grandfather. And all the talk, all the bizarre speculation.

The grandfather story, horrible as it was, wasn't really something she could relate to. Both her grandfathers were still alive. One in Odessa, Texas. The other in Barstow, California. She never saw either one anymore, hadn't for years. So if some crazy man decided to strangle either one of them with a nylon, it would be a really horrible thing. But she'd survive it.

It was the other story that had gotten all the way into her head. It was the reason she'd left the little radio on in her cubicle all afternoon, barely loud enough to hear, but more than loud enough to scare the hell out of her.

The picnic table girl. She didn't really know her. But she could have easily enough been one of her friends. She could have easily enough been *her*. For that reason, in that way, she did know her. After listening to the radio, she knew her name. It kept spinning through her head. *Cassandra Langford*.

She pulled her car into the mall parking ramp, stopped, took the ticket from the ticket spitter. She worked her way up the ramp, her thoughts never far from Cassandra Langford, but her left brain at least distracted in the search for the one elusive parking space she could claim as hers. At the fifth level, there were a number of them. And this being a relief of sorts to her, Kelly Gratchen opted not to take the first available space. Instead, she luxuriated for a moment in the options. She took the tenth, maybe the eleventh, next available space.

On the radio, the four o'clock news was just coming on. The newscaster, in his darkly excited, big-story news voice, began to inform her all over again.

The moment she heard the words *picnic table*, she shut the engine off. Exiting the car, she felt a strange feeling in her mouth, and a taste that was foreign, metallic.

She locked the car, looked around as a couple of other vehicles turned into the parking spaces she had passed up. She reached into her purse for a stick of gum, to get rid of the strange metal taste, and started toward the mall entrance, chewing, thinking, turning Cassandra Langford over in her mind.

Halfway to the entrance, her ears and the back of her neck felt a chill. There was no breeze, but she turned in the direction it would have come from. For an instant, she thought she saw someone. Some shape, some form of someone, looking out from behind one of the concrete pillars. She waited for the form, *the person*, to reemerge. Within a second or two, it did. And instantly, her mind relaxed.

Old lady. A nice old lady.

The old lady looked at her. But there was no nice old lady smile. And when there wasn't, Kelly Gratchen registered the fact that while her mind had relaxed, her neck and shoulders hadn't, and the chill against her skin had gotten colder.

Across the concrete ramp, the old lady turned and looked back to the place she'd just been, behind the pillar, with a look of concern. As if—but it couldn't be that—as if she had seen something there too. But then, just as quickly, she turned back again and proceeded to the mall entrance, more annoyed than anything when Kelly just stood there staring, watching her go.

She followed her inside, to the welcoming smell of chocolate chip cookies baking, harboring the thought of approaching the woman to ask if she had seen something. But the woman, for an old lady, was a fast walker. Faster still, when at the turn past the Gap, she looked over her shoulder to see the young woman from the parking lot tailing her.

And that was enough, that look the woman gave her. Because Kelly Gratchen knew that this time the shadowy figure was none other than herself. The ridiculousness of that made her push out a purging sigh. She almost smiled, and would have almost laughed if she hadn't, in the next few steps of her shoes against the tile floor, looked through the window of the Electronics Emporium to see a bank of TVs all tuned to the same image from the four o'clock news.

It was a picture she knew immediately. A picture of the picnic table girl. But from that distance, through the slight warping of mall light through the panes of glass, it could have been any number of girls. It could have been her.

CHAPTER 9

HEWITT had to be careful. While it was enticing to connect the two sets of homicides, her experience informed her that it was always a good idea to leave the door open to the possibility of the unimaginable. This one, though, if it ended up in that category, would've still required a seriously hyped-up imagination to get there.

She was on the Tri-State, headed for home, with her Friday Good Samaritan call to make on the way. Her attaché bag was filled with the known elements of the quartet of cases that had come to rule her planet. Obviously, it was going to be a working weekend. Brady would be working the weekend too. So it wasn't as if she had any big getaway planned. If he got off early enough and wasn't too fried on Saturday night, she'd settle for a fifteen-minute Stearns and Foster getaway.

The music was up in the car. Thelonius Monk. "Well You Needn't." The melodic dissonance of Monk was the perfect brain accompaniment as Hewitt began her mental work-up of the facts she had to go on—with, of course, her sprinkles of conjecture, her own dissonant voicings beyond the known, the expected.

In jazz, a little dissonance could go a long way. In serial homicide, a detective's musings, hers at least, were like a long, sustained jazz improvisation. To keep the improv alive through a series of choruses, you couldn't let yourself get too comfortable, too linear. You had to keep it fresh, keep surprising yourself. Because it was a Goddamn lock that the bad brain you were jamming with had laid down an unpredictable, unrepeatable, *unimaginable* solo before you ever played your first note.

Fifteen minutes, and she was hitting the speed bump at the end of Ed Spangler's driveway. It wasn't an intentional speed bump. Just a questionable job of grading when the city of Skokie had put in the curb and gutter. Hewitt caught a glimpse of him at the front window, standing there in the blue Puma warm-up suit she knew he was in the habit of wearing a lot. At least every Friday. As her car passed the crabapple tree, the visage evaporated quickly and the captain evanesced into the afternoon shadows of the house.

He met her at the back door. She could tell he'd showered that day. But the blue warm-up gave off a stale, dusty smell. He'd been wearing it more than a lot.

They held their meeting at the kitchen table. This was where Hewitt's Friday briefings were conducted. The briefings were done for the benefit of his state of mind. To Hewitt, it was considerably closer to visiting a sick friend.

"I bought some more," he said. "If you have need. I assume you haven't done rehab for it since the last time I saw you. Check that. My daughter was the one who went out and bought it. I think she's been using. Must be good stuff."

By then Hewitt was up and into the cupboard, procuring the box. "I can make you one if you'd like to experience the high."

Hewitt put a cup of water in the big old Kenmore microwave, hit START. Turning back to Spangler at the table, her eyes caught the presence of the high chair in the corner, next to the refrigerator. *Parked* was more accurate. Even though Spangler's daughter, Jen, and her year-old daughter had been living with him since the baby's birth, the parking of the high chair, as opposed to leaving it at the table, was a clear sign of the captain's comfort level with the whole arrangement. Especially the single mom part of it.

"How's the extended family?" Hewitt asked over the big old hum of the microwave.

"They're good," Spangler said, a little deflated. "They're good. It's all good."

"How about you? You saw your cardiologist yesterday, right?"

"Oh, he's good too. The picture of health."

Hewitt could feel her face giving him a look she'd often given her dad. The *okay Dad it's funny but let's get real* look. From Spangler's reaction, his acquiescence, she knew he was no stranger to receiving the same look from his daughter.

"He says what he always says. Some progress. Could be better. The way I see it, if you've got something wrong with you, it pretty much comes down to three H-Os. Home. Hospital. Or hospice. Right now this is where I am. And it's a hell of a lot better than the other options."

The big old bell rang in the microwave.

"You know those aren't the only H-O places to convalesce," Hewitt said as she took the cup of water from the Kenmore. "There's the Ho-tel California. And my favorite, the Ho-Ho-Ho Christmas Shop and Brothel in Reno."

She didn't even bother to look at him as she stirred in the chocolate powder. She could feel him grinning. When she did turn back to the table, she saw his mouth, still in a semismile, but his eyes serious, anxious.

"My main regret on the slow progress report, other than not being able to put my granddaughter up on my shoulder and run around like a jackass, is that I can't get that prick Lattimore out of your life."

"He's just one prick," Hewitt said as she slid into the chair across the table from him.

"You know what they say, though. It only takes one prick to pop the whole balloon."

Now Hewitt was the one grinning. "Who says that?"

"I don't know. I guess maybe just me."

He reached out, took a butterscotch candy from the beveled glass bowl of them on the table, unwrapped it. "There's a news conference scheduled for five o'clock. Unless you can get back to HQ in three minutes, you're going to be embarrassingly late."

He popped the candy in his mouth, enjoyed it as he waited for Hewitt's response.

"I was told my presence wouldn't be required."

"Well, that's some Goddamn good thinking. I mean you're only the most media-savvy person the division has. So of course it makes perfect sense to keep you on the sidelines so he can have his little moment in the sun."

"Now don't get all fired up over that," Hewitt said, aware, even as she was saying it, that it wasn't the right thing to say.

"Right," Spangler said. "Because if my last thought before the big gripper takes me is what an asshole Lattimore is for not including you, that would be such a pointless way to go. Is that what you're suggesting?"

Hewitt finished the last of a long sip of Swiss Miss. "No," she said. "I want you to die happy."

The smile didn't manifest at his mouth. But it did show in his eyes. The worry lines in his forehead quieted down a notch too. He pushed his chair away from the table, got up, went to the counter where the small Panasonic television was mounted under the cupboard—one of those space-saving ideas from decades past that had made sense at the time. He switched on the TV, waited patiently as it warmed up. Sound came well in advance of picture. The *Jeopardy* theme song. The version of it they played at the end-of-show credits.

"*Live at Five* with Richie Lattimore," Spangler said. "This should be good."

On the TV, a commercial pod was unfolding prior to the switch to the news. Spangler paused for a moment to consider the second commercial that came up, an ad for an erection-stimulating drug.

"With a heart condition, you can take that off the table now too," he mused.

"It's all part of the recovery," Hewitt said.

Spangler didn't respond. His eyes were on the little Panasonic as the *Live at Five* opening graphics and music came trumpeting bombastically from the speakers. The coanchors trumpeted their own announcement that they would be going immediately to State Police Headquarters for breaking news.

Spangler looked at Hewitt. His mouth smiled weakly, but his eyes lit up with the best sardonic twinkle she had seen from him since before the heart attack.

"Lattimore's first big speech on the way to running for state office," he said.

"I've heard the rumors," Hewitt offered.

"Ritchie Lattimore has had political hack written all over him since he took his First Communion. He might as well have been wearing a *Future Political Hack* tank top to his workouts all these freaking years."

Spangler got up from the table, approached the TV as the picture cut from the *Live at Five* set to the official podium in the ISP media room. Captain Lattimore was already at the podium, by himself, in a nice gray suit coat over his broad shoulders that seemed perfectly coordinated with the gray-white brush cut atop his head. Spangler was right. With that look, and without the usual cadre of support people huddled around, Richard Lattimore did give the appearance of someone who was about to deliver a political address.

"Good afternoon," he intoned importantly into the microphone.

And that was it, the end of the speech. Because Captain Spangler had just made the executive decision to kill the TV volume. He turned to Hewitt. "Okay, now tell me what the hell is really going on."

CHAPTER 10

HEWITT gave Spangler everything she could. She always did. Of course, she couldn't always share every detail, couldn't actually give him the backstage pass to her show, the ACCESS TO ALL AREAS tag he could clip to the pocket of one of his white Arrow shirts. Because the bottom line was that she never did that, couldn't do that, with anyone.

So she'd given him everything she could. And as she drove away from his nice suburban split-level ranch, she knew that if Captain Spangler didn't make it to the top of the hill with his heart condition, someday she'd give him everything she could in the folded shadows of some nice suburban funeral home.

And just as she'd been forced to withhold aspects, angles of cases she'd investigated for him, at his wake she would be forced to withhold a few critical things too. Like, for starters, her actual feelings. Oh, she'd be sad. There would be plenty of that. And she'd mill around and meet and greet with that empathetic death mask on her face. But how much it really hurt, how much it killed her that her captain was gone, that wouldn't be made available to the public—any more than she had made Elizabeth Taylor Hewitt emotionally available to the world when her real dad died.

With Ed Spangler appointed her surrogate father by the gods of reciprocity, his death would be borne by a similar balling of hands, clenching of jaw and constricting of bronchial tubes.

Spangler's death. Jesus Christ, his split-level ranch, his multigenerational domestic scene, was less than a mile in her rearview mirror and already she was counting him with the carefree spirits on the other side of the sky.

He was still here, for God's sake. Still here, for her. Saying, doing the right things. Like turning off the sound on his little TV, letting the diminutive version of Lattimore prattle on like some little robot law enforcement action figure in the window of FAO Schwarz. So she could have *her* moment.

With his back to that image of Lattimore, Captain Spangler had listened to Hewitt's detailing of the case. To Hewitt's mind, the cases pivoted on two essential elements. *To her mind.* She was always aware, always plugged in to her tendency to take information, findings into a deeper psychic scan of the bad brain in question. In this case, it was under the big black umbrella of profiling, but several compass points off the generally accepted line of reasoning. It was in the archetype she was beginning to perceive at work, a Jungian kind of expression of it. But if you were up against one very serious head case—at least one—why not start there?

So, with her technical superior explicating in TV picture only next to a Bunn-o-Matic home brewer, Hewitt had laid out her thinking at Spangler's kitchen table. She began with the two young women, Jenna Neuheisel and Cassandra Langford. With the look, the prettiness, the lovely, flowing hair, and from the nature in which they were laid out for public viewing, for all the world, they were the archetype of *The Princess*.

In a conjoining time frame, the grim fairy tale had manifested two other bodies, which, yes, beginning with the eyebrows, had evoked the look, the persona of authority figures. To Hewitt, the embodiment of *The King*.

Two dead princesses. Two dead kings.

As for the third figure in the drama, Hewitt had no physical body. No palpable body of evidence. But clearly, she had a figure, a type, ensconced in shadow as he was. In his place, his time, his moment, he was the most powerful member of any kingdom, controlling the exactitude of the final moments between life and death. And in such moments, at such times, all eyes would be on him. He would conduct his work with an efficiency of effort, an efficiency of thought, an efficiency of emotion. Because this was the business, the purpose of, *The Executioner*.

Hewitt shared this thinking, all of it, with the orange-juice-sipping

Ed Spangler, while Ritchie Lattimore ran for public office on a silent mini-TV screen under the cupboard.

"The big question," Spangler offered between sips of citrus, "is how many executioners are working in this little kingdom of yours?"

Hewitt told him she didn't know, admitted she wasn't close to being in a position to know. This, of course, was where she held back. Because she knew. Or everything in her intuitive matrix told her she knew. And her first step in corroborating her imagined version of events was to pay a visit to the execution scene of the first victim, Terrence McCullough. King Terry.

SHE arrived at the McCullough residence a few minutes before six. Which meant that everywhere else in Greater Chicago, from the boutique eatery-drinkeries on Rush Street, to the big-breasted hotel lounges that flanked O'Hare, it was Happy Hour. With the sun starting to sag behind the big willow that stood like an arthritic colossus at the end of the McCullough property, it was hard to imagine that happiness, even an hour's worth, would ever be felt on this parcel of land again.

Like Delbert Rasmussen, Terrence McCullough had lived alone. With the investigation ongoing, the residence remained a sealed crime scene. So Hewitt had phoned ahead for assistance from a local plainclothes to unlock the padlocked door so she could have her look around.

The plainclothes was waiting in an unmarked car out front, an all-business type in her late twenties who Hewitt thought was a bit too mannish and weight-trained for the nice engagement ring on her finger. The woman let Hewitt in and returned to her vehicle, with maybe fifty perfunctory words between them.

Stepping into the house, Hewitt was met with a puff of terribly stale air. While the summer had yet to really warm, it had been more than enough to heat up the house during the day. Especially with the place completely sealed and the air-conditioning off.

She did a quick walk-through, starting with the kitchen, where she found a small wine rack mounted under the cupboards, with three of the six slots occupied by, from left to right, a Pinot Noir, a Merlot and a Cab. Seeing this, a thought squirted through her mind like a stomped red grape. If Terrence McCullough was a habitual red wine drinker, he would never get a chance to cash in on those purported extra years of cardiovascular health. Not now.

In the family room, she found the wall of pictures. The mosaic of differently shaped frames, all adding up to an oval pattern on the wall that suggested to Hewitt a big eyeball. Which felt appropriate for this last look into the life Terrence McCullough had been forced to leave behind.

As always, the pictures told the story. The marriage to a diminutive, bright-faced brunette. The two children that followed, one of each. The growing years. The trips, the holidays, the ceremonial rites of passage. And through it all, Hewitt couldn't help but notice that those hirsute little life-forms above Terrence McCullough's blue eyes had continued to evolve. And especially in the photographs from more recent years, the ones in which the wife, the mom, was missing. Maybe there was something about deep grief that set a man's eyebrows off.

Hewitt took her search to the living room, where the body had been discovered, where the killing had gone down, not sure of what exactly she was hoping to find. Her eyes drifted to the Bose Wave Radio on the built-in walnut bookshelf. About the nicest radio/CD player you could buy. The kind of thing a couple of adult kids could pool their money for as a special gift for an older guy who, by that time, pretty much had everything else.

Moored there in the death room, Hewitt felt a need to do something to freshen the heavy, lifeless air. Not wanting to mess with the windows, she figured she'd do the only other thing she could to improve the atmosphere.

She went to the Bose, pulled on a glove to turn it on, even though the place had already been dusted and combed. The unit was preset to RADIO, and pretty damn loud, and set to a station Hewitt wouldn't have opted for if the choice had been hers. But there was something nice, something *clean*, about the Bach piece that was currently playing on the classical station.

In the liner notes of *Kind of Blue*, the writer had referenced the influence of Johann Sebastian Bach in the compositions of Miles Dewey

Davis. And that, plus the way Bach's music did have an effect on freshening the air in the death house, was enough of an endorsement for Hewitt to allow the music to continue to flow from the beautifully balanced Bose speakers, although at a reduced volume.

From her attaché bag, Hewitt pulled the photos from the case file. Because of her travel to the FBI seminar, she hadn't been present at the original crime scene. But for the re-creation she had just conjured, the photographs would be an adequate map. Using the pictures for positioning, she went to the place in the southeast corner of the living room where Terrence McCullough had lain in state, with a pair of nylons around his neck, until his son had come by half-a-day later with the turkey sandwich and the bag of curly fries his father would never get to taste.

Hewitt stood there, stared at the spot, hovered over it with her eyes, her whirring, clicking mind. *While the rest of his face had been lying there dead all those hours, the eyebrows had continued to grow.* She was solid on the eyebrow thing. Thin as a Chinese lantern on everything else.

She had two dead kings. In a parallel universe, she had two dead princesses.

Always strange, always unnerving, no matter how long she had resided in her skin, the way her mind could convince her body to do things against which she had an initial revulsion. Stranger still, how the mind overrode the revulsion, to get where it wanted to go.

So here she was now, dropping into a kneeling position. And then, working from the crime scene photos, her body unfolding into the position Terrence McCullough had occupied, with his heart and brain shut down, but his eyebrows still reaching out to the world.

Hewitt closed her eyes, went inside. She could feel the shape of her body inside the victim's much bigger form. She could feel the shape of her face. But she couldn't tell if the next thing she felt was real or if she'd created it. A little flutter of air against her face, sensed by, as if directed to, the soft scimitars of hair above her own eyes. A little ripple of air just above floor level. But the house was sealed. Which left two possible sources. Either the sounds of Bach had the metaphysical power to rearrange air molecules. Or it was her own boomeranging breath.

She inhaled and exhaled through her mouth several times, nice and easy. She had never conducted a homicide investigation where she hadn't attempted to get inside the case as penetratingly as she could, to get inside the victim, to *be* the victim. But prior to this, it had always occurred within the relatively friendly confines of her own head. This, however, this assuming the position thing, was totally different.

As for instant revelations, she wasn't expecting any. But she'd done enough inner-mind work to know that the brain did some of its best processing in sleep, in daydreams, inside a Miles Davis solo, inside a Bach concerto.

So she lay there on the king's ethereal deathbed, wondering why on God's green earth a killer had inspired himself to strangle Terrence Mc-Cullough with a pair of nylons and leave him lying in this exact spot for the human carrion that would follow.

Her mind hit something then, stuck itself to a barb of the one element she had that was potentially the most telling. There had been no signs of a struggle in the upstairs bedroom. So whatever had motivated Terrence McCullough to come downstairs in the middle of the night had been something that *lured* him. Something curious, but not threatening.

Yet the longer she lay there, listening to the Bach, this ancient, courtly music, the more she began to drift from the murder of the king to the death of a princess.

CHAPTER 11

HEWITT awoke not to her clock-radio, but to her own inner atomic clock which, on a Saturday morning, had allowed her thirty-five minutes of additional sleep. On a normal Saturday, normal being about as relative a term as there was in her life, she would have slept in. But even on a sliding scale of normal, this Saturday, this weekend, this next chapter in her life, was already off the charts.

Her actress friend greeted her at the breakfast table. Smartly dressed. Face perfectly made. The night before, Hewitt had dressed Little Liz in the canary yellow pedal pushers and matching top. Sick of TV, sick of the notes and sketches she was laying down in the notebook, sick of the Time-Life jazz disc she'd looped on her stereo—she'd turned it off on the third playing of "Killer Joe"—Hewitt had opted to play with her paper doll to while away the time until her mind settled down enough to attempt sleep.

Little Liz. What an exquisite existence. Your sole purpose each day was to look sweet, happy and perfectly comfortable in your paper skin. Because it didn't matter. Because you could look perfectly fetching in canary yellow pants and top, or an oversized gray sweat suit.

Hewitt did the visual transference, superimposed the gray warm-ups she was wearing onto the cardboard body of Little Liz. And damned if the little actress didn't look as smart and confident as a girl could look in such a getup.

Brady was working. So she had the whole day to herself. He'd probably try to arrange for his Saturday night thing. Deliver a pizza and a cheap but well-considered Chard. On the phone, he would ask her what she wanted on the pizza. She would give him her usual choices. He would counter. They'd negotiate. And ultimately, they'd end up with the same hybrid they always ended up with. Two-thirds of the pizza would be eaten. The Chard would go down. And it would be nice. And they'd end up in bed without pausing to brush their teeth. Because that made it fair. They'd have the same hybrid pizza breath. With an oaky finish.

If he called. If her mind was free enough to take his call when he did.

She had breakfast with the movie star. Nothing fancy. Certainly not by movie star standards. One poached egg. Jelly toast. The big mug of Swiss Miss. As she ate, she thought of her convalescent news conference with Captain Spangler. Briefly, she replayed the information she'd shared with him. But what she dwelled on, all the way to the final sips of hot chocolate, was what she hadn't told him. The little directive she'd gotten from Lattimore when he'd given her the news that she wasn't needed at the media briefing. The little directive that, on his watch, Special Agent Hewitt wouldn't enjoy the same Diners Club carte blanche she'd enjoyed under the leadership of Mr. Ed Spangler. The fact that Lattimore had referred to him as "Mr." rather than "Captain" hadn't been lost on Hewitt either.

Putting him out to civilian pasture before anything official had even reached a rough draft. It had been a pretty Goddamn cocky thing for Lattimore to do. Spangler had suffered a serious cardiovascular event, after which four segments of blood vessel were removed from his legs to replace the clogged ones that serviced his heart. So shit yes, there was a chance Spangler was done. But the chance that he could come back hadn't been taken off the table. Given that, the churlishness of Lattimore's statement made Hewitt wonder if maybe he had some kind of inside information about the true status of Spangler's medical condition.

Of course, Lattimore's poison-tipped verbal arrows hadn't stopped there. And this was the part Hewitt hated the most, that *hurt her* the most. Enough that she had buried it so deep in her well of self-doubt that Captain Spangler would never know, let alone even sense the effect of the missive that followed. Given the nature of the case and the resemblance it bore to Hewitt's other extremely high-profile case, the Poe homicides, Lattimore was going to keep Hewitt on a short leash—and these were the words that cut her to the bone—*to prevent the personal and departmental embarrassment of having a lead investigator engage in intimate activity with a killer during the course of an investigation.*

Definitely a good idea Hewitt had kept that part to herself. With Spangler's hackles already elevated to full alert, that might have put his heart right off the EKG chart. And any chance of his return to the division would turn to dust. And the bad guy would win. And the world would go to hell.

She rewarmed her half-mug of Swiss Miss, added some more mini-marshmallows. Anything to sweeten the pot of the hand she'd been dealt. She absorbed the artificial sweetness in its entirety, in three protracted sips. Then she laced up her hikers and took her brain for a walk. The two-and-a-half miles were what she needed, a respite from the case, a little breathing room.

The walk also gave her a chance to get caught up on the progress of the June foliage. It was the twenty-first, the day before the summer solstice, which would actually hit during the early morning hours of the twenty-second, and the Midwest, *her Midwest*, was showing all the signs of a successful spring fling between Mother Nature and the Sun God. As she moved beyond the condo grounds, the wild summer grasses that flanked the road sprang up with a fecundity that felt to her unabashedly sexual. The morning breeze and the undulating grass drew a pang of horniness from her, and she missed Brady, missed waking up with him that morning, ribbon-adorned or not.

The dandelions that had splotched the landscape with their aggressive yellows had faded and given way to patches of daisies, bee balm and chicory. And it was all very nice to Hewitt, very comforting. Because it reaffirmed for her that despite all the bad brain craziness that was blooming around her professional life, there was still another world out there that she could not only recognize but give a shit about.

Upon her return to the condo complex, as the wild grasses once again relented to the kept lawns, she decided to check the mail she'd been neglecting the last couple of days. The first of those days had been her birthday, a day she'd skipped to avoid the disappointment of the dearth of birthday cards that had become an annual tradition.

So, nerved up to face that and whatever else, she went to the big bank of mailboxes, took a small bundle of pieces from hers, shuffled through them. She did find a couple of birthday cards, but not exactly anything to write home about. One was from her life insurance guy. With the life she was living and the premiums she was paying on long-term disability, death and dismemberment—whichever came first—he should have included some kind of Goddamn gift certificate. The other card was from a massage therapist she visited a handful of times a year, when the stresses of her earthly existence ganged up to force her spine into any number of untenable positions.

An insurance agent she paid to care about her life. A therapist she paid to touch her. It was nice to be remembered.

She was just letting go of that thought when her fingers found another greeting card–shaped envelope. And when she saw a name she recognized and the words *Treasurer* and *Class of*, her heart wobbled for a couple of beats.

Approaching her front door, she slowed to a stop, opened the envelope. She sat down on the porch step to read the card inside. It was the second and final attempt by her Wheaton West High School class to contact her in the hope she would honor them with her presence at their impending twentieth reunion. As she considered the message, Hewitt could feel her lips pressed tight together. She blew a burst of air through the seal that gave out a worrisome and depressing wheeze.

She had the case from hell—double hell. A politically motivated boss who saw her as damaged goods. And she had a younger boyfriend who would not only turn heads but turn catty commentary into an art form around the punchbowl. But another line of reasoning told her that a high school reunion was like the wild Midwestern grasses, the daisies, bee balm, chicory and all the other life-forms she'd just encountered. If your job, if your way of living, ever totally eclipsed your ability to participate in those ancillary expressions of life, what exactly was the point of being alive?

If she went, though, if she did find a way to show up for her twentieth, she was well aware it would be the first time she'd see most of her Wheaton West High School class since the night she wore a cap and gown and, on a dare, nothing else but a pair of black pumps.

CHAPTER 12

I T was a choice of beef tenderloin or stuffed chicken breast, and Hewitt was mulling it while Chet Baker sang "My Funny Valentine" and Saturday morning traffic ignored the speed limit only slightly less than it did on a normal, full-stress commuter day. Of course, there was the obligatory vegetarian offering that had been included in the menu options for the Wheaton West reunion. But that was always such a hit or miss at such functions, eggplant not being the easiest thing in the world to mass-produce.

It would be the chicken. Always a solid choice. Not that Hewitt had a problem with beef. Some of her more succulent childhood memories were of the big beef roast sizzling away in her mother's Frigidaire oven. The way the wild-burnt smell of it would fill the air and paint the walls of the house. The way she would watch it through the glass window of the oven, juicing and tenderizing, flanked by the three baking potatoes, doing their own steaming, puffing, breathing. The way her dad would rip into the finished beef at the table, like some wild castaway rescued from a desert island, invited to the captain's table, getting his first taste of meat in years.

So, the chicken. She would send in the reply card telling the class treasurer that she would, in fact, grace them by dragging her ass to their twentieth freaking reunion.

"My Funny Valentine" faded, and with it, Hewitt's thoughts of roast beef, high school treasurers, being naked as a plucked chicken under her cap and gown.

In the Mazda, with Chet Baker blowing the horn intro to "Let's Get Lost," she might as well have been naked now. That way, the nicotine-faced trucker who rolled up alongside her wouldn't have had to use his imagination. Her life felt that exposed. Like she had nothing left to hide. Nowhere to hide it if she did.

Let's get lost . . .

Chet Baker was singing now. The smoking trucker had faded into her rearview mirror. There was a time in the aftermath of the Scott Gregory-Raven case when she'd likened herself to a *Playboy* model. Elizabeth Taylor Hewitt, out there, uncovered, for all the world to see. But at least the photography could still be tasteful. At least she still had the dignity of looking good. Christ, she'd killed the bad guy, hadn't she?

But the more time that had elapsed, the more the tabloids had exaggerated and invented the details, the more Hewitt felt she'd moved into the *Penthouse* model camp. Knees wide, fully exposed, in your face. And just when you thought the world had finally seen all there was to see, there was this latest development. Your de facto superior suggesting, implying, damn near stating that you were not just a liability to yourself, but some kind of freak that had to be fitted with a neck bell.

So in that scheme of things, in that world, she was a Larry Flynt girl now. In the classic shot-from-behind, butt raised, head-turned-back-to-camera *Hustler* pose. Posed so that even where the sun never shined, the bright lights did.

Hello world.

WHEN Hewitt arrived at the restaurant, she was happy to be fully clothed. Megna and Patterson were already seated together at a wall table in the back.

"Hey, chief," Pete Megna issued, pulling back the chair they'd appropriated for her, the one that faced away from the rest of the restaurant. The *Special Agent Hewitt Seat.*

Hewitt took off her sunglasses, set them down next to her perspiring water glass.

"Thanks for showing up on a day off," she told them as she sat down.

"Is there any other way?" Megna said, hunching his shoulders in the way that always made Hewitt hunch hers.

"That's what friends are for," Val Patterson chimed in. And for a moment, both Hewitt and Megna paused as if they expected Patterson to chime in with the rest, in full chorus.

Val got that, smiled. "Not going there. Not on a Saturday morning. Now Saturday night, that's a whole 'nother matter."

"You guys order?" Hewitt asked.

"Turkey club for the gentleman," Megna answered, with another hunch Hewitt managed to fight off. "Power bagel for the lady."

"Correction." Val Patterson half-smiled. "*Black Power* bagel."

"How nineteen sixty-eight of you," Hewitt offered, with a half-smile back.

Their waitress approached, recognized Hewitt, left it at that.

"Roast beef au jus on a French roll," Hewitt ordered.

Megna's eyebrows rose. Hewitt watched them settle back into place.

"Isn't it a little early in the day for roast beef?" he asked.

"The Turkey Club opened the door," Hewitt responded. "Serial homicides always make me ratchet up my intake of red."

"Good source of iron. Excellent protein," Megna said.

"Don't you ever worry about Mad Cow?" Patterson queried.

"With all the mad humans, who has time?" Hewitt said.

Megna's eyebrows were on the move again. "You sure seem to find 'em. Or they find you."

"It's like looking for night crawlers when you're a kid," Hewitt explained. "Until you get down there in the dark and switch on the flashlight, you have no idea what's waiting for you."

"You always find the analogies too," Patterson weighed in.

Minutes later, their food weighed in too. By then, Hewitt had neatly laid out her top-line thoughts on what they were looking for, what they might find waiting for them when they got the chance to turn on their flashlights in the dark.

The first thing that jumped out to her colleagues and, for that matter, upon hearing it stated for the first time, *her*, was the bad brain count. Hewitt felt there was more than a reasonable possibility there were two. Given the timing of the two sets of killings, she couldn't get past the notion that each pair of acts had been synchronized somehow. And probably not synchronized by one actor.

Now, over the smell of sliced roast beef and freshly spilled *jus*, Hewitt listened to Pete Megna's next shoulder-rounding question.

"So in this scenario, we're looking at two killers working in tandem? Working with some kind of common goal?"

"I'm saying that's one scenario," Hewitt answered. "There are, of course, two others. One, that a single actor committed all four murders. And the other, that the two sets of murders have nothing in common other than the coincidence of dates and times. Of the three, that seems the most remote. Though not impossible."

"That's a little like all nine planets lining up in a row," Val Patterson interjected. "If you want to get a picture of that, you're going to be waiting a long-ass time."

Pleased with her analogy, she celebrated with a bite of power bagel.

Megna was already deep into his turkey club. But he paused to illustrate his take. "Like they say. You put a chimpanzee on a word processor and let him pound the keys, eventually he'll write *The Brothers Karamazov*."

"I thought it was *War and Peace*," Patterson said.

"Any Russian novel will complete the thought," Megna clarified.

"Like I say," Hewitt offered—she'd taken her first bite of roast beef. "Highly freaking unlikely."

"And the MOs on the two sets are so different," Patterson projected, "a single perp seems pretty out there too."

They were, the three of them, eating with great proficiency as they dialogued, having worked together enough that waiting for an empty mouth before speaking wasn't necessary. But they didn't go full-mouth either. The tacitly agreed upon principle was between half and three-quarters clear.

"The MOs are totally different," Hewitt said. "But not mutually ex-

clusive. And if you let your mind circle above the bodies long enough—
if you *go vulture*—you might be able to see a connection or two."

"Sounds to me like you've been spending some serious time in the
sky," Val Patterson posited.

"The higher you go," Hewitt chewed, "the prettier the world looks."

CHAPTER 13

THERE was something beautiful about a beef burrito. Not just as something you could put in your mouth and enjoy. But as something you could hold in your hand, hold up to the light and admire. For its simplicity. Its complexity. Its beauty.

The beef, perfectly browned and seasoned. The cheese. Melted. Layered. And all of it wrapped so nicely, so neatly, in the soft tortilla, itself warmed to the perfect feel, with the little brown baking marks here and there. Beauty marks.

Ah, what the hell. He was getting goofy on himself again. Here he was, Jerry "The Sub" Walker, sitting on his fat ass in the middle of a shopping mall food court. With the buzz of other excited mouths all around him. With the smells of his beloved beef burrito curling into his nose. With the sounds of the mall piano swirling in his ears. Sitting here, extolling the virtues of a Manny's Mexican beef burrito.

Ah, shit. It was one of the things he did. One of the things a semi-retired substitute teacher with a wife in heaven did. When the one real, concrete thing of beauty in your life passed on, you had to take your substitute beauty wherever you could. So if it was here, with all the smells and the voices and the piano, well, that's where the hell it was.

His upper and lower front teeth connected, and with a pretty good bang, as he physically entered the burrito for the first time. Instantly, the spices melded with the inside of his mouth and, through it, his entire nervous system.

He felt his eyes tear up. And it wasn't until his third bite that they cleared enough for him to find himself caught in the return look of the piano player seated on the little riser in the middle of the food court, less than fifty feet away. He was playing a piece Jerry Walker recognized the moment he heard it, while he was making the walk from the Manny's Mexican pickup line to the first open table. This one. The one that had put him right in the sightline of the man at the piano. And while he had recognized the piece the man was playing, he didn't know the name, didn't know if he'd ever known it.

For a few bites of burrito, Jerry Walker thought of going up and asking the pianist the name of the song. Something about the way the young man with the pleasant face and the big shoulders continued to hold his eye contact with him made Jerry Walker think he would be more than happy to answer the question. But it struck him then that the man wasn't exactly making *eye contact* with him. More, it was as if he was looking higher. Above the eyes. Just a little. Looking at what felt like his forehead. And with the music of the familiar piece continuing to pour from the fingers of the pianist, it felt, for a moment, as if the musician were reading his forehead for the musical notes his hands were playing.

Without altering his pleasant expression, the pianist withdrew his eyes and returned his gaze to the notation on his music stand. Two minutes later, the burrito was history, and so was the piece of music.

Jerry "The Sub" Walker took the last aerated straw sip of his soft drink, applied the virtually nonabsorbent Manny's Mexican napkin to his face, piled the aftermath of the meal on the tray and got up to cross to the nearest receptacle to dump it. Releasing the mess of it into the big open mouth of the trash bin, he noticed that the pianist was taking a long time between songs. Longer than usual.

He set the tray atop the stack on the receptacle and turned, expecting to see the piano player preparing to take a break between sets. But the young man with the big shoulders was still seated at the piano, poised to play his next piece, but not quite ready to do so. Because, of all the damn things, he was once again looking at Jerry "The Sub" Walker. Looking at him as if he was already anticipating that he would make the walk from the trash receptacle across the terra-cotta ceramic tile to the piano station. To ask him the question that was not only on his mind, but apparently on his face.

Jerry Walker did approach the piano, was more than halfway there when he saw the brightening, the keening of the pianist's eyes. That look, intensifying, as he neared the piano. A flash of teeth, nearly as keen as the eyes, as Jerry Walker's big shoes came to a stop on the tile.

He opened his mouth to address the glowing eyes of the pianist. But no sooner had he done so than the lights of the eyes went dark. And instead of the words of Jerry Walker entering the space above the piano in the shape of a question, it was the strings of the instrument, struck by a multitude of little padded hammers, that riddled the air.

Jerry Walker hovered at the piano for a moment, much as he would have hovered at a student's desk, anticipating a verbal response to one of his substitute teacher's questions. But by then, the piano player had turned his face and his big shoulders to the page of music again.   ·

There would be no question, no answer. The song Jerry Walker knew but didn't know would remain a mystery.

CHAPTER 14

A S was her custom, if not her complex, Hewitt had given herself the
most difficult of the assignments.

Val Patterson would interview Cassandra Langford's close circle of
girlfriends. To Hewitt, it was pretty clear the killer or killers were ap-
plying a targeted screening process in selecting the victims. This would
have involved a considerable amount of preplanning, stalking, maybe
even *interviewing* prospective victims. If there had been any sensing or
experiencing of that kind of pressure by Cassandra Langford, Hewitt
knew the girlfriends were the most likely to have been told. Either under the premise of *You're gonna think I'm nuts*, or if it had been Hewitt
with any of her long-lost buds, *There's something that's scaring the shit
out of me.*

Pete Megna's Saturday would be spent, in similar fashion, with
some of Delbert Rasmussen's male compatriots. Guys he went to ball
games with, or fished with, or preferably, tipped a few beers with, alcohol being the closest thing to a male truth serum.

So Megna and Patterson would talk to the friends of the victims.
And it would be difficult. It was always difficult. That kind of thing
would never cease being difficult. No matter how many times you did
it. No matter how much you insulated yourself against it professionally.
Yet Hewitt's job on this increasingly moody June afternoon, with its
chance of thunderstorms, was the real ball-buster. Because it would be
her job to spend some time with Delbert Rasmussen's daughter, Megan
Charlton. And that, of course, would draw the whole hive of bees to the
sorrowful nectar of the relationship dynamic that continued to rule her
own psyche.

Daughters who missed their dads. The recurring theme that she knew, deep down, would always be the recurring theme in her life. Because if it ever stopped being a theme, her life, at least as far as she knew it, would have ended.

Hewitt parked her car on the linden tree–lined street in Barrington. In a true visual sense, there was nothing different about a house that was in abject mourning, compared, for instance, to the houses on either side of it where mourning wasn't a factor, or if it was, wasn't as fresh. But as Hewitt paused on the sidewalk and took in the look and, especially, the feel of the Charlton home, why did the Cape Cod windows look back at her so sadly? Why did the roof seem so heavy it could collapse at any moment? Why did the front door seem so permanently sealed?

Upon the ringing of the bell, the front door unsealed within seconds. Hewitt had called ahead to arrange the interview. So there was no surprise on Megan Charlton's face. Her eyes recognized Hewitt. But the rest of her face didn't follow. It stayed exactly where it was, loose to the bone, numb, unwilling to respond to the nervous system's prompts to convey feeling.

"Sorry to have to disturb your family like this," Hewitt offered as she stepped into the foyer.

"The rest of them are gone," Megan Charlton answered in a voice that reflected her face. "My husband took Maggie out. To the Lincoln Park Zoo. We were all going to go. We made plans. At the beginning of the week."

"I'm sorry," Hewitt said, intending to say more. But Megan Charlton didn't leave room.

"No, I wouldn't have gone. I don't think the monkeys were going to get many laughs out of me today."

The thought of it knocked Hewitt back. The woman's father had been found brutally murdered the day before—*she had found him*— and yet here she was, reaching out and grabbing a tether to her human cortex and tossing out a self-deprecating zinger. *Jesus.*

Midwesterners were incredibly tough, resilient that way. To a fault. Or to a heroic level, depending on how you looked at it. Later, her mind replaying the thinking, Hewitt would recall the funeral of her aunt Carla, her father's sister. How, as the cemetery technician was cranking the vault down into the grave, the crank started sticking, squealing, fighting back. One of Hewitt's cousins had offered the line, "She always had to have the last word." And it had pumped a charge of laughter through the group assembled around the funeral canopy.

Ashes to ashes. Dust to dust. And make sure someone picks up my dry-cleaning when I'm gone.

They sat at the kitchen table, Hewitt and the victim's daughter. Only there was nothing funny about what she was saying now.

"The thing about it, the worst thing, is that I don't know if Maggie saw him."

There wasn't a monkey on earth that could've made Hewitt laugh now either.

"When I walked into the living room. When I saw . . ."

Hewitt watched the woman's eyes sharpen in retro-disbelief.

"I know my voice made a sound. I heard Maggie's feet . . . running . . . behind me. And I turned and grabbed her, picked her up. Instinctively. I didn't think she'd seen him. I told her later that Grandpa went to sleep on the floor and didn't wake up. At first I thought she was okay with that. But now . . . looks she's given me. I think maybe she did see."

Hewitt's right hand opened to the place on the table where a warm mug might have been, on a better day, in a more hospitable world.

"Children are resilient," Hewitt said.

"Do you really believe that?"

It was more an accusation than a question. For the answer, Hewitt had her own history to draw from. She had only seconds to debate internally whether she should open that book.

"I lost my mother when I was eight. At the time, I was just told she died. Eventually I found out she had taken her own life. Did it hurt? Worse than anything I've ever felt. Did it destroy me? Apparently not. Not completely."

Hewitt rendered the statement in her head, compressed in a sad breeze of thought. She left it there, let it blow through, until she couldn't see it anymore.

"I wish I could undo all of it," she told Megan Charlton. "That's the most difficult thing about coming into people's lives when I do. I can't rewind the tape to before. But what I can do is get you to an ending. Where we understand what happened. Not necessarily why. But we *know*. And from there, we know at least there's been some justice."

Hewitt's honesty spree had a measurable effect on the enervated soul across the table from her. Megan Charlton's eyes softened. There appeared to be a break in the private horror movie she was watching. She offered Hewitt something to drink. What she had in the house. Cranberry juice cocktail. Hewitt accepted gratefully, sipped politely as she proceeded through the interview.

Not surprisingly, there was nothing palpable in the *suspicious character/visible stalker* category. At least nothing Delbert Rasmussen had shared with his daughter. Hewitt felt there would be more fertile ground in the *profile/victim selection* area. She pushed into habits, activities, geographic tendencies. Del Rasmussen was a walker. His walks were primarily confined to his own neighborhood and its surrounding arterials. He walked every day. In the cold months, he took some of his walking indoors, to either of the two shopping malls in the area. In the summer, he liked to wander down to the local ball field and watch the little league games. He had shopped at the same grocery store, on Fridays, mostly, for years. He had his favorite hardware store, his favorite drugstore, his favorite place for lunch.

It had been a pleasantly unremarkable life, now made sensational for the most abysmal of reasons. While alive, Delbert Rasmussen's story had been incredibly normal. Now it had become Hewitt's job to help his daughter and, eventually, his granddaughter understand why the story had ended in such an incredibly abnormal way.

As the Q&A wrapped and Hewitt took a last sip of cranberry juice, she could see Megan Charlton was the one with one last question.

"I've heard, there's been talk, this theory that the victims—the young women and the older men—that they're somehow related."

Hewitt picked up her glass, tried to claim one last sip of cranberry juice, sipped cranberry air. "I've heard that theory too. I can't prove it's true. But right now, I'd have an even harder time proving it's not."

CHAPTER 15

"**Y**OU could put out a five-county warning that all men with bushy eyebrows either go in for a trim or beef up their security."

His statement completed, Brady Richter swallowed the last one-third or so of his original mouthful of pizza. He took a sip of the wine Hewitt had opened. For him. She had held off to this point, and with some difficulty, it being a cheap but intriguing-smelling Chard. Or maybe it was more intriguing because she was denying herself access to it. It was Saturday evening. She'd been off the clock since the previous day at five. She wasn't due at ISP headquarters until 8:30 Monday morning.

The reality was that she wouldn't be off duty for as long as it took to provide Megan Charlton and her daughter with an end to their story and whatever stories were yet to be written. So the Chard, no matter how vexing the bouquet, would have to go stag.

"You could also put out a warning that any young women who ever dreamed of playing Aurora in *Sleeping Beauty* not go out without an escort."

They were sitting on the living room floor, on the lavender throw blanket, the pizza box positioned elegantly on the coffee table. The Saturday night pizza picnic.

"I'm a little surprised, impressed, that you know Sleeping Beauty's real name."

"I grew up with sisters. Two of 'em. Older. Between all the videos and the dress-up, there isn't a fictional princess I haven't met."

They'd been dating for months. They'd been intimate. Very intimate. Pizza-and-wine-parties-on-the-living-room-floor intimate. But this was the first time Hewitt had heard about the sisters. Maybe that explained a few things. About him. His almost Saint Bernard–like loyalty to her. Maybe it explained a few things about her. Some of the curious mutations in her own recent behavior. Special ribbon-tying ceremonies, for one.

"Even if I had the power to cast it, there isn't a net that wide," Hewitt told him. "My gut tells me this one's so twisted there really is the possibility of more than one actor."

Brady had just taken a bite of his sausage and mushroom. This time, he didn't pause to swallow. "You're saying two stalkers, two killers. Working as some kind of unit?"

"It sounds crazier when you say it. Especially with your mouth full."

"But you're talking about crazy in the land of the crazy. You're talking what—*crazy squared?* You get into exponential craziness and anything's possible. I mean look what happened in the . . ."

Brady cut himself off where he always cut himself off. Hewitt knew damn well where it was going, what memory card was waiting to be played if she laid down her cards first.

"You're right," Hewitt said. "If the primary investigator can end up with legs wide and face smiling in the killer's bed, hell, the realm of possibility just expanded exponentially."

Her fellow picnicker seemed to slip on the blanket, even though he was seated as firmly as he could be.

"Christ, Hewitt. Where the hell is that coming from?"

"Just helping a friend finish a thought."

"Now you're just getting goofy. Make that goofy *squared.*"

"I guess I'll take goofy squared. In the nicest sense of the term."

"That's the way I meant it."

They returned their focus to the pizza. But it, like the room, seemed to have cooled to a less appealing temperature. After wolfing down an entire new piece, Brady broke the silence.

"What the hell, Hewitt? You got him. However you got there, whatever the hell you had to do, you got him."

"And so that makes it forgivable."

It was a question. But Hewitt hadn't inflected it that way.

"I wouldn't be sitting here otherwise."

The words had barely hit the air when Brady Richter wished he could suck them back in and swallow them forever. But it wasn't his own cognition that made his throat want to turn in on itself. It was the look on Hewitt's face.

She could feel the contortions of it herself, at the corners of the eyes especially, the corners of the mouth. In a nice, sugar-plum-fairy world, Brady's answer would have been, *Hell, Hewitt, it never even crossed by mind.* But clearly it had. Clearly there'd been some internal dialogue. Some internal negotiating. Christ, there might've been a full-blown jury trial. With expert witnesses. Powerful closing arguments. The whole freaking thing, right there in the courtroom of his head.

"That was really fucked up," she heard him say. He waited to say the rest until she looked up. "Right after it happened, when I came to see you in the hospital, that was it. That was me. There. Because of you. *You.* Exactly as you were."

For several minutes, Hewitt had been holding her body so tight that now when she felt his big hands on her shoulders, her upper back, she let it all go, let the wild, angry wave wash back out to sea.

Brady's hands found their way to her low back, to where her hoody sweatshirt fell just short of reaching the top of her jeans. He lifted the shirt, a little tentative. Hewitt nuzzled her face into the front of his shoulder, while the rest of her body said *go ahead.*

She let him undress her, didn't react to his fumbling first attempts at her belt buckle, the tiny hooks of her bra. Once the pants were undone and the bra came loose, the animal in Brady Richter left its cage.

He was all over her. All over all of her. His mouth tasting her skin, finding her lips, consuming them. His hands ripping at his own clothes like a wolfman in the shocking light of a full moon. And once they were off, the big bare arms and shoulders engulfing her, possessing her. And it made Hewitt wonder, even in the shudder of the first of his incursions inside her, what it was in a man that made him hold on to a woman so fiercely.

CHAPTER 16

SHE woke up naked, on her back, on top of the sheets. The blanket and comforter had been kicked off. She rolled onto her side, the top sheet rolling with her, sticking to her skin.

She was sweating. Sweating her ass off.

There was an obvious reason for this. It was hot in the apartment. Hotter than the June night could have made possible.

Hotter than hell.

She got out of bed, the sheet finally letting go of her on the third step across the wood floor of the bedroom. The floor, way too warm too.

When she got to the thermostat in the hallway, the nightlight from the bathroom illuminated the wall box enough that she was able to read it without the need to switch on the hall light.

It was eighty-nine degrees. Which made no freaking sense whatsoever. And now here she was. Up in the middle of the night. Sweating. And pissed. And she needed her damn sleep. This sucked. This really sucked. And it sucked all the more because she couldn't make any sense of it.

She looked at the setting on the thermostat. Set to HEAT. She rewound her thoughts to the last few minutes before she went to bed. The apartment had been warm. Too warm. And stuffy. But the damn neighbor's dog was always put outside at 5:00 A.M. So it could empty its thirteen-year-old bladder, and its throat of a hundred Goddamn howls. Because of that, the windows had stayed closed and she'd gone with the AC, even though the night was cool.

But clearly she hadn't. Dumbass she was, she'd moved the setting button from the middle to the right instead of the left. In the third week of June, she'd turned on the heat. Setting it to eighty-nine freaking degrees, though. That she didn't remember.

Whatever. Whatever the hell. She set the thing to seventy-five now. And this time, on the A-freaking-C.

Cooling the apartment would take a while. She was too sweaty to go back to bed anyway. So, by the orange-moon-glow of the nightlight, she took a cool, middle-of-the-night shower. And that helped. Rinsing away all of the sweat, most of the anger.

Turning the thing to HEAT, that she got. But setting it to eighty-nine, that she didn't get, wouldn't get, no matter how long she thought about it. So she stopped thinking. Inhaled the smell of the strawberry soap. Stopped thinking some more.

Life got so much easier that way. When she stopped thinking. If she could just stop thinking, life would be perfect, heavenly. Maybe that's what heaven was. A place you went when you were done with all the Goddamn thinking. A place where you never had to do any thinking again. All you had to do was stand there in your innocence in a soft, warm waterfall, smelling the wild strawberries, feeling peaceful, sleepy.

Kelly Gratchen fell asleep. Standing right there. In the shower. For maybe a few seconds, she figured. But wonderful seconds they were. Heavenly seconds. Blissful seconds. Away from the thinking. Away from the thinking that always ended up in the pissed-off places her thoughts would go.

Her knees had buckled. That's what woke her. Standing there in the shower, sleeping, her knees had been the first thing to go. She wouldn't have made a very good cow. Cows could sleep standing up. Of course, they had four legs. And three stomachs. And enough nipples to take on a hockey team.

Fuck. She was doing it again. Thinking. She was out of heaven, officially out of heaven.

As she toweled off in the orange-moon-glow of the nightlight, she noticed that the bathroom door she'd left open just a crack had opened almost halfway. From the wind, her thinking told her. But that couldn't be. Because she'd turned on the AC. And the windows in the apartment were still closed to the dog from hell.

CHAPTER 17

HE wasn't going to let her go. Whoever he was, he wasn't going to let her go. And she knew, if this held true, that he was the last human being that would ever hold her at all.

He held her, but so far he had not touched her. He had wrapped her in a blanket—several blankets, then tied it tight with ropes. He had done this while she was unconscious. But her mind was awake again, even if her body couldn't move. Her mind was clear to what was happening. And she knew the man who continued to hold her down against the carpet of this unfamiliar floor was the same man whose presence she had sensed and felt in the parking ramp. The shadow of a man. The shadow of a shadow.

Why had he been watching her? Why had he wanted her?

"*Why me?*" she heard her wild, terrified voice cry. And again, even louder. "*Why me?*"

She knew he would not answer. There had been no response to any of her previous cries, her shouts, her calls to be let go or at least be told why she was being held.

Her face was pressed into the floor, into the dust of the rug, in this place he had taken her. After watching her in her house. After waiting while she dressed in her pajamas after the shower. Waiting with the towel he forced over her face. The chemical towel.

"*Please, what do you want from me?*"

Hot burn of surprise then, as she felt him release her head. She heard him unzip something, a bag, a backpack. She heard his hands taking something from it.

Though her body was subdued, her voice was not. And she heard it again, frantic, faraway. *"Please, tell me why. Please! What if I'm not the right one? What if I'm not the one you want?"*

She felt his hands on her feet now. Her bare feet. She felt the plastic of the gloves he was wearing. Handling her carefully. *Gently.* But in a way that didn't feel right. In a way that didn't seem to come easily to his hands.

The voice that came from him then was not the voice of a sick man. But the voice of a sad boy.

"I'm sorry. I'm sorry this is what he does to you."

The apology struck her, touched her. And her mind began to lose its clarity. Like a kaleidoscope twisted, shuffled, exploded. Because for this impossible moment, she felt like there might be a chance, a hope that he might still have a soul.

But even as the kaleidoscope was spinning, as the fears of her body punched through the hold of her mind, the spell of it all was broken by a feeling she had never felt, in a part of her body she never thought of. A pressure, a pushing of something cold, inside, *underneath*, the nail of her big toe. Followed by a sharp poke, a piercing of that strange skin. And she thought, as the kaleidoscope froze in a brilliant red pattern, of a finger, a spindle, a single drop of blood.

CHAPTER 18

THEY had crashed on the living room floor, on the Oriental rug, in a post-sex torpor, partially covered by the lavender throw, Hewitt more so than Brady.

At a little after one, she stirred, opened her eyes to the VCR clock, didn't like the idea that she could have been asleep in the big soft bed. But that, at least on this night, was the price of not being alone.

Hewitt got up, tiptoed past Brady and went to the kitchen for a glass of water. Returning to the living room, she saw that Brady had stirred too, in the instinctual pursuit of sustenance. And he'd found it, not far away. On the coffee table. Beneath the cardboard lid. In all its leftover, room-temperature glory.

"Hate to see it go to waste," he said to Hewitt, looking up, catching her in a shard of streetlight through the drawn drapes.

"Yeah, who would want to see that?" Hewitt said. "Can I get you anything else? A side salad? Something from the bar?"

"Nah, I'm good. Better than good. Almost perfect. Eating cold pizza naked. While looking at you naked. I could die a happy man. Right now. Well, maybe after one more piece."

"What would make it perfect?" Hewitt asked.

Brady just looked at her, chewing with a half-drunk, half-recently-laid look.

"You said naked pizza and me standing here was *almost* perfect," Hewitt said. "What would make it perfect?"

"If you turned around a couple of times and let me see that too."

Stupid as it was, although seemingly less stupid at two o'clock in the morning, Hewitt indulged him.

A half-turn, with a pause. Then a full revolution. With another pause, for effect.

"I believe perfection is well within our grasp," she heard Brady say in a low, middle-of-the-night voice. And from there, she just went with it. Bought into it, believed it, sold it.

In that minute between 1:09 and 1:10 A.M., Elizabeth Taylor Hewitt learned something. Performing in that thin ray of spotlight. Moving, turning, touching into the cell memory of all the ballet classes from her childhood. Pirouetting. In the altogether. In the middle of the night. With an audience of one who desperately wanted her to achieve perfection, no matter how subjective, no matter how short-lived.

And she realized, Hewitt did, on her eleventh, twelfth revolution, that perfection wasn't something measured. It wasn't something achieved. It wasn't something attached to an end result.

Perfection was, had always been, could never be anything but, a totally naked feeling in the middle of nowhere.

CHAPTER 19

I T begins with a music box. The vision. The dream. A lovely music box. A sweet music box. A perfect music box.

The equally lovely, equally sweet, equally perfect hands open the exquisite music box, their pale flesh tone paler still against the dark walnut veneer of the box.

Even before the lid is open, the music has begun. By the time the lid reaches its perpendicular angle to the red velvet stage, the ballerina is in her second pirouette.

This is her one pose, her one attitude, her one grace. This slow, agonizingly slow turning to the music that never changes, the music in this tinny pizzicato version once composed for personal adornment on the smiling teeth and dark spaces of a Pleyel piano.

It is not difficult to imagine the sound of the original Pleyel. Nor is it a great leap to imagine the ballerina breaking free of the set *passé* and beginning to exercise her artistic will on the mother-of-pearl stand that rises from the red velvet like the pedestal of a sea nymph pressed up by the hand of Poseidon below.

Thus she begins to move. Always mindful of the vision. Not just the rhythm, the tempo, but more so, the mood, the wistfulness, the sweet sorrow, the hope, the longing, the love, the fear.

The nocturne.

A single electronic beep breaks the spell. The player of memories checks his watch to make certain the beep has sounded at the prearranged time. The temporary glow of the watch illuminates the player's face. He cannot see this. But he feels it. This sallow, distant hint of warmth against his face.

A sunrise on Pluto.

Yes, the watch has performed its function properly. Which means he is within a minute now. This wide universe of scattering seconds until he will experience the second and final piece of music of the evening.

A lot can happen in less than a minute. Kings crowned. Presidents assassinated. Love lost. Love found. Love made.

He opens his eyes to the room, to the reality that he is not alone, to the warm, shivering comfort of that.

The seconds peel off, one by one. He hears them pass. Each one hanging for a beat in the heavy air, then ripping away from the uterine wall of time, to be subsumed by another, and another.

Across the room, the tiny jewels of green light beckon, entice. But there is no hurry. Not now. Now that they are together in this place. In the night. In the welcoming coils of darkness.

UPSTAIRS, the sleeper is awake. But only in the barest essence of awakening. It has begun with a nudging of his sleep state, a permeation of his most recent dream by the musical air that enters the caves of his ears.

For several measures the music takes the form of coloration and visual interpretation in the context of the dream. But the dreamer's mind begins to discover, in ascending order, the presence, the sound, the tone, the tempo, the structure, the instrument, the piano.

But I don't have a piano.

It is this thought that punctures the dream. And in the wake of its dissolution, Jerry Walker is sitting up in his bed, truly awake, truly alive. As alive as he will ever be.

DOWNSTAIRS, the window of time has closed. And with it, time has accelerated. Time has exploded. It all happens, as it has happened each time before, with amazing swiftness.

Not even eight measures have played, but already the body is active upstairs, is taking the first steps it will take to deliver itself to him.

On the staircase now. The body coming. The breathing still the labored breathing of sleep, with a rattle of confusion at the edges of the inhalations.

At the bottom of the stairs, the body pauses. As if it, he, has stopped to listen to the music. But no, he is on the move again. Floorboards cracking, wincing beneath his feet. The sound of it preceding him into the living room. Where he pauses again, his eyes finding the little green jewels of light. And then, finding the lovely one who sits waiting for him on the sofa, as if she has been seated there waiting for him forever.

The breathing stops. The flow of blood between heart and limbs seems to have stopped too. And there is only the music. The music. And the three of them. Together, once more.

So stunned, so taken is he by the loveliness, that he does not even feel the presence of the other man in the room until, in the twenty-sixth measure of the composition, the stockings seal around his throat.

CHAPTER 20

I T was the perfect evening for a man. Pizza. Sex. Minimal conversation. A little sleep. A little pizza revisited.

Brady hadn't stayed the night. He was on his weekend shift, and that included Sunday, which had already come. So he'd left about 2:30. And Hewitt was fine with that. She'd grown so accustomed to sleeping alone that the presence of another large mammal in the bed with her was still a major cause of sleep interruptus. Maybe she'd have to upgrade the queen-sized bed to a king. With, for sleeping purposes, a long body pillow down the center.

All things considered, it had been a good night for her too. The kind of thing you still needed to grab a piece of, even when the hunt was on. Her father had handed down a tale to her that had been handed down in his family from the clan's farming days. It was the story of the guy who could skin half a horse, take a break to eat his lunch while sitting on the unskinned half, then finish the job over a cup of coffee.

The lesson of that was no matter how intense or grim the gig, you still had to take your breaks. You had to eat. Eating, of course, being a relative term. As Hewitt knew, there was more than one way to feed yourself.

So she was up, ready to feed again before getting back on the horse. She microwaved the water. Added the brown powder. Made the toast. Buttered. Jellied. At the desk with her breakfast, she summoned the Mac, went to her messages. One each from Patterson and Megna. Nothing earth-shattering from either the girlfriends of Cassandra Langford or the buddies of Delbert Rasmussen. Each had another interview or two to run down. Hewitt thought of telling them to hold off until

Monday. But when she typed in her reply, she found herself telling them to stay after it.

What the hell? She was going to stay after it. Although, as she picked up her plate and licked up the spilled jelly, she had no idea that it was the case itself that was coming after her via the first incoming call of the day.

Lattimore. In his Sunday morning preacher's voice. And it was clear from his opening inflections, that humanity had gone to hell again.

That another princess had turned up at another roadside tribute didn't surprise Hewitt. The fact that it had occurred just forty-eight hours since the last one did. Something had squeezed the bad brain's juice beyond what the glass could hold. And now, on a pretty Sunday morning, June twenty-second, the summer freaking solstice, it was Hewitt's horse to skin.

Lattimore had made that clear in his closing missive. "Hewitt, do whatever the hell you have to."

"Does that mean sleeping with the enemy is back on the table?" Hewitt posed.

"Everything's on the table," Lattimore told her. "Including, right now, another dead girl."

SAME picnic table bier. Same blue plastic shroud. Same assemblage of the curious. But at a different wayside. In a different county. This time, Kane. And of course, this was a different princess. And Hewitt had to push her guts back down into her solar plexus when she lifted the sheet, saw the same look of destroyed innocence on a another tragically expired face.

Her name was Kelly Gratchen. And it had been her outrageous fate to have fit the bad brain's profile. But it was all there, as impossible for Hewitt to miss as it had been for the killer. The delicate features of the face. The doll-like mouth. The thick, flowing locks. Seeing the hair this way, in the morning glow of the summer solstice sun, pulled Hewitt's musical mind into a chamber she rarely entered. *French Impressionism.* Mr. Claude Debussy. "The Girl with the Flaxen Hair." In the liner notes of *Sketches of Spain*, there had been a reference to the way the impressionistic compositions of Debussy had influenced Miles Davis.

Standing there over the surrendered form of Kelly Gratchen, Hewitt was having this disembodied thought. But only for a moment, as a man's voice pushed its way through the picnic table crowd. Hewitt knew immediately. The voice of the father.

As is often the case with an attractive daughter, there were no readily observable signs that the father was the carrier of the pretty gene. And even if he had been one of the leading male models of the 1970s, the sudden onset of the first stage of grief was very efficient at draining the handsomeness from a man's face.

A couple of county deputies reacted to his approach as if they planned to restrain him. But Hewitt shook them off, said softly, "Let him."

The uniforms separated. The wild-faced father pushed between them, stumbling just before he reached the picnic table. Hewitt didn't try to intercept him, didn't attempt to make eye contact. If she needed, she would have her chance to meet him, to see, intimately, an aspect of him his own daughter had been spared. But now it was his time. For the *Oh, nos*, the *Oh, my Gods*. It was his time to find the thought that pummeled Hewitt's mind, the thought he expressed in a half-whisper, with his own face pressed into the side of his daughter's.

"It's the first day of summer, honey. It's the first day of summer."

CHAPTER 21

SHOE Number Two dropped that afternoon. In Mount Prospect. And it was a seriously large shoe. Viewing the body in the living room of the modestly furnished saltbox, Hewitt noted that the latest deposed king had walked his kingdom on a pair of larger-than-life feet.

Without the kind of media scrutiny the outdoor victims attracted, Gerard Walker remained on his back on the living room floor, uncovered, just as his deposer had left him. The yellow pajamas looked like they'd been made for someone else. Someone less big. Less heavy-boned. Someone with smaller feet. They had to be seventeens. Eighteens. The big toes were about the size of a baby's foot. The morgue techs were going to have to find a tag with an extra-large band.

As predominant as the feet were in the overall physiology of the latest victim, it was the face, once more, that revealed the most telling information to Hewitt. They sat there, poised above the eyes, like twin wooly caterpillars that, at any moment, could stand up on multiple legs and creep their way to a meeting point at the victim's worry crease. His *former* worry crease.

A local Mount Prospect detective, a young guy who smelled like Calvin Klein Something and cotton candy, nuzzled up alongside her without actually touching.

"Agent Hewitt?" His hand was out, expecting hers. "Matt Findorff. MPPD. I was the first one here, after the uniforms."

Hewitt shook his hand, decided *Calvin Cotton Candy* was a better name for him. *Where the hell was that smell coming from?*

The answer came not in the form of a statement, but in the form of a bubble. Or a potential bubble. Hewitt could only hope he wouldn't

actually blow the thing and pop it. He didn't. Instead, he sucked the
pink wad back into his mouth, resumed chewing.

"How's the upstairs look?" Hewitt asked.

"No indication of a struggle. Everything where you would expect.
As if the guy just got up to take a leak and never made it back."

"But he didn't get up to pee," Hewitt said. "Something drew him
out, called him out. Something got him downstairs. Where the killer
was waiting."

Detective Calvin Cotton Candy was eyeing the body on the floor.

"He's such a big guy," the detective mused.

"Big enough that he should've been able to fight back?"

"One would think."

Hewitt gave him a collegial smile. She regretted it when she read the
misinterpretation on his face.

"You ever had a pair of nylons pulled tight around your throat in
the middle of the night?"

He shook his head, not liking the tone of the question.

"My guess is it would tend to suck the fight right out of you,"
Hewitt said.

He swallowed hard, didn't like the taste of that, either.

"Thank you, Detective," Hewitt offered, in her end-of-story tone.
"I'll be in touch."

She left him there, moved toward the front hall, the staircase, feeling a little pang of guilt for having pulled down the shade on him so
fast. He was a nice-looking guy, with workout shoulders and hips. He
could've been a Brady Two, perfect for the day when Brady One either
took off on his own or was sent there by not-so-subtle suggestion.

But that was negative thinking. And on the positive side, from Detective Calvin Cotton Candy's point of view, she had probably saved
him from any number of life-altering shenanigans. Like waking up one
fine morning with a ribbon tied around Calvin Jr.

She was at the top of the staircase. Moving down the hallway, she
paused at the bathroom door, allowed herself a couple steps inside. Definitely a man's bathroom. Smells of shaving cream and inexpensive
spiced cologne, with the essence of not having been cleaned as often as

if a woman had still been living in the house. And there was the other telltale sign of being a true men's room. The toilet seat, locked and loaded at ninety degrees. Forensic and, to an equal degree, morbid curiosity directed her eyes to the rim of the bowl.

There were a couple of little, recently dried pee puddles on top of the many-days'-worth of previous ones, all made to bond to the porcelain like some uric crème-brûlée glaze. Hewitt knew that sad confection well. Her dad had been a chronic seat-up, no-clean-up type. And her mother had taken care of the wipe-up jobs. Hewitt had seen her do it. And the most amazing thing about it was the way her mother had done it without making a face, either way. There'd been no look of distaste, and no staging of a pleasant smile. Just a taking-care-of-business thing.

Once her mother had lifted off the planet, the wipe-up job had fallen to her. And she had performed her job well, right down to the taciturn face of industry she'd co-opted from her mother. That face had served her well, through the endless river of atrocities and calamities in her professional and personal lives. Standing in a man's bathroom now, she resisted the little nudge from her nervous system to pick up a couple of tissues and give them a squirt of disinfectant.

Returning to the hallway, Hewitt sniffed the air for directions to the dead man's bed. It was the first door on the left. Once again, a guy's room. Yet the impression of the woman who had once shared the boar's nest of a California king mattress wasn't completely gone. A trio of fairly florid, but artsy enough gold-framed prints on the walls. The gold tissue box cover on the dresser. The ceiling hooks in the corners, waiting patiently for the reintroduction of the hanging plants that had once freshened the room.

The room definitely needed freshening now. Hewitt flashed the thought of opening a bedroom window, which caromed her mind to the Delbert Rasmussen living room, to that crime scene, to that place on the floor where they had both lain. He, in death. She, in her living attempt to comprehend it.

She listened to the buzz and bump of activity downstairs. Listened past it, through it.

Sound.

It was sound. Whatever had first pulled Gerard Walker and Delbert Rasmussen and Terrence McCullough from sleep and then lured them to come and find the reason for it, the source of it. A voice? Couldn't have been. Not unless it had been a voice familiar to all three victims. Virtually no chance of that. And without question, an unfamiliar voice wouldn't have resulted in three grown men walking right into an ambush.

A nylon stocking ambush.

The back of her neck felt a chill. Her breathing quickened. Whatever it was, the sound had to be innocuous enough to have left them vulnerable. Harmless enough that fear hadn't fully awakened them to the potential danger. But given the context, the middle of the night, the darkness of a house, what pattern of waves and frequency could have negotiated such a détente?

CHAPTER 22

"THINKING of crawling in?"

In her inner focus on the aural world, Hewitt had failed to pick up the sound of the intruder's approach from the hallway.

"I prefer a queen," Hewitt said. "Preferably a Stearns and Foster."

Lattimore didn't smile. But he allowed, with a slight contraction of his facial muscles, that it was a good comeback.

"What brings you to the front?" Hewitt asked.

"Truth, justice," Lattimore said.

"Throw in *The American Way*, and you could put on a blue and red suit with a big *S* on your chest."

The smile muscles twitched again.

"As of this morning," Lattimore said, taking a couple of steps into the bedroom, "we've officially gone from top story to special report with every news organization on the planet."

Hewitt, feeling something eerie about Lattimore's approach, even for him, backed up a little deeper into the room.

"Six murders with choreography will do that," Hewitt said.

Now Lattimore's face let him have his smile. But it wasn't a smile of amusement. "Is that how you see it? Choreography?"

Conscious that her weight was pushing back into her heels, Hewitt tried to straighten her posture. Without some serious moving, she was out of backing-up room. Her calves were already pressed against the side beam of the bed frame.

"I see it as creativity, yes. I see it as elements of style, a calling card. Like an artist signing his work."

Lattimore took another step into the room, just enough that he could close the door behind him.

"Hewitt, I don't give a shit about art. But I do like a good story. And I need one. A new one. Right now we have the story of a killer with six notches on his belt. And the people who are pursuing him have Jack Fucking Shit."

Given his body language and the look in his deep-set eyes, Hewitt had to take a couple of quieting breaths, to reassure herself that the storyline wasn't about to change to *Supervisor murders lead detective in victim's bedroom.*

"That's where you come in, Hewitt. We need to advance a story that *we* can control. To demonstrate to the rest of the world that we might have some clue as to what the hell we're dealing with here."

Hewitt's calves were really pressing into the bed frame now, enough that she knew she'd leave the room with marks. Better there than her ass. But with the way Lattimore leered at her while she had the thought, she wasn't totally convinced she was safe there either.

"So let me see if I understand you," she said. "You want me to come up with something. I'm assuming you'd prefer something real. But in lieu of that, my educated guess is you'd settle for something less than real."

Lattimore took a moment to map his next statement.

"There are certain holy men in the world, Hewitt, who believe that none of this is real. I'm not real. You're not real. The victims. The killer. None of it. They believe this is all some kind of play of the mind. Some wildass, elaborate dream."

He took a half-step back, toward the closed door, a move Hewitt interpreted as his first step in leaving. Her hope, anyway. She felt her calves release a little from the bed frame.

"Don't you find it interesting, though, that somehow we're all having the same dream?"

Her question didn't ruffle Lattimore in the least. His response seemed preprogrammed.

"But that's just it, Hewitt," he said, his voice calm, but his eyes more active than they'd been since he'd entered the room. "We're *not* dreaming the same dream."

If it was supposed to unnerve her, it succeeded. But Hewitt didn't tell him that. Nor, from what she could discern, did she give it up non-verbally. Instead, she gave him a verbal response that couldn't have surprised him more.

"Christ, we might as well be married."

It took Lattimore a moment to reclaim his mouth muscles. "You're going to have to take me through the thought process on that, Hewitt."

"Well, here we are. In the bedroom together. You don't really want me. But life's circumstances have dictated that you need me."

It was meant to unnerve him. And it did. He tried to cover it with a couple of dominant-male shows of teeth. But that only made it more obvious.

"You know what, Hewitt? I'll take your shit. I'll take it. And if you've got any more to pile on, I'll take that too. And maybe someday we'll get together and laugh about it over beer and pretzels. And we'll laugh and pat each other on the back and talk about that crazy time when all those young women and old men were dropping like flies."

Without realizing she'd moved again, Hewitt felt her calves backed into the bed frame as if, this time, they might never get off.

"But the only way we have that special evening, Hewitt," Lattimore leered, "is if you stop fucking with me and use that charm of yours to get this piece of shit."

CHAPTER 23

TWO days hatched, staggered around and fell. And Hewitt was into early Wednesday morning when the epiphany rose up and tickled her ears. Like so many of her life's telling insights, it came when she was lying on her back, in her bed, without the reassurance of another warm body with her.

The two intervening days had seen no shortage of activity. There was Lattimore's decision to step up the monitoring of waysides by state troopers in a five-county area that included Cook, Du Page, Kane, Lake and McHenry. There was also Lattimore's latest attempt at a news conference. On that front, it was *déjà cable news* all over again. And as Hewitt had anticipated, a couple of questions had come her way, even though she wasn't on the dais to field them. Her little mousse-topped buddy from FOX had floated a question about her current role in the investigation, given her body of experience.

Lattimore had spit back an answer like: *Special Agent Hewitt is an integral part of the investigative team*—and left it at that. For some reason, the captain had decided not to share with the media any sound bites from the conversation in Gerard Walker's bedroom.

On the forensic front, the results were in on the chemical agent that had stopped Cassandra Langford's heart. As with the first princess, the killer chemical was Ketamine. The injection site, the skin beneath the nail of the right big toe. And again, it appeared there were two specific injection sites in that same patch of skin. So, for the second time, the life-taker had taken meticulous care not to mar, not to abuse, the physical form of the victim. And this, hedgerow eyebrows aside, had become the one element of the case that beguiled Hewitt the most.

It would have been one thing for the killer to have taken such care to hide the injection site if he was trying to mask the fact that the women had died by some other means. But this level of obfuscation was so obsessive that it iced Hewitt's blood thinking about it.

It was as if the killer was doing everything possible *not* to hurt the woman he was killing. As if he were sparing her. Protecting her. Preserving her. Almost as if he weren't really killing her. And the two injection points. That was curious too. Was the first one to narcotize her and the second to finish? What the hell went on in between? There were no signs of sexual abuse. So what had he done between shots? What would a monster do with a sleeping beauty?

Hewitt continued to go down her mental list of the case until she finally dropped off to an uneasy sleep. Counting sheep would have led to a more pleasant slumber. But it wasn't sheep that were being slaughtered out there.

FOUR-AND-A-HALF hours after the last butterfly of conscious thought skittered across her mind, Hewitt's brain was wide awake again. She was on her back, her skin damp against her T-shirt, her mind wet with the release of the information she'd been craving.

She felt her hands moving to her face, her eyes, finding the thin, nicely trimmed eyebrows. Her eyebrows. Sitting up, she reached to the nightstand for her notebook, her eyes rolling over the digits on the clock-radio. *5:12.* First light was only an unverified report through the cracks of her blinds. She switched on the lamp.

Sitting there in bed, her legs crossed at the ankles, Hewitt quickly knocked out two sketches, side-by-side. On the left, she rendered the image of a man in a bed, a composite of the three victims, big in the body, heavy on the eyebrows. To the right of this, she sketched the same three-in-one man laid out in composite death on the living room floor.

She paused for a moment to consider the sketches. Her mind clicked through the variables, like a safecracker listening, feeling the tumblers. When the last tumbler clicked with a little ping of resolution, she knew she had it, knew she was right.

In the notebook, between the sketches of the man asleep and the man permanently asleep, she drew five parallel, horizontal lines. Within these, she drew four solid, ascending circles, then added a straight-line tail to each. Quarter notes. In the spaces of a staff. Which, it occurred to her, and which any schoolkid with a reasonable attention span knew, spelled the word *face*.

CHAPTER 24

I T was music. Not necessarily the *do-re-mi* kind, the *f-a-c-e*. But what-ever it was that had lured those three big men out of their beds was, in essence, musical. Enough to make them listen, to make them wonder.

The spoken call of a human voice would have sent up a red flag. But a musical voice, that was something not merely nonthreatening, but in-triguing, compelling.

Her face bathed in the morning light of the microwave, Hewitt drew another example. The wind. It had a frequency, a vibration, a pitch. The wind banging a shutter against the house was a sound that communicated trouble. The sound of wind blowing through chimes, however, was a sonic event that echoed in the dells of pleasure.

The vibration and pitch of the microwave motor weren't exactly musi-cal. But the Pavlovian sense of knowing what awaited her at the end of the hum and the closing beeps resonated, in its own way, in the pleasure zone.

Forty-five minutes later, the chocolate buzz still with her, Hewitt was in the Mazda, on the Tri-State, en route to a porch step meeting with whatever deputy the Lake County Sheriff's Office dispatched to let her into the Rasmussen crime scene.

Her mind was definitely in a Miles Davis place. It was a morning like that. Sky kind of gray. Kind of white. *Kind of Blue*. And if she was in a Miles Davis kind of state, she was also, at least according to the famous liner notes, in a kind of quasi–J. S. Bach state of mind. Bach aficionado or not, she had at least become an unofficial student since her little floor exercise in Terrence McCullough's living room. Whether there was another floor exercise in the offing on this gray, white and blue morning would be born out soon enough. With "All Blues" set on

REPEAT, Hewitt made her way through the azure-slate atmosphere and into the blood-red heart of Libertyville.

The deputy was parked at the curb, with his window half-down and the rest of him half-asleep. It wasn't until the second rap of Hewitt's knuckles against his window that he looked up. Hewitt's first thought seeing his face: *Young Walter Matthau.*

"Deep in thought?" she said.

"Deep in a three-week-old baby on the home front," he told her as he stepped out of the car.

"Boy or girl?" Hewitt asked, sounding interested, even to herself.

"Little girl," he said, extending his hand. "I'm Deputy Drake. Jim."

The way he did it, between the gesture and the timing, it felt to Hewitt as if he were introducing his hand as Jim. So she took Little Jim, all five fingers of him. It was an overly aggressive handshake on Big Jim's part. Which seemed to belie the Walter Matthau look. Or maybe he was just trying to prove how wide awake he was now.

"First?"

"And based on the first three weeks, maybe last."

They were halfway up the Rasmussen driveway.

"Well, I'm afraid I can't quite relate," Hewitt said. "I haven't been there."

The deputy gave her a look as they continued toward the back of the property, a quick assessment, reading her movement, her gait, her age, in an equine kind of way. She could only hope he wouldn't try to pull her lips open and check her teeth. But she understood why he was looking at her that way. He was doing the math, figuring how much time she might still have to know the experience firsthand.

At the back steps, she was struck by the sense that this was the first time she hadn't added a *yet* when the issue had presented itself. She watched as the deputy stuck the key into the padlock, knowing it was only a matter of a few years before mother nature would slap a padlock on her.

In the glass of the backdoor window, she saw her face, couldn't imagine herself getting any older than she was right there, right then. And it made the pit of her stomach flutter, or maybe it was the uterus itself, at the thought that there was nothing she could do to stop it.

"I hope you find what you're looking for," she heard the deputy say.

"Thank you," she said. "That would be a lovely development."

The deputy swung the door open for her and stepped aside.

"I won't be long," Hewitt told him.

"Take whatever time you need."

Translated: The meter was still running on his squad car nap.

Hewitt let herself inside, smelled the smell of nobody home, of nobody having been home for a long time. Dust, old curtains, expired plants. But entering the kitchen, a little hint of life having been lived. A spice rack. On the wall, in a nook that also housed an old butcher's block. The spices, to Hewitt's mind, like a stick of incense lit in a room of bad smells the morning after a wild party.

The sole guest at this post-postmortem party made her way into the living room, where her black Steve Maddens came to a stop at the feet of the ethereal body of the victim, Delbert Rasmussen. He was still there, that aspect of him. In that sense he would always be there. Eventually new owners would come. They'd pull the carpet and pad. They'd open all the windows for days. They'd paint the place in antiseptic. But that sense, that essence of Delbert Rasmussen, would leave the house only when it was good and ready.

Hewitt's own body, ethereal and otherwise, was abandoning that space now and moving across the room to the only piece of furniture that held any interest for her. Its blond wood veneer came reasonably close to matching the shade and grain of the coffee and end tables. Hewitt took a handkerchief, used it to lift the lid, the springs and hinges voicing a squeal of protest as she did.

There was a record on the turntable, a 33$\frac{1}{3}$ LP. Hewitt leaned in to read the label. FRANK SINATRA. The first song on the platter: "The Summer Wind."

Well, now she had to. And scarcely had she articulated the rationalization in her head when she saw her handkerchief-holding right hand going about the business of switching the control to PHONO and turning on the stereo.

It took a good half-minute to warm up. And when it finally did, Hewitt pulled the lever that lifted the tone arm, swung it slowly over the record and lowered the needle to the dusty old vinyl. And dusty it was. And scratched. A forensic analysis would have probably found traces of popcorn butter, pizza sauce and Brylcreem in the grooves as well. For starters. But that only gave the music a nostalgic intimacy as the first strains of the intro hit the air.

Hewitt's eyes fell into the grooves of the vinyl, rode them like a merry-go-round, was joined on the bobbing horse next to her by one Francis Albert Sinatra as the vocal kicked in.

The summer wind came blowing in, from across the sea . . .

On the spinning vinyl, Hewitt overlaid a picture, an Instamatic photo taken by her mother, of her dad and the four-year-old retro-incarnation of herself on a carousel at a church festival. The Instamatic camera's shutter didn't have the deftness to freeze its subjects on a moving merry-go-round. But it did manage to grab enough detail of their broadly smiling faces to identify them as a father-daughter pair, she sitting rigidly on her rainbow pony, he standing beside her, his big hands around her hips and shoulders to block any chance of an accident. And the slow shutter had resulted in the wavy swaths of motion at the edges of the images, so that, years later, it paid a kind of blurry homage to the transience not only of that brief moment in the history of amusement rides, but of the transience of the whole human carnival.

The thought of that was depressing enough that Hewitt left the turntable, backed away from the stereo console. But the music had its hooks in her. And she wondered, standing there in the middle of the living room, if the sound of Sinatra crooning on some windswept oceanside party deck was the music that had tickled Delbert Rasmussen out of sleep and invited him downstairs to his strangulation.

As Hewitt approached the stereo again, she allowed herself to imagine being asphyxiated by a pair of nylons with Sinatra playing her out. But she could conjure that image for only a handful of seconds. Because once her eyes tuned themselves to the radio dial, everything else—Sinatra, the party deck, the whole damn ocean—disappeared.

It was the setting of the dial. The little red line. Positioned between

93 and 94 on the FM band. Closer to 94 than 93. With the handkerchief, she reached down to switch the stereo's setting from PHONO to
RADIO, realized as she was doing it that the control had been set to RA-
DIO from the beginning. And in her rush to hear Sinatra, she'd blown
right past the wonderfully salient fact that the last thing that had played
on this stereo was the radio.

It began to play now, Sinatra instantly preempted by a commercial
for a local Italian eatery. She had heard this radio spot before, but never
on this station. When the commercial concluded, a silent pause ensued,
and Hewitt knew it was the end of the commercial pod. A pleasant little theme on guitar bloomed up, giving Hewitt the confirmation, even
before the prerecorded, bullfrog-voiced announcer rose up from the
guitar hole and identified the station.

"Chicago's classical voice. WCLS. Ninety-three point eight. FM."

After a pause for the fade of the guitar, a live announcer chimed in,
less formal-sounding than the bullfrog, but definitely from the same
pond of enunciation.

"Next up a famous work by Franz Schubert that, no matter how
many times it's played, never quite comes to an end." He added a
squeeze of syrup to his voice then, to make sure the listeners knew his
tongue was planted against his cheek. "It's Schubert's Symphony Number Eight. The *Unfinished* Symphony. Neville Marriner conducts the
Academy of St. Martin-in-the-Fields."

Hewitt felt a surge of heat in the bone of her forehead. Perhaps, she
thought, not unlike the surge Franz Schubert had felt when the theme
for the *Unfinished* Symphony first flashed its doomed patterns across
the right side of his brain.

CHAPTER 25

THE Gerard Walker crime scene had been sealed for forty-eight hours. So again, Hewitt had to contact the locals for access. She said her quick good-bye to the blearier-than-ever Walter Matthau likeness, boarded the Mazda, and issued her request to the Mount Prospect PD.

Before turning on the radio, Hewitt lowered the two rear windows, even though, given the warmth of the day, the AC was up. She did this for acoustic reasons. Jazz was fine in a closed environment. Confined to a smoky nightclub with shitty ventilation. That was jazz. But this was classical. And classical music, a symphony especially, needed space, needed air, needed room to breathe. Especially a symphony that had died before it had ever breathed its first breath.

Unfinished though it was, Schubert's Symphony No. 8, the first movement, was up and running inside, and to a lesser degree, outside the Mazda. While nowhere near an aficionado, Hewitt appreciated classical music, respected the art. There was something sadly beautiful about the Schubert piece. *Hauntingly beautiful*, the writer of the liner notes would have no doubt chosen.

Classical music just wasn't what she did. It wasn't the music. It was the people. The patrons. The people who truly listened. The people who got it. There was always something a little ivory tower about them. Something that affected a distinction in social strata. Or maybe it was just her. Having a bug up her ass over her lack of pedigree. Thinking of herself that way.

Maybe, though, in her own sweet way, she was just as guilty of that herself. Her love of jazz. The one true American art form. In that belief, maybe there was a *haute musical* attitude of her own.

The first movement of the Schubert symphony drew to an end. The second began. And as she listened, a part of her waited, more tensely than she would have figured, for the *Unfinished* Symphony to come to some sort of abrupt, disconcerting ending. As if Schubert had just suddenly dropped his pen in the middle of an arpeggio and fallen off the piano bench. She almost expected it. The sudden cessation of the orchestra, followed by the thud of a muted kettle drum. With the high scream of a solo violin seconds later, as the wife or mistress entered the chamber to find the great composer stricken on the floor.

Hewitt had no idea what the real history had been. She felt now she would have to find out. Someday. The postsolstice sun was hot against the tops of her hands on the steering wheel. The day was blooming, igniting all around her speeding car as her hands continued to absorb the heat. She exhaled heavily a couple of times. To reduce her anxiety over Schubert's impending collapse. To soften her lungs beneath the weight of six dead and, she had every reason to believe, more to come.

Minutes later, with Franz Schubert still very much alive, she met the Mount Prospect deputy who'd been assigned to let her into the Walker house, allowed him to do exactly that. With a minimum of fuss. A minimum of cognition. Stepping through the door, hearing his *you're welcome*, her *thank you*, she realized she hadn't even registered his appearance. In Libertyville, she had looked at that deputy long enough to rename him. This guy, for all she didn't know, could have been a young Jack Lemmon. In any event, an associative reunion of *The Odd Couple* would have to wait.

She was in the living room, her eyes already on the radio, this one housed in a much more modern unit than the one in the old blond console. This radio was part of a Sony bookshelf unit. The wood on this was blond as well. Not as blond as the console. And not real wood, but a laminate.

Feeling like a vagabond magician, she pulled out the handkerchief again. Her only trick now, however, was to cover her index finger and turn on the unit.

The volume was up and the theme hit her instantly, actually pushing her back, her weight shifting into her heels. If there had been a bed frame behind her, she would have felt that too. But the middle of the living room was empty, save for the supine ghost of Gerard Walker and the theme and variations of Schubert's Eighth Symphony, the one that played from the Sony speakers, the one that still hadn't come to an end.

She let the music play, let herself turn and drift across the room to the place Gerard Walker had occupied in the hours before his discovery.

Her mind was firing off the questions, First, did it mean *anything*? Yes, it had to. But only if she could connect the dots. Or the musical notes. This killer wasn't just hooked on killing. He was hooked on music. Hooked on the classics. Or at the very least, it was his preferred accompaniment, his music to kill by.

Hell, who didn't like to have a little music playing in the background while you did your work?

Hewitt's eyes floated to the head of the invisible body, the neck. She saw the gauzy texture of the neckerchief the killer had fashioned for his host. What a freaking way to go. A pair of nylons closing off your windpipe, in the hands of an erudite psycho who had absolutely no intention of letting this, his third opus, go unfinished. And all the while your hands were gripping and pulling at the stockings, your ears were unable to ignore the sounds of beauty and passion that filled your house and your final thoughts.

Hewitt let it go, let those be her last thoughts about the final moments of Gerard Walker. It was several seconds, several ticks of an unheard metronome, before it registered that the *Unfinished* Symphony had, in fact, come to its unresolved ending.

The WCLS announcer allowed a properly reverential pause at the dissolution of the music. There was a cheerless tone to his first words, a *tisk* of regret over the genius Schubert's lousy luck.

"The Eighth Symphony of Franz Schubert. The *Unfinished* Symphony. Such a lovely work. Made even lovelier by its mystery. Why did Schubert abandon this work after composing two such exquisite movements, only to go on to compose his epic Ninth, the so-named *Great* Symphony? Perhaps Schubert intended to return to the Eighth. Perhaps he simply ran out of time. Franz Schubert lived just thirty-one years before the musical gods called him home. A little life lesson for us all, perhaps. What great unfinished works do *you* have?"

The announcer took a big inhalation, and with the volume up on the stereo, it was as if he took in some of the vanquished air in the Walker living room as well.

"I'm Jay Boniface," he intoned. "And this is WCLS, Chicago's voice of the classics."

Hewitt had left her notepad in the Mazda. She wasn't convinced she would have gotten the spelling of the last name anyway. For now, she would have to remember the way it sounded.

CHAPTER 26

IT was the first thing Hewitt had that she felt she could actually get her arms around since the last night she'd been with Brady. Which, at that point, seemed like a neoromantic century ago.

A lot could happen in a century. A lot could change. For Hewitt, the changes couldn't have been more dramatic. Beginning with her automobile. She had gone from a funky-chick jazz car to a symphony hall on wheels. Her personal life had manifested serious alterations as well. Not returning Brady's phone calls, for starters.

She knew he understood why. The problem was that she didn't exactly understand why he should have been made to. Love was love—if that's what it was with Brady. Death was death. There was no avoiding that. What she was in danger of was allowing death to rattle love's cage. At eighty-eight miles an hour on the Tri-State, that was something she could actually exercise some control over.

Brady picked up on the second ring. He was in his car too.

"I just figured you were up to your eyeballs," he said in response to her apology.

"Problem with being up to your eyeballs," she said, "is that it makes it hard to find things."

"I don't know," he offered. "If I was to make a guess, I'd say you already found something. My first clue is the tunes."

Hewitt took the phone, held it down against the car speaker beside her left knee, to let Brady listen that much more closely to whatever piece Jay B. from WCLS was playing.

"You mean that?" she said, the phone returned to her ear.

"Yeah, that. *The Swan of Tuonela,*" Brady told her. "Jean Sibelius."

"I learn new things about you every day."

"Except the days you don't return my calls."

"Up to my eyeballs."

"Eyeballs, right. So what the hell, Hewitt?"

"The music?"

"The music."

"It's the radio."

"WCLS," Brady helped. "Ninety-three point eight. I've been known to spin the dial that way on occasion."

"Why have I never been there on such an occasion?" Hewitt posed.

"You never let me drive."

In the phone, she could hear he'd tuned to the same station, the same *Swan of Whatever It Was*.

Radio waves were fast as hell. As fast as a serial killer's mind assessing a potential victim. But now she was receiving two signals, with an ever-so-slight delay between what she was hearing in her car and what the phone was playing in her ear.

They were close, she and Brady. As close as skins of an onion, touching, adhering to one another, acclimated to the same smell of life.

"It's a beautiful piece, isn't it?"—Brady's voice, from deep inside the onion. "So you gonna tell me or not?"

"If I gave you one supposition, what would it be?"

A musical interlude, a few kicks of the swan's feet as Brady loaded his words.

"I'd say your bad actor has some kind of music thing. As part of his pursuit of happiness. However measured or far away."

She liked it, almost loved it, the way he would toss out these lateral-thinking lines, little references, literary, historical, knowing her mind would be there for each zig and zag. She wished, at that moment, she was with him, inside the onion.

"Yes," Hewitt said. "You got it. Especially the faraway part."

"You gonna make me guess the rest?"

"No, I'll tell you. At the three crime scenes, in the room where murders went down, the stereos were all tuned to WCLS."

"Wow. Nylon stockings and classical tunes. Pretty eclectic. But I guess if you're going to have a fetish, why not make it interesting. What's your next move?"

"An all-expenses-paid trip to Northbrook."

"To the radio station?"

"I thought it might be a nice time to introduce myself."

"Based on what line of reasoning? Other than it's a beautiful day for wild geese?"

"Hey, one man's *Swan of Tuonela* is another man's *Wild Goose of Northbrook*."

"Not sure I've heard that piece."

"Stay tuned and you might."

CHAPTER 27

HEIDI Slocum hasn't felt right for several days. Today is just the latest of those days. Even sitting here in the brightest, warmest place in the house. In the middle of her living room floor. Seated, as she is, in the oval of sun that radiates through the circular skylight.

In the brightness of day, she can still feel the shadows of the room, waiting, watching, breathing. It is warm outside, warm, too, in the house. But Heidi Slocum reaches out and takes the white afghan from her sofa and drapes it around her upper body, as if it were a morning in mid-December.

She knows she's wrong. About all of this. Of course she's wrong. There are millions of people in Chicago. Thousands of Heidis. So the chances are so remote. It is ridiculous. It's fucking ridiculous.

She hears the words from her throat an instant after hearing them in her head.

"S'fucking ridiculous."

And her voice sounds convincing. Sounds, in its hardness, soothing. It's what she needs to hear. To hear in her own voice that it's okay.

Living alone, it isn't as if someone else is going to tell her.

She closes her eyes, tilts her face toward the skylight. This is her safest place. The center of the room. All her life she has made a little habit of avoiding the corners of rooms for anything longer than a casual pass-by. At parties. In restaurants. How many times had she made the indignant face to the restaurant host or hostess when shown to the place where the walls collided?

The light feels warm against her face, especially her eyelids. Another nice feeling. Being able to see, to sense, to feel the light even with your eyes closed.

Feeling the pleasant sense of her own body weight, she takes a breath and lets it go. Yes. Ah. This is what it feels like to relax. It's been a while. She relaxes in sleep. But only so much. The night grinding. She knows she's one bad trip to the dentist from being fitted with a night guard, a muzzle. To keep her from grinding. To keep her from fracturing her own teeth.

But all of that is far away now. In the light, her eyes closed, she breathes again, maybe feels her jaw let go a tiny bit. Right now she'll take a tiny bit. Of anything. Of this.

She can sit here as long as she likes. It's a sick day. Getting out of bed, she knew she couldn't work. Even though she's not technically sick. She's not technically well either. What does it matter? The paid day off is all. More a vacation day than anything else. A vacation day with no place to go.

There are places she can go, though. Even sitting here in the living room, in the bathing rays of the skylight. In fact, she's already going. She's already there. In her mind, behind closed eyes, she has gone to her place, her beach, her sanctuary. This is how it feels to her. The rug becomes the sand. The afghan is a giant beach towel. The sound of the refrigerator motor is the wind, the waves. The intermittent squeak of the motor, an occasional seagull. And of course, the skylight is the sun. The steady gift of light, bathing her with the affirmation that as long as the light is present, the darkness is far away.

Clouds will come. Clouds will always come . . .

For a moment, she loses contact with her thoughts. When she reconnects, she realizes she has slipped off, slipped into sleep, into a little daytime nothing zone. Returned to the beach, she recognizes the inevitable. The clouds have come, to interrupt her little sun nap. Eyes still closed, she accepts this.

Clouds will come . . .

The cloud moved.

Too fast. Too fast to make sense. Her eyes open, widen to the shape of the skylight. And her mind plays back the shape and the movement of the dark aspect she is almost certain she glimpsed withdrawing from the skylight a moment before.

She listens. But the wind, the waves, the gulls are still there. Only it isn't that anymore. It's her refrigerator. There are no refrigerators on the beach. All that is gone now. Even the sun, having been eclipsed, even if momentarily, can no longer be trusted.

A cold glaze of fear coats her body. Something is on her roof. *Someone* is on her roof.

The sun explodes, and its remnants are immediately claimed by the darkness that has been waiting in the corners all along.

CHAPTER 28

THE first speed bump in the WCLS parking lot coincided with the roll of a kettle drum in the Rimsky-Korsakov piece.

It was an unusual location for a radio station, a curious juxtaposition for *Chicago's Classical Voice*. The building was a vintage, single-story, early-nineteen-seventies, plum-colored institutional brick, nestled in all the romance of a Northbrook industrial park. At the front entrance, Hewitt assessed the security system, peeked through the tinted glass for signs of life, preferably a nice, cooperative administrative assistant.

There was a front desk. But Hewitt's first thought was that it didn't appear to be a front desk that was terribly *lived in*. There was definitely no one living in it at the moment.

Hewitt pushed the intercom button. After several seconds she heard a click, followed by the internal strains of Rimsky-Korsakov, followed by the cheerful strain of a familiar voice.

"Hi, this is Jay. How can I help you?"

"Special Agent Hewitt. Illinois State Police," she heard another familiar voice intone, nothing cheerful about it.

"Hewitt? Elizabeth Hewitt?" the voice said, the cheeriness drained, replaced by a disarmed wonder.

"Yes," Hewitt said. "I'd like to speak with someone from your management."

"Oh, my God," the voice in the intercom offered against the tinny rumble of the Rimsky-Korsakov through the speaker. "I'll buzz you in. I'll be right there."

The buzz came, and Hewitt entered the radio station to the sounds of its current selection. That, and the strong smell of hazelnut coffee, either brewing or just-brewed.

There was no one around, and no sense that anyone had been around anytime recently. Beyond the reception area, there were a couple of darkened offices which, as Hewitt thought about it, reflected the general feeling of the place. *Darkened.* She had time to reflect on this assessment. Because, despite his promise to *be right there*, the voice in the intercom was taking its sweet time showing up in person. The reason for this became clear to Hewitt as the Rimsky-Korsakov piece rose to a crescendo, then fell into the chasm of its ending.

"'Sheherazade,'" the familiar voice resonated. "Nikolai Rimsky-Korsakov. Yes, Nikolai was his first name. Not Rimsky. Rimsky-Korsakov was his hyphenated last name. So maybe Mr. Rimsky-Korsakov was a harbinger of things to come in our current hyphenated-last-name world. Maybe in that way, he was ahead of his time too."

A commercial for a local jeweler kicked in. And less than fifteen seconds into it, the body that contained the WCLS voice manifested from the darkened air.

As manifestations of the human form went, this one was a mind-blower. After not having seen him in twenty years, her mind's initial reaction was to throw a blanket over the recognition. A *no freaking way* reaction. And she actually averted her eyes from his, found an eye-shaped knot in a strip of the polished oak floor. She wasn't sure if she had actually shaken her head to clear her ocular nerves of that first picture of him, but it felt like it. From his vocal response, it seemed she must have.

"I'm afraid it's true," he said, a hum of self-deprecation behind the words.

"I didn't recognize your voice," Hewitt said, her own voice humorless, more self-conscious than she would have liked.

"We always look different than we sound on the air," Jimmy Bonson said, with the half-smile and the almost-wink two decades hadn't changed. "Are you a regular listener?"

"As of this morning," Hewitt said. "Is there somewhere we can sit and talk?"

"It'll have to be the studio," he answered. "I'm back on the air in fifteen seconds."

The quarter-minute came and went, and he was back in the studio, back on the air. And she, Elizabeth "Betsy" Hewitt, was back in high school, sitting across the control console from him, like they were lab partners thrown together in some music appreciation class.

She listened to him do his thing. He was good. He'd always been good at whatever he did.

"Next a piece by French composer, pianist, and lady about town. From the *Romances Sans Paroles*. By Cécile Chaminade. A 'Romance Without Words.' Diana Parker at the piano. With a special dedication, just this once . . ."

The look in his eyes caught her, touched her, held her.

"For *Betsy*."

CHAPTER 29

THE "Romance Without Words" served as accompaniment in the
initial stage of their conversation-interview. Hewitt wanted the interview. But Jimmy Bonson/Jay Boniface was the one who insisted on
the conversational tone. Having not spoken with her in all those post–high
school years, it was only natural Jimmy Bonson would want to talk.
About himself. About the radio station. About the role of classical music in a disintegrating society.

The "Romance Without Words" was a relatively short piece, wispy
and emotive and, to Hewitt's ears and personal radar, sexually longing.
And the thought of that, the suggestion of its relevance, was the last
thing she needed in the warm, padded coziness of the WCLS studio. But
feel it she did. Of course, the "Romance Without Words" by Cecile
Somebody wasn't the only thing creating that vibe. Any way you looked
at it, Jimmy Bonson/Jay Boniface cut an attractive figure. Either one.
Whether it was Jimmy Bonson, the smart, funny, tennis team and honor
society member whose smile in the Wheaton West yearbook was the
one your eye went to first on any page it appeared. Or whether it was,
as it was now, with his nom de radio, Jay Boniface, the voice of the classics in Chicago, weekdays, between the hours of 10:00 A.M. and 2:00 P.M.

The "Romance Without Words" came to an end, and Hewitt
watched, listened as he set up the next track, Mozart's Symphony
No. 29, shifting into his on-air persona as smoothly as tiny marshmal-
lows dissolving in steaming chocolate, a cup of which he offered after
determining her beverage preference. It wasn't her usual. It was, in fact,
something cocoa critics would have called a serious step up.

"Liquid Decadence," he informed her. "Brought some back from

New York. I have guests in the studio on occasion. Artists here to perform with the Chicago Symphony. Hillary Davis, the mind-bogglingly brilliant and, as anyone who's seen her will tell you, *beautiful*, violinist is a big fan of the stuff."

Over her steamy mug of Liquid Decadence, Hewitt laid out her reason for coming, her reason, until the case was put to rest, for living. Her coffee-sipping host reacted not with surprise to the information as much as guarded curiosity.

"I'm not sure exactly what one might deduce from the three radio settings," he said, playing to the audience, the way she remembered him doing on the tennis court as a talented, self-aware teenager. "I've been to Vegas. I'm sure you have too. Sometimes the slots actually do come up all oranges. If they didn't, Vegas wouldn't exist."

"I've never been to Las Vegas," Hewitt responded. "For my money, it might as well not exist."

"Town puts a lot of people to work," he said. "On both sides of the law."

"You sound like you're something of a regular."

"I go a couple times a year. Good for the soul. Bad for a marriage."

She glanced at his left hand, reaffirmed what she'd already seen missing from the designated finger.

"But for an entrepreneur," he continued, "rolling the dice for fun and profit is almost a form of spiritual retreat."

"You said *entrepreneur*," Hewitt posed. "I had the impression you were employed as an on-air personality."

"Yes and yes," he told her. "When I'm not on the air, I'm the owner of this popcorn stand. Actually, when I'm on the air, I own the place too. But when I'm shepherding the music, I like to think I'm working for a higher power. Certainly a higher power than me."

Hewitt was watching his hands, the way they were fiddling with the mouse cord on the console. He realized she was watching, stopped.

"I'm glad you have a higher calling than trips to Las Vegas," she said. "Speaking of which, your analogy about the oranges doesn't quite work. The three settings to your radio station would be like playing the slot and having three sun-ripened tomatoes come up."

"There are no sun-ripened tomatoes."

"I'm aware of that. I'm also aware that a little digging in the homes of the three victims didn't turn up anything that suggested they were classical music buffs either. Or even casual listeners. We had some Beatles. Some Sinatra. Willie Nelson. Beach Boys. Hell, even an Astrid Gilberto. But not so much as a Schubert, a Brahms or a Rimsky-Korsakov. And certainly no Cecile Whatever-Her-Name-Was."

"Chaminade," he provided. "So what are you saying? My radio station is somehow connected to these killings?"

"I'm not saying that. All I'm suggesting is that whoever's out there doing this might like a little accompaniment during his performances."

He got up from the console, coffee cup in hand, the Mozart seeming to lead him as he took a few steps across the room and sat down on a table cluttered with papers and discs. He looked at Hewitt with a face that could no longer contain its disquiet.

"And is this information going to become a matter of public interest?"

"That depends."

"On?"

"On how strong I feel about its efficacy. If I can get some sense of why. Even better, some sense of who."

He finished the last of his coffee, not with a sip as he'd been doing, but with a strong pull. "And you believe I can actually help you with the why and the who of half-a-dozen murders."

Hewitt's Liquid Decadence was gone. She was wishing now she'd saved a little for the home stretch.

"I'd sure love it if you could," she said. "I mean if you think about it, is there anyone you know, anyone you work with, anyone you've met during your activities in the hoi polloi?"

"I think most of the people who live in those circles would prefer *socially gifted* to *hoi polloi*," he said, plinking the side of his coffee mug with the manicured nail of his right index finger. "So basically, you're asking me of all the people I know, who's the most likely to be a homicidal maniac. It's like a line in a school yearbook. On the special predictions page. The page dedicated to that darkly secretive or weirdly overactive group of students who never quite made it on the teams or in the classroom or"—this struck him as either funny or ridiculous—"in the backseat of their father's Crown Victoria."

"Who's to say?" Hewitt said. "Maybe some of those people led more active love lives than we did."

"Maybe they still do."

"Bottom line, if there would be someone, it's not your job to identify them off the top of your head. It's my job to poke around and see if we hit anything."

"Or not."

"Absolutely. There's probably a ninety percent chance the *or not* is what we're dealing with here."

"All right," he said. "The Mozart has two more movements to go. So if you want to pursue this, let's go."

"Okay, first question's an obvious one. Any troubled or disgruntled employees you might want to tell me about?"

Upon Hewitt's query, his face went into instant cognition mode. Which sent Hewitt into fluttery chest mode.

"There's only one of those. Brad. Brad Spheeris. And thank God there's only one of him."

Hewitt wrote the name in her book. "And why would Mr. Spheeris be unhappy?"

"Well, he's a tempestuous personality to begin with. But the fact that I fired him three months ago probably didn't help his disposition."

Before she could follow up, he preempted her with his own little probe. "Would it be against protocol if I asked you something at this point?"

"I've always found that some of the most effective protocol is the improvised kind."

"Just curious," he said, flipping to his best yearbook smile. "Are you going to the reunion?"

CHAPTER 30

SHE shouldn't have gone outside. She shouldn't have gone outside. She shouldn't have gone outside.

She tells herself this, her mind banging the refrain of it against the front of her forehead. She should have stayed inside the house. Should have called someone. Should have followed what the voice inside was telling her.

The thoughts circling in her brain. Circling . . . Circling . . . Until the tigers turned into butter. In this mad place, this absolute corner of her life, her mind pinging the high wire of a childhood memory.

But she didn't. Didn't listen to the voice. Because another voice inside her head told her the worst thing in the world she could do was make a fool of herself in front of other people. In front, especially, of him. In front of her father.

So she hadn't done it, hadn't called anyone. Once it had been quiet enough in the house, on the roof, she'd convinced herself that the only *not dumb* thing to do was to go outside, car keys in hand, and to back far enough away from the house to see the skylight but to still have time to get to her car in the driveway. Because that was a much better plan than making a fool of herself.

She knew now, knew maybe for the first time in her life, that her father had been totally wrong. The worst thing in the world wasn't making a fool of yourself in front of other people. The worst thing in the world was this. Lying on her back, blindfolded, her head propped on a pillow, her body wrapped in what felt like blankets, tied on the outside with rope, tied so tightly she could still breathe, but beyond that, her movements were confined to almost nothing.

He wasn't moving either. Since the moment she'd awakened from whatever it was in the towel he'd pressed against her nose and mouth, she'd known he was there. Sitting on the floor. Not more than ten feet away. In this place, this house she didn't know. This old-smelling house. There was a smell coming from him as well. Mint, like a breath mint. And perfume. A lady's perfume.

She heard him shift his weight a few times, heard the movement of his shirt, the slide of his pants against the floor. But mostly, she heard him breathing. Slowly, rhythmically. Like a sleeping dog.

But he wasn't sleeping. Because she could feel the heat of his eyes watching her. And even though he didn't answer her in words, she knew he could hear and understand what she'd been saying to him. She knew, because of the tiny shifts in his breathing as his mind prepared the words his voice refused to deliver.

"Can you please," her own voice tried again. "Can you please say something. It isn't fair. That I'm the only one who talks. It isn't fair . . . to you. You have things to say, don't you? Don't you want to talk?"

She listens, hears the little hesitation in the breathing, hears the sound of shirt and pants. But then it all settles again. The breathing steadies, quiets, becomes the sleeping dog again.

"It must be hard not to say anything. Just to sit there and listen to me. Just to sit there and not do anything. Anything!"

She is surprised by the sudden rise of anger in her voice. She doesn't want to sound this way, knows it won't help, knows it could make things worse. Worse, even, than the worst thing in the world.

She thinks of the other girls, the ones who came before her. She wonders if they got angry too. After trying to talk to him. Did the anger just come? Did it ever leave?

"Say something, you fucking asshole!" she hears all of them yell together.

She listens. There is no hesitation in the breathing this time. No sound of shifting clothes.

But all this changes in her next heartbeat, with the sudden inward pull of his breath and outward push of two words, in a shockingly soft voice.

"I'm sorry."

CHAPTER 31

BRAD Spheeris didn't answer his phone. Nor, when Hewitt drove to his suburban Cicero home, did he answer his door. Not even after Hewitt gave up on the doorbell and went with the official State of Illinois balled fist to the door.

Jay Boniface had given Hewitt a list of places Spheeris had been known to frequent. Among them, a couple of restaurants. A bar. A bookstore on Navy Pier. A deli. Hewitt had people running it down. She had also put a twenty-four-hour watch on Spheeris's residence. Jay Boniface had informed her that Spheeris had been divorced for several years and, to his knowledge, was living alone. *Jay Boniface.* It would take some getting used to. But it was his legal name now. And James "Jimmy" Bonson was a name relegated to expired driver's licenses and archived high school transcripts.

He had never attended any of them either, the reunions. And it was kind of weird, an interesting kind of weird, how he had admitted to a decision process so similar to her own. Deciding with each decade or half-decade invitation that this would be the one she would finally attend. But each time around, in the slow dance of the psyche, finding some reason, creating some situation that kept her from going.

Upon his admission, he had tossed out a glib remark, or she had taken it as glib at the time. "Maybe all along we were just holding out for this one."

It wasn't until later, until she had ended the interview and left the radio station, that she played back the words and her reaction to them. And his reaction to her reaction. All very understandable. All very high school. But that was the thing about it. When you saw someone again after all those years, you went back, you became who you were, maybe who you'd always been.

Maybe all along we were just holding out for this one.

It hadn't really held a tuning fork to her sternum at the time. But a little something was ringing there now.

Maybe all along we were just holding out for the right escort.

He hadn't said that. It was entirely possible he hadn't implied it. But it was hanging there now, a big heavy necklace of speculation, *nice speculation*, against her chest, where the tuning fork had yet to surrender the last of its ring.

Jimmy Freaking Bonson. *Jimmy Bonbon*, as they called him behind his privileged, well-muscled back. The Wheaton West golden boy. An accessory to the deaths of three eyebrow kings. He wasn't an accessory, of course. His connection was incidental. Three radios had been set to his station in the homes of three murdered men. She wasn't sure what his penalty would be if convicted. Perhaps one night locked in an uncomfortable social setting, sharing the beef and/or chicken from the banquet plate of your coed cellmate.

Jimmy Bonbon. Maybe that would be the best way to think of him now. Until she got used to the Jay Boniface persona.

As it was, the whole Jimmy Bonbon thing was a nice diversion for her mind. But that was okay. Epiphanies in investigations rarely came from holding a gun to your head and forcing your brain into peristaltic activity. Epiphanies came, if they came at all, after a period of doing *anything but* squeezing down the case.

So thinking about Jimmy Bonbon and Wheaton West and the whole sloshed and spilled history of midcontinental, adolescent inanities wasn't an indulgence to her. It was *processing*. And as long as she kept telling herself that, she could also maintain the firewall between what she knew and what Captain Lattimore hoped she knew, nervous-colon poster child that he was.

She had something. Hell, yes. But she had extended to Jimmy Bonbon the pledge that she wouldn't go forward, go public with anything until she knew it was solid. He had impressed upon her the fact that there were better ways to turn a profit than running a classical music station. He'd tried some. And his successes there had allowed him to go off on this quasi-entrepreneurial jag of his. Yet there was a bottom line to his musical sojourn. And according to the radio station owners' handbook, homicide investigations were not a recommended way of enhancing revenue streams.

Hewitt was working up these thoughts at home, at the computer desk, with the vague sense that the dinner hour was passing her by, and with the growing sense that the WCLS website was a good place to be doing a little browsing.

Looking at the On-Air Personality bios, she was able to put names with faces. At the top of the hierarchy, there was Jimmy Bonbon starring as Jay Boniface. As he had described to her in the interview, he was one of just three on-air personalities who actually brought their voices and the rest of their physical bodies into the WCLS studio. Each of the three covered a four-hour on-air shift. Along with a brief description, there was a photo of each of them.

Jay Boniface, looking like his tennis team picture with twenty years age enhancement, handled 10 A.M. to 2 P.M. Prior to that, Ray Cameron, a large man with a shock of unkempt salt-and-pepper hair and, as Hewitt described it to herself, *a pirate face*, ran the 6:00 A.M. to 10:00 A.M. slot. As the station owner had explained it to her, Ray Cameron had been a part-time, pinch-hit announcer who had been elevated to the morning show to replace the departed Mr. Spheeris. The afternoon hours at WCLS were taken by one April Hoffs. One impeccably groomed, mid-fortyish April Hoffs. A woman with a handsome face of privilege and maybe two glasses of wine too many on a nightly basis.

Hewitt would send Megna and Patterson to interview Mr. Cameron and Ms. Hoffs, not anticipating much of a revelatory nature there. Because the staff member who remained of keenest interest was the one whose name and photo had been removed from the on-air personality page. The departed alum, Brad Spheeris. Not that he had been completely erased from the station and its airwaves. And this, to Hewitt, was where the voice of the classics thing turned very intriguing.

WCLS played classical music twenty-four hours a day. Live bodies in the studio accounted for only half of that time. For the balance, the music of past centuries was conveyed by modern technology only, with no live human component in the studio, not even a half-asleep engineer. From 6:00 P.M. to 6:00 A.M., the programming was computer-run, with preset play lists and prerecorded announcer bites. And as Jimmy Bonbon had shared with her, in a way that suggested he saw no significance in it, the prerecorded announcer was the excommunicated Brad Spheeris. Or the *virtually* excommunicated Brad Spheeris.

The reasons for keeping the spectral version of a terminated announcer around were, according to his ex-boss, a combination of practicality and public relations. On the practical side was the fact that the robot-DJ had been part of Spheeris's job description for several years. And he, more so than anyone else at the station, was a master of the kind of anecdotes and information bits the listeners enjoyed at the open and close of pieces. He was a walking, talking encyclopedia of classical music. And as such, he had handled the responsibilities of selecting, formatting and producing the automated part of the WCLS schedule. Further to the practical side, Brad Spheeris was typically several months out in front of the on-air schedule with his preprogrammed material. So to Jimmy Bonbon's way of thinking, the stuff was paid for and he was going to let the music play.

The PR component of this was practical as well. Upon Brad Spheeris's *leaving* the morning show, there had been considerable reaction from the listenership. So to placate that external audience and to appease his inner entrepreneur, Jay Boniface had allowed Mr. Spheeris to stay on the air in this more manageable form.

When Hewitt had questioned her studio host as to whether that arrangement had left the door open for Spheeris to return, his answer had been eminently logical, but not entirely edifying. "I'm hoping it hasn't. Because this is the perfect way to work with Brad Spheeris. He's here without really being here. And he's gone without really being gone."

Which had left Hewitt with the one burning question. "If it's kosher to ask, I'd love to know why you let him go."

"Oh, it's kosher," Jimmy Bonbon responded. "I fired him because he's a world-class asshole."

That was it. All he was going to give. Normally Hewitt would have pressed a subject to drop the gamesmanship and give her a freaking break. But these weren't exactly normal circumstances. This was Neverland Revisited. Not the Neverland of London and Sir James Barrie. But the Neverland of Wheaton West Senior High, where, even twenty years later, Jimmy Bonson still had social power and Betsy Hewitt was still waiting for her opening.

At the computer, Hewitt clicked on the WCLS program schedule. The day's playlist bloomed up on the screen. The pieces were slotted by clock time, running time, composition title, name of composer and a performance credit. Hewitt scrolled down the listing to the current time. As she did, her eyes fell into the stream of composer names, each one sounding a little chime in the concert hall of her memory.

Schubert

Verdi

Rachmaninoff

Brahms

Rimsky-Korsakov

Chaminade

Scarlatti

Mendelssohn

Offenbach

Respighi

Mozart

Saint-Saëns

Liszt

Schumann

Chopin

Paganini

Glazunov

Strauss

Berlioz

Albeniz

Tchaikovsky

In Hewitt's mind, the scroll of names shifted, turned and began to alternate in red and black slots, circling, circling, with a little silver ball countercircling on an inside track. When the great composers sat at their pianos or composition desks, they could have had no inkling that centuries later their compositions would be spinning on a musical roulette wheel, the invisible signals of it passing through Earth's atmosphere to be translated, first, by a radio receiver, and then transmuted by the ears of a man who was madder than any mad musical genius, into his own hideous interpretation, his music to kill by.

The roulette wheel was spinning even now—she scrolled down to the current time slot—spinning on *John Field*, a name Hewitt hadn't heard before. Curious, she got up from the desk and went to turn on the radio on her living room stereo. She punched in the numbers, 93.8, and hit the MEMORY button to assign it a permanent place in her preset programming.

It was piano. Just piano. A quiet, moody, almost accidental piano music that gave her a strange sense of wanting, longing, of missing something, someone.

Of the tens of thousands of sets of ears listening to the piece as she was, Hewitt wondered if two of them were connected to the brain that was responsible for the musical deaths that had already occurred and those that already existed in potential, depending on the spin of the wheel, the stopping of the little silver ball.

Hewitt sat down on the sofa, in her curl-up corner, listening to the clicks of the wheel, the roll of the ball, the soft, yearning tones of a piano that moved farther and farther away the closer she listened.

CHAPTER 32

HE apologizes to her feet. Since the first *I'm sorry*, he has continued to do this, slowly making his way across the floor toward her. Until the point that, now, he is right here. Right behind her. Apologizing to her feet.

She knows at some point he will touch them. She will feel his fingers on them. But until then, he will continue to speak to them, in the low, soft voice.

"Why?"—she hears her own voice. "Why are you sorry?"

He makes no verbal response. Yet she hears a reaction, a change again in his breathing, a hesitation, a cooling in the temperature of his physical approach.

If she can just say something that gets him to say something back. To change the direction of his thinking. She has to try. Because at some point, the hands will come. At some point the apologizing will stop.

"You don't have to be sorry. You can stop feeling sorry. You can. If you want to."

She listens, hears the sound of him listening back.

"I know it feels bad. It feels bad to feel sorry. I know. Because I've done things that have made me feel sorry."

She hears him listening, even more closely. He's thinking now. She can hear him thinking. She opens her mouth to draw in a breath. But as her next words are forming in her throat, she realizes he has breathed in just ahead of her, and his words crackle brightly across the dark universe.

"What did you do?"

The victory of it thrills her wholly, but only for the moment it takes to realize she must now provide an answer. In her mind, there is a thick notebook with the stories of all the things she has done in her life for which the world has made her feel sorry. A mental wind rushes in to blow open the pages of the notebook. Somewhere inside is the right story. But she doesn't have time to look. She doesn't have time.

"What did you do?"

The notebook closes.

"In the Christmas play, at my church," she says. "I forgot what I was supposed to say. I was the angel. The angel who came to the shepherds. I practiced my line. For weeks. But when it came time, all the lights were in my eyes. I couldn't see. I couldn't see the shepherds. And my mind went blank. And I just stood there. On the stage. In my angel costume. I just stood there. Staring into the lights."

It isn't until the end of this that she hears the tears in her voice, feels them on her face. She waits for her captor to say something, waits on the stage in her angel costume, unable to see, knowing her father is out there on the other side of the light, looking at her with his disappointed eyes, his face of cold nonlove.

"You have nothing to fear," she says in her child's voice. *"I come to proclaim good news to you, tidings of great joy to be shared by the whole people . . ."*

It is several words into her next sentence before the child's voice is replaced by her own. "Those were the words I was supposed to say. But I didn't say them. And for that, I was sorry. I *am* sorry."

"Say them again."

In his voice, the sound not of a demand, but of a sincere request. As if—oh God she can only hope for this—she has touched him.

"You have nothing to fear. I come to proclaim good news to you, tidings of great joy to be shared by the whole people . . ."

She hears a slight rustling of clothing. Not movement. But the preparation for movement.

"And these words, forgetting them. This makes you sorry."

"Yes."

"Say it."

"I'm sorry?"

"Yes, say it."

"I'm sorry."

"Again."

"I'm sorry."

"And now, please, say it with me."

Another rustle of clothing, louder. *Movement.* But she can't think about this, can only think of the two words.

"I'm sorry."

His voice joining hers in an exact, even complement.

"Again, please," he says.

"I'm sorry."

This time his voice is the louder of the two. Not because hers has become softer.

"Again, please."

"I'm sorry."

But this time, it is only his voice she hears. Because he has taken her foot and pulled off her shoe.

CHAPTER 33

A S it would in moments like this, Hewitt's mind sprang from sleep. The force of it lifted her into a sitting position and threw her into a momentary panic until she ran her palms and fingers over the cool reassurance of the fitted sheet and the soft, grooved pattern of the mattress pad beneath.

She had taken the roulette wheel and its musical accompaniment to bed. She didn't recall any specific dream in which the music and, with it, the little steel ball, had come to a stop. But it didn't matter. The wheel had stopped. That much her somnambular and, now, waking mind knew.

She checked the clock-radio, saw it was a few minutes before 2:00. Though her higher mind was wide awake, her base brain was still pumping melatonin. And her body was fighting back to reclaim its supine position in the bed. But her higher mind managed to drag her body to the bathroom, and the dragging proceeded downstairs, to the computer desk.

She had already attributed her gambling thinking to Jimmy Bonbon's Las Vegas comments. But a period of significant rest, and some significant pillow hugging, had bounced the notion back to her that it might not be roulette at all, might not be a game of pure chance. Instead, it was entirely possible that the game she'd been sucked into was more specific, one where chance was involved, but with a much more defined purpose, a more predictable probability. So eminently predictable, in fact, that players were known to successfully count cards, to the point that the really successful ones were often banned from the casinos where they plied their skills.

The game was *Blackjack*.

On the WCLS website, Hewitt was clicking on the program schedule, and from there, clicking through to the program schedule archives.

Someone, maybe Jimmy Bonbon, maybe Brad Spheeris, had decided to archive past program schedules for up to sixty days for the reference of the WCLS listeners. Hewitt didn't need her case file to reference the three dates she was interested in.

She archived back to June ninth, the date the first king was executed. She selected the two pages of the schedule, printed both, then followed the same procedure for the dates of kings two and three. With the sheets of paper in hand, she went to the kitchen, turned the dimmer light up to halfway, enough that she could read, and set the pages on the table.

She was looking for a pattern, and her pattern recognition skills were always enhanced significantly by the cocoa bean. So she took the action, created the steaming mug, sat down at the table two minutes later to figure out what the hell, if anything, she had.

Forensics had estimated the times of death for the three kings as all having occurred during the night, most probably between the hours of midnight and 4 A.M. On the printed program schedule, Hewitt's eyes ran down the dark hours for June ninth. Looking for a pattern. Or something encoded in a pattern. The first one emerged quickly. Between the hours of 2:30 and 3:00 A.M. *Brahms. Beethoven. Bach.* Back to back to back. Three *B*'s. Followed by a *C. Chopin*, at a little after the top of the hour, after, what she assumed, was a commercial pod. At 3:03 A.M.

She took her first sip of the hot chocolate. There was a time when what she felt would have registered as way too hot. But she had built an immunity, or a heat-resistant shield of cells on her tongue . . .

Jesus Christ. She had turned to the June twentieth schedule, looking for a pattern of *B*'s there too. But she saw something else. Something that made all her little hairs tingle.

Chopin. Again, Frédéric Chopin. But it wasn't just the composer's name. It was the time. Three-oh-fucking-three. And the clincher, the hair-tingling screamer, was a single word in the title of the composition. The word *Nocturne*.

She'd seen it in the composition title in the listing for June ninth.

Her hands and eyes were already back to that page. She found the title. The "Nocturne in E flat." It was a pattern. A nuts-on solid pattern. To her middle-of-the-night thinking, as solid as the body of a grand piano.

She knew now. Knew she had something. And she felt so juiced, so buzzed, she took a congratulatory sip of perfect-temperature chocolate. It was only a formality now. Finding the third match. She set the mug down, turned the pages to the June twenty-second schedule. She found the time slot a moment before some of the last hot chocolate pushed back up into her throat.

Shit.

What the hell was this? *Scriabin?* Alexander Fucking Scriabin? Masquerading in the 3:03 slot. And thereby allowing the house to keep the winnings she'd already started to blow.

Tasting the hot chocolate redux, she felt like gagging the rest of it back up. She saw her hands pawing at the pages of the schedule, to put them back in order. Like Jackie Kennedy climbing up on the back of the limo, trying to reclaim the pieces of the dying president's head, her mind racing away under the overpass, sirens going off, faces in shock.

In the madness, Jackie's forearm caught the side of Hewitt's mug, tipped it, dumped it. Chocolate pages. Chocolate Chopin. Chocolate Scriabin.

Hewitt shuttled to the kitchen counter, grabbed the roll of paper towels, came back to the table, dabbed at the mess, couldn't help going back to the President Kennedy scenario. The Parkland Hospital gurney. The autopsy papers. Dabbing at the spill. Dabbing at the end of the world as she knew it. And with all that potential . . .

The sheets of paper, the schedules were still too wet to pick up and toss out without dripping presidential blood on the floor. So Hewitt pulled another couple of paper towels, doubled them up and held them to the pages. As she did, she saw a number at the top of the autopsy sheet. A number that didn't make sense, that wasn't part of the Kennedy report.

New life in the wake of all that spilled brown blood. She'd screwed up. She'd totally screwed up. She had printed the schedule for June twenty-first, the day *before* the third king had been killed.

Back to the computer desk, pulling up the schedule. Screening. Eyes alive. Mind alive. And yes, hell yes, hope alive.

It was right there, for all the world to see. Even if the whole world was only her. On the night of June twenty-second. In the 3:03 slot. The "Nocturne in E flat," by Frédéric Jesus Christ Chopin.

As she slid into the desk chair, she felt the thud of two huge questions landing in her lap. Was it the person programming the pieces who was now the most interesting individual in the world to her? Or was it still some nameless, faceless listener out there, playing Charles Manson to some classical version of "Helter Skelter"?

She didn't have an intuitive draw either way. And while her intuition was still hair-tinglingly convinced that this was the crack in the case she was so desperate for, there was always the chance that outrageous happenstance had routed its parade onto her little street once again.

There was one way, of course, in which the efficacy of her theory would be borne out. If another Chopin piece played at 3:03 in the morning in the coming days and another princess and king turned up dead, that would pretty much seal it. But that wasn't going to happen. It was time for a moratorium on Frédéric Chopin in the middle of the night. Because if she was right, there was one sick maestro waiting for the right piece of music to call him back to the stage for an encore. Whether it was a maestro working alone or in concert with some special guest artist, she wasn't sure, didn't have a solid sense of. Either way, the moratorium had to go into effect.

Or maybe not. There was one other way to play it. If she procured the WCLS schedule for the coming days and weeks and there was another Chopin listing at 3:03, she could put surveillance on Brad Spheeris twenty-four hours out. She could track him, observe him and take him down before he began to act.

But Hewitt knew, even as she was thinking it, that she couldn't do it. No Nocturne in F-ing way. If she let the music play and Spheeris wasn't the guy, then she would've given her tacit approval to another set of royal homicides.

No, the Chopin moratorium had to start as soon as she could get the station owner on the phone and have him begin whatever steps were necessary to purge and replace any upcoming pieces from the play list.

She pulled out Jimmy Bonbon's business card, picked up her phone, dialed the home number he'd written in black pen.

Five rings, and his voice mail kicked in. Another five rings when she redialed. In the interim, she had returned to the WCLS program list on the website. To her brain-humming delight, she found that she could conduct her look into the crystal ball right now. At least for the seven days of advanced schedule the station offered its devoted listeners. And right now, there was no more devoted listener in the listening universe than Elizabeth Taylor Hewitt.

She was into her third set of five rings. This time, after Jimmy Bonbon delivered his entire recorded message, she began hers.

"Jimmy—Jay—it's Elizabeth Hewitt. I need you to get back to me as soon as possible. I think there may be a problem, a connection with . . . *Jesus Christ.*"

She could feel her heart beating in her eyeballs as she focused on the monitor screen. In the predawn hours of June twenty-sixth, in the 3:03 slot, as if the words had just been freshly entered into tonight's schedule, was the title of the composition the sane world couldn't afford to hear.

Frédéric Chopin. The "Nocturne in E flat."

Which meant Special Agent Hewitt and her ship of fools had forty-one minutes to kill the music.

CHAPTER 34

T HE Roadmaster slows in front of the two-story Cape Cod, which is white with green trim by day, but gray with black trim in the dead of night.

This is the dead of night. So aptly termed. At such a time, such a quiet, peaceful interval of time, it is the perfect time to be that, to be dead.

Dead asleep. Dead to the world.

In such a state of sleep, that deep, imponderable nothingness, were the sleeper to stay there, to not awaken, *to die*, the morning that would come would never have been. The sleeper wouldn't have missed a thing, would never miss a thing again.

To miss something, you had to remember it.

By now the Roadmaster has continued past the Cape Cod. It will continue two blocks farther, will, at that time, slow again and begin to circle back to repeat the approach to the gray and black Cape Cod. And unlike the recent night when this same exercise was practiced, this time the Roadmaster will not only slow, but stop.

The "Cantata and Fugue." The piece has been playing during this entire time. When Bach expired, when Bach at last surrendered to the formless, dreamless sleep, where did all the music go? Did the music simply cease? Or did the music journey with him? Not the compositions already written, performed in life. But *the music*. The music of a mind that was itself music.

The music, not dependent on the fingers of players, the extinguishable breath of performers. The music, not beholden to the pen and page for its documentation.

The music, not of this physical plain, but as a self-perpetuating string of inspiration across the faintly glowing staff lines of the universe.

Where Bach was now, there was no dead of night. There was no dawn. Yet there was music, was there not? There had to be. For the angels among them, at least, there had to be.

Little Chip Chip is there. Little Chip Chip has his music. He has his prize. And soon the angel he guided, for her short time in the world of day and night, soon she will have her prize. Soon she will hear the music as accompanies the dance of recompense.

The engine of the Roadmaster shuts down. But the music continues to play, inside the car. The "Cantata and Fugue." The music of Bach lives on.

The listener watches as his hand reaches to the volume control on the radio, turns the round dial to the right. The music rising. Bach rising.

He will listen for a bit. According to the preparation, the Roadmaster is well concealed.

His eyes alight upon the car clock. There is time enough. Time for him to listen.

Time for *them* to listen.

CHAPTER 35

H EWITT had never shut down a radio station. And after the flurry of calls to Jay Boniface's phones went unanswered, she was questioning her chances of closing this one.

With the metronome ticking, Hewitt made two executive calls. The first directive was to HQ to dispatch a trooper unit to Jay Boniface's Lake Forest residence. That directive came with the additional instructions to haul the property owner's ass out of bed, if that's where it was, and deliver it to the radio station immediately.

The second directive was to herself, to get to WCLS and position herself to do whatever she had to do to get inside and disable the broadcasting robot.

If she couldn't figure out how to do that on the way, she'd slam something together when she got there. What she would do, and the degree to which she would do it, would be determined by whether or not she had either Jimmy Bonson's presence or permission. If she could get his ass there, he could just take care of it. Hell, he could probably substitute another song, without the audience missing a beat, except for those who played along at home. She was dead sure there was at least one of those listeners up and running at that hour, raptly anticipating his cue. Though, shit, maybe it would be better if the WCLS air just went dead at that moment. Maybe the shock of that would screw up the freak enough to make him close the show early.

But that was if the troopers delivered Jimmy Bonbon in person. If they picked him up but couldn't deliver him to the station in time, she figured Jimmy could direct her via phone to, first, disarm security and get inside and, second, to shut off the music before the "Nocturne in E flat" sounded its first killing note.

Drawing a bead on Northbrook, from the speed lane of the Tri-State, with the Mazda doing everything it could short of dropping engine parts on the road, Hewitt advised herself of the third potential scenario. That Jimmy Bonbon wouldn't appear in the flesh or via the phone, and she would be alone in the studio in the middle of the night— having gotten in by whatever means was necessary—like some Phantom of the Radio Station, ready to kill, but not knowing who, or how.

"HE'S either not home or he's dead inside the residence," the trooper's voice tolled inside her phone ear. "But the one thing I can rule out is that he's here but not responding."

A state trooper had a way of getting a response. It wasn't like pretending there was no one home to avoid trick-or-treaters.

"Then I'm pretty much down to breaking and entering," Hewitt said—in her head.

"Agent Hewitt?"

"Not what I wanted to hear, but thank you for the effort."

She clicked off, sighed, let her body sink into the seat of the Mazda, thinking how nice and, at that hour, how sensible it would be to just go to sleep. But a snooze in the WCLS parking lot was absolutely not in the realm of the possible. She checked her car clock, the same way she'd checked it fifteen seconds earlier, and a quarter minute before that.

Her options had dwindled to two. Doing nothing, and hoping she was wrong. Or going in, right or wrong, legal or not. Of course she knew damn well there was nothing legal about option B. There would be no legal precedent for such an entry in a heaven-high stack of law books. But just because there was no law advising it didn't mean it wasn't right.

Double, triple negatives in support of her convoluted internal logic.

Fuck it. Law. Logic. Fuck 'em both. This was life and death. There was definitely a heaven-high precedent for that.

She got out of her car, reached inside her jacket to feel the nighttime coldness of her service revolver. A small comfort in the middle of the night. In the middle of the preposterous plan she was about to execute.

She checked her watch. Depressing glow of indigo bearing distressing news.

It was 2:47.

Sixteen minutes to Chopin. Sixteen minutes to the "Nocturne in E Flat."

CHAPTER 36

THEY are sitting in silence. In the same silence that held them before either of them was born. In the same silence that held them in the aftermath of her terrible ending. She, by then, had gone to the place beyond silence. To the place, or places, where silence was something other than what it was on earth.

Where silence was sound. And sound was light. And light was love. And love was God. And God was music.

And music was silence.

Of course, on earth it can never be truly silent. There is always the hum and the churn and the crawling. Even when it is still, when it is quiet as can be, there is always, at some level, the sound.

In the heavy stillness of the living room, there is still that sense of the yearning, the needful advance, the crawling desire of the human soul. The sense of it, in this place, stronger than in any of the previous ones. Strong enough that the unseen aspect of it is threatening to become seen.

He hears it now. The earth sound.

Movement upstairs. *Premature* movement. He is up. He is up too early. The sound of him. His big feet scraping against the floor. Unsteady in the first two steps. As if he might not keep his balance for a third.

It is an unsteady step, the third one. But a fourth, steadier, follows.

In the downstairs, they sit quietly. As quietly as two visitors can sit. For now, he is doing the listening for both of them. Soon, when the music begins, she will commence her own listening. She will be the eyes, the ears, the witness.

But not if they are intruded upon by the premature riser. Already, his feet have moved him to the upstairs hallway.

Downstairs, the male visitor does not stir, does not move to take a position. He does not blink as he looks across the room at the face of the one for whom this moment has been tendered. She is calm as well, as unconcerned as a theater patron perusing the pages of the program ten minutes before the opening curtain.

Upstairs, the heavy feet approach the staircase, then stop. He stands there, listening. Downstairs, the visitor waits, listens to him listening. In the undeclared armistice, they listen now, each to the other, but hearing nothing. And when the nothingness is substantial enough, the big feet turn away from the staircase and proceed down the hallway, to the bathroom, where, out of old habit, he closes the door to the squeal and grind of a dislocated hinge.

CHAPTER 37

SHE had assessed the exterior and chosen a place to break into the radio station that would cause the least amount of damage and require the State of Illinois to pay the least amount of compensation.

It was only after she had broken out the window of a storage room in the back of the building and crawled inside that she registered the totality of her commitment to the Chopin theory, standing there in a dusty room populated with long-since-replaced studio equipment and office furniture, while the security alarm whined its looping whine across the building.

Moments earlier, she had almost talked herself out of it. Having circled the building and returned to the front entrance, she tried all of Jimmy Bonson's phone numbers one last time. She stood there observing her dimly lit reflection in the front-door glass. She waited, checking again the pale glow of indigo that rose from her watch.

The ten-minute mark had been her make or break. So at 2:53, she had hustled to the back of the building again and used the butt of her service revolver to break the pane of glass.

By then it was nine minutes to Chopin. Nine minutes to the "Nocturne in E flat."

Moving quickly down the hallway, toward the studio, her mind a thunderhead of thoughts. How long would it take the security system to elicit a police response? Would killing Chopin actually keep the killer from killing again? If you had eight-and-a-half minutes to disable a radio station, what would be your first move?

Disabling the damn alarm would help. A relentless electronic yelping in your ears was never conducive to problem-solving.

Unplug everything. Her last thought as she entered the studio, as the sounds of the music greeted her ears. The current selection. The track that would lead to the top of the hour and the three-minute commercial pod that would set up the 3:03 slot. Not that she needed reminding.

She unplugged everything she could find. The console. Computer. Monitors. Speakers. Even Jimmy Bonbon's coffee cup warm-up pad.

But the music, the "Polovtsian Dances" of Borodin—as the monitor informed her before she shut it down—played on.

She had to get to the ultimate source. The control room. So she abandoned the studio, made her way down the hall, pushing in doors, until the third one she came to opened to the techno-brain of *Chicago's Classical Voice.*

If it was plugged into a power strip or wall socket, Hewitt pulled it out. She found the breaker box, shut everything down. But still, Borodin would not go down. The "Polovtsian Dances" continued to play.

With every Goddamn cord in the place unplugged, it finally hit her. Radio stations were immune to power shutdowns. In an electrical storm, a brown-out or a nuclear attack, radio stations had to stay on the freaking air. Radio stations had backup power, an auxiliary source of juice. At least one.

Hewitt had heard the "Polovtsian Dances" a handful of times before. Not enough to really know the piece. But enough to know it was in the home stretch now. Which would leave only three minutes of radio station commerce between life and death and whatever hell there would be to pay at 3:03.

It struck her then. The mental equivalent of stepping on a metal rake and having the handle fly up to smack you in the face. Her eyes pulled inward as the thought formed a bruise behind her forehead.

The radio station was like the killer, *was* the killer. And she was in hand-to-hand combat with it. And it was bigger than her. Stronger than her. Its extremities wrapping around her like a quartet of pythons. The mouth of one of them, in the form of the killer's hand, pushing toward her throat.

There was only one move left to her. She had to put a bullet through the radio station's heart.

CHAPTER 38

THERE are so many things that can keep the time besides a clock. The drip of a faucet. The movement of the moon. The beating of a heart.

All three are at work at this moment. All three are heralding the arrival of the three o'clock hour.

Sitting in the living room, the excitement of the unexpected urination now a postscript, he knows the time, feels the quickening of it. Nonetheless, he pulls back the sleeve of his jacket, his synthetic gloves making a mouselike squeak against the glass face of his watch as he reaches to push the tiny button of illumination.

The face of the watch lights, the glow plainly present but equally distant. The final faint gasp of a dying star. To an angel flying nearby, it would be mesmeric, as if God had flashed a final keepsake photo. Yet to the same angel, flying a much more distant path, the glow would seem insignificant. A single falling tear of God, lit for a moment by a fugitive ember from hell.

It is three o'clock, and twenty-nine seconds.

The moon hurries through the window.

His heart beats against the bone of his chest.

In the kitchen, the faucet drips holy tears.

He allows the cycle to repeat four more times before he rises from the chair and crosses the living room to the bay window, where the old Bakelite radio has been waiting, preset upon his arrival, its next piece programmed weeks in advance. For that matter, programmed since the first tiny flash of light ejaculated the entire universe.

CHAPTER 39

IF she couldn't stop the flow of the blood, she had to stop the heart.

Two sixty-second commercials had run. A third had just started—for a funeral home. As long as we've got you lying awake at 3:00 A.M., let's talk mortality, eternity and price. But it only fit the program. The world was murmuring death. And here she was, standing in a radio station control room, her gun drawn, her mind ingesting the message of the inexorable dignity of eternal rest, her eyes struggling with the image of the techno-wound the first bullet had put in the center of the control panel.

She fired a second shot into the machine, waited for the high-tech debris to cease its clattering around the room.

But the voice of death was still talking, with a helpful lilt now as it offered a phone number.

A third shot greeted the humming pause at the end of the commercial.

And incredibly, mind-blowingly, the pause held. Where the announcer, where *Brad Spheeris* should have entered with his introduction to the "Nocturne in E flat," there was nothing but the sound of all that unleavened ether.

She had done it. She had killed Chopin. Whether that would stop the real killer was something she could only hope. But without killing Chopin, there wasn't even that.

In the distance, she could hear the sound of the first squad car. It was interesting the way the high-pitched emergency tones harmonized with the piano that was playing on the purple-gray horizon of her thoughts.

Somewhere beyond that horizon, her mind's terra firma gave way to the great psychological ocean. And it was into that black sea that her heart fell as she distilled the sounds into their clear forms.

The emergency siren.

The security alarm.

The very undead Frédéric Chopin.

There had been no introduction, no fascinating tidbit, no charming anecdote.

Just the soft, subtle sounds of the "Nocturne in E flat" refusing to die.

CHAPTER 40

THE first flutter of movement in the upstairs bedroom has announced itself to the rest of the house.

Thirteen measures into the nocturne, and the body has left the bed. From the sound of the movements, more awake this time than in the previous flight, the urinary excursion.

Hitting the hallway, a hastening of the step, a suggestion of aggression. Irritation, more than anything else. A slightly more pronounced version of the irritation he'd felt from that persistently nudging bladder. *Empty me. Empty me.*

And now this music. This intrusion. *Listen to me. Listen to me.*

Why it was enough to piss a man off.

"What in the Goddamn hell?"

The words of the awakened one resonate down the stairs. An angry belch with syllables.

Who would dare disturb such a great man? Who would dare place the playing of the piano, this delicately arranged music of the evening, above the night dreams of the lord of the house?

Measure twenty of the nocturne, as the feet make initial contact with the staircase.

Who would propagate such a notion? Who would commit such a transgression? Who would defy the natural law of the behemoth?

He looks across the room to where the perfect one awaits the behemoth as well. He nods to her.

We do, he says with his smile. *We do.*

And with that expressed, he stretches the stockings in his hands, pulls them to a maximal tautness, lifts the smooth thick string of nylon to his face and plucks it with his chin.

A low, dying butterfly of a note, quickly swallowed by the left hand of Chopin's piano. But not before it has its moment to accompany, to harmonize. This one-note prelude to the grand orchestration to come.

Nearing the bottom of the staircase. Measure twenty-seven of the nocturne. By the thirty-first measure he will have seen her. He will *know* her.

Yes, here. He encounters her now. Stopping. Disbelieving that she has returned.

Chopin fills the air.

And then, in the middle of measure thirty-four, Chopin vanishes.

His eyes fly to the old radio. Still glowing. Still on.

In the velvet silence, the voice smacks him in the ears an instant before a large, claw-shaped hand strikes his right eye and temple.

"Who the hell are you?"

Another swing of the opposite hand that grazes his nose and lips.

Forty-two measures. They should be forty-two measures inside the nocturne by now.

"Get out or I'll kill you."

The void of the forty-third measure is filled by a burst of laughter.

"Kill me?" he hears the laughing voice say. "After all you have killed, you can kill me?"

The body that flies at the killing giant is not his own. And yet he feels himself a quick, perfect shadow to that body as he circles for position, as he opens his shadow mouth to mimic the great shrieking laugh that resonates from the physical body and transforms into words.

"Kill *me*?"

"Kill *me*?"

"Kill *me*?"

CHAPTER 41

TWO officers from the Northbrook PD had responded, only to find the breaker and enterer waiting for them on the concrete step of the WCLS entrance. They approached aggressively. But when they caught sight of Hewitt's face, they fell off and reacted, facially, as if to say: "Oh, *you*."

As if that explained everything.

Hewitt didn't care what they thought, couldn't care what anybody thought in the coming minutes, hours, days.

She wasn't sure which bullet fired into the machine had been the kill shot. All she knew was that at some point, amid the frenzy of unloading her entire clip, the pianist had simply quit. She opted not to share the details of her shooting spree with the officers. And to their credit, and Hewitt's gratitude, they didn't press her.

Both officers were inside thirty. And Hewitt figured it had to be about the most crazy-assed anticrime measure either one of them had ever seen. When she had concluded their tour of WCLS with a stop in the control room, neither of the guys seemed interested in writing it up as much as mentally archiving it for the stories they would tell later.

The officers stayed until Jimmy Bonbon arrived, having been alerted at his downtown condo by the security company that monitored the station. Of course, the downtown condo was news to Hewitt. When she finally had a chance to ask him why he hadn't shared that information with her previously, his answer had been eminently logical.

"I guess I just never figured you'd need to blow me off the air in the middle of the night."

Once the attending officers had gone, as she and Jimmy stood to-gether amid the techno-carnage of the control room, Hewitt did her best to help him understand why the hell she had done what she'd done. Jimmy Bonbon listened, digested her story, his face passive, despite the fact that one of his favorite machines had been shot dead by a mad-woman with credentials.

"Okay," he sighed at story's end, more to the dead machine than to Hewitt. "You've got three radios tuned to my station at three death scenes."

His eyes seemed to reflect some sort of probability table he was mapping in his mind. The pause gave Hewitt a moment to consider some-thing odd in his choice of words. *Death scene.* As opposed to *crime scene.* Why so theatrical? Why the unscripted reference to the choreo-graphed nature of it?

"And you've found a pattern of Chopin nocturnes in the three-oh-three slot that coincides with the nights the male victims were killed."

"That," Hewitt said, "and one of the more seismic gut feelings I've ever had."

He smiled at the slaughtered control panel, intending it for Hewitt, but waiting a moment to turn and deliver it. "That's the thing about you."

"What?"

"Seismic."

"What about it?"

"Who the hell says *seismic*?"

"People."

"People who study geology."

"And people who have really strong gut feelings."

"And apparently people who don't have a problem with firing a gun into an innocent automaton."

Now it was her turn to deliver what would have to pass for a smile. To her mind's inner circle, there was nothing, absolutely nothing, to smile about. She had stopped the music. But she had no idea if she'd stopped the bad brain.

"And that's the thing about you," she said.

"How so?"

"Automaton."

"YOU know I'm sorry."

They were sipping beverages in the studio, in the same positions where the original interview had been conducted.

"I know you're saying that," he offered. "But I know deep down—down where the seismic activity starts—you're not. You're a gambler. No, you're a *riverboat* gambler. You're out there on the water with one purpose in mind. And that's to win."

She knew he was right, was impressed as hell by how immaculately right he was.

"When you get a hunch, you roll the dice," he continued. "Only when *you* roll the dice, you're not just trying to beat the house. You're trying to beat the devil."

Hewitt sipped her Liquid Decadence. "So is there some kind of point at the end of this elaborate analogy?"

"I've already made it," he said, no shadow of a smile this time. "The point is that deep down you're not sorry for shooting up my control room. It was a roll of the dice. A very loud, very expensive roll of the dice. But you're not sorry for the roll. You're not sorry at all."

Hewitt was in midsip. She left her face in the cup longer than was natural. It was not a good hiding place.

"Okay," she said. "The State of Illinois is sorry."

"That's a little more believable. And when can I expect a thank-you note and flowers from the governor?"

She didn't respond to this. Mainly because she was tired of responding to his cavalier demeanor. He was just too damn accepting of what had just gone down with his radio station. It wasn't as if she had come into his station and knocked his favorite lamp off a table. Yet his whole way of acting made it seem it was no bigger thing than that.

"Hey, nobody got killed," he said. "I'm here. You're here. We have relatively hot beverages. My engineer is en route. I have backup equipment. We'll be back on the air before sunrise."

"What about the automaton?" Hewitt posed.

"In automaton purgatory," Jimmy Bonbon answered. "There are a lot worse places to end up."

Hewitt had seen some of them. She could only hope her actions had kept any new souls from being added to those places.

"So what's your next move? Now that the dice have been rolled."

Hewitt took her final sip of Liquid Decadence, more decadence now than liquid.

"If I'm a riverboat gambler, I wait to see if any bodies wash up on shore."

CHAPTER 42

T HE music woke Hewitt at 5:42. It wasn't solo piano, wasn't, as far as she could tell, a nocturne. Whatever it was, it was filling the house, from, as she knew only too well, its only possible source.

Her living room stereo.

She wrested herself from the bed, went to turn the radio off. Or at least down. Entering the living room, a cold invisible hand stroked the back of her neck. In the tepid, gray, predawn light, Hewitt did a quick three-sixty, a spin that wasn't choreographed to the music but might have been.

There was nobody there. Of course, there couldn't have been. She was outside the MO, outside the profile. No matter how much she let herself go in the next twenty years, she would never be confused for Leonid Brezhnev, no matter how confused the mind was that was doing the perceiving.

She played back the events that had led to this unexpected morning serenade.

When she had finally come home from the studio, the first thing she had done was check the radio. To see if *Chicago's Classical Voice* was still off the air. Turning on the radio, turning the volume up, she was greeted, not by the white noise she would have expected, but by something much closer to silence than sound. And she liked it, distant, muffled, odd as it was. Odder still, when she stood there listening to it, listening to the barely perceptible hum, the almost nothing.

That it relaxed her enough to recommend sleep was the reason she was back in the living room now. She'd relaxed so suddenly, so completely, she had proceeded to the bedroom without shutting the thing off.

Jimmy Bonbon had been right. He was back on the air by sunrise. Whatever other discoveries might be made by members of the public that morning, the faithful WCLS listeners who would wake up to their clock-radios from that point on would discover that nothing was wrong with the world. Or at least the slice of it located between 93.7 and 93.9 on their FM dial.

As she waited at the microwave a few minutes later, the ISP phone went off. Hearing it, Hewitt smelled the Illinois countryside. Instantly. That early summer potpourri the air conveyed after blowing across the fresh green fields, the cool streams, the warming pines. In her personal Pavlovian conditioning, she didn't salivate at the dinner bell; she smelled an Illinois wayside in June.

"Hewitt."

On the other end, Lattimore inhaled his bad news inhalation. But when he spoke, it wasn't bad news. Because it wasn't Lattimore.

"Agent Hewitt," a mellifluous, low voice said. "My name is Brad Spheeris. I understand you've been looking for me."

CHAPTER 43

THE crows were singing. Despite the fact crows couldn't sing.

An untrained ear would have insisted that a crow was a crow, and a caw was a caw. Not that she had an impeccably trained ear. But the thousands of times she had gotten up in the predawn hours in pursuit of ornithological education put her in a seat of primacy above the casual birder. Or at least it put her middle-aged butt into her foldout canvas seat to listen to the fine-feathered overture.

Right now the only seat she was interested in was the one she would find in the ladies' bathroom. *Singing crows*. She could contemplate them there.

But she didn't. Dr. Melinda Fawcett went into the public restroom the way she always did. Function over form. In and out. And it was the out part when it got interesting again. With the crows. The reprise. The damn singing crows.

The chorus of them—*chorus*—was coming from behind the park pavilion. She checked her watch. If she hadn't been fifteen minutes early for her meeting with the birders group, she wouldn't have bothered making the walk around the shelter to see what the crow action was about.

But she did. She did.

Songbirds were songbirds. Carrion were carrion. Nature had made this eminently clear. Songbirds assumed their little territory, their little stage on which to perform. Carrion jockeyed for position. A songbird was a brilliant soloist. Carrion were a light-deprived, atonal chorus.

She had circled the better half of the building.

But that was just it, what had drawn her to this nuance of nature.

There was something in their voices, individually and collectively, that was different, that was surprising. Pleasantly surprising. As if the crows had shed some of their darkness. As if the crows had found a reason to celebrate.

As if the crows were *singing*.

Her scientific mind was amused by what came next. That little chemical reaction in her brain that fired off a relational childhood memory. A little diaphanous ditty. A silly musical rhyme.

> *Sing a song of sixpence. A pocketful of rye.*
> *Four-and-twenty blackbirds baked in a pie.*

In the predawn shadows, she stumbled a bit as her well-cushioned hikers made the transition from the asphalt walkway to the gravel path that led to, from what she could make, a picnic area.

From the center of her body, her diaphragm gave a sudden spring upward, like a trampoline just released from the plunging feet of its jumper. The vocalization she emitted as a result was half-songbird, half-carrion. And the volume of it not only startled her, but surprised the crows enough that, for a moment, the inglorious chorus fell silent.

CHAPTER 44

OTHER than his willingness to meet with her at that ridiculously early hour, the thing that surprised her most from her initial conversation with Bradley Spheeris was the fact that his former employer had been the one who had inveigled him to contact her. After all the phone calls and door pounds and trail-sniffing, Jimmy Freaking Bonbon had apparently done or said the right thing to get his disgruntled ex-employee to pick up the phone and volunteer for an interview.

Hewitt had tried to contact the WCLS owner for the lowdown on all that, but he had returned once again to the Bermuda Triangle of classical music, or to sleep. Which left her with Brad Spheeris, who had advised her of his habit of taking morning walks at Navy Pier. So the place for their meeting had been the easiest decision she'd made since the last time she consented to let Brady fumble with her bra.

Christ, *Brady*. Who would have ever thought she'd be craving pizza and a half-assed bottle of wine at seven o'clock in the morning?

But here she was, jonesing for exactly that, with a coitus chaser, as she walked into the sun's unsteady rays, on the great big pier, looking for a man with a Chicago Cubs cap, a black leather jacket and a little talking devil on his shoulder.

At least that was the impression his phone voice had given her. She had already heard the on-air voice in which he affected his professional tone. A mix of authority and intrigue. With an unspoken suggestion that if you listened to him long enough and really paid attention, he might reveal something about the universe you would've otherwise died without knowing.

His phone voice, however, wasn't as subtle as that. His phone voice had a ring of something Hewitt could only describe to herself as mischief.

To Hewitt, the official entrance to Navy Pier was the Bob Newhart statue, with Newhart, as Dr. Bob Hartley, seated in his chair, an empty couch alongside him. Walking past, Hewitt had to override her usual feeling of wanting to sit down with Dr. Bob for a little heart-to-heart. But she and her designer bag of complexes continued east toward the big lake.

Whether Brad Spheeris's in-person voice would present any peculiarities not revealed in his phone or radio voices, she would know soon enough. Within thirty seconds, at the rate she was walking. The blue baseball cap and the black jacket had just pulled into her field of vision. There was no face attached. Not yet. Because the subject of the still-wet watercolor landscape had his back to Hewitt. He was tall, ruggedly well built. His body language appeared relaxed to Hewitt, most likely the result of the activity he was currently engaged in. Staring at Lake Michigan.

"Brad Spheeris?"

He took longer than he should have to turn around, to Hewitt's mind. Playing games right from the start. This was going to be good.

"Yes. And knowing that, you could only be Agent Hewitt. Although as a patron of the media, I would have recognized your face from a hundred paces."

"It's hard to recognize something when you have your back turned," Hewitt posited.

"I have nothing to fear from the world, or from you, do I?" he posited back. "I mean, it's not as if you were going to sneak up and take a bite of me like some hungry lioness."

The remark pushed Hewitt's weight into the back of her shoes. This guy was really good. Smooth. Charming. Articulate. In that respect, he was cut from the same cloth as Jimmy Bonbon. For all she knew, they could have been doubles partners in tennis going back to high school. But while she had been a little buzzed in her head and more than a little naked under her gown, she would have definitely remembered seeing this guy on the graduation podium.

Unlike Jimmy Bonbon, Brad Spheeris definitely had a face for radio.

And yet there was that ruggedness thing, that tough, weathered, born-to-ride look that turned a lot of women on.

"I know," he said. "I don't look like my voice. None of us on radio ever does. Except for the occasional lucky son-of-a-bitch like Boniface. Or whatever it is you call him."

"What do you mean by that?"

It was the first question she'd asked him, and definitely not the one you'd start an interview with.

"I understand the two of you have a history."

"I don't know what you were told. But if it was anything other than *we attended the same high school*, it would've been due to the story-teller's embellishments."

Standing there against Lake Michigan, using it as a backdrop, Brad Spheeris let out a plume of big, showy laughter, the tail of which turned into the words: "That's an excellent rejoinder."

For a policewoman.

Hewitt added the second line in her head, based on the tone of the first.

"I'm glad you appreciated it. And I want to thank you for coming out here so early."

"For me this isn't early. I did the morning shift for so many years. I don't think I'll ever have the capacity to sleep in."

"That's something I need to ask you about," Hewitt said. "Your time at WCLS. Your leaving. The fact that you're still on the air—at least by means of your recorded voice."

He was moving now, abandoning the still-life pose, starting to walk. Hewitt's segue to direct questions had triggered it.

"Walk with me and I'll tell you all about it," he said. "There's a lit-tle coffee cart down this way. And for those of us who don't drink cof-fee, I know they'll be happy to set us up with something else."

This required no particular sixth sense on his part. As a patron of the media, he had ample access to the stories, the profiles that had been written and produced about her. It was a readily available factoid—that, in addition to dating the occasional serial killer, Special Agent Hewitt had a thing for hot cocoa.

Whether knowledge of that idiosyncrasy was responsible for the little spring in Brad Spheeris's long legs or the half-grin on his face as they
strolled the pier, Hewitt couldn't tell. What she did know was that the
piece of cool hardware against her left rib cage was a welcome chaperone on the promenade.

CHAPTER 45

"**M**R. Boniface let me go because, well, I guess because I had become a bit too much of an irritant to him. He seemed to feel I was getting a little too big for my breeches. I made it clear I wanted more of a stake in the station's future. A little more self-determination."

"He told me he fired you because you're a world-class asshole."

Brad Spheeris's face froze. But only for the length of time it took for a seagull to wail in the distance. After that, he was all grins.

"Well, there *is* that. But I always feel if you're going to do something, be world-class."

Hewitt swirled the contents of her cup. "In your opinion, who's the greatest composer?"

From his reaction to the question, Spheeris couldn't have been more surprised if a water lily had suddenly risen from his coffee cup.

"There's no way I can answer that question without more detail," he said, reaching for his coffee, inhaling a sip as Hewitt responded.

"It's just a question. I mean we all have favorites. Movies, for instance. Mine is *The Wizard of Oz*."

He took another sip, his inward-roving eyes carefully locating his next words.

"To my mind, *The Wizard of Oz* would fall into the category of children's films. Which isn't to say there's anything wrong with having a children's film as your all-time favorite."

"Then what are you saying?"

"Simply that there are categories to be considered. It's not like asking who's your favorite supreme being."

They were seated outside at a patio table, one-hundred-eighty degrees across from one another. Precise that way. Like rivals in a chess match.

Hewitt set her cup on the table. "Who's your all-time favorite baseball player?"

"Ernie Banks. He's also my favorite supreme being."

"Okay."

"Okay what?"

"There were no categories there. I didn't say who's your favorite Cub?"

Brad Spheeris had his response all picked out. He took a cocky sip of coffee just to make her wait.

"In that case, the category had already been established. You asked a man wearing a Chicago Cubs cap. But please, to get back to your original question on composers, if you had said, for instance, 'Who's your favorite operatic composer?' I would have said 'Puccini.'"

"Fine. Who's your favorite composer for the piano?"

All the charming repartee had led to this moment. Brad Spheeris took a few beats either to compose himself or to consider the question at face value. It was Hewitt's job to discern which. In the interval that ensued, her ears drifted down to the water. To the sound of Lake Michigan. Big as it was, it would never have the pulse and verve of an ocean.

"Well, that's an easy one," Spheeris said. "Chopin."

Hewitt had been reading him all along. But this was where she conducted her first deep read. She was looking for two possible reactions. One, that Jimmy Bonbon had already told him about her presumed Chopin connection to the case. The second, that for whatever vibrations the music of Chopin generated in the intricate piano wiring of his brain, he, Bradley Spheeris, was the one who had been orchestrating the gruesome concert.

She saw neither. Or perhaps Brad Spheeris refused to let her see. As the seconds ticked by, as the big lake continued to do its best to impersonate an ocean, Hewitt felt herself becoming less and less sure of what she was looking for.

She wasn't even sure she was still looking at Brad Spheeris. Because there was such a shift in him, a softening of his body, his eyes. And especially his voice. Which he offered her then. His on-air voice. Given its quality, combined with the look in his eyes, it would almost certainly have been his bedroom voice as well.

"Frédéric Chopin was an unparalleled genius of the keyboard. Now you'll note I didn't say Chopin was unrivaled. There were others who composed for piano with phenomenal brilliance. Schubert. Brahms. For God's sake, Beethoven. So many great ones. Yet Chopin, as a composer for piano, was unparalleled."

He was looking right through her. That was Hewitt's initial description of it. But she quickly realized that wasn't accurate. He wasn't looking through her as much as he was vaporizing her so she could fall harmlessly to the earth. As rain. Falling into the vastness of Lake Michigan.

"I'm not sure I understand the difference," Hewitt said, watching her words disappear into the reflected water of his eyes.

"I'm not Noah Webster," he said gauzily. "But I'll give you my best understanding. *Unrivaled* means you're without peer. *Unparalleled* means you're the absolute master of your own special sphere."

Hewitt knew the latter definition would have fit neatly inside the braincase of any creative genius. She also knew it would have fit in the profile of any number of psychopaths.

"I've looked back through your programming archives," Hewitt said. "Something you've been doing regularly for some time. Programming a Chopin nocturne in the middle of the night, in the three o'clock slot. I have a feeling there's a fascinating story behind that."

Spheeris took his time in crafting a response. Not, Hewitt sensed, to create a smoke screen, but to make his answer as clear as possible.

"F. Scott Fitzgerald, no stranger to the wee hours himself, once described it this way: *In a truly dark night of the soul, it's always three o'clock in the morning.*"

He sat back, sipped his coffee.

"I guess I'm left hoping for a little elaboration," Hewitt said.

The elaboration came instantly. As if by rote.

"The nocturne," he gleamed. "The longing, the loneliness, the passion, the sorrow, the frailty, the power, the despair. This is the world in the middle of the night. This is the perfect music for that darkly radiant hour. And Frédéric Chopin was its god-king."

Hewitt felt the inside pocket of her jacket begin to vibrate, on the opposite side from her service revolver.

"Excuse me," she said, reaching inside to field the phone call.

As she listened to the worst possible news, she read Spheeris's eyes for any glint of knowing what she was hearing. But his eyes showed nothing, other than his continued gaze out over the lake, at what Hewitt imagined to be a middle-of-the-night dreamscape, composed of a grand piano and a frocked man with penetrating eyes and beautiful hands making love to it.

CHAPTER 46

CHUCK Radke had never been dead before. So the experience was nothing less than a shock. Especially to be dead like this. On the floor of his living room. Lying there like the fallen boxer who had battled with everything he had. But everything had not been enough.

The opponent had been more than he could have ever prepared for.

There had been the preparation earlier in his life. Preparation for hand-to-hand, toe-to-toe combat. Chuck Radke had done some boxing. As an amateur only. Some Golden Gloves. Some AAU. He had lost his share of fights. But he'd never been knocked out. He'd never been stopped.

It had carried over to the rest of his life. The willingness to get in there and duke it out. To take a shot to the nose, a thumb to the eye. A high-strung, high-maintenance wife. Three kids, translated eventually to three difficult teenagers. The death of one from a college alcohol binge. The high-maintenance, high-strung final days of a wife dying of cancer.

Through all of it, Chuck Radke could have never imagined his own end would come this way. Taking the count in the supposed sanctuary of his living room.

Counted out.

Stopped.

Bill Radke knows there is no hurry to call 911. There is no emergency here. Not anymore. This fight had been over for a long time. He knows who the other fighter was. He knows who stopped his brother. He reads the papers. He watches the news. The nylons. Everybody in the whole Goddamn country knows about the nylons.

The minnows are swimming in the car. They will be swimming there a long time now. In the back cubby of the blue Explorer. In the metal minnow bucket, wedged into the corner with the Coleman cooler, heavy with ice and mostly Diet Pepsi. Just four cans of Bud. For health and driving reasons, they were both down to two a day.

He could drink all four now if he wanted.

There were a lot of things in the brother-brother world that suddenly no longer held. Chuck would never outfish him again. Chuck would never beat him in poker. Chuck would never clean his clock pitching horseshoes. Chuck would never earn more money in a fiscal year than he would. Chuck would never get the better seats at Soldier Field.

Chuck would never beat him at anything again. Because Chuck was done. Chuck was finished. Chuck had lost.

He had lost to the most ridiculous of all possible opponents. Chuck Radke had lost to against-all-odds bad luck. Chuck had been claimed by chance. Chuck had been knocked out by a fluke punch.

And here he was now, the younger brother. The brother who was good, but never quite as good. Looking down at his brother. The older. The better. But now, the fallen.

Here he was, Bill Radke, the younger brother, the last one standing.

Over his fallen brother.

Like he was what—the winner?

Then why wasn't he raising his arms in the air in victory? Why instead was he kneeling down? And not the way a referee would drop down to count a fighter out. Kneeling more the way they used to kneel together between their mom and dad in church. Kneeling for the God neither one of them ever fully accepted.

But if that was true, why had his mind entered into the recitation of the Our Father? Why was he doing something now he couldn't remember ever having done during all their competitive years together on earth?

Why was he reaching out to touch his brother's hair?

CHAPTER 47

EITHER Brad Spheeris wasn't the guy or he was a master of obfuscation. That, and facial muscle control. There was also a third possibility. That he was the guy, but in his mind, he wasn't. The stealth psychopath. Hey, another part of me, over which I have absolutely no influence, is the one doing this. Not me.

It was hard to tell with this man. When his face didn't move. And his eyes bled into the same deep blue nothingness as Lake Michigan.

Hewitt had taken the bad news—the discovery at a Kane County park—with the intention of executing some facial muscle control of her own. There were questions she still wanted to run down with Spheeris. But a fresh princess had turned up. If royal protocol held form, a king would follow. And she had to ask herself, sitting there at the patio table, in the relentless sunshine of Navy Pier, if the placid, dreamy man sitting across from her was the killer of one, or the other. Or both.

"Did Jimmy—Jay Boniface—mention why I wanted to talk to you?"

"He said you had questions about the overnight programming. I think it's pretty clear now what you're after."

The water was gone from his eyes, and in its place had come fire. Blue fire.

"Since I program the evening selections, you may very well think I could be cueing myself to murder younger women and older men for no reason other than a way to kill a few nocturnal hours."

Now it was Hewitt's turn to stare placidly, dreamily across the table at him, *through* him. To reveal nothing of her thoughts. Or to reveal nothing more than what had already been revealed.

"You've given me no reason to think that," she told him.

A seagull chose that moment to call out. And the high, plaintive tone of it seemed to drain some of the credibility from Hewitt's claim.

"I can only hope that's true," he said. "Of course, you're not exactly in the business of telling the truth. At least not all the time."

"I'm as truthful as the people I deal with allow me to be."

His smile became a grin, and then a laugh. Her mouth mirrored none of it. But the damn seagull took the opportunity to chime in again. When he and the gull were both done, Spheeris shaded to his version of serious.

"Most human beings are so preoccupied with fabricating their own existences, they wouldn't know truth if it stuck its tongue in their mouth."

It was the first thing he'd said that made Hewitt's pulse quicken, that gave her a glimpse of what else might be hidden in the deep fissures of his mind.

"I just have one more thing to ask you," she said, in the most non-threatening voice she could fabricate.

"You want to know my whereabouts from last night," he volunteered, in a sufficiently unthreatened tone.

"It's one of the questions they taught us to ask in detective school," Hewitt responded.

"You probably already know that I didn't spend the night at home."

Hewitt knew. She had the overnight report. She didn't try to hide that fact from Spheeris.

"Okay, fine. Enough said. If you must know, I was staying with a lady friend. Am I required to tell you who at this point?"

"No. I was just wondering where you were. I know where you are now. That's all that matters."

It *was* all that mattered. She had him in her sights now, and she wasn't going to let him get away. Chances were he had actually been with a girlfriend. Her gut kept insisting that he wasn't the killer. Killers had a certain smell, like a death pheromone they gave off. It was something she'd always had a sense for. Except the one time her own pheromones had gotten pulled into the spray bottle and masked the killer's.

"If you'd like to ask the next question, please do," she heard him say. "Not to be presumptuous, but it's kind of written all over your face."

"Okay, this one's hypothetical," she said pleasantly—enough to surprise both of them. "And it has to do with a name you know. Frédéric Chopin. Based on what you know about him, if there was one person in Chopin's life he would have murdered if given the chance, who would it have been?"

Spheeris's response came as involuntarily as the left eyebrow tremor that accompanied it.

"George Sand."

Hewitt ran the name through the little gray supercomputer.

"I don't believe I'm familiar with him."

This arched both of his eyebrows and drew a mild snort from his nostrils.

"You *definitely* aren't familiar with him. Because he was actually a *she*."

"A woman named George?"

"A woman with the nom de plume *George*," he clarified. "She was a novelist. At that time in Europe it was extremely difficult for a woman to attract serious interest in the arts and letters. So *Amantine Aurore Lucile Dupin* began to circulate her writing under the name *George Sand*."

"When I first started as a detective, I worked under the name *Lenny Hewitt*."

She couldn't immediately quantify who was more surprised by the glibness of the comment. She had a fresh murder scene to get to. She might have had the killer right there in front of her, sipping coffee and waxing artsy. But there was absolutely nothing solid about him she could bag, cuff or take down by physical means. He'd programmed the music she suspected of being a trigger in the murder of the kings. He was an unusual character. An esoterically odd man. A deep thinker. But atop that depth, he was a very creative jester.

If she was going to get anywhere with him—if there was anywhere to get—an occasional jab from her might be just what the joker in him was looking for.

"So why would George Sand have been the one? Why, in a hypothetical world, would Chopin have taken her life?"

There was no jingle of merriment in the jester's eyes now. Just a brooding tightening, a setting of the pupils on a pinpoint in the center of Hewitt's chest.

"Because in a nonhypothetical world, she took his."

Hewitt waited for him to elaborate. When he didn't, she opened up some additional space for him to do so, picking up her paper cup and acting as if the air in the cup actually contained one last swallow of HC. Doing so, she got the sense she could fake-swallow for an hour and all he would do was sit and watch her.

"I guess once again I'm hoping for a little elucidation."

Spheeris's eyes blazed at the challenge.

"As Frédéric François Chopin—as that beautiful, perfect genius lay dying in his Paris apartment of consumption, drowning in the fluid of his own lungs—this woman, this longtime love, this privileged confidant, didn't so much as take the time to come and wish him a decent bon voyage."

His answer was just settling into the folds of Hewitt's brain when her phone went off again. The news she took was a depressing, but not surprising coda to Spheeris's story. She said little on her end to the news that the king's head had officially rolled into the public square. And when she clicked off, Brad Spheeris was there with his condolences, unsolicited, but not entirely unwelcome.

"I'm sorry," he said. "Your eyes are much too lovely to reflect such pain. Whatever it was in those phone calls, I'm truly sorry."

CHAPTER 48

IF she could've done it, Hewitt would've bought a cup of top 'o the morning blend for Pete Megna, with room for cream. But as it was, when she had left the patio table of the coffee stand, she had also left Brad Spheeris contemplating a refill and any number of other steaming topics.

For his part, Megna was one of the many people—probably half of America—who wasn't worth a shit until he got those first twelve fluid ounces into his bloodstream. Hewitt's call had gone in to him early enough that he should've had time to spike himself somewhere on the way to Navy Pier. If not, it must've killed him to watch Spheeris sipping merrily away, close up, through the high-tech opera glasses.

As Hewitt neared the shore end of the pier, she called him to check in.

"Sorry I didn't get a chance to do much with my hair," she told him after snuffled greetings.

"You're on a pier in *The Windy City*," Megna said into her ear. "I'm not sure it would've mattered. If it's any consolation, you looked a lot better than he does right now."

"Is he still there?"

"Like he's planning to make a day of it."

"In other words, maybe not in a big hurry to go kill anyone."

"At least not until he finishes the crumb cake he just treated himself to."

Hewitt could see her car now, still illegally parked. No ticket. One positive thing.

"Where are you?"

"You know the T-shirt place that got in trouble for selling Richard Speck tank tops?"

"Yeah."

"I'm standing out in front like I own it."

"Let's hope you won't have to stand there all day," Hewitt said, closer to a sigh than a statement.

"Why am I sensing maybe you're not so sure he's the guy?" Megna posed.

"I suppose that's how I sound."

"That's how you sound. How do you feel?"

"To the cool side of ambivalent."

She had arrived at her car, wasn't looking forward to taking it where she needed to go next.

"Who knows?" Megna offered. "Maybe he'll finish his crumb cake and lead me right to the next potential victim."

Hewitt got in the car. "If he doesn't, maybe he'll do something nice like take you to the Art Institute. Or at least Crate and Barrel."

"If I'm really lucky, Mr. Beef," Megna said. "I can't toss down a beer. But there's no department reg against heaping piles of meat during a surveillance operation."

"If you do, have an Italian special for me."

"Sweet peppers or hot?"

"Both," Hewitt answered.

She had pulled out, U-turned and was heading west toward the expressway, and her trip not to a wayside this time, but a park in Kane County, on the banks of the Fox River, where apparently they had picnic tables too.

"Anything to get the taste of death out of my mouth," she said. "Anything."

BRADY'S call came in at the perfect time. As if he'd coordinated it by some extrasensory means. To Hewitt it was a good sign. A sign that she was actually in sync with somebody. Not just physically. But in all those mysterious little electrons of communication that could hold the nucleus of a relationship together after the physical thing lost some of its hold.

"Did I catch you at a bad time?"

"No," she said, backing away from the main group a little more than she already had. "I was just finishing picnic table duty."

Though it was as second nature to her as breathing, it still startled her when she would say things like that, fashioning those euphemistic phrases, while the reality of what she had just seen and felt and tasted was still searing, smoking like a branding iron against the skin of her soul. But shit, if you didn't keep one foot on the good humor side of the door, the angry-as-hell side would claim you for good.

"I heard your psycho has expanded his activities beyond waysides," Brady offered.

"Probably didn't help that the stepped-up monitoring was the lead story on last night's ten o'clock news."

"Can I do anything to help?"

"You're already doing it. Please keep talking. Any topic is acceptable."

"Okay, let's go with this . . . I'm ready for something else."

His voice was so small in her ear—and the Illinois countryside was so wide—that the true size of his statement didn't hit her at first.

"I'm sorry"—she saw Spheeris's face at the pier—"I'm sorry. What did you say?"

Panic on panic. On top of what was already on the picnic table, under the royal blue shroud.

"Pizza Night," he said. "I'm ready for something else. Like maybe some Philly cheese steaks."

"You bring the Philly. I'll bring the cheese."

Love in the park. It beat the living hell out of death. But with a body on the table in front of her, and another one on a living room floor in Palatine, death wasn't going anywhere. And with Brady at his desk in another county, love wasn't either.

"I know your day-to-day couldn't be any more outrageous than it is right now, but . . ."

She listened as he exhaled a sigh at the end of the thought, wished she was with him to let the breeze of it blow against her eyelids.

"Right now that *but* would go a long way toward making me feel human again."

"That's what buts are for."

In her head, she heard the same words in a Val Patterson/Whitney Houston duet.

"The parents are at the scene," Hewitt said, changing tack, backing farther away from the gathering. "An older sister too. The thing I notice is that the shock of it doesn't seem quite as total as it was with the next of kin of the earlier victims. I mean the shock of the death is the same. Total. But the shock of the situation, the circumstances—it's a model they've already seen. And somehow that makes the horror of it less horrific. That their daughter, their sister wasn't just some isolated, incomprehensible case. But that she's part of a bigger picture. A performance. A program."

"It's the reason support groups form," Brady responded. "Knowing someone else who knows the experience. No matter how beyond belief."

The older sister was looking in Hewitt's direction. Just staring. Eyes not knowing where to go. Until they actually landed on Hewitt's eyes, struck a deal with her for a few seconds of contact. Hewitt knew she couldn't give the woman anything but her own eyes for as long as it lasted. Whatever message they imparted. And she was going to be damned if she would be the first one to look away.

The sister was the first to go, abandoning Hewitt for the yellow streak that ripped suddenly between them. Hewitt followed it then too, as the goldfinch found a tree branch, fixed its claws to it, perched there looking out at the human commotion.

The intervention of the bird pushed Hewitt's mind to acknowledge the persistent calling of the crows in the trees above. Those damn black birds. Would they ever leave her alone? Would they ever let the world have a little peace?

CHAPTER 49

THE world is watching. He knows this. He has known this all along. And so they watch. They watch, but they do not see. This is the difference. The difference between himself and the rest of the world. They do not see because they have no idea of what they are looking for. He, however, knows. He knows precisely.

There is no secret to any of this. No great esoteric mystery. It is simply a matter of opening your eyes, truly opening them. For the first time in his life, he sees now what he is truly meant to see.

Believing is seeing.

There is an entire sky above them. *An entire sky.* But here, on this ground, on this sidewalk, these people who walk with him do not even pause to consider it, to give it even a momentary reflection. Can the lifeless, hopeless concrete beneath their feet be more interesting to them than the brilliant sky above?

An entire sky.

On this morning, not just brilliant but rapturous, the sky. And what makes it more stimulating to him: it is all there for the taking. So if they do not wish to have it, he feels no guilt in claiming it for himself. Had he a flag, a flag of his one-person nation, he would plant it in the center of the sky.

Occasionally, as they approach, one of them will notice, even acknowledge, the fact that he alone among them has his face turned skyward as he walks. Invariably, he will draw his face down to meet theirs, to make the acquaintance of their curiosity, their almost ashamed interest in what a skyward face might suggest.

Why so terrible to break away from the herd? When and by whom were such seeds of fear sewn?

Why can no one else bring themselves to look where he is looking, to see what he dares to see?

The walk continues. For a time he imitates them, looking down at the sidewalk to see his feet making their invisible tracks in the concrete.

Of course, they are watching these tracks of his too. But again, they see nothing. Nothing they can follow. Nothing that will help them.

There is no help for them. Not here on the fuzzy gray world they walk. Not in the brilliant sky they occasionally look at but fail to recognize. Not beyond the great blue ceiling. That place, that realm few can ever even begin to envision.

There are days when he can do little else but envision it. For that is where she lives now. That is where she plays.

There had always been the tiniest speck of blue in her otherwise hazel right eye. Not just a typical blue, an eye-blue. But a much lighter, a much more luminous blue.

A top-of-the-sky blue.

When her life left her body, and the music with it, he imagined it had passed through that tiny blue speck. And not unlike the universe exploding from a tiny point of energy, her essence, her soul, expanded instantly to fill the entire sky.

This is where she plays for him now. Not at times like this when the sky is present. But at night, when the sky is no longer there. When the earth is still. When the music passes most easily through the membrane. When the piano transcends the wood of the sleeping floor. When her nocturnes fill his lonely mind with love.

CHAPTER 50

TWO things Hewitt had never understood: the art of fishing, and *Entertainment Tonight*.

Not that she had anything against either. Her dad had enjoyed fishing, or had at least paid lip service to its virtues as a relaxing pastime. And *Entertainment Tonight*. She had colleagues, Val Patterson at the head of the class, who got TiVo for the purpose of never missing an episode.

Hewitt had lived more than ten thousand days on the earth, and never before had one of those days featured the topics of fishing and *ET* at the same time. But this day, in late June, in her thirty-eighth year, for reasons known only to the universal planning committee, had brought them together.

Beginning with the princess crime scene. Beginning with Sybil Jenks, mother of the victim, Juliette Jenks. Her daughter fit the profile, hit the marks of the princess archetype as envisioned by her killer. And without the intercession of that killer, she would have someday hit her marks on the set of *ET*. At least that had been her dream, her passion, her short life's calling. It was, as Sybil Jenks had described to Hewitt, the reason she had taken her grandmother's inheritance, left her job and enrolled at the Columbia School of Broadcasting while she lived in her grandmother's vacated home.

Mary Hart. Leeza Gibbons. Juliette Jenks.

Why the hell not?

That the mother, destroyed as she was, had wanted to make sure Hewitt knew all this about her daughter was one of those investigational nuances that made Hewitt's mind spin and her eyes water. But she'd seen it before, and she knew it fell into the category of *Things you should know so you really care about this loved one of mine and what was not only taken from me but from her.*

If Juliette Jenks's father had been able to stop muttering some strange, shocked reprimand to himself—or his daughter—under his breath, maybe he would have offered another personal story to help Hewitt understand who his daughter had been. As for Juliette Jenks's sister, Jeanette, eye contact would remain the only communication she would share with Hewitt on this occasion.

At the second crime scene, Hewitt met the fallen king's brother, who, being the surviving younger brother, was now the king himself. But that wasn't what he talked about. Because the thing Bill Radke wanted to make sure Hewitt understood and took with her was the fact his big brother, Chuck, would never go fishing again. This was a crime not only against humanity, but against natural law, man's God-given right to fish.

Hewitt got that, made sure Bill Radke knew she got it. She could have told him the whole story. How her own father's death, on the night they were scheduled to go out for their all-you-can-eat spaghetti night, had taken spaghetti off her personal menu ever since, and from her best projections, for the rest of her life.

Yes, she got it. And because she got it, she was going to do everything in her power to get every last bit of justice she could for him, even if she couldn't get him a refund for those two dozen minnows that would never see the waters of Lake Zurich.

OF the two WCLS people she'd interviewed, Jay Boniface was in the better physical shape. He obviously worked at it, and wore it as a suit of armor. Brad Spheeris was actually the bigger of the two men, but not as well defined.

She still didn't have a clear read on Spheeris. Which meant it was entirely possible he was the guy, but equally possible his odd, suspicious demeanor was merely the result of having an odd, suspicious personality. He was a classical music expert, a quasi-celebrity, by his very nature steeped in eccentricity. But that and three bucks would get Hewitt a venti hot chocolate and a wooden stir stick.

If Brad Spheeris had been suppressing an entire volcano of bubbling, raging psychosis, he hadn't made so much as a gurgle. For the life of her, she hadn't gotten the sense that he was holding back anything of that magnitude. Of course, a world-class psychopath could have pulled that off. She'd seen it before. She'd hugged, kissed and stroked it before.

She was in her car, headed for HQ and a sit-down with Lattimore as she processed the case through the windshield of the Mazda. It was that time in summer in the Midwest when the dead bugs really started showing up on the glass. The washer fluid and wipers only pushed the carnage around, made it into a disgusting, protein paste. She needed a carwash, needed even more the thinking time it would give her.

Jimmy Bonbon wasn't an issue. Former high school studs, especially tennis-playing studs, didn't go off and run a series of successful businesses and then one day just start strangling old men in their living rooms and displaying young murdered women on public picnic tables. Yet of the two radio personalities, why did it seem to her that Jimmy B was the one who was more mysterious?

The front wheels of the Mazda had just rolled into the bay of the Super Spray Carwash when she received a phone call and her first opportunity to sneak a feel of whatever Jimmy Bonbon had in his secret pocket. But before she could do any of that, Jimmy B had hauled off and invited her to dinner.

Dinner would've been one thing. And if it had just been that, she wouldn't have bumped Brady Richter, who was already penciled into her evening slot, if such a slot was even a possibility given the day's unfolding to that point.

No, despite the fact that she, like most girls at Wheaton West, had had a crush on Jimmy Bonbon and, more than once, had closed her eyes and taken her hand down Fuzzy Lane over him, dinner alone on this night wouldn't have been enough. But having the opportunity to poke at him a little and probe for more about the DJ he'd fired, well, she had no choice but to serve and protect.

"Your shootout with the machine didn't have the desired effect," Jimmy Bonbon reminded her.

"I killed a machine. That's all."

"Do you really think Spheeris is involved in this?"

"I don't know. I hope to hell he is."

"Why would you hope?"

The Mazda was starting to shake from the two-sided assault of the air blowers.

"If he's not, I have absolutely no idea who is."

Another call was coming in. Hewitt signed off on the dinner invitation, agreed to his restaurant suggestion, shifted the meeting time to 8:00, padding it for any additional insanity the universe might throw her way in the meantime.

Hewitt clicked the incoming call. Megna. His voice excited. Shoulder-hunchingly excited.

"After a series of mundane pursuits—breakfast, a run on personal items at Walgreens and a layover at home—your man just got a lot more interesting."

Hewitt felt a thrill in her chest that immediately pushed upstairs to flush her face. It was an eighty-twenty flush. Eighty percent excitement over the thought that Spheeris might be opening a secret passage. Twenty percent over the fact that she now had a viable reason to avoid Lattimore.

"Where and what?" Hewitt heard her night-before-Christmas voice inquire.

"He left his place about twenty minutes ago. I followed him to a residence in Highland Park. He parked on the street and let himself in the house. Front door. But not before he did something that was pretty Goddamn wacky."

"How so?"

"Well, before he went in, he did a quick turn and survey. Like: I hope nobody sees that I'm obviously walking into this house in broad f-ing daylight."

"So it couldn't have looked more suspicious."

"The way you'd draw it up in a B movie."

Hewitt had exited the carwash, all clean and shiny for her next expressway sortie.

"Anything since?"

"All quiet?"

"Too quiet?"

"I'm not sure how to quantify that," Megna responded. "It just feels weird."

"I can be there in fifteen," Hewitt said as the Mazda banged out from the pitched drive of the carwash. "In the meantime, any way you can get close enough for a look inside?"

"Well, that's the other thing. The place isn't exactly letting the sun shine in. For a summer day, it's pretty well draped up."

"What kind of place?"

"English Tudor. *Big* English Tudor."

"Get me whatever you can on the owner."

"Or to save time," Megna said, "I could just go up and ring the bell and tell them I'm lost."

"Wait till I get there," Hewitt said as she hammered the accelerator. "We can show up lost together. The way this is going, it's not like we'd be lying."

CHAPTER 51

HE watches them, this man and this woman. He watches as if he is right there with them. He watches as if he is not there at all, as if this activity he views is little more than a lucid dream brought forth by an absence of sexual gratification and the presence of a mild fever.

He is present, but he is not present. He is here, but also nowhere. He is a body in the room, but also a nonbody, an ethereal entity, a shade, a sprite, a ghost, a hologram of his own projection.

Inhaling, he watches the man's hands on the woman's neck. He can feel the breathing of the woman, can feel it in his hands.

The angle and the light prevent him from seeing the woman's face. But this is no matter. He has seen the face before. Soon enough he will see it again, up close, contorted in its mask of privileged pain.

He will hear the music then too. Not terribly unlike the music that plays now. But terribly more significant. The hands of the man, the fingers, the thumbs, playing the woman's neck almost as if it is a musical instrument, mirroring for a time the hands of the piano, the Rachmaninoff that plays, the gentleness of his *Variations on a Theme of Corelli.*

When he begins with her, *truly begins*, he will change the music, using the power he has to change it. The Rachmaninoff may continue to play. But he will listen to the music that prepares the truth for him. The music that touches and holds the invisibleness that is his true nature, that is the true nature of all men.

For a moment he is the one there, the one with his hands on the woman's neck. He feels the pulse of his heart in his palms, feels the tingle of absolute life in his fingertips. He feels the life pulsing back to him from her neck. The life never more truthfully felt, more truthfully lived.

He knows this not just from the feeling in his hands, but from the feeling expressed in the woman's face. If indeed this is the precursor, the foreplay, then she has much to look forward to. For already there is the sense she has become sensually enhanced, psychically charged.

When the time is right—and that time will come soon—he will fulfill that promise for her. He will take her there on the dark, winged horse she has been grooming in the wild fields of her soul all along.

Deep in the hindquarters of that dark horse, he feels the first charges of electricity.

The tug of a smile comes to his lips, his cheeks. In this strange new world the fates have fashioned for him, he is really beginning to find his way. He is, as they would say, hitting his stride.

CHAPTER 52

THE princely home was actually owned by a princess, and not a young one. Gloria Martindale was fifty-four years old, about double the age of the previous female victims. But that didn't rule out a daughter who might be living with her. With Brad Spheeris as her houseguest, Hewitt wasn't in a position to rule out anything.

Calls to Gloria Martindale's home phone had gone unanswered. Which didn't rule anything in. People ignored phone calls for all kinds of reasons. Not necessarily because they were hosting a psychopath. So that, by itself, wouldn't have been enough for Hewitt and Megna to seek entry into the home. What invited them in was the visual Hewitt encountered when she slipped inside the ivy-choked lattice on the south side of the house and managed a look through a finger's-width of space between the drawn curtain and the window frame.

From a three-quarters angle, she saw the back and side of Brad Spheeris with his hands around the neck of a female with very long, very blond hair. Hewitt couldn't see the woman's face, couldn't tell how much life, if any, the face still contained. But after Megna kicked in the door, she had her answer in a matter of seconds.

Gloria Martindale was alive, but also in shock. She was seated on a high-backed chair in the center of her sumptuous living room, with Brad Spheeris standing over her, behind her, his hands still on the shocked neck and shoulders. In the instant photo Hewitt processed, the expression on Spheeris's face was less shocked, but the surprise was total, as was the duck and cover look of having been caught in the act.

Hewitt's *Freeze!* rang out and rattled against the high walls and tall ceiling. But the volume of her voice was supplanted by the sound of Brad Spheeris's instant reply.

"Trust me, we're already frozen."

The next impression Hewitt recorded wasn't so much a photo as a multimedia show.

First, there was the realization that Spheeris's voice wasn't big and sonorous and *house-filling* because she had gone temporarily insane. It was because he, for some insane reason, was wearing a small headset microphone that was projecting his amplified voice through speakers.

Second, she quickly located not only the twin speakers, but a portable audio mixing board in the room.

Third, she finally registered that the lush dramatic music that had been filling the house was emanating from the little sound system. *Little* being a bit misleading. Since the sound that came from the system was as big as the damn house.

"I'm not sure what you were hoping to find," the house said to her as Brad Spheeris's mouth moved in sync with the words. "But I'm fairly confident this is not where you want to be right now."

By now Hewitt was sensing a fourth element in the multimedia blitz. And that was the unmistakable air of carnal pursuit.

Of course, none of it made any sense, at least not in the context through which Hewitt had decided to enter the home without anything remotely approaching a *Captain, may I?* But she needed a few moments more to assess what she saw before she could consider lowering her service revolver.

In that interval, the piece of piano music came to an end, with a landing that couldn't have been softer had it been placed on hallowed ground by the hands of a dying priest.

Before Hewitt could summon her own voice, the voice of Brad Spheeris filled the house again.

"Variations on a Theme of Corelli. By the great Russian composer, Sergey Rachmaninoff. Another great Russian, Vladimir Ashkenazy, at the piano."

Hewitt and Megna had seen enough. Enough to make them withdraw their weapons. Brad Spheeris took that to mean it was okay to withdraw a tiny remote from the chest pocket of his shirt.

"Next, another work of thoughtful, intelligent and, yes, sensual piano. The 'Fantasy in A Minor,' by Johannes Brahms." He paused to look at Hewitt. "Let's all take a deep breath now. That's right. Ahhh."

CHAPTER 53

SITTING across the dinner table from him, she couldn't help thinking how much easier it would have been to have kept her date with Brady. Easier and more pleasurable in an end-of-the-night kind of way.

It would have been easier and more pleasurable had she been able to keep her appointment with Jimmy Bonbon too. But clearly, neither the gods of pleasure or easiness were booking her social calendar.

Hewitt had been plugged into the media world long enough to know that the influence of celebrity and the cult of personality could manifest in all kinds of outrageous behavior. What she had seen at the suburban castle had been a case for the psychology books, especially once she had received a preliminary explanation from Brad Spheeris as to what the hell had been going on beneath those great Tudor ceilings.

Across the dinner table, between flickers of a candle in a gondola and bites of linguini in a clam sauce, Brad Spheeris continued his explanation.

"My audience loved me. That's something people don't realize. It's something I don't think even I realized until after the fact. After the unceremonious canning."

Hewitt was still short on details about the unceremonious canning. That could come. Right now she had him talking about himself, over a meal he had suggested they share. Right now there was no better place to be.

"Within an hour of the announcement, the phone calls started coming in, the e-mails."

He took a sip of his Chianti Reserva. Hewitt smiled a subtle smile of approval as he did. The same way she'd smiled after he'd taken her suggestion to order a bottle.

Truth serum, with an earthy bouquet.

"Music listeners don't just open their ears to us on the radio. They open their minds. Some even open their hearts. A special few open their souls."

He sank his fork into the linguini, gave it a couple of quick turns, lifted a neatly knit forkful to his mouth. It struck Hewitt that he had a certain dexterity, a deftness, not unlike the recorded musicians who accompanied him on the air and, at least lately, in selected living rooms.

"So when you left, some of your faithful listeners went into withdrawal," Hewitt said as he chewed.

He didn't hurry his eating to accommodate her. More so, he waited until his mouth was fully empty before answering.

"You don't accompany people into their thoughts, their moods, their secret lives without creating a deep bond, an intimate relationship."

"And you decided to take this relationship, this *understanding*, into the real world. Like a service contractor."

Spheeris smiled a linguini-thin smile. "That would not be an inaccurate description of it."

"I'm just curious," Hewitt said, with her own angel-hair width of a grin. "Do you have business cards?"

He was in the middle of knitting another bundle of pasta. The question caused him to settle for a less tidy forkful this time.

"I mean, what would it say?" Hewitt pressed. "'Classical DJ and deep tissue massage in the privacy of your own mansion.'"

Spheeris set his fork down, took his napkin and dabbed at the corners of his mouth. "No, I don't carry a card for that. But if I ever do, that'll be on it. And I'll make sure you get one."

He made it sound humorous. But why did it feel like a thinly veiled threat to her? As if somewhere inside the subtext was the real message: *Trust me, honey, the last thing you want is to be on my mailing list.*

She let her eyes lower to her plate. If the intensity of her focus had been converted to heat, she could have reheated the room-temperature surface of her lobster pizza.

"Do you cook?"

The question was such a sudden right turn into the personal, he might as well have asked Hewitt whether she waxed or shaved.

"I don't cook so much as I wave," she told him.

"Wave?"

"As in micro."

He pushed out a short, prideful sniff—like a poodle that needed to go outside.

"So for you this is a treat."

What a prick, her mind pushed out, in its own prideful sniff.

"Lobster pizza is always a treat," she said. "It's one of the entrées Stouffer's doesn't offer."

He finished another swallow of Chianti Reserva. "You might have to upgrade to Wolfgang Puck."

He swirled his wine, took a satisfied sip, held it long enough, hard enough for it to be a swig. The cockiest gesture he'd displayed to that point.

"And what kind of wine would you recommend with a Wolfgang Puck frozen pizza?"

"With or without a dinner salad from a plastic bag?"

"Let's say with."

"What kind of dressing?"

"Vinaigrette."

"Well, that makes it easy. A nice California Shiraz."

"Thank you," Hewitt said. "I'll remember that for my next pizza party."

"And do you throw many of those?"

"I try to have at least one a week."

Hewitt was glad Spheeris's mouth was devoid of food at that point. Had that not been the case, the deeply pulmonary laugh he expectorated would have come with a garnish.

"This is so charming," he said after a couple of settling breaths. "The two of us. Trading fours like this."

The jazz reference threw her a little.

"I mean here we are," he continued, his eyes deepening and lighting up at the same time, in a way that made Hewitt's hairline buck. "Here we are exchanging all the finely tuned rejoinders. Together, in the light of this ludicrous candle. You sitting there suspecting me of being a very dark and dangerous man."

"I'm sure you're sitting there thinking some interesting thoughts of me as well," Hewitt offered, aware she was poking a stick in the beehive.

"Oh, I am," he said, his eyes going deep and luminous and exercising their voodoo on Hewitt's scalp again. "I'm thinking that you're a potentially dark and dangerous woman. Especially when the lights go off and the candle goes out."

"So in the dark and dangerous category, does that make us even?"

"It makes us even in every way. As the PR people in your business are fond of saying, I'm a person of interest to you. In a reciprocal way, you're a person of interest to me."

"Well, given your interest, I hope I haven't disappointed you."

For a moment, Hewitt thought another lung expulsion might be coming. He inhaled that way. But all he exhaled was a sigh of resignation. As if he knew their verbal foreplay was coming to an end and there was no after-play anywhere on the menu.

"Disappointment was never even a possibility," he told her. "Now as far as your interest in me, I'm afraid disappointment is an inevitability. Because this creature you're interested in simply isn't here. There may be things that mimic it, even parallel it. That's why you've been drawn to me. But the thing you seek doesn't live in me. Any more than the thing I seek in you could ever be there for me."

Hewitt needed more bread. To soak up some of the acid her stomach jets had just fired into her gut.

She looked at him, not just at his physical presence, but at his countenance. Physically, there was his bigness, the strong, angular nature of it. Facially, there was no beauty there whatsoever. But in the beauty vacuum, there was a sort of amusedly suffering wisdom. Beyond that, it was the valence of persona around him that drove Hewitt's mind, in those seconds, to add a character to her king-princess-executioner. The one palace character still remaining for assignment. The one character that had eluded her thinking.

It was the royal mystic. And looking at Brad Spheeris now, she saw, in the face, the body, the aura, the only comparison she could draw.

Her mind tossed her the words, the description, the moniker.

Rasputin, with a salon haircut.

CHAPTER 54

IT was nuts. Totally preposterous. As totally preposterous as a restau-
rateur's decision to put candles in the hulls of miniature gondolas.
But it had worked. It had worked dreamily. Every best-case-scenario
projection from her initial acceptance of his dinner invitation had produced a sweet bite of tiramisu.

She had taken his bait. She had dangled hers for him. He had happily
sucked it in. She'd gotten him a little drunk, a little cocky. And with the
combination, she'd gotten him more than a little sensually stimulated.

But at the point when all of that should have pushed him into the
executioner's chamber, instead he had wandered off to the mystic's cave.

She was in her car, heading for home, still shaking her head, even
though her neck and shoulders were frozen, her jaw was locked, her
eyes were fixed on the nothingness of her bright headlights, and her
mind was focused on the brilliantly detailed nothingness of her dinner
with Bradley.

Her gut was shaking its head too. Only down there, there was actually some action. Her gut was shaking its head *no*. It would have been
infinitely easier if it hadn't been the case. But while he was an eccentric
brainiac who had a side business broadcasting classical music in lonely
rich women's living rooms—and whatever else was included in the
package—Brad Spheeris just didn't feel like a killer. He didn't feel like
the guy.

She'd been riding in silence, audio system–wise, since she'd left the
restaurant. She turned the system on. Still set to WCLS.

For a moment, she thought of popping in some Miles, maybe
"Sketches of Spain." But she didn't, instead letting the car fill with the

piano piece that was playing. A melodic, but quizzical piece she'd heard before. Listening to a few more measures, she identified it. The composer anyway. A French composer. *Eric Satie*, she thought.

And while the radio played the odd piece, Hewitt allowed herself to be pulled back ever-so-slightly into overriding her gut and leaving the bedroom door if not open just a crack, then at least unlocked to the possibility that Brad Spheeris was still a player in this psychotic psychodrama.

In the genus of homicidal freaks, there was a subspecies that had, as the centerpiece of its profile, a fascination with the police work and the machinations, media included, pursuant to the investigation. This fascination often manifested in the killer's desire to *be around* the various aspects of the investigation. To cooperate. To even pretend to assist the investigators.

Brad Spheeris, even if he wasn't a homicidal freak, could have easily faked his way into chapter meetings of that depraved subspecies. Given that, he would continue to enjoy the honor of a twenty-four-hour tail, courtesy of ISP.

IT was dark déjà vu when Hewitt left her car in the lot and made her way up the sidewalk to her condo unit. Extremely dark déjà vu. Blood-freezing, skin-screaming déjà vu.

On the front porch. Sitting on the top step. The figure of a man. A strong, well-cut man, peering through the gathered haze of grays and blacks in the evening air, the only thing that separated him from her.

It could have been him. It could have been Scott Gregory. The only thing keeping him from being Scott Gregory was the fact Scott Gregory was dead. But this man, the déjà vu interloper, showed he was anything but dead as he cocked his head to one side. *Not smoothly*. Rather, almost grudgingly. Painfully.

Her hand was in her jacket. Her head was registering the cold reassurance of the service revolver against her fingertips.

"Whoever you are, you need to know I'm not real big on surprises."

Her feet had come to a stop on the walk just before the last of her words bounced back at her from the condo façade.

The porch light was off. But a little swath of streetlight was casting a glow over parts of the porch. By design or chance—but likely design— her visitor was sitting in a place that evaded illumination. When he rose now, his face ascended into the part of the night she could see.

Scott Gregory, *The Raven*, was dead. But as the face of the visitor began to reflect the light, it sent Hewitt a picture of Scott Gregory as he would look now, risen from the grave. Because the face she saw was decomposed, wasn't, in fact, even a face anymore.

The nonface opened, revealing a tongue, still very much intact, very much viable.

"At this point, I'm afraid I'm a walking surprise," the tongue informed her.

Hearing the voice confirmed what her eyes had already registered. Her visitor was not a corpse that had come to life. It was a living man who had lost a piece of himself to death while the rest of him lived on.

"I was hoping I wouldn't frighten you," John Davidoff said next. "I was hoping of all the women in the world, you would be the one who couldn't be frightened."

"I'm not frightened," Hewitt said. She began to move her feet in his direction again. Her right hand, however, remained tucked inside her jacket. "Thirty seconds ago, I was. But I'm not now. Unless you give me a reason to be."

She knew he had been thinking about her—and probably obsessively—not just for several days, but for years. Thinking about her, experiencing her in his imagination from every angle, outside and in.

In that moment, in that light, in that gap between rational thoughts, Hewitt projected a picture in her mind she could have never imagined herself seeing.

It was John Davidoff's face, the face that had given its life in the line of duty, in a puddle of burning fuel, a small puddle just large enough to drown a human face. She saw it, the face of death, not from a safe distance, but from a precarious closeness. In a space, hovering above her, but not touching, while the rest of his body, his death-virgin body, touched her in every way.

CHAPTER 55

H E was doing her. Death was doing her. And now, not only was he above her. He was in her.

Though she had her eyes closed, she could see every nuance of the landscape of his face. Landscape of a planet without an atmosphere, without anything to slow the fire and brimstone the heavens so relentlessly sent its way.

It was still shocking to her that she had ended up here. But as long as she kept her eyes closed, she would be okay. She might even, before she climaxed, drift back to one of the bodies she'd been doing before death.

She had started with Brady. After all, she was in a relationship with him. But when Brady had faded, she had gone through a partner montage. Ghosts, all of them. Ghosts of her mind. Ghosts that reached out to her libidinous center, to put a finger to her button and turn it on.

Maybe she'd get one of those picture frames with all the various-shaped spaces for displaying the faces of loved ones. She could fill it with her men. That collection of fine fellows who inevitably came to assist her when she was trying to get off under the wise but never quite warm enough direction of her own hand.

Tonight's roster included the old reliables. And right before she so shockingly segued to John "the face of death" Davidoff, Jimmy Bonbon had taken a special guest slot.

She was done. It had been Davidoff at the end.

The sudden quiet of the house filled her ears, covered her shivering body. Living without roommates, it made no sense not to make noise. Now that the noise had subsided, it was as if it had never been there.

If a tree falls in the woods . . .

If a woman goes Big O in the privacy of her condo . . .

For his part, death had not gone quietly. Not just now in her mind's eye. But earlier, on her front porch.

Rolling onto her side, pulling up the sheet and blanket, she played back pieces of the porch incident. John Davidoff was not a stalker. He insisted on this, right out of the box. And Hewitt had tried hard to believe him.

To John Davidoff's mind, he was just responding to a communication. It had all come down to several seconds of shared space between them at the Cassandra Langford crime scene. It had germinated from a look Hewitt had given him, or his perception of a look, or some Ping-Pong sequence of both.

It was, he claimed, a look he hadn't seen since he'd lost his face.

Closing her eyes, her mind fighting off the biochemical torpor her body was being pulled into, she heard his voice again.

"You looked like you could see through it. Like you didn't stop there. Like you could see through it to the other side."

She slept. For five seconds. For five minutes. She didn't open her eyes to look at the clock, didn't need to open them to hear the voice that had awakened her inside her head.

"If you knew how much my thoughts of your face kept me alive. Kept me interested in life. I wish there was some way I could make you understand. I wish there was some way for me to express it."

Of course there wasn't. At least not flesh to flesh, face to face. Crumpled here on the porch step of sleep, she was wondering if he had taken her gentle rejection and returned to make love to her in his mind. If so, perhaps some angel of sex had hovered over both of them, helping to coordinate the release so it timed out perfectly, together, the way it almost never happened in the nonimaginary world.

THE angel of sex did not visit her dreams. But an angel of music did. An angel who played the piano. What accompanied her on her little trip through the dark hours was a seemingly endless stream of piano music her mind provided as background to a series of dreams.

Piano. Dreamy. Lavish. Hauntingly lovely. Hauntingly lonely. It was the music of the nocturne. The music of Chopin.

Yet being a dream, and being that an angel was playing the instrument, the music that came from the piano was amorphous, mystifying, so that the dreamer who heard it couldn't connect it with any piece or pieces she recognized. It was as if the music coming from that realm was not confined to the tonal shaping or mathematical order of what the same piece would have been if performed in the waking world.

There were no hooks, no repeated themes, no motifs. There was just the steady precipitation of soft, sad piano—as if a Steinway had been raised to the clouds, tipped over, and its music allowed to fall to the earth.

She hummed these thoughts, saw these images against the two-way mirrors of her eyes that were seeing, simultaneously, the ceramic mug slowly turning on the carousel of the microwave.

She remembered one of the dreams specifically. A lucid dream. With lucid pictures. Not just in the dream, but in the dream's primary prop. She remembered the thing from her grandparents' house—her father's parents. An antique stereoscope, a nineteenth-century invention that was a precursor to the Viewmasters of her childhood. On visits to her grandparents' home, they would take the thing out and let her play with it. She would put the various picture cards into the slot on the end and look through the dual eyepieces for the 3-D effect. To her little-girl mind, the effect was mesmerizing.

In the dream, one picture in particular had been as mesmerizing as any in her childhood. As the microwave beeped, she opened her eyes. The inside light went off, leaving a darkened screen against which to project the first images of the stereoscope dream.

She was in her grandparents' house, in their bedroom, a room she had rarely been permitted to enter. Sitting on the polished wood floor, she held the stereoscope in one hand while the other reached into the old shoebox that held the picture cards, in no particular order—piled, not stacked.

Out of the pile, little Betsy selected a card and, without looking at the image, placed it in the curved metal bracket of the viewer.

While the music of an ethereal Chopin fell all around her, she moved the stereoscope to her eyes. An instant later, she was in Paris.

In her immediate visual field she could see the Arc de Triomphe, the Champs-Elysées. Her dream body moved then, transcutaneously, through the skin of the photograph and into the physiognomy of Paris, into that outrageous world, hovering above the streets in that perspective, floating as if she were an angel, held aloft by the furious beating of invisible wings.

There were people in the streets below. But there was someone there, in the streets, or in some apartment. Someone she needed to reach. Someone she needed to talk to. Someone she needed *to help*?

She felt the pull of that, the call of that, from somewhere in the Parisian landscape. And she felt it for the first time, recognized that this was, in fact, an old Paris, a Paris that no longer lived. And upon this realization came another—that no matter how strongly her intuition told her to begin a search of the locus over which she was suspended, she was unable to do so, was unable *to move*.

She was just there, treading air, paralyzed except for the constant beating of her silent wings.

I can't keep doing this . . .

She remembered the sinking feeling of that thought, the way it had first presented itself in the dream. She knew she couldn't keep beating her wings. She couldn't stay there in the air above Paris. As the inevitability hit her, her acquiescence accelerated. And she felt herself doing something she never, ever did. She felt herself giving up.

As she fell, the dream fell with her, down a chute of slippery velveteen fear.

Standing at the darkened microwave, in the light of a new day, she felt it again, the descent into failure, the descent into fear, even as the phone rang for the second time on the kitchen table. The cell. The business line.

It broke her fall. But only temporarily.

In journalistic descriptions of people hit by sudden trauma, the word *ashen* was often used to describe a person's face. When Hewitt heard Jimmy Bonbon on the other end of the line, the tone of his voice was unmistakably *ashen*.

"Something happened last night," the voice told her. "Something happened to the program schedule."

CHAPTER 56

T HEY had been through this. They had been fucking through this. They had talked it out on the phone. He had identified four times in the coming weeks when a Chopin nocturne was programmed to air at 3:03. To preempt the flow of community slaughter and to throw the bad brain off maybe just enough to push him into a mistake, Hewitt had asked Jimmy Bonbon to delete the Chopin pieces, replacing them with something else, something less conducive to atrocity.

"I took care of it," Jimmy Bonbon said in her right ear. "I checked it three times. I did a dry run. Twice."

"Then what the fuck happened?"

"Someone got into the system and edited the schedule," Jimmy Bonbon told her. "Someone changed it back."

The spoon stopped stirring. Everything stopped stirring. Even her angel wings. And all at once, all over again, she was plummeting toward the streets of Paris. This time she hit, felt the roundhouse punch of the street against her face. It would have been easier if the fall had killed her. But it hadn't. And now she had to get up and start walking.

"Someone programmed a Chopin nocturne at three-oh-three," Hewitt supplied as she wobbled up. "Please tell me I'm wrong."

"You're not wrong."

"No, really. Please tell me I'm totally full of shit. This is all totally full of shit."

"I wish I could."

Hewitt could see ripples on the surface of her hot chocolate, the source of which was her central nervous system. The conduit, her folded hands on the table.

"Okay, what the hell *can* you tell me?" she said, pulling herself back inside, but leaving her hands folded. If she was ever going to formally ask for divine intervention during a case, this would be the time.

"All I can tell you is somebody got into the program. Our security system keeps a log of people who come and go with security cards during automated hours. I've checked it. No one did."

"Which means somebody accessed it from outside. Or somebody hacked in."

"I don't know any other way it could have gone down."

Gone down? That wasn't Jimmy Bonbon–speak. Was he trying to impress her? Influence her?

"Does anyone have authorized access to your system from outside?"

Her question was still half in her mouth when the answer came.

"Just one. Bradley Allen Spheeris."

Hewitt didn't like the way it sounded. Not that it was Bradley Allen Spheeris. But the way Jimmy Bonbon said it. The three names. That was the kind of hyperbole she would expect to hear if Spheeris was ever identified as a suspect on FOX News.

John Wilkes Booth. Lee Harvey Oswald. Bradley Allen Spheeris.

"But tell me, James Parker Bonson, why would Brad Spheeris, knowing he was a person of interest, do something so outrageously obvious?"

She articulated the complete question in her head, but allowed Jimmy Bonbon to hear nothing but her pause. Which he promptly ended by acing the exam as he usually did.

"Which begs the question—why the hell would someone under suspicion do something so brazen?"

There was an obvious, brazen answer for this. Hewitt waited a moment to see if Jimmy B would anticipate the correct response for this too. When he didn't, she supplied it.

"People who do things like that do things like that because they can't *not* do things like that. It's like a program running. A program that runs and runs and runs."

"I hate to ask the next question . . ."

"No need. It's already been asked."

"What do you think?"

"What I always think. Worst-case scenario. Then if I'm wrong, it's actually a little victory."

The dull ache in the bones of her pelvis and the heavy feeling against her chest made her think there would be few, if any, small victories that day. Because she feared the spoils—two of them—had already been claimed.

CHAPTER 57

DANCE, ballerina, dance. It is a source of satisfaction, of comfort, that he can summon images of the dancer, the princess, even while engaged in serious conversation, or playing to the audience, or both.

He sees her now. The delicate form of the pink and white princess. In the perfect passé. Posed, poised to return to life so gracefully, at the simple pull of the peg that has been holding back the energy of the tightly wound spring.

He keeps her this way. In his mind, and otherwise. This tightly wound music box that brings her to life when he chooses to release the little peg that holds the world so breathlessly in balance. He keeps her poised this way. The spring always wound as tightly as the cranking of the key will allow.

It is only in the dance that the spring is liberated, and with it, the soul of the dancer. Upon the completion of each dancerly flight of fancy, the spring is rewound, moving easily at the beginning, the gears clicking passively, agreeably. Midway, however, the tension begins. And it is here that the work becomes delicate. For, as with every spring-wound music box, there is a point, a delicate point, where the keeper of the key must sense he is approaching the last turns, the final clicks. This is delicate work. Delicate, *delicate* work. To become excited, to desire too much, at this critical point will result in the breaking of the mechanism, the destruction of the dance, the death of the dancer, and the silencing of the sweet, sad music that gives life not only to the dancer, but to those who worship at her feet.

If all the great beasts on the face of the earth howled at the same time, that is the sound he would hear, the sound he would make if the music ever ceased, if the dancer died, if the winding of the spring was taken that one click too far.

He sees her this way as only he can. As the keeper of the key, he alone understands what is at stake, what exists inside the graceful pose, beneath the charmingly poised surface. Only he knows how fully the spring is wound. Only he can feel how close the music box is to catastrophe.

The conversation has ended. But the image of the little dancer remains. The music begins again, flowing from his mind by way of the original mind. As a coda to the dark brilliant night just passed, he releases the music once more.

Opus 9, Number 2.

The "Nocturne in E flat."

CHAPTER 58

AARON Morrison smoked Dunhill Menthols, wore way too much *Tag* and had a tremendously annoying habit of sticking his index finger into his ear and secretly smelling it. The last of which would have been fine if he'd actually been able to keep it a secret.

But Hewitt was more than happy to put up with all of it if the ISP's best IT guy could help her determine who had hacked into WCLS to program another death opus while the rest of the radio world slept.

He was basically an overgrown kid, Aaron Morrison. Twenty-five, twenty-six. And overgrown kids who had a savant-like talent for tech work that paid well were pretty much allowed to stay overgrown kids as long as they wanted.

Hewitt had contacted Aaron Morrison at home, had picked him up at his Lincolnwood Apartment, indulged him in his Starbucks run and delivered him to the WCLS studios, where Jimmy Bonbon greeted them less like a harried radio station owner and more like a helpful tour guide. He gave Aaron Morrison the run of the house, and IT Boy quickly disappeared with his vanilla latte into the sinuses of Chicago's Classical Voice.

Hewitt accepted her host's invitation to join her for the traditional libations. Hewitt was good with that. There were a number of things about Jimmy Bonbon's Jay Boniface that bothered her. At the head of that privileged rap sheet was the fact that she was still turning on to him physically every time they shared the same physical space. In this case again, the WCLS kitchen.

"How long do you think it'll take Mr. Morrison to find what he's after?"

His low-end tenor voice blended with the hum of the water-heating microwave in a way that felt warm on Hewitt's exposed skin.

"Why are you smiling?" he followed up.

"I've never heard him called Mr. Morrison before."

"Blame it on my mother. She had a thing for manners."

"The world could use more mothers like that," Hewitt said. The sound of her own voice against the microwave wasn't nearly as pleasant as his.

"To me it's pretty clear our civilization could benefit greatly from a little civilization," he offered.

The microwave had completed its work, and he was reaching inside to take Hewitt's heated mug.

"Less littering at public picnicking sites would be a nice place to start," Hewitt volunteered.

He turned, gave her a look that troubled her—because she couldn't check it off against anything she'd seen previously in the Jimmy Bonbon gallery.

He held the look, held it long enough to distract himself from his hold on the steaming mug, which dipped the few degrees it took for some of the water to spill on his hand.

He glanced down at the spillage, winced—with his eyes only—before resuming the look.

"You know, a more appropriate response would've been *Shit!*" Hewitt coached.

He turned away from her, to the canister of Liquid Decadence on the counter.

"Shall I? Or did you want to mix it yourself?" he said, more to the canister than to Hewitt.

"I trust you."

There was a little hitch to his motion as he took a tablespoon and scooped some of the powder.

"You'll have to excuse me," he said. "But I feel like the cartoon character who just got hit in the face with a frying pan."

He deposited the contents of the spoon into the mug, didn't start stirring as soon as Hewitt would have liked.

"You'll have to bear with me until my face returns to its normal shape."

He finished stirring, stepped away from the counter, leaving the spoon in the mug. Hewitt quietly filled the vacuum, moving to the counter, taking the mug, extracting the spoon. She lifted the spoon to her face, made quick work of not wasting the chocolate skin that coated it.

Not that Jimmy Bonbon would have noticed the indulgence. He was staring across the room, at the sink, as if he were seeing Niagara Falls for the first time.

"I did this."

It was as if Jimmy B had just gone over Niagara Falls in a barrel. Like one moment he was there, still the person he was, and the next he was totally gone.

Hewitt set the spoon down, her body still savoring the sneak taste, but her mind tasting only the confused air of the radio station kitchen.

"You did this," Hewitt said, meaning to leave it with a leading tone, an expectation of further explanation. But she had left it sounding flat, unsure.

Jimmy Bonbon turned his face toward hers, but his eyes dropped to her feet.

"If I had stayed off the air, this couldn't have happened. No one could've changed the program. Because there wouldn't have been any-thing to change."

Hewitt needed him to look at her. If she was taking his photo, she would have gone to the old children's trick. *Hey look, there's a monkey on my head.*

"*Hey, look*," Hewitt said. "We don't know that something hap-pened last night. So unless we hear something, there's nothing to hear."

The monkey on her head must've squeaked. Because Jimmy B's head snapped up. "But that's just it. If there's nothing to hear, there's nothing to hear."

There was something to hear down the hallway—Aaron Morrison letting out a technically frustrated *Fuck!*

"Who's to say if you'd shut down it would've made any differ-ence?" Hewitt posed. "Who's to say the killer wouldn't have come up with some other excuse to kill? I mean it's not like the guy needs a whole lot of encouragement."

Something quizzical fluttered beneath the skin of his forehead. "You said *the guy*. Does that mean you think it's a single actor committing both sets of murders?"

Hewitt took a sip of her beverage, allowing the question to hang, allowing the subcutaneous forehead thing a little more fluttering time.

"I don't know," she said. "You could make a case for it. But it just doesn't seem likely that two bad brains could work that closely together, that many times, that smoothly, without some kind of fuckup."

The forehead thing stopped.

"So where are you coming out on Spheeris?"

Hewitt sipped her beverage, let him wait a little. For one, because she wanted to see if it would make him anxious. And two, because she didn't have an answer. Until she heard a report on the overnight surveillance, it was impossible for her to comment to Jimmy Bonbon. Or even to herself.

"Motherfucker."

Another less-than-promising report from Aaron Morrison down the hall as Hewitt's phone went off.

"Maybe that's Spheeris calling in with a confession."

Jimmy Bonbon was fidgeting oddly with his hands—as if, to Hewitt, he was checking the strings of an imaginary tennis racket.

"Hewitt."

It was Megna, reporting in with a tone in his voice she rarely heard from him. *Panic.*

"Nick Groener's missing."

"What?" Hewitt reacted, loud, alarmed—no chance to filter it for Jimmy Bonbon's consumption.

"I know. Totally off-the-charts nuts. But Groener is missing."

"Surveillance people don't go missing."

"Not in the normal world, no," Megna said.

"Fuck," Aaron Morrison called out.

"Fuck," Hewitt echoed.

CHAPTER 59

THERE were only nine chapters left. And Sadie Miller was planning to savor each one. She'd started the book after dinner the night before. Her reading had taken her into her bathtub and, finally, into her bed. If her brain had been able to stay awake, she would have finished right there with her head on the pillow and her feet in the fuzzy ankle socks she wore under the covers because her circulation wasn't as good as it once had been.

Not much of her was. Nothing, in fact. Except her mind. That part of her had never been more alive. It had definitely been awake while the rest of her slumbered. Such that when her body stirred at a little before seven, her mind was already telling her she needed to find her glasses and her paperback novel within the turmoil of bedding as soon as humanly possible.

Living alone did such things to a person. When her husband was alive, she would have never been given the luxury to just pop out of bed and go for a drive to a special place where, over her little thermos of Italian roast coffee and a Danish, she could hold the book in her hands and lick nine chapters' worth of frosting from the tips of her fingers.

She was in the restroom, having decided to free her bladder of any distraction that might infringe upon her total immersion into her book. With business taken care of, she took her day pack from the hook on the door, exited the stall, washed up and stood for a moment at the mirror.

She was alone in the public restroom. Alone in her private world.

Was she crazy? She looked a little bit that way. Maybe more than she thought. Maybe more than she knew. It was a little crazy, wasn't it? To take your fictional thriller into the real world of a killer.

But she didn't care. She was sixty-eight years old. There was a new day ahead of her. There were nine chapters left. There was a plot line and endgame to be enjoyed. And the sun was shining. If she was a little crazy, hallelujah.

She left the bathroom, went outside, the day bag slung over her shoulder, the paperback held protectively in both hands.

There were a couple of other cars in the parking lot now. But no one, from what she could see, had ventured back behind the shelter. She would have the place to herself. Which meant she could pick any of the tables on the natural green patio. She could pick any of the tables that sat in the dappled light. She could have any table but the one farthest away, the one at the outer edge of the picnicking area. The one with a dead girl lying on top of it.

Her feet stopped moving. The paperback hit the ground.

The coffee, the Danish, the last nine chapters would have to wait.

CHAPTER 60

NICK Groener had a wife, two young sons, a baby daughter. He had a dog named Barry, three siblings, both parents, one living grandmother. And he had a squash partner who was expecting to see him over the lunch hour for the latest in a series of grudge matches where the loser bought the hoagies and the beer.

Whether or not any of the people on the list still had Nick Groener was the question on Hewitt's breakfast plate, though the asking of it, and the potential answer, put Hewitt in a place where the only nutrition she could have stomached would have been the type that came via feeding tube.

Surveillance people didn't disappear. They didn't abandon an unmarked vehicle on a city street with the doors unlocked, the keys still in and the radio station tuned to classic rock.

All hell had broken loose in Hewitt's life before. But never to the degree to which Captain Richard Lattimore had informed her while she stood with Jimmy Bonbon in the WCLS kitchen and listened to the intermittent expletives from the tech savant down the hall. For his part, Lattimore had left a few bad words ringing in her ears too.

Now that the killer had crossed the blue line from the public to one of his own, Lattimore's tone had gone from desperate to despotic. He had ordered Hewitt to an audience in his office. He had informed her that if Nick Groener turned up dead, it was on her. Hewitt informed him back that she'd already assigned herself that distinction.

• • •

DESPERATE for air, Hewitt told herself it would be okay to duck in at the condo, to fix her face, to smear whatever salve she could find on her disheveled psyche.

On the approach to the condo lot, she saw the first emergency vehicle, figured one of the old-timers in the place had suffered some kind of fall or cardiac event. It was on the sidewalk that led to her porch that she realized the problem wasn't with any of the neighbors. Because the emergency people were huddled around the entrance to *her* place.

Through the citadel of legs, she was able to see the object over which they were all swarming. Which meant the inconceivable.

There was a body on her porch.

Halfway up the walk, she saw the faces of fellow residents turning toward her like balloons in a breezy dream.

Separating out from them was the round face of the condo manager, all flushed and disbelieving and desperately hoping Hewitt could wave her magic wand or the barrel of her gun and make it all disappear.

"I tried to reach you," Sal Parente cried out. "I called your emergency number. The one from your application."

The one I gave you five years ago, Hewitt responded in her head.

"Who is it?" she called as she hustled up to the porch.

"They say he's a police officer," Sal Parente called back.

Hewitt mind-flashed a short list. Very short.

John Davidoff.

He had come back and made a self-immolating statement at her front door. To symbolize the romantic threshold he imagined they were standing on before his face went missing . . .

Shit. *Shit.*

The circle of observers opened for her and she stepped inside the scrum to see she had left one very important person off her short list. The person all Chicago law enforcement was looking for.

Lying on his back, his dead eyes open to the gorgeous June morning, Detective Nick Groener.

CHAPTER 61

THE Roadmaster rolls along the suburban arterial, just another car, an older-model station wagon taking its driver to work. There is still some time before he is due at his first job of the day. Almost an hour.

His car is not so much a station wagon as it is a coach for the transport of very important people. He is not the driver as much as the coachman.

The coachman smiles to himself.

In the fairy tales—Cinderella especially—coachmen were depicted as relentlessly smiling, utterly subservient drones. As if they were some kind of neutered subspecies of order-followers, existing solely to stand by, waiting patiently and without desire, while the rest of the world suckled noisily at the teats of life right in front of them.

A coachman had no life. In the stories, there was never a subplot involving the secret life of a coachman, his secret passions, his secret dreams. But coachmen did have these things, these capacities. This coachman does.

Another smile ripples his face.

As Cinderella rode in the carriage on her way to the ball, could she have had any idea of the thoughts swirling in the mind of the man who handled the reins on her behalf? What would have happened to the tone of her thinking, the feel of her skin, had she known how deeply he desired her? Later, dancing with the prince, would she have been able to fully give herself to his lead? Or would the dark secret of the coachman thrill her heart just enough to make her hold back, to cause an imperfect moment, an incident of courtly clumsiness that would have blown the whole romance?

For all they knew, coachmen could have been some of the most fascinating people in the kingdom.

Right now, rolling down the road, this coachman knows he is the most fascinating person in this kingdom. The stir he has caused, the attention he has generated. Consider the latest delivery. The most recent transport. The Roadmaster still holds some of the overcologned essence of the man who had insisted on watching him. Funny how the watcher became the watched. No doubt they have discovered him by now. And it is their turn to smell him.

He will never forget the startle of the man's body, the wriggle of recognition that snapped his nervous system as he realized a force had come to change everything in the world as he knew it.

A similar jolt will radiate through the law enforcement world when the discovery is made. It will excite them greatly to find him, to reclaim him. It will excite, especially, the one who seeks him most, whose porch is no doubt serving now as a dais for her internal speechmaking on the need to save humanity, from him, from the terrible evil.

A dog is running on the sidewalk. A huge dog. A Saint Bernard. An overweight woman is chasing it, arms outstretched as if, with a sudden burst of speed, she might swoop in and scoop the giant dog into her rambling bosom.

Where is the terrible evil now as he begins to apply pressure to the brakes, to bring the Roadmaster under the control he will need if the Saint Bernard and his pursuer should career into the road, into the path of the shining carriage and its smiling coachman?

CHAPTER 62

WELL, God dammit then. You want to invade my privacy, I'll invade yours. I'll kick in every fucking secret door it takes to get to the center of your sick fucking brain and then I'll scream so fucking loud and long it'll make you slam your head into the floor as many times as it takes to make it stop.

It was scary. The invective that sprang from her head once the bad brain got some of his own brainwaves through the force field that protected her sanity.

But what the hell? What the living hell?

She had to calm down, needed something to calm her down. An antidote to all of it. Not something hot this time. A nice cool glass of water, preferably holy.

The only beverage being consumed on her front porch was coffee. A couple of the local detectives had their paper cups in hand. The saline solution being dripped into Nick Groener's right arm wasn't quite the same.

Yes, Nick Groener was alive. Incredibly, he was still alive. Even more incredible was the manner in which he was still alive.

Standing on her porch, looking over him, having received the download from the EMT, Hewitt knew exactly what had happened. The undercover detective had survived, but not in the truest sense of the word. Nick Groener hadn't cheated death. Death had cheated him.

Had the executioner chosen to take his life, it would have been easily accomplished. No, at the last moment, the executioner had pulled up, had chosen not to deliver the fatal blow. But rather, to use his prisoner as a symbol, to make a statement to the kingdom.

With no visible signs of a physical struggle on him, Hewitt knew

Detective Nick Groener had been taken for processing in a manner similar to the princesses. The chloroform, the hidden entry point of the syringe. It was the contents of the syringe that had differed. Not the substance. The amount.

Ketamine when used with such intent was lethal, generously lethal. If the administrator wanted a lethal hit, it would be a lethal hit. There were no near misses. Unless the administrator wanted a near miss. Unless the killer wanted to seriously fuck with the pursuer. To send a message. That he'd done his assessment. And she wasn't even in his league.

"We're not having the same dream, Hewitt."

It was Lattimore's comment from days before. Reiterated. But not by her memory. By Lattimore himself. He'd been there on the condo grounds—in her yard—for a couple of minutes already. She had even shot a line or two of comment back to him. And now he had chosen to repeat the line. Not just for the echo. But as a reminder, a banging of the drum. Not a statement as much as a theme. Like a campaign theme. Like he was trying to stay on message. Trying to make the message stick.

Hewitt came out of her internal dialogue, stepped into the full bale of Lattimore's stare.

"If Groener makes it," he informed her, "that doesn't mean you will too."

The words were like knives thrown at a spinning board, sticking around the outline of Hewitt's strapped-down body.

"If that's not a personal threat, you'll have to explain why," she said, her voice in self-defense mode.

"You're free to interpret it any way you want. But let me share my interpretation. Life is short, Hewitt. Just ask these girls, these men. Ask yourself. They need answers. We need answers. But more than anyone, you need answers."

The look he was giving her was as cold and sightless as any she had ever seen, her entire roster of bad brains included. She needed her dad. She needed him to come bounding up the sidewalk again, just when the big kid in the neighborhood was starting to put his hands on her.

Hewitt knew it was time to release Brad Spheeris to the media. She'd seen enough. The dumping of the detective at her doorstep was a classic in-your-face, nah-nah-nah-nah-nah, *you clueless fucking idiot* stunt. The only actor she knew, whom she'd actually interacted with, was Spheeris. Unless it was something absolutely preposterous going on that was invisible to her, or that she'd allowed to remain invisible.

"I can give you a partial answer right now," Hewitt said. "Call a conference. Release Bradley Spheeris as a person of interest. We also need to get into his home and go through it. But I've gotta tell you, if he's the guy, he hasn't left any big cookies lying out on the table for us. He's planned. He's staged. He's got some elaborate endgame already worked out."

"I'll call the conference," Lattimore said. "And we'll get the order for the search. I'll do that in the next half hour. And after that, you've got twenty-four to show me something on Spheeris or I'm taking you off."

"And what exactly am I supposed to show you?" Hewitt asked, feeling her adrenals conducting a symphony of fight-or-flight throughout her body, skewing heavily toward fight.

"How 'bout the killer's head in a bag. With his balls stuffed in his mouth."

Hewitt made a mental note of it, would probably draw a sketch of it eventually. But she didn't let it rattle her the way he wanted.

"I don't know how you expect me to impose your timetable on this," Hewitt said.

"Oh, trust me," Lattimore leered. "This isn't my timetable, Hewitt. As of right now, it's yours."

As Lattimore's phone went off, he gave Hewitt a look that suggested he might be changing his mind on the twenty-four-hour thing, that he was going to take her sorry ass off the case right now.

"Lattimore."

The look shifted only slightly as he took the incoming message. But it was clear that the news was enough to make him know he needed every sorry ass he had. Even hers.

CHAPTER 63

T HE first piece of the day shall be a tribute. It is only fitting to do this. To do this for them. But especially, for her.

Already the sun is climbing the trees to tree house level. The heat of it against the right side of his face is a strange comfort. Were he to turn around on the bench, would the left side of his face experience the same strange comfort?

He cannot explore this. Because the tribute awaits. Reaching into the paper bag beside him, he takes a handful of white confetti and throws it to the murmuring listeners who have already assembled at his feet.

The murmuring increases, becomes an adoring dialect of its own as the listeners push forward excitedly. They will have their tribute. And he will have his.

His hands lift from his lap, gathering energy, drawing from the well once more, the fingers pulsating, warming.

The tribute shall be Chopin. Already the listeners seem to know this, as they settle in, waiting for the first voicing of the composition.

He withdraws his hands. The smile that comes to his face seems to pull away some of the energy from them. He considers the music in the offing. This most shadowy of nocturnes, in the broadest of daylight.

Sometimes life is simply brilliant.

He infuses his hands once again, occupies them. The nocturne begins.

With its commencement, his fingers deftly take to their work. His mind begins an equally dexterous performance. The outside world becomes a wall, shedding its third dimension to create a reflective surface by which the light of day may travel through his eyes and inside his head, to cast the proper light on the figure that dwells there always. Dark or light. Conscious or unconscious. Dead or alive.

The dancer. The sweet little dancer. In her perfect passé. She has waited here for him. Waited since the last time he performed. The ballerina in his brain. So perfectly balanced in her pose. And his mind, the perfect stage.

He releases her now. *Or is it she who releases him?* He feels this, feels the release. As she pirouettes, as she performs for him. As she dances in his brain. As his mind dances with her. As his brain anticipates her movements, opening itself, maneuvering its walls, its folds to accommodate her, to give her support, to give her audience, to give her life.

So deep inside his head is he now that he must force his eyes open to look down at his hands, to see that they are still playing. And as he does, his mind slips away from the ballerina just long enough that he glimpses the disturbing vision of his hands playing nothing but the air above the park bench, while a gallery of pigeons enjoys the scattering of popcorn at his feet.

CHAPTER 64

TWENTY-FOUR hours could be a lifetime. It was to a mayfly. Maybe not the most rewarding life—the main purpose of your existence being as food for birds and fish and the occasional mouth-breathing kid on a bike. But it was a life. And that was better than never having lived at all. Wasn't it?

Next time a mayfly hit her windshield, she'd ask it.

She was headed west on Half Day Road, to pay her respects to the newest member of the worst club in the world. She had nothing but the victim's name. Daphne Nemovitz. But she already knew her. Knew the way she would look. The way her hair would fall away from her face and pile in velvet hills around her shoulders. She knew the way her overapplied perfume would give the illusion that she hadn't completely expired, that death was still slightly on hold.

Hewitt looked at herself in the mirror, saw that death was still on hold for her too. Much less so, it seemed, than a week ago. She turned on the radio, joined a WCLS morning classic in midstream. A Mozart symphony. Which number, she wasn't sure. About as far removed from the Chopin nocturnes as it could be. With Aaron Morrison still on the premises at WCLS, and just down the hall from the broadcast studio, Hewitt figured there was a good chance the morning DJ's comments at the completion of the symphony might include a special word or two.

"Music by Wolfgang Amadeus Mozart. The Symphony in *Fuck!*"

So there was that front, the continuing search for the Chopin re-programmer. The second front was more widespread, and included any of the known pockets of life where Brad Spheeris had been doing his living. Megna and Patterson were driving that bus, with a posse of ISP detectives and the jurisdictional cooperation of local law enforcement pretty much wherever the sun was shining on that cloudless morning.

On the radio, the Mozart piece had shifted movements. *Andante. Allegro. Alfredo* . . . She wanted to join in the Spheeris hunt. But her job was calling her to picnic table duty, at a wayside once again, in the service of the Vanquished Princess Society.

Betsy Hewitt had wanted to be a princess someday too. She hadn't been vanquished by a serial killer. Junior high school had done the job there. Reality had injected its princess poison into her. And while she'd rested on her back in the glass box all those years, no prince had ever come by with the kind of magic lips she needed to fully reanimate her pretty little self. Although Brady was the closest in a long time.

The Mazda was at the top of a rise that gave her a good one-mile view to the west. Already she could see them. The emergency vehicles— gleaming, *buzzing* at the wayside.

She knew the instantaneous revulsion was coming from the pit of her stomach. What she didn't know, wasn't sure how to even gauge it, was how low the pit of her stomach had sunken after all the repeated episodes.

She had to stop it. She had to stop it. And she wasn't thinking of the killer. That she knew. What she had to stop—this moment—was the picnic table visitation. She had to stop seeing them, these girls laid out, displayed, desecrated.

She could feel her right foot easing off the accelerator. The space created by this minisurrender was instantly filled by the ringing of her phone, the triad notes finding acceptance in the melodic structure of the Mozart.

What Aaron Morrison initiated in her ear then wasn't a conversation. It was an oral dissertation on his findings, with F-bombs in lieu of punctuation.

CHAPTER 65

"THE fucker thought he had a free skate. But when I found his little fuckup, I said, 'Fuck you, Sam. That's right, *fuck you*.'"

The technical explication was white noise to the music that came to
Hewitt's ears in the form of URL number, name of owner and home address.

From the originating URL of the WCLS hack job, everything else
ratcheted into place. The cable TV account by which the hack had been
committed belonged to one Mary Frances Eau Claire of Highland Park.
On the drive there, Hewitt tried her best not to gut herself with guilt
over leaving the Daphne Nemovitz crime scene with nothing more than
a U-turn in the parking lot to show for it.

She promised herself she would make it up to Daphne Nemovitz
somehow. Maybe some fresh-cut flowers at the funeral. An angel teddy
bear on her headstone. Or better yet, way better, by sticking a gun up
the ass of her killer and squeezing the trigger. At least once.

A pattern emerged the moment Hewitt's eyes made contact with the
Mary Frances Eau Claire property. The Mary Frances Eau Claire *manor*
would have been more appropriate. As such, the massive French Country mansion with its undulating grounds was part of the same privileged-
place subset as the beamed fortress that housed Gloria Martindale and
her passion for, at the very least, classical music broadcast live in her living room.

At the front door, having failed to respond until Hewitt went to the
official balled fist entreaty, Mary Frances Eau Claire gave every effer-

vescence of a woman who was no stranger to the forces of cultural eccentricity.

She was also no stranger to the electronic and print media. So she recognized Hewitt instantly. Or as Hewitt surmised, instantly for the second time. A glimpse from a window upon Hewitt's approach had probably been the woman's first clue. And Hewitt's pounding fist had confirmed that this would be a little more complicated than waiting out a Jehovah's Witness.

At first blush—and she used a hell of a lot of it—Mary Frances Eau Claire was erudite and evasive. An equal mixture. No matter what Hewitt had for sale, she was above buying. And the middle-class girl in Hewitt bristled at the scent of Chanel and condescension in the air as she was allowed into the marble and cherry-wood foyer.

"In connection with what exactly?" was the terse response to Hewitt's floater about answering a few questions.

"In connection with an Internet security breech that may have originated from this address. Specifically, from a personal computer on the premises."

Hewitt read her carefully. But there was no sign Mary Frances Eau Claire was connecting the dots. From the look on the woman's face, Hewitt might as well have been there on behalf of Jehovah. However, she quickly established that Mary Frances Eau Claire was the lone resident. Her husband had died two years earlier. She had cleaning help and lawn care. Other than that, she was on her own.

"I've seen you. I know what you're investigating. But how in the hell can something that happened with my computer have anything to do with that?"

Mary Frances Eau Claire said it as if she were seated on a nice plaid car blanket on a hill high above it all, enjoying a cool drink and well-made sandwich while her driver waited in the Bentley.

"I was hoping you could tell *me*."

The look she shot Hewitt then was from the same category as looks she had given her now deceased husband a moment before sealing the lid on an argument. Hewitt's take.

"Well, I can't tell you anything if I don't know anything, can I?"

Unlike her dead husband, Hewitt could still fight back. "Do you know a gentleman by the name of Brad Spheeris?"

Mary Frances Eau Claire couldn't mask her answer to this question with any mixture of erudition and evasion.

"Please don't say no," Hewitt followed up. "Because I know you do."

"Anyone in Chicago who listens to classical music knows Brad Spheeris."

"But not everyone who knows Brad Spheeris gets personal visits from him," Hewitt offered. "Very personal visits." And she knew that somewhere in the culturally elite section of heaven—or wherever he was—Mary Frances Eau Claire's husband was high-fiving every passive dead husband he could find.

Mary Frances Eau Claire was her own king and queen. And when the queen was no longer able to defend her king, she stood there in the foyer, rigid, erect and as unmoving as a checkmated king on a chess-board. But unlike the chessboard in such a predicament, there was still one evasive move left for her in the 3-D board game of her stately manor.

Against the far wall of the foyer there was a decanter of brandy and a couple of sparkling clean snifters on a credenza—the kind of old-school alcohol altar you didn't see much anymore. But there it was. And it was there that Mary Frances Eau Claire's eyes and then the rest of her went. Or appeared to go. Because at the moment Hewitt expected her to reach for a snifter, her left hand pulled open the credenza's top drawer. In one clean movement, her right hand took a small handgun—silver with a pearl inlay—raised it to her temple and shattered her king and queen all over the marble and cherrywood chessboard.

CHAPTER 66

"**W**HAT are you doing for lunch?"

She didn't know if he was trying to be funny, sweet or stupid. Mary Frances Eau Claire's brains were still warm in the foyer. Emergency services were en route, although Hewitt had already made it clear there was no reason to hurry.

"A woman just shot herself in the head. Right in front of me."

"What?"

"Yeah, that's my morning. How's yours?"

Hewitt could hear the first sounds of the emergency vehicles.

"The word is Nick Groener's going to make it."

"There was never any chance he wouldn't," she told him.

"How so?"

"The killer titrated down just to fuck with us."

The emergency response was within a handful of blocks now.

"Just to fuck with *you*," she heard Brady say. "I don't know what he'd have to do to make it any clearer that you're in the crosshairs now."

"Is that what this is about?"

"What's that?"

"Big brother keeping an eye on little sister."

Brady didn't answer right away. The pause made her conscious of the fact that certain recent wall hangings in the foyer were starting to lose their hold.

"Even if I wanted it to be that, I'm afraid it couldn't. Last time I checked, you were still a couple months older than me."

He gave Hewitt a small space in which to respond. When she didn't fill it, he did.

"Sounds like your friends are arriving."

They were. Within a block now.

"Yeah, I suppose I should be a good host and greet them at the door."

She knew from the bone of regret that was lodged in her throat that she was leaving the door open for Brady.

"I'll pick something up," he said. "I'll meet you wherever you are. We'll do it in the car."

"Do it?"

"Lunch. What do you want? Name it. I'll go fetch. I'll call you wherever you are. We'll do it on the fly."

The emergencies were pulling up outside. Hewitt looked at the body on the floor, the human spackling on the wall.

"Something light," she said. "Something vegetarian."

AARON Morrison was downstairs in the den, examining the contents of Mary Frances Eau Claire's hard drive. The promise of a carton of Dunhill Menthols and a Starbucks gift card had gotten him to the scene at least a half-hour earlier than would have been normal. Hewitt had already had the keyboard and surrounding area at the computer desk dusted for prints. But it was clear some enterprising soul had already done a thorough and, apparently unscented, cleaning of the area in anticipation of such a visit.

Hewitt was upstairs now, in the one place where Mary Frances Eau Claire's hidden secrets were most likely to be hidden. Only a few miles away, Pete Megna was leading the search of Brad Spheeris's residence. A part of Hewitt wished she could be there. But a bigger part of her, led by her heart and mind, told her the most critical search was the one that was under way right under her feet.

She had no real idea what she was looking for. Which, in a way, made her even with the victim. Because she was pretty sure Mary Frances Eau Claire didn't have any idea of what kind of future she was looking at when she signed on for the first encounter with Brad Spheeris that would, through whatever twists and shimmies, cause her to take the terrible action she'd taken at the first sign that it was all going to be dug up, unwrapped and exposed for all the world.

It was about ten minutes into the search and on a top shelf of the dressing room closet that she found a Gucci shoebox with what appeared to be nothing more interesting than some audio cassette tapes inside. But the tapes were personally labeled. And the paucity of information on the labels drew Hewitt's interest.

It was dates. Just dates. Month. Date. Year. All within the last twelve months. Just that. As if that was enough. Enough to trigger a memory of whatever it was in the audio world that had transpired on that date.

Hewitt took the tapes—eleven of them—and put them into her bag. She exited the house, leaving the local cops, the tech crew and Aaron Morrison to hold down the manor.

In the private listening pod of her car, she began with the most recent date, just five days earlier. After the opening tape hiss, a piece of classical music was joined in progress. But it wasn't classical music dubbed from another direct source. It was an ambient recording, made with a microphone. And right away, Hewitt knew the tape hadn't been made to record music as much as to capture a setting, an event, an experience.

The piece of music was unfamiliar to her. A string quartet, she thought. But as to name, composer, she had no idea. After less than three minutes, however, the answers came when, at track's end, the voice of Brad Spheeris rose up from a place removed from the microphone. A room, maybe two away.

"The String Quartet in F Major, by Antonin Dvorák. Also known as the 'American.' Which, of course, makes perfect sense when you understand that it was composed in 1893, during Dvorák's famous sojourn to the United States, during which he wrote another little piece known as the *New World* Symphony."

Brad Spheeris paused there—to cue his next selection, Hewitt assumed. Moments later, from a location much closer to the microphone, Hewitt heard the sound of what could have only been a zipper. Unzipping.

Followed by—to Hewitt's ears—the rustling of clothing, shoes being kicked off. There were additional sounds. But they were rendered indecipherable when Brad Spheeris resumed his announcing.

"Next, three nocturnes by Chopin . . ."

It was amazing how quickly the adrenal glands could get their juice to the heart.

"The nocturne form was created by England's John Field. But it was perfected and taken to a place beyond perfection by Mr. Frédéric Chopin. Or as he was known by the one who knew him most intimately, *Little Chip Chip.*"

It was equally amazing how quickly the heart could distribute the adrenaline to the network of capillaries at the surface of the skin.

Given the relatively crude nature of the recording and the fact that the amplified music was coming from a room or two away, the Chopin piano that began to play felt unquestioningly ethereal, as if a ghost had come to sit and play at the house piano Hewitt remembered seeing in the parlor. As if—and Hewitt wasn't sure why it struck her this way, why her mind went there—as if the ghost of Chopin himself, with some sort of unfinished business, some statement left unspoken, had sat down, stretched his long, facile fingers and conjured once more the music he had once conceived.

Chopin's ghost or not, the nocturnes were not the only music that would play on this recording. Although it was the most artful, and, definitely, the most melodic.

Hewitt had never been much of a porn person. But she'd seen a few things—one guy she'd dated, briefly, had a thing for multimedia wine and cheese parties—so she certainly recognized the soundtrack when she heard one. And there was no mistaking, on this recording, the sound of a woman's voice lowing, then rising, *and repeating*, against the melancholy echoes of Chopin's ghost piano.

CHAPTER 67

THE sex act continued through the first two Chopin pieces. It was in the third piece that Mary Frances Eau Claire—by now Hewitt had heard enough of her passionate voice to match it with the dispassionate one she'd heard in the foyer—reached her crescendo, during a wild flourish in the nocturne, one of those sections common to the form where the lighter, more enchanting motifs exploded into a kind of unbridled fury. The way it had exploded in Chopin's mind when he composed it. And perhaps, the same way it affected the killer's mind, this wild swing from sweet-sad to ecstatic-raging when the acts went down.

After the climax, the room returned to quiet, except for the deeply articulated breathing of Mary Frances Eau Claire. The man who had accompanied her to the top of Mount Chopin, in body but not in voice, was either so still as to not have been captured on the mike, or no longer in the room.

In less than a minute's time, as the third Chopin nocturne ended, Brad Spheeris was back in announcer mode. Not that he had necessarily stepped away from his original position in the makeshift studio. Or if he had, not to have traversed the room or two necessary to appear at Mary Frances Eau Claire's bedroom door, ready to interpret Chopin in his own inventive way.

And while Hewitt wasn't a porn person, she was enough of a sex person to know a few things about the fine art of doing it. And doing it, at least the way it sounded through the mouthpiece of Mary Frances Eau Claire, and the accompaniment of the mattress and box spring, would have been a world-class performance for a guy Brad Spheeris's age.

There were drugs, of course, that could help a guy like Spheeris. But that was more in the missile-raising department. As far as the rest of him—abs, glutes, legs, flexible low back and pelvis—that would have required rejuvenation on a more epic scale. The kind that, really, only a fountain of youth, or *actual youth* could provide.

There was one way to sort out the who and how. And that effort was currently under way, with the tech who was going over Mary Frances Eau Claire's bed for any souvenirs that had been left behind.

In her car now, headed for Northbrook, Hewitt was staring through her windshield at a bumper sticker on the Volkswagen Jetta in front of her that advised: COMMIT RANDOM KINDNESS AND SENSELESS ACTS OF BEAUTY. If the killer was currently out on the road with her, she figured she could at least eliminate that vehicle from suspicion. Though it didn't eliminate it from her consternation, rolling in the speed lane at about sixty. Which wouldn't have been so bad if she wasn't wedged in by dueling semis.

If Brad Spheeris wasn't pulling double duty as voice and dick talent, what the hell kind of carnal circus was he running?

CHAPTER 68

JIMMY Bonbon was waiting for her on the concrete slab outside the WCLS entrance, a diminished version of his normal self. The confident smile not quite as confident. The body was moving, for the first time she'd noticed, with a suggestion of middle-aged stiffness.

Hewitt knew she wasn't her normal self either. She doubted there was much of anything normal left about her to reclaim. She wanted the chance, though. If she ever got to the other side of this case. If she lived to tell herself about it.

"Can I get you a refill?" Jimmy Bonbon greeted her.

"I don't want to take the time."

"It's already made. Steam still rising."

The steam continued to be active moments later when Hewitt lifted the WCLS mug to her face in the fluorescent glow of the kitchen. Jimmy Bonbon wasn't sipping with her this time. And the laser-like way he was focused on her as she drank flipped her the ridiculous thought that he could have just poisoned her without the slightest bit of trouble.

She smacked her lips, lolled her tongue to retaste the brew—a mostly involuntary response to that thought.

"You look like someone tasting a ten-year-old cabernet."

"Trust me, I'd rather be doing that."

"You and me both," he gleamed suggestively. For show, she knew. But also, to some degree, for real. "The idea of getting out of this drama from hell and getting drunk as a skunk has its appeal right now."

"What kind of hors d'oeuvres go best with Beaujolais?"

He liked the question, loved that she was the one who'd asked it.

"I'm always partial to those little tenderloin sandwiches with a horseradish sauce."

"Throw in a plate of those and it's a date."

"Consider this your rain check."

He stepped forward, much too forward, and kissed her on her unpoisoned chocolate mouth.

Given the context, and the setting, it was outrageous. But not as outrageous as her reaction. Not the reaction she showed him, but the one she actually felt. Because that one freaking kiss, that elusive, exclusive kiss, was the one brand she'd been waiting for all her life. Or at least since the time in her adolescence when life's true happiness was measured in such a brand of kisses. Though she, like a hundred other girls, had had a crush on Jimmy Bonbon in her Wheaton West incarnation, it wasn't that the kiss had come from him that was the earthmover. It was what that little mouth-to-mouth finally represented.

The unreachable freaking star. Nothing less. The recognition, the acknowledgment, the physical tête-à-tête from one of the dream boys. One of the future kings.

There were some girls who routinely traveled the rose-strewn path in the company of a prince. But those privileged princesses were far removed from the world in which Betsy Hewitt and all the rest of them dwelled.

"I'm sorry," she heard Prince Jimmy say from a couple of decades away.

She looked at him, watched him say the rest of it in the streetlight that came through the windshield of the white Camaro his parents gave him for his sixteenth birthday.

"I'm sure that was totally inappropriate. But you just had a look. I'm sorry if I got it wrong."

"The way my life is right now," Hewitt heard herself say, with a twenty-year echo on her voice, "I'm not sure there's a wrong way to get anything."

Her gut instinct—augmented by her mouth—was that she wanted another white Camaro kiss from him immediately. And probably another one after that. And then it was just a matter of doing what you did till the windows steamed over and the outside world didn't matter anymore.

She could see he was feeling all of that too. She could tell from the spectrum shift in his skin tone—toward the orange-red. And for a moment, for a few frames of washed-out Super 8mm, she saw them all the way at it. He, standing. She, sitting on the WCLS kitchen counter, among the plastic straws, the artificial sweeteners, the nondairy creamers.

"Did Brad Spheeris ever have any kind of special listeners group? Or fan club? Or people who weren't satisfied with the amount of Brad Spheeris they were getting on the air?"

Mentally she was still sitting on the countertop. But physically she had to stand her ground and ask the questions she'd come there to ask, before Jimmy Bonbon interpreted the look in her eyes and the pheromone mist from her skin as the invitation it probably was.

He closed his eyes, held them that way. Long enough to start the engine of the Camaro and shift it into gear.

"The Queens Club," he offered.

"The what?"

She had understood perfectly well. But she wanted to see if he would say it with any less regret the second time.

CHAPTER 69

THE piano is playing. And this time it is he who is playing it. Not his mind. Not his mother. Not little Chip Chip.

No, this time it is only him. His brain. His heart. His hands. With his right foot on the pedal as the music dictated.

In his final illness, Frédéric Chopin had continued to compose brilliantly, to play inspiringly. In his final loneliness, he had continued to dream, even as the loneliness consumed him.

He closes his eyes, closes his mind around the dying genius, lets him go, lets him have his peace.

Chopin is instantly transported to the musical sphere, that place at the far end of the universe where loves can be loved without hurt, where music can be composed without fear. As Chopin scatters to that place, a trail of spilled musical notes is left in his wake, glowing like the tail of a comet.

Eyes closed, he focuses on the streaking celestial body. This light smudge of hope against the dark inner mouth of the universe. This solo voyager. This lonely traveler. So lonely. So distant. So lovely. So brilliant.

As the observer, the discoverer, he must give it a name.

Comet Frédéric.

But the sound of this seems too formal to him. The piano plays. He thinks. Something a little more personal.

Comet Chip Chip.

More piano. More thinking. But is that too personal? Too private? Perhaps something a little more familiar, a bit sweeter. The piano plays, then rises in a flourish. The thinking follows the same arc . . .

Comet Freddy.

Eyes closed, he watches him go. Watches him streak fuzzily across the light-swallowing universe. He watches *Comet Freddy* go, the trail of particles in the million-mile tail composed not of ice and dust, but of the infinitude of piano notes in all their potential chords, arpeggios, sequences, arrangements, voicings.

Eyes closed, he listens to the final voicing of the piano on earth. The final chord decays. His right foot lifts from the pedal. *Comet Freddy* disappears down the muscular gullet of God.

Eyes open now, he sees the hands of the only person in the universe who is applauding. He nods at her, this matron, this middle-aged woman with the wild, unfocused eyes. He smiles at her, licks his lips, lifts his right hand away from the keyboard and uses it to take hold of an invisible drinking cup.

The middle-aged woman takes his cue, her wild eyes giving the appearance of focusing for the briefest of moments. Dutifully, she turns from him and embarks on her mission to supply him with another cup of finely crushed ice.

CHAPTER 70

THE Queens Club had no formal set of membership guidelines, no stated code of conduct. It was a club made possible, first of all, by the gargantuan ego of Brad Spheeris. And that, more than any physical room or hall, was its official meeting place.

The music was off in Hewitt's car. But the engine was singing, pushing ninety on the Kennedy Expressway, while Pete Megna pushed the bad news in her phone ear.

"He's an eccentric guy. Eccentric-and-a-half. His decorating style is a mix of postmodern and early tree house. And he has a music collection that could fill Soldier Field. And I'm not even going to get into the umbrella collection. But unfortunately, no smoking guns. No smoking syringes. And no smoking computer. Because there was *no* computer, period."

"Because he's moved it," Hewitt said. "If he's into this thing, he's moved *whatever*. And he's got some other staging area. If he's into this, he didn't go to all that trouble so we could waltz right in and help ourselves to the wet bar."

"He did have one of those too," Megna told her. "But bottom line, even with a personal tour of his personal space, the Spheeris trail is still cold."

"On the hottest day of the summer so far," Hewitt said.

"Irony sucks," Megna replied. "Especially when it makes me sweat my ass off."

He was going to be sweating a little more. Because Hewitt proceeded to hold a quick, over-the-phone knighting ceremony, in which Megna was put in charge of assembling a brigade to pay separate visits to the twelve members of Brad Spheeris's well-heeled musical ego trip. Which meant that, within the hour, in the most silver-polished local enclaves, a bunch of crappy sedans in need of a wash were going to disgrace the circular drives of the surviving royals who made up the Queens Club.

It had all started out so innocently, according to the story Jimmy Bonbon told her. Though WCLS was a for-profit enterprise, making that profit, or even breaking even with a classical music format, was asking a lot. So once a year, WCLS management asked its most affluent listeners to pass the hat—the fancy, feathered kind.

During one such venture several years earlier, Brad Spheeris and the full committee of his Delusions of Grandeur had dreamed up the idea of auctioning off his services for a one-time, in-home guest DJ appearance, wherein the winning bidder could select his or her favorite classical pieces. The *his or her* aspect hadn't been an issue. The responding bids had all come from women.

Jimmy Bonbon had remembered the name of the original winner without much trouble. Mary Eau Claire. *Mary Frances Eau Claire.* What he had serious trouble with was the news that the original winner had just blown her brains out in the foyer of her mansion while Hewitt watched.

The look on Jimmy Bonbon's face went beyond seriously troubled when Hewitt informed him that Mary Frances Eau Claire's home computer had been the originating site of the cyber break-and-enter that had resulted in the airing of another fatal nocturne.

Hewitt opted to withhold the audio sex tape discovery. Not because she was reluctant to heap more troubling thoughts on him, but because she wanted to see if he would show any sign that he might already know. She read his face. But if there was anything there for her edification, it eluded her.

Her phone went off, and with it, a run of panic skittered up her low back. It wasn't panic over the news she was about to receive, news that was made only slightly less God-awful because it was so utterly expected. The king, of course, had been found, to complete the royal set.

Hewitt noted the king's name, his address, the circumstances that attended his discovery. She noted how, once again, she felt her heart constrict at the information, and the blood it pumped thicken, darken. But the feeling of that, consumptive as it was, hadn't been the sole source of her spinal freak-out. Rather, it had been a series of revelatory questions her innermost mind had shot her in the moment before her phone began to chirp.

What if the Queens Club was just a diversion? What if it was something less than a direct connection to the murders of the kings and princesses? What if there had been some kind of inside-out job, some setup of Mary Frances Eau Claire and her home computer? The whole live announcer/live sex thing could've been nothing more than a middle-aged celebrity and some older ladies being morally outrageous in the northern suburbs.

A titillating story for the local news. Sex, suicide and the music of dead geniuses. Who wouldn't want to know more about that? But as a news story, it couldn't hold a match to the conflagration that would continue to rage out of control, in classic Chicago style, if all her expressway speeding, and that of her colleagues, was headed for a Blues Brothers police car pile-up at the same dead end.

If all the interviews with the extended royal family failed to produce an incrimination of Brad Spheeris, or an accomplice, it would be Hewitt's head that would be the one to drop into the basket in the public square.

Maybe she'd be lucky and land face-up, so that in those last few beats of time before her screen went blank, she could take in one last view of the sky that still stood watch over Chopin's Paris.

CHAPTER 71

BRADY'S interpretation of a vegetarian lunch was a couple of grilled cheese and tomato sandwiches, with a side order of sea salt and vinegar chips. In separate bags. No wine. In fact, no beverages. But Hewitt had solved that problem by co-opting the foam cup of ice water on Nick Groener's tray table. From the looks of him, despite the report she had received to the contrary, it didn't look like he'd be getting to it for a while.

Groener had been moved from the ICU to a regular private room. His attending physician had advised Hewitt, during her telephone query, that it was only a matter of time until he regained consciousness. A short time. And the information Hewitt wanted from Groener was so critical that the inside-an-hour the doc had projected was absolutely worth her while. Because to that date, Nick Groener was the only human being on record who'd danced with the killer and lived to tell about it.

"So what do you make of this Queens Club?" Brady asked from the visitor's chair on the other side of Nick Groener's bed.

Hewitt had downloaded all the newsworthy items she had on their walk from the parking lot to Groener's room. While they'd taken a moment to start their vegetarian lunches, Brady digested the download.

"Right now, I'm up for theories," Hewitt said. "I was hoping a fresh eye—fresh brain—could throw a couple into the ring."

Brady took another bite of grilled cheese and tomato as a thought-starter. While he chewed, Hewitt scoped Nick Groener's face for any sign of progress. To her optimistic eyes, he did look a little less pallid, less slack-muscled.

"The suicide means there's something there," Brady offered. "But does it mean this very rich and obviously troubled woman was connected to the killer? Or was she just pursuing happiness with an extra pickle on the side?"

"So maybe it's just some creepy middle-aged sex circus," Hewitt said, her voice sounding more disappointed than she wanted.

"Or maybe the pickle's just sitting there innocently—as innocently as a pickle can sit—alongside a killer corned beef sandwich."

"Next time we go vegetarian, get yourself the meat version," Hewitt said, neither bitchy nor funny. "Because if we have to talk in delicatessen analogies, we're going nowhere fast."

"What I mean by way of analogy," Brady reloaded, "is that the sex thing could be ancillary to the . . ."

He stopped himself, the toes of his oxfords up against the analogy out-of-bounds line.

"Just say it."

"The whole enchilada," Brady proffered, with a lazy grin that was quickly wiped out by a handful of chips.

"Beef or chicken," Hewitt queried. "Christ."

"Food makes people do strange things."

Brady gestured for Hewitt to share some of the ice water with him. She handed the beverage to him over the bed.

"You could say the same thing about sex," Hewitt offered as he sipped.

"You could say a lot more than that."

"Speaking from experience?"

"The human experience. Your interview team should be able to scare up some details."

"That would be the desired effect. Depends on how willing they are to let us drill down."

"I'd start drilling in their underwear drawer."

"Believe me, if I could get a court order, I'd swab every one of them."

"What a lovely image that is while I'm eating."

Hewitt looked down at her own sandwich, half-eaten on her lap. The smell of the hospital room wasn't exactly helping her appetite. And the thought of swabbing down the entire Queens Club, to Brady's point, wasn't doing much for her either. But she knew the day had the potential to be a long one. So she began to force the rest of the food down.

"Where are his wife and kids?" Brady asked, nodding at the body in the sheets.

"Visiting her parents in Colorado. Summer vacation thing. They get the trip. He gets out of dealing with the in-laws."

"How many kids?"

"Three. Want names? I've got 'em."

"Let me guess."

Hewitt was chewing. With a push-out of her lips, she said *have at it*.

"Peter. Paul. And . . . ah, what the hell, Mary."

"It's two girls and a boy."

Brady thought. Hewitt finished the last bite of her sandwich, reached into her bag of sea salt and vinegar, her eyes looking for the biggest one first.

"Rachel, Sarah and Jake."

The correct answer startled Hewitt. But not because it was Brady's guess.

Detective Nick Groener, father of three, was conscious. At least enough to remember the names of his kids.

Hewitt leaned in, transferred some sea salt and vinegar to Groener's right hand.

"I'm Hewitt, Nick. You were on night surveillance. You relieved Pete Megna. An assailant—possibly the man you were tracking—jumped you, knocked you out with chloroform, then injected you with a barbiturate."

Groener was trying to focus on Hewitt's mouth as she spoke, with occasional forays into her eyes. But he still had one foot in the Black Forest. So he did better with Hewitt's mouth, following it like a bouncing ball that highlighted her words.

"Do you remember anything, Nick? Anything about the assailant? Did you see him? Did you hear his voice?"

Hewitt watched the detective's eyes, the way they sharpened in reverse, irising inward. As if he was actually trying to look inside his brain for the images, the audio files. He was a good soldier. Just a little shell-shocked.

"Who's the guy?"

"I'm her lunch buddy," Brady said, extending his hand and another serving of sea salt and vinegar to Groener. "Brady Richter."

"Boyfriend?" Groener said.

"Sometimes that too," Hewitt answered, getting into his eyes with hers again. "Nick, I want you to try to remember the last things that happened to you last night. The last things you recall. Do you remember getting out of the car?"

She watched as he navigated deeper into his brain files.

"I was listening to the radio," he said. "Stupid. But, you know, long night."

"You were listening to WROC—classic rock," Hewitt assisted, knowing any sensory cue might help trigger things.

Groener's face darkened, aged. To the point that, to Hewitt's mind, it was like asking a vintage model Keith Richard, the morning after, if he remembered the set list from the night before.

"Steely Dan," Groener said sleepily. "'Rikki Don't Lose That Number.'"

Nicky don't lose that suspect—in Hewitt's mind only. Although from the look Brady gave her, it was as if he was sending her a telepathic text message of the same thing.

"Did you listen to the whole song?" Hewitt asked.

Groener's eyes sharpened. "Yeah. A commercial came on and I turned it off. And almost right away—a few seconds—a bird, a mourning dove landed on the hood of the car."

"Dead?" Brady asked, looking to Hewitt for permission after the fact.

"No," Groener answered. "If it was dead, I wouldn't have gotten out of the car. At least not like I did. Not that fast."

Hewitt saw the whole scenario now. The perfect setup, the invitation. A surprise dove, flopping on the hood of your car. A sudden, flopping dove that had never presented itself in your training, your experience, your wildest freaking dreams.

"I'm sorry," Groener said. "I'm sorry I fucked up."

"If I had a buck for every time I've said that in this business, I'd own the fucking Wrigley Building."

Groener didn't smile at Hewitt's comment. But he finally let out the breath he'd been holding.

"I got out of the car. And he hit me right away. Got his arms underneath mine—you know, from behind—like a full nelson. And he got the towel in my face . . ."

Groener's face went blank, totally, for the second time in twenty-four hours.

"That's it," he muttered.

But Hewitt knew it wasn't. "So you didn't get a look at him?"

"No."

"Did he say anything? Did you hear his voice?"

"No."

Sight and sound were dead. She knew the only thing he'd tasted was the chemical towel.

"Okay, Nick. I want you to think. When he grabbed you, when he got his arms on you, around you, how did he feel?"

"How did he feel?"

"What was your first thought—what did your instinct tell you about this guy?"

Groener's mind trolled his memory banks.

"He was strong . . . Wild-strong. You know, crazy-strong."

"How old was he? Younger, older?"

"Younger."

"How young?"

"I . . ."

"Best guess."

"Inside thirty-five."

Hewitt went to the last sense she had left. "Before he got the towel in your face, do you remember smelling anything? Like a cologne."

Groener closed his eyes. Through the lids, Hewitt could tell he found something.

"Yeah. Yeah. Something strong. But not a guy's. It was perfume. Like a high-end woman's perfume."

CHAPTER 72

H E is in a Chopin state of mind, having just completed the "Waltz in B Minor" and pausing now to consider his next. But first, a break for the crushed ice.

Raising the cup to his face, he feels the cold of a winter morning in Paris. He inhales, sucks in that cold Paris morning, holds it there, closes his eyes, feels the apartment around him, the comfort of all his familiar things, especially the Pleyel piano.

He breathes in again, feels the lungs shudder at the cold, heavy air, feels his heart pull back from his chest and roll backward into itself, and roll again, and . . . fall.

The fear hits, the panic. He swallows the scream that would otherwise come. Yet, upon opening his eyes, he realizes not all of the scream has been contained. Because around him, the faces are all turned to reflect the same angle of sun that streams through the skylights. But these are not sun worshippers synchronized in a moment of devotion. No, this audience is an audience of scream fearers, fearing even this partial scream, this accidental scream, this scream of the constricted lungs, the scream of the broken heart.

The turned faces wait for him, in all their sunshine. They wait for him, as their musical interpreter, to explain the sound that has pulled them from their plates, their beverage cups, the fantasies and visions they have witnessed in the green-shaded glass of their tabletops.

The sound of his voice-box implosion has yet to fade completely, finding extended expression in its traveling to the outer walls and, especially, the high glass ceiling of his music hall.

The gift of the musical God on this morning, the gift on behalf of his beloved, brokenhearted son, is the fact that the inside-out scream has sounded in a familiar key.

E flat.

As the last of his cold-Paris-morning cry disintegrates in the public air, his right thumb descends on the black key between A and B, in the octave above middle C.

CHAPTER 73

THERE was a beverage her father had been partial to. An old school cocktail called a Brandy Old Fashioned Sweet. It was made with four specific ingredients that had to be mixed—according to her father—in just the right way to make it work.

To Hewitt's mind, she now had the equivalent of the four ingredients necessary to make her investigational cocktail work.

The first ingredient, the *one-and-a-half ounces of brandy*, was the sex, the over-the-top energy of it. Now she had a witness, the *six ounces of Seven-Up*, corroborating what she'd detected on the sex tape. Sort of. But a younger man was a younger man. And Bradley Spheeris was not a younger man. No matter how much Human Growth Hormone or Cialis Extra Strength he popped.

The third element of the cocktail, the *six drops of bitters*, was Spheeris himself. More specifically, the lack of him. People of interest who just disappeared did so for one of two reasons. Either they wanted to disappear. Or someone else wanted it. Her gut told her Spheeris was still walking the earth, casting his tall, angular shadow. And developments that would come during the noon hour would convince her there was a second shadow, a shadow's shadow, walking with Spheeris.

This development would be the *Maraschino cherry* to the cocktail. A Maraschino cherry in the form of some spilled body fluid, since dried, on the fitted sheet of Mary Frances Eau Claire's bed. Alone, that wouldn't have been enough to put Hewitt on a personal manhunt for the rightful owner of that lost love juice. What set her off was the computer photo shrine Ms. Eau Claire or someone she knew very closely had created for a young man named *Piotr*. A little on-site digging through Mary Frances Eau Claire's hard drive had revealed that Piotr had a Russian surname as well. *Nikolai.*

Now it was up to Hewitt—she had taken it upon herself—to match the rest. DNA culled from the semen to match DNA drawn from Piotr Nikolai's body. Hewitt knew she didn't have enough for a court order to obtain the blood. But Piotr Nikolai didn't know that. If she could jump him, get in his face, inside his head, she might be able to get him to spill a little truth on the spot. Or at least supply the right kind of fight-or-flight behavior to help her understand what she was dealing with.

It would all come down to her ability to pull off the drama, the opening act of which would be a surprise visit to the Prospect Square Mall, where Piotr Nikolai was not only currently employed but punched in.

CHAPTER 74

A S Chopin lay dying in his Paris apartment, did his love bring him cool water to wet his mouth, to soothe his throat? Did his love offer a cool, wet cloth to his exhausted face?

Where was his love in these final moments?

Was it present in a vase of flowers on the bedside table? Was it flowing from the mouth of a music-loving countess as she prayed for him in the candlelight of the cathedral? Was it dancing on the brainwaves of the fading genius in the form of notes and chords and phrasing that would never be written down, never performed, never heard?

If such love was present, it was the only manifestation sanctioned by a God who was known for keeping a respectful distance at such times. And one wonders—*he* wonders now, playing these imagined notes of the dying Chopin—if God had closed that distance and appeared directly to the eyes of George Sand, with a direct plea to attend to the bedside of her "Little Chip Chip," would she have torn herself away from her creative indulgence, whatever it was, to bring one last gasp of love to the lungs of that lovesick soul?

The *Deathbed Chopin* is having its predictable effect on the audience. This is especially noticeable when he compares the reaction to the one generated by the "Nocturne in E flat"—a piece with which they were familiar, if not from hearing it performed on piano, then surely from a music box.

Whatever the case, the familiar, the known piece had followed a checklist of listener-response subtleties. Their chewing had become rhythmic and less aggressive. Their sipping had become, in essence, more measured, more graceful. Other movements—from the dabbing of napkins to the licking of fingers—took on a certain synchronization, all falling into rhythm with the cadence and, at an even subtler level, the timbre of Chopin, imperfect though the rendition might have been.

It was as if they had become players themselves in a Chopin ensemble. Crude musicians, yes. But musical in their own base way? Absolutely. Even those among them who hummed and cooed at the tactile stimulation of their ingestions would pitch their lows and murmurs to harmonize with certain chords and phrases.

It was Chopin—imperfect as it was—served in an eminently palatable fashion in the courtly place where palatability was very much the desired fare.

But that was the known, the embraced. That was the "Nocturne in E flat." This, however, this music he played now, this had no title, no opus, no music box rendition.

This was the deathbed music of Frédéric François Chopin. These final musical passages. Fragile as fading breath. Quiet as a barely beating heart.

Looking up from the keyboard, he sees the audience struggling to assimilate the passages, uncertain of where to find the next downbeat, unsure, with their consuming hums and coos, of how to modulate them into harmony with the chords and notes that fall, like brittle tears, to the tile floor.

CHAPTER 75

HEWITT had slept with a serial killer before. So the possibility of engaging in some foreplay with another one wasn't as off the charts for her as it would have been for most women in the law enforcement community.

Of course, there was still one big if—whether Piotr Nikolai was, in fact, a killer. The obvious disconnect on that count was the location to which she had traveled for the encounter. The Prospect Square Mall. More specifically, the Gap at Prospect Square, where Piotr Nikolai worked as an assistant manager. Serial killers didn't work at the Gap. And special agents, no matter how loudly the clock was ticking inside a twenty-four-hour timetable, didn't stalk assistant managers of the Gap.

She was sitting in her car, putting the finishing touches on her less-than-stellar attempt at going undercover. She had a Chicago Bulls cap pulled down over her forehead and a big pair of blue-tinted Oakleys over her eyes, less like a pair of shades and more like a cowl Catwoman would have worn for a meeting with Batman.

She got out of the car and almost immediately inhaled—and tasted—something metallic. Like heated metal. A construction site smell. There was a Mrs. Fields just inside the entrance. As she made her way inside, the two smells combined in her head, forming a smell-image that would've made her laugh if she wasn't about to do something so antifunny.

Little toy cars, baking in an oven.

Once she had exhaled that from her mind, the smell of the building was pure mall. People. Perfume. Plastic. And one more thing to add to the alliteration medley. Piano. Coming from the upper level. From the food court.

Hewitt couldn't tell if it was a professional or just someone who'd sat down to mess around. It was weirdly improvisational, and it bothered Hewitt that she couldn't shape it into more of a rhythm, a melody. But she didn't have time for remedial music exercises. Because the physical presence of the Gap was looming in her immediate future.

She knew him instantly, didn't have to scan the cargo shorts and halter tops to determine his whereabouts. Piotr Nikolai had a Russian look. The broadly handsome face. The little wild streak in the otherwise Americanized hair.

Piotr Nikolai didn't have to spend much time combing the racks, either, to identify Hewitt as a prospect. For a Gap shopping spree. Or—who knew?—a little spree of a clothing-optional kind.

"Hello, I'm Pete," he said in a voice that had relinquished the thickest part of its accent. Chatting up hypercasual Americans all day would've accelerated that.

He didn't extend his hand. But in a way maybe only an older woman looking for a younger man would notice, he definitely projected the rest of his body.

"How can I help you?"

"That depends," Hewitt said.

She gave him a look through the Catwoman cowl, felt an invisible tail curling up and grazing her shoulder blades.

"Depends . . ." he said in what should have been a question but was more of an agreement.

"Yes. That depends on what kind of personal attention I can get for, oh, a thousand dollars."

There were expansive skylights at the top of the mall. From the way the young man's face lit up, it was as if the incoming light had just doubled.

Piotr Nikolai smiled at her with his big Americanized smile, his deal-sealing smile. "If this is the case, you will be taken care of in the way you so richly deserve."

Difficult as it was, she peered through the solar panels of his smile to read his eyes. She was thrilled by what she saw, and a little unnerved by the powerful pull of his brain. The way it invited her, in such an insistent way, to climb into the hot air balloon with him for a little ride in the clouds.

They spent a few minutes picking out a handful of items, which he held for her gently, in his big hands, before leading her to the back of the store, to the fitting rooms.

To the slaughter. To the slaugh-ter.

Hewitt played that refrain in her head, attached it to the cadence of Piotr Nikolai's footsteps on the tile floor. The question for the non-gallows-humor side of her mind was: Who was leading whom to the slaughter? The one who led or the one who followed?

The rules of engagement always changed when you left the main floor and transitioned to the fitting rooms. Back there, store personnel could *monitor* you while you undressed, dressed and undressed again. And you, for your part, could do pretty much any damn thing you wanted, in whatever stage of undress you chose, as long as you kept the little saloon door closed.

The perfect Americanized gentleman, he led her through the transition and paused dutifully at the second door they came to. He held out the clothing to be tried on, and Hewitt let him hold it. And hold it. And hold it.

Until it started to feel too heavy for both of them.

"Are you changing your mind?" he asked.

"I guess I'm still deciding," Hewitt told him.

"Can I show you something else?"

She didn't bother to monitor his face to see if it was a legitimate offer or code for another retail operation. Because by that time she was already entering the fitting room, pulling him in behind her, kicking closed the little saloon door.

CHAPTER 76

CHOPIN is still alive. But barely. His dying musical thoughts project through the mind and hands and the instrument of the player, who holds on, fighting for the last breaths, knowing their remaining number has dwindled, is dwindling. How many left? More than a dozen? Less than fifty?

Chopin is still alive. And so, his musical thoughts.

Remnant chords.

Scattered notes.

A slow, falling arpeggio. Falling. Falling . . .

As life wanes. As music fades. As God goes to sleep.

IT is later. Minutes. Hours. Centuries. All the same, really, when measured in the immortality of genius.

He opens his eyes. Chopin is not dead. But he has passed. And in his wake there is a great silence. In his transition, there is a universal clumsiness. As if, in his passing from one world to the next, the world of his exit has been drained of its rhythm, its harmony, its ability to move from one moment to the next without stopping to confront the utterly paralyzing truth that good and evil are secret lovers drawn to a Paris apartment and a Pleyel piano, one to play the left hand and one to play the right, with the sanity of humanity to be determined by the impromptu.

The world needs help. The world needs cheering. The world needs a song.

Or the ghost of one.

Summoning the spirit, he prepares his hands at the keys. Chest up like a soldier, he breathes in. Before the breath is out, the piece has begun. The ghost has risen. The lost souls of a clumsy world rise to greet him, to cheer him, to love him.

CHAPTER 77

HEWITT was in the car, in the parking ramp, still parked, listening to the Miles solo on "So What," waiting what she considered a reasonable length of time to convince Piotr Nikolai she'd had time to drop off her little bag of evidence at an appropriate lab location.

The evidence bag—with its wad of crimson Kleenex—was on the seat beside her. It was a disturbing sight. Everything, from the moment she'd pulled Piotr Nikolai into the fitting room with her, had been disturbing. But a good kind of disturbing.

While Miles played on, followed by Cannonball Adderly, followed by Coltrane, Hewitt's mind played back the highlights of the fitting room romp.

The first surprise had been the utter lack of surprise on Piotr Nikolai's part. Which had flashed the thought in her mind that either this wasn't the young man's first fitting room encounter, or he had mapped in his mind that it would only be a matter of time until the first one went down.

There was, however, more than a little glimmer of novelty in his eyes when Hewitt pulled the ten one-hundred-dollar bills from her purse.

"Just so you know I'm good," she said.

"I have no doubt you are very good," was the assistant manager's response.

The bills were in the air by then, dropping like propaganda leaflets thrown by a bushy-eyed man atop the Kremlin wall.

The green leaflets worked perfectly. As had her choreography of the two moves that came next. The first was her dropping down immediately to reclaim the bills. The second, her sudden and, to Piotr Nikolai's eyes, surprising snap back upward. It was even more surprising to his nose when the back of Hewitt's head smacked him there like a KGB fist.

Of course, as Hewitt had anticipated—*bet the freaking farm on*—Piotr Nikolai had started to bend down himself, to make sure none of the leaflets went unaccounted for. So the positioning was perfect, and the impact solid enough to create the accidental nosebleed Hewitt was looking for.

Hewitt had apologized profusely. Not just for the accident, but for accidentally ruining the mood of what could have been a beautiful thing. She'd provided the Kleenex, helped him clean up. Once that was done, she left with the suggestion of taking a rain check. For his trouble, she slipped him one of the hundreds.

Exiting the store, she nodded appreciatively to a mall rat across the way who looked a lot like Val Patterson impersonating a mall rat. From there, weird as this mall visit had been, it took on a tincture of weirdness only an ironic, theatrical God could have provided. Walking toward the exit, bloody Kleenex stowed safely in her bag, Hewitt had reconnected with the mall music again. And she'd almost laughed at the selection that was not only playing her out, but had been echoing during her fitting room fiasco with Piotr Nikolai.

It was a less-than-perfect but passionate rendition of a classical standard, a piece she remembered an ancient Vladimir Horowitz playing for Mike Wallace on *60 Minutes* in a previous century.

The "Polonaise in A Flat," by Chopin. "The Heroic."

Hewitt figured she'd need to listen to car versions of "Freddy the Freeloader" and "In Your Own Sweet Way" before heading back into the mall for an encore.

It was already clear to her that while Piotr "Pete" Nikolai may have been a lady killer, he wasn't a killer of kings and princesses. That much she had discerned well before she had turned the Gap fitting room into her own personal mosh pit. Her half-assed attempt at going undercover had been purposefully half-assed. With the dumping of Nick Groener's body on her porch, it was a rude reality that at least one bad brain had targeted her for its leave-behind message, its threat, its come-and-get-me.

If Piotr Nikolai had been the bringer of such gifts, or one of the co-presenters, he would have known Hewitt, recognized her. The disguise was intended to be her little surprise. Had he seen her walking up fully exposed, he would have had a moment to prepare his mask of cluelessness before she got a chance to catch his eyes close up.

With no credible sign of recognition, she could have abandoned the plan there, bought a pair of marked-down shorts and a top and gotten the hell out of there. But during her pantomime between the racks, a secondary use for the visit had struck her, a secondary use for the assistant manager, a forensic value to be derived from Piotr "Pete" Nikolai's Americanized blood. Guilt by association. Guilt by being in the wrong place at the wrong time with your pants pulled down for all the wrong reasons.

She did her own volume fade for "In Your Own Sweet Way," got out of the car, made her own sweet way to the mall, the Gap, with no pretense of being undercover this time. And of course, the assistant manager reacted with predictable dread as she made her entrance. Banging heads with a man had a way of marking a woman.

This time Hewitt fully identified herself and suggested they take a little walk to the coffee shop down the way. For a moment, Peter the Bloody exhibited a classic fight-or-flight look to his eyes. But Patterson had materialized out of the perfume-and-plastic as an obvious backup at the entranceway.

At this, Nikolai's body tensed up in f-or-f one more time, then relented. Where the sigh of resignation should have sounded, there was, instead, a word.

"Shit."

The assistant manager wasn't feeling any better about things as Hewitt walked him down the mall concourse, with Patterson trailing silently behind them.

"We'll have a nice warm beverage," Hewitt told him. "I'll buy you anything you want, lover-boy. As long as there's no bullshit at the bottom of the cup."

The cognition came to his eyes. "Do I need a lawyer?"

"To have a cup of coffee and a scone, hell no," Hewitt said.

Behind them, Patterson responded with a failed attempt to suppress a snort.

"Who's she?" Nikolai asked.

"The truth fairy," Hewitt said, drawing another snort from Patterson.

With his gaze, Piotr Nikolai polished the floor for several steps.

"I don't want to lose my job," he said.

"You and me both," Hewitt offered. "Funny how that shit works."

CHAPTER 78

"JUST between us, that blood sample you volunteered earlier—I'm having it cross-matched for DNA with a pretty impressive semen stain we found in the bed of a Ms. Mary Frances Eau Claire."

They were in the coffee shop, beverages on the table, and with Hewitt's statement, Piotr Nikolai's balls in his throat.

"By the way, whatever happened to the concept of protection in that business?"

He looked at her straight-up, gave her his best liar's face.

"I'm sorry. I don't understand what—"

"What protection is? There I can help you. It's where you put this stretchy plastic thing over Pete Junior. So you don't do something really stupid like dump a puddle of evidence in some rich lady's bed."

He looked at her now with his bedroom eyes, his best version of them under the circumstances.

"It is wrong for a younger man to bring intense pleasure to an older woman?"

"As a science project, no. As a way to make money, yes."

The science project he didn't get. The money he did. The bedroom eyes folded up and returned to the nightstand drawer.

"If making money is the problem, why are you acting like I killed someone?"

"Because the woman to whom you were bringing such intense pleasure has been killed."

There was a little ad placard on the table between them, with a photo of a serene woman serenely sipping her steamy tea. At the news of Mary Frances Eau Claire's death, Hewitt wasn't sure who displayed less emotion—the tea-sipping model or the coffee-drinking call boy.

"I can assure you I did not kill her."

"Oh, I know you didn't. Because I was there when it happened. She killed herself."

Another contest of nonemotions between the model and the prostitute. A draw this time as well.

"I can see you're really broken up about the way she died too."

"I am sad. I show you little because I don't understand how this involves me."

Hewitt took a sip from her cup, got a little too much froth on her lip, licked it clean.

"Oh, I'd imagine you're involved in all kinds of interesting ways. And I believe it all goes back to the day you met a man named Brad Spheeris."

What startled Hewitt then wasn't the look on his face, but the look of Brad Spheeris that seemed to channel through Piotr Nikolai's features. The way a younger man would manifest the face of his father in a moment of extreme challenge.

"You *do* know him," Hewitt pressed.

Nikolai-Spheeris didn't answer.

"Pete. Petey. *Sweet Pea.* We know you know him."

"Okay," he said softly. *"Okay."*

"And how long have you known Mr. Spheeris?"

Piotr Nikolai sighed as the Spheeris demon drained from his face. "One day too long."

CHAPTER 79

H E is in an American shopping mall, not a Middle Eastern desert. Yet the image he sees, the image he holds with his eyes, *this mirage*, can only be that.

Yet the longer he watches her, shifting as he has from one hidden angle to the next, the more he understands that mirages sometimes become warm, breathing beings in the flesh. Warm, breathing beings who sit in mall cafés and sip drinks from paper cups. Warm, breathing beings who, in the female form, volunteer to become the sweet, silent witness.

Beauty—there is no other way to describe it—witnessing the beast. But not the beast as it terrorized, through false love, the beauty. But the beast, through the twitching of its own heart, turned against itself.

He relaxes his unsightly grip on the handrail. All that will come. For now he will be content with being the witness himself, observing the beauty—through eyes true, and eyes beyond true. To see her as she was. To take these warm, breathing beings and transfuse them with enough of her blood, her soul, to make them viable.

Once done, of course, the viability would be set, cast, *enabled*. The entire dance would be set in motion, set to music.

He hears the music now, hears the playing of the piano. Not as he would ever hear it in such a setting as this, this American shopping mall. But rather, the concert hall of his mind, where the only performer is beauty. And the only audience, the boy with perfect hands.

CHAPTER 80

IT was becoming a theme. As compelling, as provocative as any the-matic in a Chopin nocturne. It was the theme so recently articulated by Piotr Nikolai, his eyes closed, his balls in his throat. The realization that he had known Brad Spheeris one day too long. Thinking back, Hewitt knew Mary Frances Eau Claire had been the first to articulate the notion. Not in so many words. But with one little hammer strike that ended the world.

How many others had been swallowed in that theme? How many others had rued that one extra day?

Jimmy Bonbon had been there. The one day too many when he de-cided to cut Brad Spheeris loose from the radio station. Hewitt knew now that neither the excommunicated DJ nor his employer had been entirely forthright on the reason for Spheeris's termination. She knew because of the edifying but disheartening story Piotr Nikolai had im-parted to her over his three successive cups of chai.

Hewitt had burned off the buzz of the mall hot chocolate. But to continue to feed the need, she'd gone to a Three Musketeers bar, pur-chased from one of the wayside vending machines.

It was the scene of the most recent princess display. The one honoring Princess Daphne Nemovitz. The crime scene personnel were gone now. As was the table where Princess Daphne had been displayed. So Hewitt had plunked herself down at the table nearest the space of the missing one.

At 2:00 on a late June afternoon, in the unfiltered light of the sun, the half-life of a Three Musketeers bar was about a minute. After tak-ing the first bite, Hewitt had been staring into space for at least two.

Based on his story and her reading of the chai leaves, Piotr "Pete"

Nikolai wasn't part of the psychopathology that had caused the picnic table replacement. Piotr Nikolai was an enterprising vagabond with a green card who wanted an apartment upgrade, a nicer car and a more happening lifestyle than assistant-managing the Gap could provide. Brad Spheeris was his father figure pimp, not his Satanic advisor. He'd been recruited by Spheeris along with some other male models from a Russian-owned modeling agency. That was big news to Hewitt, bigger news when she shared it with Pete Megna.

Hewitt took a tissue from her pocket, wiped the chocolate from her hand, dabbed at her mouth. Not as if anyone was keeping an eye on her personal appearance. Not out here. Taking a moment to make herself look nice. It was something Little Liz never had to do. At the thought of that, she felt a white-hot burn in a previously sealed corner of her mind. She focused, tried to connect to it, to open a secret door or two.

Little Liz didn't have to worry about fixing her face. Because Little Liz was a paper doll. You could have smeared all the chocolate you wanted on her face and Little Liz wouldn't have flinched. Her eyes wouldn't have shifted. Her mouth wouldn't have moved.

You could've laid Little Liz on her back on a picnic table and she would've stared up into the wild blue infinity, undeterred, for as long as you left her lying there.

Hewitt wiped her fingers again with the tissue, used it to wrap the remains of the Three Musketeers.

The liquid heat that infused her muscles did the rest, lifting and positioning her as she climbed onto the table, sat down in the middle of it, then laid herself flat, in the *Dead Princess* position.

More white heat erupted down the hallways of the intuitive wing of her mind, this time blowing out trap doors, hidden panels.

What had the dead princesses seen? Not while they were alive, but after they had cashed in the luxury of being able to care about the way their faces looked to the rest of the world.

What had the princesses seen between the final time they blinked their eyes and the first moment they stared into the blue infinity?

The princesses had been killed, but they had also been left alive. Innocently between worlds. Each one.

The killer had needed the princesses dead. But he had also needed them in a doll-like state so he could continue to play with them.

Lying on the picnic table, Hewitt tried to help them remember, to try to coax them to speak to her. So deep did she go into her dead princess séance that she didn't become aware of a car's approach on the highway until it had actually begun to slow down for the outrageous image she was presenting.

The car continued slowing until her body movements sent its driver the only signal possible. That this was some deranged woman's idea of a sick joke.

She had just laid her head down on the table again, having waited for the sound of the vehicle to pass, when the phone rang. It was Megna reporting in.

"I sure hope you're calling to tell me Spheeris turned up and he's dying to talk to me."

"I can't give you Spheeris yet," Megna told her. "But we might be able to build a human chain to him. A human chain with a Russian accent."

The blue sky came raining down on Hewitt in one big biblical splash. She sat up on the table as she listened to the rest of his report.

When she was done with the download, she left the picnic table, hurried toward her car, caught the sight of a little patch of wood violets.

Two minutes later, the Mazda spun out of the parking lot, leaving a plume of dust that would eventually settle on the purple bouquet she'd left on a patch of sun-deprived grass.

CHAPTER 81

HIS hands hurt. They always hurt when he drives the car, when he holds them in one position too long, folded around the steering wheel. Not the beautiful hands that had once received so much attention. But the pink fleshy talons they have become. Especially when their grasp on the wheel tightens in sympathy with the tightening of the mind that attempts to control them.

There is that difference. With him. A difference he long sensed. But one he has now come to understand. To accept. Even, strange as it might be to the rest of the world, to understand.

He makes suggestions to his hands. He does not control them. Some might say his hands have a mind of their own. But that wouldn't be true. He knows this because he knows the truth of his hands. It is not that they have their own mind. The truth is they have their own soul. And while hands can be broken, he knows souls cannot.

Souls live on.

The soul of Little Chip Chip lived on after the hands, the perfect hands, were stilled. He feels that soul stirring in his right hand now. The hand of the father.

His left hand, of course, holds the other unbreakable soul.

He unwraps it, the left hand, from the steering wheel, turns its palm toward his face. The palm, this part of it, still perfect.

The inner soul is what moves the hand the remainder of the distance to his face. It is not the perfect skin he begins to kiss, but the perfect soul inside.

She is there. In her soul-form, she is there. The closest he can come to kissing her now is to kiss this part of the hand to which only she could have given life. This perfect part. This perfect little piece of her that remains.

To an observer, he would look like a strange, even a sick, person, kissing his own hand. But to an inner being, an inner being who understands, he can only be a son of the universe expressing his unbroken love.

A rabbit darts into the road, stops when it feels the approach of the car, freezes. To avoid the animal, he knows he must return his left hand to the wheel. He knows this in a fraction of a second. But in the next fraction, he also knows the hand is not finished with its work.

So the display of affection continues. As he continues to kiss her soul. As he kisses the soul of the rabbit just liberated from its crushed body. As he kisses the fresh memory of the woman on the table. This vision. This gift. This dream before the dream.

CHAPTER 82

INCLUDING Piotr "Pete" Nikolai, there were five of them in the Russian callboy count. To Hewitt, the number was a nice confirmation. Because not only did it give her hope that there could be mad, passionate love after age sixty, but it also kept alive the theory—the only theory—she had running. That among all those good bodies there was one very bad brain.

After getting Megna's info dump on the Queens Club and their extracurricular activities, Hewitt was mulling the notion of releasing Spheeris to the media as an official person of interest. She figured at the very least Spheeris would get a kick out of hearing the phrase applied to his name. If he was getting any kicks at all. She had a sense that if one of the members of the callboy club was the freak in question, Brad Spheeris might already be a postscript. It was one thing to be missing when a friend or family member was trying to find you. It was another when a legion of law enforcement was hunting your ass.

The timing of it, the way he'd dropped off the face of the earth at the same time Nick Groener went missing, was a big red flag. A big red flag atop the Navy Pier Ferris wheel.

In the Mazda now, Hewitt inserted a CD into the player. Sonny Rollins. "St. Thomas." It was time to live a little. Her theory still had a pulse.

Megna and his posse had done a bang-up job squeezing down the surviving members of the Queens Club. Women of that echelon had a way of not being terribly forthcoming at the suggestion of personal impropriety—especially paying young men to make them see God. But Megna and his charges also had the big icebreaker they could drop. The breaking news that one of the queens, one of their own, had blown her brains out when confronted with the story.

The other factor in Megna and Company's favor was that with Mary Frances Eau Claire already dead, there wasn't a fear of retribution if one of the ladies decided to point a heavily bejeweled finger her way as the leader of their little upper-class sex ring. It also hadn't hurt that they'd been given a strong whiff of serial killer with their Q&A potpourri. The notion that their carnal cotillions included a homicidal freak might've motivated them to get the bad brain, if not off the streets, at least out of their Jacuzzis.

It was quite a neat little operation, the Queens Club. At the top of the organization you had CEO and pimp, Brad Spheeris. Sitting alongside him, if not on his lap on special occasions, was the chairwoman and haute madame, Mary Frances Eau Claire. Beneath her, when they weren't on top, was the labor force, a group separated by only a single generation from a once-visionary social system that would have implored these workers of the world to unite. Well, unite they had. With a very privileged upper class.

Hewitt was sketching the organizational chart in her notebook, as if she were roughing out the pages of an annual report, with insets of Brad Spheeris and Mary Frances Eau Claire, and smaller shots of two key employees Megna's posse had rounded up, both of whom were inadvertently posing for her, at that moment, in the interrogation veal pen at the ISP's Villa Park Division.

Megna had already presented the young men with his good cop version of the Q&A, which Hewitt had observed from the other side of the glass. It was Hewitt's turn now. The bad cop looked up from her notebook, looked at the place on the other side of the mirror where she figured Megna was observing her. She gave the visualized Megna an appreciative hunch of her shoulders.

"You guys like the taste of American cigarettes?"

Both subjects paused in their nervous smoking, eyed their cigarettes as if they'd never considered the taste before. Each gave a nonverbal yes.

"You see, I have no fucking idea. Because I don't smoke. And between you and me, I hate the smell of cigarette smoke."

She pushed away from the wall she'd been leaning against, approached the table where the two of them sat, still paused between puffs.

"But I especially hate the smell of smoke when it comes from the mouths of young guys who eat old pussy for cash."

She glanced at the invisible Megna, rolled her shoulders again.

"And what makes it even worse is when the smell of that mixes with the smell of cheap, shitty green card cologne."

She pulled out the chair, sat down.

"Would you please put those things out?"

She nodded at the Diet Coke can ashtray. The subject on her right, Dmitri "Timmy" Pisetsky, the one with the dishwater blond hair with platinum highlights—and the better skin—put his cigarette in the can first. Right behind him, Pavel "Paulie" Belov, the more muscular one, with the Bambi eyelashes and the early Ringo Starr hairdo, extinguished his.

Both of them were well-cut and good-looking. *Model looks.* Or close enough to get into the parties.

"You guys do have your green cards, right?"

Both nodded, throated something between a *yeah* and a *dah.*

"Now Detective Megna, your 'Uncle Pete,' explained to you that despite this little social embarrassment, there might be a way for you to hold on to those useful little cards."

Hewitt took her notebook and laid it on the table, open as it was to the schematic that included the sketched faces of the two of them.

"Okay, you see your names there on the chart, along with two others. Those gentlemen are being gathered up right now. I've already had the pleasure of meeting with Mr. Nikolai. So, gentlemen, now you need to tell me—you *really* need to tell me—if there are any names missing from this group."

There was a hesitation from them. Both looked at the Diet Coke can as if they wanted their cigarettes back. Their eyes and faces acted as if they wanted to turn and consult. But the Eurasian mountains of their shoulders held them back—the Urals for Timmy, the Carpathians for Paulie.

It thrilled Hewitt totally that there was something there. That there was something in it that scared the Americanized shit out of them.

"Okay, guys. Words don't seem to be working. So let's try pictures. I want you to visualize this. A great big toilet. And there's a hand holding two green cards. That hand belongs to, not your Uncle Pete, but your Uncle Sam. You know, old guy with the white beard and the tall hat. Tends to dress in red, white and blue. Well, gentlemen, in ten seconds he's going to reach out with his other hand and flush that toilet. And your cards are headed for the big INS sewer. Starting now. *Ten. Nine. Eight . . .*"

The Carpathians were the first to surrender their hold. *Seven*. The Urals followed. *Six*.

"*Five. Four . . .*"

At three, the deal between them was consummated.

"*Two. One . . .*"

"Mee-sha," platinum highlights offered.

"Mee-sha," Ringo Starr agreed.

CHAPTER 83

WITH Misha Sharapov, the callboy count was an even half-dozen. Five of the six had known addresses. Misha Sharapov was the anomaly. Three of them currently shared an apartment. The other two had shared one with Misha. Until he'd moved out. With Brad Spheeris's help.

Hewitt was shuttling through heavy midafternoon traffic, heading for Northbrook, her shuttling accompanied by Felix Mendelssohn. It was a piece she knew as "The Hebrides Overture." She knew because a minute earlier Jay Boniface had cued it up for public consumption.

She'd tried Jimmy B's studio line. But he hadn't picked up. Which was just as well. For the pointed questions she would have to ask him, showing up unannounced would be the better approach.

Megna, Patterson and most of the rest of the division were pursuing a face-to-face with Misha Sharapov, beginning with the freaking mall where he played the food court piano. *That* freaking mall. Hell yes, it would have been infinitely easier if she had just ridden the escalator upstairs after her head bump with Piotr Nikolai. Especially if Nikolai had ridden along, bloody nose and all, and pointed to the guy at the piano and said: "*He's another one. Just like me. The only difference is he can sight-read Chopin, while I'm stuck with waist size, inseam and laundry instructions.*"

For information on Misha Sharapov, Hewitt would have laid down a food court smorgasbord for the assistant manager that could've fed a hungry Marxist republic. As it was, she didn't expect much for her people to chew on at the Prospect Square Mall. Calls to management indicated Misha had left the building. Worse, they couldn't provide a home address. On his employment application, the pianist had listed his residence as 1200 S. Lake Shore Drive. Which was fine if you believed the Shedd Aquarium was renting rooms. Or tanks.

HEWITT covered the distance from car to front entrance at a half-run. For all the security she'd encountered on previous visits to WCLS, it riddled her brain when, after a couple of unanswered buzzes, her curious right hand found the door curiously unlocked.

Inside, it was business as usual, with the current musical selection—the final passages of the Mendelssohn—playing in the lobby. On her way to the studio, Hewitt loaded three questions into the linear chamber of her mind, questions generated by the statements she'd drawn out of her Russian boy toy duo half-an-hour earlier.

Do you recall a young male intern who might have worked for Brad Spheeris within the last couple of years, a young male intern with a Russian accent?

She was at the closed door to the studio. She knocked at the same time she pushed inside.

The studio, filled with Mendelssohn. But totally absent the on-air personality.

Her next stop had to be the kitchen. In the hallway, she loaded question two into the chamber, assuming a yes to question one.

As an intern, would the young man with the Russian accent have been given access to any security codes or Internet passwords to access the radio station's programming equipment?

The lights were on in the kitchen. So was a full-carafe of WCLS Late-Afternoon Blend. Signs of intelligent life. But no living DJ.

Did the young man with the Russian accent strike you in any way as unusual, secretive or just plain fucking weird? And if you're not in the men's room right now, where the hell are you?

She knocked on the bathroom door, didn't wait for a response.

"Jay? Jimmy?"

Neither one was standing at the urinal, which she fixated on for a couple blinks of her eyes—that forbidden men's place. Then she was out, the door closing behind her as the Mendelssohn came to an end.

She felt a silent scream beginning to build in her solar plexus. But the scream was doused by the oaky white wine of a soothing voice.

"'The Hebrides Overture' by Felix Mendelssohn. Also known as 'Fingal's Cave,'" Jay Boniface intoned. "The inspiration for the piece arose from a trip to Scotland when the composer was in his early twenties. It was on the famed Staffa Island that Mendelssohn encountered Fingal's Cave, with its rock pillars rising high out of the sea. On calm days, the rocks are serene. On stormy days, one can hear the crashing of the sea against the rocks across the entire island. You heard in the overture how beautifully Mendelssohn captured that. The interplay of calm . . . and violence. *Calm . . . and violence.*"

Hewitt had made her way back to the studio.

"Coming up," she heard the announcer say as she pushed the door open, "a famous symphony with an out-of-this-world nickname. Mozart's Symphony Number 41. The *Jupiter* Symphony."

Empty chair. Empty studio. Empty largest planet in the solar system.

"But first, two idylls by the English composer George Butterworth."

Pre-corded Boniface. Bogus Bonbon.

CHAPTER 84

JEN Spangler had a pot of Rice-A-Roni on the stove, her baby girl hanging on her neck and a father who was lying down in the bedroom again, looking like shit, but insisting he was fine.

She picked up the old wall phone, knowing her dad wouldn't pick up the cordless from his nightstand, the cordless that had rung and rung and rung during the night for all those years. Well, at least the nighttime calls had stopped. But how weird, how freaking weird, that at the same time the phone stopped interrupting their sleep, a baby started.

It was a familiar voice on the other end. Familiar to Jen, but not exactly comforting. Given what the caller did for a living, she doubted her voice was ever truly comforting to anyone.

"Yes, he's here. But he's resting," she told Hewitt. "Just a minute."

As she set the phone on the counter, she heard Hewitt's little voice call, "How's the baby?"

The Rice-A-Roni was just hitting a full boil in her ears as she reached the half-cracked door to her father's room.

"Nobody," his dry voice greeted her as she and the baby poked their conjoined heads into the room. "I really can't talk to anyone."

"It's Hewitt."

His face gave up a little of its gauntness. He gave her the cupped-hands gesture he'd been giving her since she was old enough to crawl. Come to Daddy. And just like she'd done every time all those years, she went.

Jen Spangler knew her dad had never forgotten the high school tantrum she threw over his preoccupation, his *fondness* for Hewitt. The kiss he put to her face as she leaned over the bed now was another reminder that he hadn't forgotten. She picked up the cordless, clicked it on, handed it to him. She left the room, hip-carried the baby to the kitchen, got the Rice-A-Roni under control.

The wall phone was still lying on its back on the counter. She felt a burn in her gut, knowing she shouldn't, but also knowing she would. Taking a clean towel from the drawer, she wetted it under the faucet, gave it to the baby to suck on, quietly picked up the receiver.

"Don't sweat it. You can stop by next Friday," she heard her father say. "And the Friday after that. Despite what my cardiovascular system keeps implying, I'm not going anywhere. Contrary to conventional wisdom, I'm not going to follow my heart."

"Why start getting sentimental now?" Hewitt responded in her bumpy car voice.

"How close are you?"

"Could be right there. Could be a thousand miles from home. I wish I could give you the full download. But I'm coming into port for an interview."

"Even so," Jen Spangler's father said—insistence, worry in his voice, "let me leave you with one little thought."

"Sometimes that's what detonates the big ones."

"Do what you do, Elizabeth. Do what you've done before. Go to your gut. Ask yourself, 'What's the one thing I might've missed?' If it's there to find, you'll know it. Knowing you, you're probably already halfway there."

The baby had thrown the wet towel to the floor. She scrunched her little face—the warning shot to the crying to come. As gently as possible, Jen Spangler hung up the phone, knowing she shouldn't have listened, but knowing if her dad didn't pull through this, she'd have a better understanding of him for having done so.

It was just a shame that the daughter he never had was the one who could make him show it.

CHAPTER 85

THE needle goes in with surprising ease. Easier than with the previous recipients. He knows there is no real need for such specific placement this time. Perhaps that is what makes it seem easier—knowing that if he is less than immaculate in the entry, no one will be hurt. No one who matters. Oh, everybody mattered to someone. Yet there were degrees. Degrees of mattering.

He takes a moment to consider this as he withdraws the needle, as he feels the body, already slowed, submit now to the peace.

The degrees of mattering, yes. An otherwise bright, intelligent person could sit in his easy chair, watching a news report of a million starving, dying people on the other side of an ocean, blink a couple of times, then reach out for a piece of pizza, turning it around to eat it backward because the crust was stuffed with cheese and that was the fastest way to gorge.

Yet this same pizza-eating TV watcher could fly into a rage upon coming home from work to find that a spouse had been slow to put on the family dinner and they were all starving, dammit.

The degrees of mattering. It was all a case of how close the subject matter was to you. There were billions of women in the world. But in the heat of the passion, in the heat of remembering, all of them, young, old, beautiful or not, would be as cold as an abandoned body in winter, compared to the one who mattered.

You could feel empathy. You could even bring yourself to apologize for the ruthlessness of the world. But that wouldn't warm one bit the body that had already gone cold.

No amount of cheese in a crust could ever fill that emptiness.

CHAPTER 86

IN the twenty minutes she had between her conversation with Spangler and her arrival at the Highland Park PD, Hewitt could have given Captain Spangler, if not the complete download, more than enough for him to voice an opinion. She had the time. It was the voicing of the opinion she couldn't afford.

Which meant what? In his current state, she didn't think he could bring it anymore? Faded as he'd become, had she moved on now? Was she humoring him? Pretending to listen to the advice of some doddering parent while planning in her head what she was actually going to do?

"Agent Hewitt?"

In addition to her name, she heard the slide of an envelope on the countertop that separated her from the inner workings of the HPPD desk job hive.

"Key and code," the desk sergeant said, the pained, vacant look on his face a reflection of what she knew he was seeing on hers.

"Thank you," she said. "I'll try not to make a habit of it."

"It's not exactly like anybody else is using the place," he offered.

Not unless the ghost of Mary Frances Eau Claire had returned in search of one more wild ride on the Beautyrest.

Crazy thoughts as Hewitt left the air-conditioning of the building and reconnected with the late afternoon heat.

Did ghosts have desires like that? Did ghosts ever feel horny?

In the car, it was the ghost of John Coltrane rising up to greet her. It had been forty years since JC had blown his last note on earth. Then why, every time she listened to this track, "Alabama," did it feel so strongly like some of his smoky breath was leaking from the sax and rising against her face?

ED Spangler wasn't a ghost yet, but his last advice had been pretty damn prescient. All day, the whole Mary Frances Eau Claire thing had been banging at the edges of her mind. Not the notion that they'd missed something there. But the sense that Ms. Eau Claire hadn't missed the target of her single shot for a damn good reason. A reason, to this point, Hewitt had been unsuccessful in raising from the invisible world to the world she could actually see through the latest bug art on her windshield.

A rich socialite caught with her pantsuit down, the alpha female for a pack of aging doyennes who weren't above paying good money for stud services. Exposed, yes. But enough to gun yourself down without a second thought about spin control? Hell, celebrities survived sex videos. Presidents survived cigar sex.

Who the hell knew? Maybe all those decades earlier, her mother had walked in on her little gazebo party with some high school boy. Maybe she'd been reminded of what an awful girl she was ever since. First, by her mother's real voice. Later, by the voice in her head.

Funny how the voice in the head was always worse. More insidiously vindictive. More creatively mean.

She turned on the wipers, summoned the washer fluid, got rid of the worst of the insects.

What was Mary Frances Eau Claire so deadly ashamed about? There were the tapes, sure. If the media, if the Internet got ahold of those, it would make for some serious squirming. From the start, Hewitt sensed there was more. But if there was, the top-to-bottom search of the house by the CS team hadn't given it up.

She was looking at it again now, top to bottom—the façade of the French Country monstrosity—as she pulled into the long, tree-lined driveway. Approaching the front entrance, she had the sense it would be a long time until this big house was lived in again. A long time before it became a living, breathing home and ceased being what it was now. A death museum.

With that assessment, Hewitt had assigned herself yet another title to add to her business card. *Death Museum Curator*. No, that was too grandiose. *Death Museum Maintenance Manager*. Yeah, that was it. That sounded like a position she could grow into.

The head of maintenance entered the pass code, waited for the little green light, then inserted her key into the heavy-duty deadbolt, rang the atonal chimes of the inner workings of that, opened the door and entered the foyer.

After a sudden death, some houses still maintained a weird energy that made you feel it was possible the former resident was still residing in the home, in some form. The Eau Claire manor did not. There was no feeling of that, of a loitering entity. Rather, it was just an emphatic sense of emptiness. Of someone having gotten the hell out of there, with no forwarding address.

The lying-in-state thing was becoming a habit. But the thought of that was so unsavory, she actually eyed the brandy decanter on the credenza as a quick fix for getting rid of the sick taste it left in her mouth.

Much more tasteful, she thought, to simply visualize the post-gunshot body. Her brain reprinted the image of the fallen contortionist. The splayed right knee. The left elbow that looked like she'd been caught in the follow-through of throwing a curveball. The chin upturned toward the ceiling, at an angle she would have never been able to realize alive. Not even in the haughtiest moment of her life.

Even if she'd been so inclined, Hewitt knew she would've needed several years of serious yoga to approximate the pose herself. So she took her posing interests elsewhere, passing through the foyer and making her way up the unlit staircase.

It was here that her mind and her body closed around the memory of the manor's departed owner. When Mary Frances Eau Claire had entertained the special bedroom guest, had she and her lover-for-hire climbed the staircase together—like a couple just returned from dinner and a show, ready, each, to make a late-night liqueur of the other?

Or given her queenly persona, was it more of the come-hither approach? Waiting in her chamber, lying naked under the royal sheet, playing Catherine the Great to his Gregory Orloff.

Or maybe it wasn't as interesting as either. Maybe it never got anything more romantic than what she'd heard on the tapes. A live DJ. A couple of live bodies. One older. One newer.

Standing at the door to Mary Frances Eau Claire's bedroom, Hewitt was unable to stop herself from imagining the two bodies in that big cushioned spiderweb of a bed. With the master of ceremonies, Mr. Spheeris, doing *what exactly* while the pay-to-play love was being made? Spheeris was spinning the discs, yes. But classical pieces were usually pretty damn lengthy. Did he stay on his little announcer's perch? Or did he set up the piece, and in pursuit of whatever floated his bizarre boat, did he then move to a more advantageous position?

If Mary Frances Eau Claire had just made like a good Hollywood celebrity and videotaped the proceedings, instead of recording sound only, it would've made things so damn much easier.

Hewitt began to move around the room, circling the bed, eventually settling on a decent place where a camera and tripod could've been set. Through her head's stereoscopic viewfinder, she saw what Mary Frances Eau Claire might have seen if she had opted for video. After a moment, Hewitt understood why she hadn't.

Without the steady presence of a personal trainer and some bodywork of the surgical kind, the stacking of decades didn't exactly build a pedestal for the displaying of Aristotelian beauty. Given that, it only made sense to Hewitt that Mary Frances Eau Claire would capture and replay the audio only, allowing her mind to insert whatever pictures of herself she could conjure.

With your eyes closed, you could make things however you wanted them to be.

Whatever the hell that was worth. In context, she wasn't sure. Wasn't sure what any of her retro-voyeuristic musings were worth.

Well, that was one benefit she and the sane world had already realized. All that thinking, all that imagining, had at least kept her off Mary Frances Eau Claire's bed.

She started across the room, toward the doorway, caught her image in the three faces of the vanity mirror, saw her own face reflected back to her in triplicate.

Three faces.

One for each of them.

The synapses in her brain all lined up to face the direction of her next idea—like pods to a mother ship.

If Brad Spheeris had ever entered the bedroom to observe or participate, there was a mirror for him, a mirror for the lady of the house and a mirror for her lover boy.

With her eyes closed, Mary Frances Eau Claire wouldn't have had to see the faces of the two significant men in her life. She could've remained blissfully ignorant in those moments of what was really going on. Not just in this boudoir, but in others. She could have remained detached from suspicions of bigger dealings, darker workings that might have crossed her mind based on things she might have heard, behavior she might have seen.

But with Hewitt's surprise appearance in her foyer, the deeper, darker, sicker nature of all that would have screamed out at her all at once, screamed for her to cross to the credenza, skip the brandy and opt for the ultimate escape.

CHAPTER 87

WAITING is never easy. Knowing what you want to happen but having to wait for someone else's actions to determine when it will happen is the slowest kind of waiting.

As he waits this way, he remembers, as he always remembers in these slow-ticking times, how he waited on the night of his mother's ascension.

He was lying in wait that night too. Literally. Lying on the floor, in the corner of the living room, curled up like a dead person, like a person who couldn't be hurt anymore. As much as he had already been hurt, as much as had been taken from him, he knew he couldn't afford to show that there was anything left of him to take.

And so he had waited.

Waiting now, he remembers his hands. In those first moments after they had been altered. He remembers how his hands screamed out for help. How his hands screamed out for love.

They are screaming still. And he is thankful he is the only one who can hear them.

He looks across the room, to the old bed, where the first body rests, awaiting the arrival of the next. The two of them to enjoy one final dance. One final dance to honor the wishes of the good father.

CHAPTER 88

HEWITT did a sweep of the house. From checking the pockets of the billiards table in the basement to discovering all the little caches of Imitrex in the five bathrooms, including the one off the loft/office space in what had once been the attic.

When she came away empty-handed, she wasn't exactly crushed. Sometimes finding nothing was actually a significant find. Because at least it would get you off the dead-end street you were on. Or in the case of the northern suburbs, the dead cul-de-sac.

As she exited through the front door, two notions struck her. One, that she wasn't necessarily closing the door on the hunch Spangler had encouraged her to act on. And two, that she should have helped herself to one of those Imitrex tablets. She knew they were prescribed for headaches. Maybe they would have a similar therapeutic effect on the mind-ache that had been gathering in intensity under the crown of her head.

As she stood on the front porch, looking at how pathetically lost her little car appeared against the wide expanse of cobbled driveway, the earth's atmosphere couldn't have been calmer. Even the sound, the normal live soundtrack of birds and background rumble and distant dogs, seemed to have been turned down.

Hewitt didn't like it, the way it mimicked the vacuum, the hole in the world the case had become. She had no choice but to step into it, her shoes hitting the cobblestone, her breathing becoming tight, almost pained.

It wasn't until she got to her car that she understood the physical reason behind the constricting of the breath. Because it was there, just outside the monolithic shadow of the house, that she first felt the two eyes watching her. Two large, rectangular eyes fifteen feet apart.

There was a big detached garage approximately a hundred feet west of the main house. At some point during Mary Frances Eau Claire's reign over the manor, she or her husband had seen fit to hire an architect and contractor to add an attached garage to the big house. But the original garage had stayed. Architecturally, it was nice enough to keep, having the same design features as the living quarters, including the twin dormers that that continued to gaze down at Hewitt.

In the verbal download Hewitt had gotten from the head of the tech team, he'd reported that the big garage was used for storing lawn and garden equipment and other odd and ends.

Hewitt had no reason to doubt any of that. And after crossing that little section of real estate and lifting the first of the three garage doors, the report was confirmed. She stepped inside to the smell of oil, gasoline, fertilizer and a hint of pesticide. Given the report, exactly what you'd expect.

What wasn't expected, what gave Hewitt pause, was the finished ceiling. The finished ceiling that seemed to eclipse any access to the space upstairs. The space that, for whatever reasons, remained connected to the outside world through the panes of glass of the two big windows.

But of course, that didn't mean anything. Old spaces were often sealed over and left to the spiders, the rodents, the squirrels, the mourning doves. Any creature that claimed squatter's rights. Hewitt planted her feet, stilled her body, held her breath, listened. For any aural evidence of the presence of such denizens.

Either they were listening to her the same way, or there was no one home.

For a moment, she thought of just leaving it. What the hell would it matter? But she knew that wasn't a good enough reason. And she was too tired to think of a better one.

With the stand of pine trees that flanked the back of the building, the already fading sun was diminished even more. To the point that, even with one garage door open and some light coming through the side windows, she still didn't have enough illumination to see the detail of the ceiling, especially toward the back.

She tried a light switch, pronounced it dead. So she went back to the car, retrieved her State of Illinois flashlight, resumed the scoping.

First, she checked the back part of the garage, closest to the open door, looking for some kind of opening, some trap door, but finding nothing. Moving into the middle of the structure, the flashlight found some dark stains against the white paint of the ceiling. Dark brown. *Not blood, for Christ's sake.* A water leak from upstairs. A freaking water leak.

Her head was getting a little goofy. She needed to eat. With all the time she'd put in on the property, she could've raided something from Mary Frances Eau Claire's freezer. Maybe she would've lucked into that Wolfgang Puck pizza.

Fuck. There it was. In the southeast corner of the ceiling. Not just a little push-up trap, but the kind that looked like it could pull down and swing out into hinged steps. But what the hell? If you had the money, why hold back?

It surprised her a little that her predecessors hadn't seen it, or if they had, had failed to report it. But people were people, crime scene or not. And technically, it wasn't even a crime scene. The tech who checked it probably took a quick look, smelled the gas and fertilizer, said, "Yeah, that's a big ass old garage," and moved on. She had asked them to look for anything connecting Mary Frances Eau Claire to a classical disc jockey. She hadn't said anything about secret gardeners.

Her flashlight caught the metallic glint of a step-up ladder in the corner, against the wall. The condition of it—much too clean, with its Home Depot sticker still attached—caused a cold whisper against the back of her neck.

She maneuvered the ladder into place, stepped up and pulled down on the handle of the foldaway door. It dropped. Not as heavy as she figured. It was aluminum, held together by some kind of pneumatic braces that made it move smoothly, easily, almost in a kind of hardware slow motion.

Hewitt unfolded the two sections of steps until they reached the floor. She felt the cold whisper against the back of her neck again. But she didn't have time to decipher it. Because her feet were on the steps, and her service revolver was already warming in her hand.

CHAPTER 89

A s abandoned spaces went, this one deserved a spread in *Architectural Digest*. Hewitt could only hope if her life went south someday and she was forced into living in found space, she could find something like this.

Somebody had been living here, and living pretty well. That was no crime. But if they were using it as a stage from which to act out canonical death dramas, she needed to know that fast. She needed to know that completely. She needed to know that before anyone learned they had a visitor.

The room was remarkably well appointed. Hewitt's take was that it was comprised of discards from an interior decorating purge in the big house. Some very classy discards that included a couple of nice Persian rugs and a nice armoire that was the focal point of the room.

To Hewitt's eyes, however, the true focal point was another piece of furniture. A rolltop desk positioned against the west wall, *centered* against the west wall. A rolltop desk that was no recent Ethan Allen classic. This was an old one. Hewitt knew, even in the repressed light, within ten feet of her approach, knew by the unmistakable smell of old wood and passed time and dead owners.

There was no chair at the desk, which she found odd. So she stood where the chair would have been and extended her hands to the rolltop, listened to the dozens of wooden plinks too rapid to count, too fast to separate into anything but an antique protest as she rolled it up.

The writing surface of the desk was barren. There were no pencils, no tablets. No handwritten notes in the language of dead poets. The reason for this became disturbingly clear as Hewitt's eyes found the

centerpiece of what was no longer a classic desk but a personal reliquary—
with its most precious relic positioned in the center of the desk's main
shelf, flanked by two photographs. One of the mother. The other of
mother and child. And Hewitt knew that the music box between them
was the one thing in the universe that connected the two photographs
in a way that not only transcended death, but transcended whatever life
was still being lived by one of them.

Hewitt considered the little blond ballerina atop the pedestal,
poised in her eternal passé. She thought of putting on a pair of gloves so
she could take the music box and wind it. But something about it—the
tension in the base, the pedestal, the frozen body of the dancer—gave
her the sense that the box had already been wound.

Taking a tissue from her pocket, she pinched it into a workable
shape, reached out to the wooden peg and released the tension.

There was no hesitation between the first note of the music and the
first flutter of the ballerina's chiffon tutu. She had danced to this piece
before. She had danced to this piece forever.

Hewitt knew she had danced for a very special audience. An exclusive audience. An audience of one. She knew because of the musical selection that accompanied the pretty little thing. Note by plinking note.
Turn by graceful turn.

If Frédéric Chopin had been shrunken down, reduced to a minia-
turization that allowed him to fit comfortably inside the housing beneath the pedestal, the master himself could have been playing this
simple, tinny, percussive version of his "Nocturne in E flat."

Hewitt felt a wild rush of adrenaline fill her limbs, her hands, her
face. She had narrowed the universe of the bad brain to this tiny space
inside the music box, where a tiny Chopin played his nocturne for the
little blond dancer.

A younger version of herself would have thrilled even more at the
notion that she had reduced the bad brain universe to a single suspect.
But she couldn't afford to risk that miscalculation. So she would take
care to be every bit as precise as the music flowing from the box, as the
pirouetting of the figurine.

In her processing, her deliberating, she became so focused on the dancer, the music, that she didn't react to the first footstep on the fold-out staircase. By the second step, her cerebral cortex was yelling at her body to move in every direction at the same time. But her higher brain told her to ease away from the desk and get down behind the glass-topped coffee table.

The caller was halfway up the steps now as she moved soundlessly across the room. The special guest approaching the top step as she got herself into position.

With the darkness that clung to the atmosphere inside and outside the room, she was able to see only a muddy outline of the figure that rose up through the floor.

She drew her revolver, calculated the odds of using it were one hundred percent.

Music box Chopin rattled the air around her ears. At the extreme edge of her peripheral vision, the dancer did a final turn before her brain screamed an alarm that quickly flattened out, hiccupped, became the syllables of the thought her mind articulated.

Brady was the killer.

Her finger on the trigger. *Jesus Christ she was going to shoot him.*

The shot ripped the darkness, slammed every key of Chopin's miniature piano.

The ring-out was still holding the room when Brady's body hit the floor. A flesh-filled kettle drum.

Against the relentless music box, Hewitt's brain alarm screamed again.

It wasn't me.

A third scream.

It wasn't him.

The fourth scream sounded at the same time the skin of her back detected a surge of black energy behind her.

The blow to the back of her head never happened.

CHAPTER 90

S HE can't move her legs. In the dream, the hallucination, her legs re-
fuse to move. And she stands there on the recital stage, in the itchy
pink leotard and the tutu that smells like an old bandage.

She can't move her legs. And she knows the faces are beginning to
frown. She can't see them. She can't see them because the lights are shining in her eyes. The lights are shining on her legs. Shining on the muscles that have stopped understanding what she wants them to do.

More than anything she has ever wanted in her life, she wants them
to move. The music is playing. It is time for the dance to begin. But
something inside is keeping it from happening. As if strong hands are
holding her legs. Not wrapped around the outside. But grabbing her
from the inside. Holding on to her bones. Pulling them down. Making
them heavy. Making that part of her body feel like it might never be
alive again.

The piano is playing. The sweet sad song of this recital. A song she
has heard but can't recognize. Because it is not the music she rehearsed to.

On the other side of the light, she feels the faces, feels the frowning
shift from anger to hatred. She must say something. To explain to them.
To tell them what has gone wrong inside her. Her mouth is already
open—it has been open all along. But the death that has occurred in her
legs has occurred, also, inside her mouth.

She panics now. For the first time feels what might be the truth.
That not only is she unable to dance. She is unable to live.

Her eyes are still working. At least she has that. She sees the light.
But this only brings more panic. Because her brain tells her that her eyes
are closed. They have been closed all along. So the light she sees might

not be the stage light. It could be the light at the end of her life. And the faces that frown aren't the faces of the audience, but the faces of angels who do not welcome her, who do not forgive her for the things she has done on earth.

Something new now. Something terrible. The curtain is closing. The light is going away. *They have given up on her.* And she wonders. She wonders horribly. If the light on the other side goes away, what is left? Is anything left?

Is there anything left of her for heaven?

The light fades. And she feels the last little piece of her fading with it. This tiny island of herself, so remote now in the great dark ocean. So little. So lost.

But then, like a single drop of rain falling against the surface of that dark ocean, she detects one last little thought at the end of the world. That one drop of rain puncturing the dark water and drawing up a tone collected from the drowning voices of a thousand souls.

The sound of it, as it collects, seems to make the fading world hold on to its final gasp of light.

And it is precisely this to which her eyes flutter open. The light of the world reduced to a single teardrop of fire.

CHAPTER 91

HE watches her. He has been watching her all along. He has been watching her, he has been watching *them*, for years. For what feels to him forever.

Perhaps it is. Perhaps forever is nothing more than a perfectly realized moment never let go of.

He loves this moment. He lives for it. The reanimation. The rebirth.

Her eyes flutter in an attempt to reestablish contact with the world. Focusing on the flame, the stillness of it. This element he has added, not for purposes of illumination as much as for the indulgence of romance.

Her eyes find the candle. It is highly unlikely her mind has found it too. The blow to her head was unfortunate. It was wrong. But it was necessary. He understands this now. When arrangements aren't planned as much as they are imposed, decisions must be made quickly.

So perhaps it is the added effect of the head blow that is causing such a struggle for her to find the candle, to register the room, to see the world as she has never seen it before.

If anything, it is the music that appears to be pulling her into consciousness. There is a movement now of her hands and fingers. Subtle movement. A slight, rhythmic motion of her hands. As if moving to the cadence of the piece. Could that be possible?

Does she understand what she hears? Does she recognize a continuity from the simple music box to the complete *as-written* rendition?

If she does, does it surprise her? Or does it make some ultimate sense to her? Did, once again, the song of the music box arc over the valley of death to reestablish itself in the music of the next world? This world beyond death where the taken can be returned to see the love that still lives in their lives, to witness the love turned ultimately against the violator, the taker of life.

The hands, slightly more active now. Slight, but indicating every potential to become more active still. The fingers beginning to show the first signs of life beyond the prelife. Like an embryonic bird lifting its head for the first time, sensing the need to start pecking at the wall of the dark universe that held it.

CHAPTER 92

A candle on a table. A table in a living room. In an old person's house. This she can tell from the furniture. From the smell. Of air having gone stale long after the residents were able to do anything about it.

Maybe they knew the air was stale. Maybe they simply couldn't respond. Maybe they sat like her, a stroke victim on a sofa, aware that a window needed opening, that the drapes needed to be replaced.

It is clear to Hewitt that the last resident who lived here was a woman. An old woman. And now here she is, a younger woman, unable to move from the sofa to draw the drapes, to lift a window, to confront the scenario that has been staged for her.

He drugged her. Like he had drugged the rest of them. A thought rippled across her mind. She was on the verge of figuring it out. Almost had it. Lost it.

The candle. Focus on the candle. *Hands.* Move the fingers. *Feet.* Move the toes. Make the connection. Force the flow. Wake up the nerves. Move the blood.

There. Coming at her again. Slithering between the arpeggios of Chopin. She'd been drugged. And she understood now about the two needle entry points in the female victims. The first was to make them cooperative participants in the performance. The second, to make them take the memory of it to the next world.

But she is still here. She is in this world. It is night in her world. She cannot move to bring her eyes and her wristwatch into the same plane. But to know the time, she doesn't need a watch. It is the middle of the night. A few minutes after three.

The flame of the candle, steady for so long, *startles*.

The movement of it shifts everything. Shifts the space-time pocket of her mind. Pushes her back to the time before her reawakening in this old person's house.

Brady is dead.

She knows now, knows the bullet that took him didn't come from her gun. But if there is a relief in this, she has yet to feel it. She will silently scream over this for years, maybe forever. But she can't start now. Because the flame is moving. There is movement in the house. Movement of another form, beyond the muted gesticulations of her hands, the echo of the recorded Chopin. The sound of steps being taken in a room connected to this one.

Heavy steps. The steps of a man.

She wills her neck to move, but it ignores her. It is with her eyes, as she lets them roll into their corners, that she is able to see the portal through which the next actor will enter her life—the closed door that leads to the kitchen, a swinging door, the kind of swinging door that once led to her grandmother's kitchen.

The heavy steps slowing at the approach to the door. The sounds of hands, heavy hands, *deliberate hands*, touching the wood.

The candle dancing insanely even before the first inward push of the door. The dim, reclusive angle of candlelight on the face of the wood shifting, diminishing, as the door swings open and hell enters the living room.

CHAPTER 93

THOUGH his form is no more than a lighter shadow against a darker one, Hewitt knows, immediately, the identity of the figure that approaches. Her brain begins to circle like the dancer on the music box, but at a thousand times the speed, until the pedestal can no longer hold and it all begins to shake apart.

In her mind, James Parker Bonson had two distinctive identities. Jimmy Bonbon, the privileged high school boy who eventually grew up. And Jay Boniface, the character he grew into. She now must add a third personality. Jimmy Manson Bonson. Psychopathic killer.

The way he is approaching, the way his body seems to be something other than what it has always been, he is about to become *her* killer.

Was that it? When he transmogrified into the killer, did his body change with his mind?

The walk, zombie-like, as he makes his way through the layers of shadows. Why isn't he looking at her? Why isn't he turning toward her?

The adrenaline surge from the appearance of the monster clears her mind just enough to realize how clouded her thinking has been. Because until this moment, she has been his zombie sister.

They had never done drugs together in high school. But they had done them together tonight. And this event, this gathering, is going to have to pass for it. Their final reunion.

He is almost halfway across the room when he turns his head in her direction, the candle lighting all of his face, but not his eyes. Before the wavering light can find them, he turns away again, walks three more rigor mortis steps, then slows, turns back to her once more.

This time the candle finds his eyes, installing a flame in each.

But the flames only flicker to the music of the nocturne. Recognition, if it is coming, will come from a deeper place.

There is a darkness approaching, a shade, a quality darker than any previously present in the room. It is a darkness she can taste, a darkness she can feel entering her.

A darkness so pure it has evaded her visual sense entirely. The only way she knows it has entered the room with them is the deplorable fact that it has raised, as its flag, a pair of nylon stockings.

CHAPTER 94

FROM behind, this is fine. Unfair perhaps. But this is the agreement. As he expected, there is less struggle than with the others, even though they were older and in worse physical condition.

He knows, however, that as the asphyxiation comes closer to conclusion, this man will find a greater level of resistance to the death that has come to claim him.

There has never been a candle before. But this is fine too. The candle is here for her benefit. *The better to see you.* And more importantly, the better for you to see me. To see him. The way he struggles for his life before you. The way his body fights, but also pleads.

The struggling man has dropped to his knees now, allowing a better view of the woman who watches. He does not like what has happened to her. He understands why it was necessary to bring her here. But he wishes there had been a way to avoid the hitting.

He hates the hitting. He will always hate the hitting.

"I'm sorry."

The sound of his voice surprises him, confuses him. He has offered the words to the woman on the sofa. But the sound of the words mixes with the two other sources of sound in the room. The piano, more distantly. And rising up from this struggling, kicking body on the floor, the gasps and cries of a man unwilling to accept the circumstances of his final moments on earth.

As anticipated, the will of the body is fighting back now. What he didn't anticipate was the degree of the fight.

The fighting body shifts, rolls over suddenly, so that the air from its gasps is pushed in the direction of the candle. Each outpouring of breath causing the flame to scatter wildly. Causing, in turn, the eyes of the woman on the sofa to burn with their own wild light.

For a moment, it appears she will say something. In response to his words of regret? Everything about her mouth and the way it connects with the burning in her eyes suggests she will speak.

But she doesn't. Of course, she can't. It is not permitted. The chemistry of her bloodstream will not allow it.

It is the necessary silence. The silence of peace. The precursor to the total silence, the ultimate peace that awaits her. The return to the beautiful, pain-free place. Where thoughts are love. Where words are music.

His hands, beginning to throb now as the struggle nears its conclusion.

His eyes, however, remaining peaceful, engaged, locked as they are now with the eyes of the lovely being on the sofa.

This lovely being. Different from the others. But through metamorphosis becoming now the image of them, the image of *her*.

"*I'm sorry,*" he tells her, not in the English he has used with the others. But in the Russian he saves only for her.

"*Ya sozhaleyoo.*"

He looks closely for a sign of understanding. Reading her face. Reading her eyes.

He waits.

Waits.

The tiniest dip of her chin then. Her face following the movement. Her mouth quivering to an almost invisible smile. Her eyes steadying as the fire inside them calms.

But beneath him, the calm is not yet fixed. And the body jerks, kicks, violently fighting back one last time, violently fighting to turn over, to see him, to see the face of the one who has finally come to defend her.

CHAPTER 95

HEWITT had never imagined that a killer could kill with such a detachment, a poise, a grace. And she knew, by the nonverbal information he had already shared with her, that the killing wasn't being done for him.

It was being done for her.

Because she was the undead. On temporary loan from the other side. It was clear to her that she would be sent back just as soon as this recital in her honor was completed.

Who would've ever guessed? Betsy Hewitt and Jimmy Bonbon—the most likely to be found drugged and murdered.

The eyes of the killer had abandoned her now. They were focused on Jimmy—really focused—as if he was willing his victim to end the struggle, to accept his fate.

So appalling was it to witness that Hewitt didn't connect with the presence of the form that emerged from the other side of the shadows until it was standing right there with them. Like some chaperone from hell, there to ensure the dead didn't violate their curfew.

Brad Spheeris bloomed up behind the strangulation scene and assumed a stance, an attitude like a proud father come to praise his son's work in a high school play.

Hewitt knew whatever twisted father-son masquerade was being played out, a key point of the performance was this moment. When the father emerged to relish the son's accomplishment.

It was right there in the beaming expression on Brad Spheeris's face. Not maniacal, satisfied murder-lust. But a look of pride. Pure unadulterated pride.

The beaming face nodded lovingly as the son looked up from the last of his work for the affirmation he craved.

For a moment, it held. This utterly human exchange.

Father to son.

Son to father.

Then something in the universe twitched, as if cued by a dissonant phrase in the Chopin. It preceded by no more than a second the shift on the face of Brad Spheeris. Which told Hewitt the universe's twitch had as its origin the face and, almost certainly, the eyes of the almost-son.

For the first time Hewitt noticed the way the killer's hands had seemingly aged during the strangulation. Older. Gnarled. Arthritic. Hands that hurt. She noticed because the hands were beginning to hold the ends of the stockings with a resolve that was, for the first time, less than absolute.

The hands released a few degrees more at the same time their controller's head cocked to the right—as if he was adjusting his vantage point to see his almost-father's face.

The coliseum of murdered souls that ringed Hewitt's brain began to stir.

Brad Spheeris, veteran showman that he was, attempted to reclaim the confident, approving face he had offered seconds earlier. But in the mad dancing light of the candle, his eyes betrayed him. And Hewitt, though she couldn't see the eyes of the almost-son, understood for the first time what they were looking at with such intent.

Slowly, Misha Sharapov looked down at the remains of Jimmy Bonson—his face, the upper part of it. *A snap.* As the killer's head popped back, aligned once more with the face of Brad Spheeris, the upper part of it. *Another snap.* Of something else. From the cerebral-spinal funhouse of Misha Sharapov's brain.

What followed was so rapid, Hewitt's senses were forced to process it in a delayed slow motion. But in the real world, it was deftly orchestrated, with the closing measures of Chopin's nocturne providing the musical score.

The prematurely old hands withdrew from their death grip, prompting Brad Spheeris to bend forward as if to correct what he considered a still-correctable situation. Like a father adjusting his son's grip on a baseball bat. But the son no longer wanted to play. Not this game. Not by these rules.

In the next sway of candle flame, the ends of the stockings floated through the atmosphere. Tandem windsocks on a gentle breeze. But the breeze stiffened. And the stockings flew into the startled face of Brad Spheeris. The arthritic hands reanimated, wrapping the nylons around Spheeris's neck, making the last words that escaped his lungs and throat sound as if they came from some lower form of animal with a higher vocal range.

"Your mother, Misha. Your mother says no."

With what she could summon from the ongoing reclamation of her nervous system, Hewitt pushed a small smile onto her face just as the young man turned to her.

She managed to draw enough juice to barely nod her head. Once. Twice. Each time, making it clear, even in the minimal movement, that she was granting her approval.

A smile bounced back to her, through the candle's illumination. Becoming a grin. The teeth picking up light. The mouth glowing. Until the jack-o'-lantern was burning at full intensity.

And Hewitt, knowing she had only this to offer, grinned back the perfect reflection, as the coliseum of murdered souls rose in an ovation that quietly drowned the final measures of Chopin's piano.

CHAPTER 96

THE beast has died. So he celebrates—*they celebrate*—enjoying this moment of triumph when it has been made good, it has been made right between the three of them.

And so he stands and begins to undress before her. Unafraid, unashamed, unhurt, undamaged. As he was in her eyes, in her hands, before the beast entered their lives.

He watches closely her eyes. Waiting to see if she recognizes him, this quality of him, this nature.

Her smile appears again. The perfect expression of it. As if, totally comfortable with his nakedness, she will be equally comfortable with what is to follow.

The house is quiet now. Chopin is silent. The house version of him. The Chopin that is heard with the world's ears. The outside ears.

For what he is to do next, he will need only his inner ears.

He steps around the outstretched body on the floor. The bad body. The other body—the mistake—this he has returned to the shadows in the corner of the room.

Standing before her in the light, he feels the energy climb his legs, erupt in his pelvis. He hears the first scattered notes of the unwritten Chopin. And with that, he positions his arms and allows himself to be filled with the blood of the dance.

CHAPTER 97

HE danced for what felt like several minutes. But he could have danced for eternity and still she wouldn't have been able to reconcile what she was witnessing.

Serial killers often celebrated their acts in various forms of depraved ritual. But this. This was beyond that. The way he moved around the body. The way he danced around the body. Circling it. In a way that suggested the movements of ballet. But with something else thrown into the choreography. Something more primal. More animal. More bestial.

She could hear it too in his vocalizations. Breathy. Guttural. But with a pattern. As if he were trying to sing without the actual mechanism for song. An ape attempting an aria.

As she read his face, as his eyes fed her the information, she knew he wasn't just celebrating the death for himself. He was celebrating for both of them. And what she feared most, what she feared in the deepest root of her being, was that once the celebrating reached its climax, the final act of her life would begin immediately.

When the ape song ceased. When the demented dancing came to an end. As it was threatening to do. As it was *doing*. Now.

The last dance movements rattled to silence, leaving him standing, perfectly still, with his back to her, on the near side of Brad Spheeris's corpse, so close she could smell him through the burning wax of the candle. She could smell the animal. The animal that would kill her.

She listened to him breathing, knowing the killing would not come with an animalistic attack, but with the softness, the dexterity of a piano-playing angel.

Standing naked in the light of the candle, he held his position. *Meditative*. His head nodding occasionally. Having a conversation with himself. Or like an athlete visualizing his steps.

A final nod, and he began to move to his right. But instead of turning all the way to face her, he stopped midpoint and walked out of the light and into the shadowy recess of the room.

Hewitt heard from the shadows the sound of a zipper, a bag being opened. Then four barefoot steps until he remanifested in the light. A sad smile on his face. A dripping syringe in his right hand.

The show was over. Not just this performance. But the whole run. The staging, the reenactment had been completed. The retribution had been taken. What she was meant to see she had seen.

The world had been made right. The universe was in balance. Except for one missing angel, on loan from God's personal Hummel shelf.

But this angel wasn't ready to fly. She hadn't earned her wings. Yet the smiling, naked monster was kneeling down now at her feet. And she didn't have legs to run away.

It hit her in a crash of thought. How he was going to undress her, undress her at the feet. The way he had done it the first time. For the first injection. The small death. Not the small death the French referred to—the *après orgasm*. Another crash of thought. Dying here now. The death, too, of all that. A sickened regret of having been too much of a good girl. How many orgasms left on the table. A hundred? A thousand?

Amazing, the things you thought of when you were being killed.

He had put her shoes back on after the first syringe. Now he was taking them off. First the left. Then the right—the one she knew, from the feeling, he'd injected the first time. Jesus Christ. This was how she was going to meet it. A paper doll in the hands of a psychopath.

With her foot in his hand, he regarded it, *caressed it*. His head bobbed in the path between her eyes and the candle flame, eclipsing it, eclipsing with it her last contact with hope.

His hand stopped moving, just holding it now. So the other hand could take the syringe.

He began to lift the foot toward his face. He was going to kiss it.

She could feel the heat of his face as the distance closed. Then the feeling of something not as warm as she anticipated. Because it was, at the same time, warm and wet.

His tongue worked her big toe for several seconds, stopped, resumed. Until it became clear to her that this wasn't sexual as much as clinical. He was preparing her, swabbing her. And the feel of that, and what it meant, sent a shudder of protest from her solar plexus that rattled her voice box, numb as it was, enough to emit a small groan. Small, but by far, the most dynamic sound the house had heard since the ending of the Chopin.

The licking stopped. His eyes rose to meet hers.

A flutter of recognition. Not of what she was. But of what he needed her to be.

A flat stone of hope skipped across the pond of Hewitt's mind. Maybe there was some way, some nonverbal way, she could negotiate some more time. Whatever it was, she had to figure it out in the next precious seconds.

But that plan was already dead. Because her little vocalization hadn't deterred him at all. The syringe, trembling, in his dying oak tree of a hand.

Words. Pooling in her head. The arguments against what he was going to do. The way she could spin them into psychological manipulation. Flattery. Sweet nothings. Letters from home. A message in a bottle.

Christ. He was positioning the needle now. Just inches from the nail of her toe. The details of her final pedicure dancing happily in the light. The little flowers. God damn them. What she needed now was a little printed message there instead.

I love you.

At death's door. Hand on the faceted doorknob from her dead grandmother's house. Warmth of her little-girl hand on the cool glass surface.

She could feel him squeezing the top of the toe. Curving the nail. Opening the door.

CHAPTER 98

HE sees the needle pierce the skin of the toe, even before the tip has made contact, sees it as it has appeared in his waking dreams time after time.

Touching the skin, the needle makes a surprising sound. The sound of a human voice. Singing. *Humming.* A single note. A note he recognizes instantly. B flat, above middle C.

The voice holds the note. He holds on the injection, holds to learn if this is an intentional B flat, as opposed to her previous utterance. But this is no utterance. Any more than the G that follows. Again, held longer than expected. But sounded at a pitch that makes it virtually impossible to have been accidental.

This, confirmed with the next note. Yes, they are notes now. The F. The G. The F. The E flat.

His right thumb presses against the top of the syringe. He observes this at the same time his mind positions the thumb on the B flat for the next phrase.

She hums him this note, again, followed by the corresponding G. The middle C. Then, the octave shift above middle C that she manages to carry, slightly sharp, but well enough to proceed.

He looks up, slowly, sees the sheen of appreciation in her eyes, which he knows is reflecting what she sees from him. He does appreciate this. He adores this. Her serenity. Her willingness to return to heaven on the wings of this abridged right hand melody of the nocturne. *Their nocturne.*

Performing it for him this one last time. Not as a fine lady of the keyboard. But as a weary mother, near final sleep, summoning soothing tones for the benefit of her only child.

CHAPTER 99

NEARING the completion of the first round of the melody, she panicked horribly, on two fronts. First, she didn't know enough from the next section to make it viable. Second, the one who would pass judgment on its viability was now not only seated next to her on the sofa, but was leaning against her, *into her*, his head having dropped to her chest, his face pressed insistently against the flesh of her right breast.

Desperation had spit out the only strategy there was. *Stretch the time frame*. Stretch the time by any means possible. Lengthen your wasted life by minutes, seconds, by any Goddamn increment you could grab.

The only weapon she could muster—maternal humming—had granted her a stay. But the fact she'd rolled the dice on an identifiable melody, on a preciously held melody, was the thing that could accelerate the closing of the music book.

It was her worst nightmare. Being in recital, with instant death the penalty for a bad performance.

She was at the end of the part of the nocturne she knew, holding the last notes as long as she could. To the point where it was obviously too long. Because her jury of one made a movement of his shoulders she took as dissatisfaction.

Her eyes found the syringe, still held in his right hand, resting against his thigh. She saw the veins of the top of his hand inflate, saw the tendons twitch.

CHAPTER 100

S HE doesn't smell perfect. But that is the thing about mothers. They don't smell perfect, but that is what makes them perfect.

The singing of a mother is never perfect either. Not even a mother with the great gift of music in her hands and heart and mind. But again, it is the imperfection in the voice that makes the mother's singing perfect.

He returns his head to her chest, lets his ear settle into a quiet place beyond the rustling of the fabric of her shirt.

Her singing has paused. So he hears only the heart. The beat of it loud and banging and *fast*.

As if she is afraid.

He can help her here, can assist her through the transition.

And so he, the son, begins to sing, to hum, picking up the right hand melody, his hummed version of the right hand of Little Chip Chip.

Perhaps this will calm her thoughts, her heart. Enough to let her sing with him one last time.

He nuzzles her breast with his face as he continues to hum. The muscles of his neck, his jaw, initiate the movement that takes his mouth to the center of the breast, the same way it did again and again, relentlessly, in infancy.

He feels the urge to bite. But he does not.

Not yet.

For now he will be content to hum, to offer his song to her. To return the music of Little Chip Chip to its original source.

There. Yes. There now. The mother's song has made its return. With his help. His encouragement.

He leads her. And she follows.

They harmonize. Not perfect. But because of this imperfect musical union of mother and child, they are more perfect than Chopin's angel and the mother of God.

CHAPTER 101

THERE was an angel in the room with her. There had to be. He had withdrawn the needle and set the syringe on the cushion of the sofa. Without having fired the kill shot.

She was still alive. Alive and humming and smelling the mousse in his hair and feeling his mouth nibbling at her nipple.

But she wasn't dead. And for that, she had an angel to thank.

He was on her, like a baby on its mother. He had lifted her shirt, freed the bra. And it was repulsive. It was one of the most instantly repulsive things that had ever happened to her. But taking the needle and going permanently into the night would have been infinitely worse.

The way she calculated it, she had wasted years of her life. Good years. Years that, if she hadn't been so stupid, could've been the best years of her life.

She felt those years now, felt them as she battled to extend her life. For whatever more she could suck out of the world. Even as a killer sucked her tit like there was no tomorrow.

The sick irony of going childless only to end up suckling this man-baby, this killer man-baby. But like any good mother, she played her role.

And so he fed. On the milk that wasn't there. On the memory of a mother long ago remanded to the care of the unseen, unheard angels. A representative of whom Hewitt could only hope was still in the room.

Maybe the suckling son was in heaven too. Already there. If heaven wasn't a place. If heaven was a state of being, maybe this was his. In a perfect fusion of his infantile bliss and his adult ecstasy. Like any mother looking to quiet her infant's cries, she had done her job.

She listened to his contentedness. In the milk-less mimicry, she had mothered him into a position of temporary dependence. And if she could only will her dead arms and hands to move, she could put a chokehold on him that would send him to Limbo.

But she didn't have her hands and arms. Her only weapons continued to be her mind and her voice. So she followed his lead back to the top of the nocturne, did her best to harmonize with him—not just the hummed sounds, but the breathing, the communion. The mother-child bond. So repulsive it made her want to scream her head off. But she couldn't. The baby was content. If the stasis was broken, her umbilical cord to mother earth would be severed forever.

CHAPTER 102

THE piece is complete, and so, too, his feeding.

On both accounts, he is satisfied. And grateful. For this final rendition they have shared. And for the body she has shared and sacrificed for him.

It is time now to release the body and share her with the angels and the muses and the piano-playing satyr who curls up to sleep at God's feet, to keep them warm during the cold nights in heaven.

Her breasts are warm against his face. They are like twin planets facing the sun, basking in the warmth. But night is coming. And it is time for the planets to turn to their dark side.

He feels a quickening of the double-drum that pounds between the planets.

The wild beating of her heart calms his. The peacefulness he craves begins to fill him. He feels the liberation, the acceptance he can only feel when the bad father has been sent to hell and the good mother returns to the starlit concert hall of God.

All is well. He smiles at this thought. Of a town crier walking in the ether of deep space, with his glowing lantern, calling out to the void.

It could be him. This lantern-bearer. Lighting the way for her.

All is well.

He sees this now and smiles again, certain that the movement of his smile muscles can be felt by the skin and nerves of her breasts.

This sweet musical pillow upon which he rests his head.

CHAPTER 103

THE dream ends. And with it, his mother's singing. And in its place has come a scream. A scream, half-dream, half-awake. But not from her throat. Not from his. This piercing noise is coming from his leg.

Awake in the candlelight. Wide screaming awake.

He sees everything, understands everything in his next gasp of breath.

She is wide awake too. And there is nothing about her he recognizes. Her breasts are misshapen. Not the perfect forms they were. Her face is wearing a mask of foreign flesh, her mouth and face pressed into a terrible grimace.

He grabs her cold, skeletal hand, pulls it away from his thigh, pulling with it the needle she has put into him.

He will kill her now. He is free to kill her. The syringe is in his control. There is no fight in her to take it back. No fight . . .

God damn you.

He has flashed the syringe to the light, assessed its contents. Not enough to finish her. Not enough to send her on.

His legs and hips begin to lift him from the sofa. His left hand pushes away from her body, away from the body he had allowed himself to trust.

Across the floor, the candle spilling its flame in the wake of his sudden movement.

The nylons are still there, still attached to the neck of the dead stinking father. He pulls them free, causing the head to turn suddenly to its right, as if to gain a better view for the death.

The stockings flutter, shudder, like the shed skins of twin snakes, as he turns to face her. He freezes in astonishment. The serpent skins fall limp.

She is standing. Standing to receive him. She does not move as he steps toward her, except for a single twitch of her face that reshuffles her eyes, her mouth, her skin into a mask of acceptance, of *peace.*

He will give her this. He will grant her this.

Feet across the floor. Feet, sounding louder than his own feet. From behind him, his mother's voice cries *No* at the same time the mouth of the standing woman forms around the echo of the word.

He is taking the final steps to free her. But someone is walking next to him. Leaning into him. Trying to beat him to her. To *steal* her from him. To keep him from taking what is only his to take.

He reaches out, swings his hand at the nothing that is there. The nothing that is fighting him. The nothing that is pushing him into her. The nothing that is forcing his face between her breasts.

He feels his hands reaching out, finding the top of her head with the stockings, pulling them down until they snag hard against the back of her neck.

Someone is kicking his legs. Down there. Where he can't see. Invisible legs, kicking his.

His hands on the stockings. One twist is all he needs. One more twist. But his legs are falling. His legs are falling. He is pissing. But there is no wet. There is no anything.

His hands, searching desperately for the feel of the stockings. The feel . . .

He grabs at the great twin planets. Hooks his fingers into them. Wills the fingers to be his claws.

God smiles to him across the dark. Through her face. Grants him this.

He holds on.

He will not let go.

Beneath him, the floor, opening. The plasma door to a glowing world below. The strong hands of the dead reaching up to touch him, to take him.

He holds on.

But his claws are hands. Hands that hurt. Hands that will never be perfect again.

CHAPTER 104

ER face wasn't wrapped in bandages. But it felt like it should have been. To make this modern version of *The Twilight Zone* more historically accurate. Then again, the visitor to whom she'd just opened her eyes wasn't historically accurate himself. He wasn't the pig-face from the original Rod Serling nightmare. He was worse. Any panel of leading dermatologists or beauticians would've reached the same conclusion.

"You have one hell of a life."

Hearing the horribly normal voice of John Davidoff speak the words pulled her out of the Twilight Zone and into the hospital room.

"I think the key word there is *hell*," Hewitt managed—weak-voiced, mung-mouthed. She could feel the back of her head throbbing, the stitches pulled too tight.

Davidoff considered her words, the scarred muscle of his face twitching with the movement of his thoughts.

"Don't lose sight of the other key word," he said. *"Life."*

He had gone the full loop around the lake, from stalker to sooth-sayer. Hewitt was glad she'd waited to write her final report on him.

"Are you surprised to see me?"

He was smiling, self-deprecatingly, before he completed the question.

"I guess you can't *not be*," he said. "The whole world is surprised to see me."

It beat the living shit out of waking up to Ritchie Lattimore, Hewitt told herself. Oh, the prick had shown up at the crime scene at the old house, the stunned neighborhood in Berwyn. He'd shaken her hand, said "Nice work." Then he'd crated her flopping fish of a body for immediate shipment, like she was being flown in fresh for the evening meal at Cook County Medical Center.

Someday she'd watch the tape or read the transcript of the news conference he held in her absence. Someday, when she was sure she had plenty of saltines and Seven-Up to counteract the nausea.

But life wasn't fair. Five princesses, five kings could tell you that. From wherever they were. If the afterlife was fair, some lovely castle in the sky.

Officer John Davidoff could tell you about the fairness of life too. He was telling Hewitt now. Not in so many words. But in the spaces between them.

"I just wanted you to know . . ."

Lying there in the hospital room, it felt like a tonsillectomy could have been performed in the pause that ensued.

". . . I think a hell of a lot of you."

Hewitt hadn't felt real live tears in her eyes in a while. There was no *not* feeling them now.

"I also want you to know . . ."

Similar pause. An appendectomy this time.

". . . that I'm not some crazy stalker."

"I already know that," Hewitt told him.

Behind the mask, his eyes softened and seemed to lose their ability to focus—like a newborn's.

"Now that you know that, I won't bother you again."

"It's okay," Hewitt said. "Bother me again."

It was like a condor dropping suddenly from a low perch. The way he came at her from across the bed.

His mouth touched her cheek. A kiss. But harder, tougher, because of his lips. A love-peck from the same condor.

She knew he had been waiting a long time to do that. And she could tell, as he withdrew and turned and silently exited the room, that that was enough. That he was satisfied. Relieved. Happy as hell with himself.

CHAPTER 105

"I have two hands. I want you to take the one without the IV and hold it."

Hewitt let the words bang around in the back of her memory.

"Yes," Hewitt said. "I remember saying that."

She reached out over the clean white landscape of hospital cotton, took Brady's hand, the right one, the same one he'd used to knock on heaven's door while the rest of him had lain there bleeding to death. But apparently God hadn't been home. And there was evidence he'd made a little visit to the garage loft of Misha Sharapov.

"So how hilarious is it that you're there and I'm here? And I can say the same damn thing to you. Which I probably shouldn't have done. But the drugs are empowering me to say whatever the hell I think."

Hewitt gave Brady's noninfused hand a little squeeze. But only for the second and a half Brady let her before he pulled the hand back.

"No way," he said. "The last thing I need from you right now is that."

Something about the configuration of those words made his painkiller slurring sound more pronounced to Hewitt.

"Because the next thing you know I'll start relaxing. And a few minutes after that I'll be out. And that's the one thing in life I can't afford."

He paused to take a couple of breaths. Even that seemed affected by the painkillers. As if his breathing were slurred too.

Hewitt didn't press him to continue. Because she already knew where it was going.

"The only thing that scares me more than a psychopath putting a hot one in my gut is a crazy woman getting artsy with my privates again."

He wasn't going to dump her over this. Not over something as superficial as a gunshot wound to his abdomen that required nine hours of surgery to save his life. It was the price you paid for keeping an eye on your little sister. A little sister who would somehow always manage to be older than you.

"That's a relief." Hewitt smiled. "For a minute there I thought you were going to give me my walking papers."

"It's the painkillers talking," he said, extending his hand again.

Hewitt took it. Held it. Inhaled. Exhaled. Breathed with him, in his rhythm, for several cycles, as if they were attached to the same breathing machine.

Maybe they were attached in that way, she thought. Maybe a couple of near-death experiences in the same twenty-four hours were the kind of thing you could build a real relationship on.

A little more than ten minutes later, Brady dropped off into a deep pain-killed sleep. He'd definitely earned it. Not only for fighting to stay alive, but for fighting to stay awake long enough to help Hewitt fill in the blanks for what had transpired in the attic apartment of Mary Frances Eau Claire's garage.

Misha Sharapov hadn't been the shooter, hadn't even been there. Brad Spheeris had fired the gun. Spheeris had smacked Hewitt on the back of the head with the same firearm. Spheeris had been the one hidden away in the armoire. Of course, people didn't hide unless they knew someone was seeking. Which meant Spheeris had been following her. When she'd stopped at the Highland Park PD, he had made the jump ahead to her visit to the Eau Claire estate. So he went there. Waited. Hid his vehicle on the grounds. Set himself up in Misha Sharapov's little dream world.

But none of it mattered now. All it meant for Hewitt was an affirmation that Misha Sharapov couldn't have been the one who hit her. After whatever hellacious violence he had seen done to his own mother, he couldn't hurt a woman. He could only put them to sleep. He could only send them back to heaven.

Brady had been knocking on that door himself. Hewitt was happy as hell he'd come back. The angels, especially the unmarried ones, would have to wait.

CHAPTER 106

JIMMY Bonson lived too. But not to tell about it. At least not at first. And from what his ears, nose and throat doctor told him—with an emphasis on throat—probably never in the same mellifluous tones again.

Which wasn't so bad if you played the trumpet for a living. But if you crooned classically over the airwaves on a daily basis, it was a little more problematic.

For Hewitt, it was problematic as well. Because Jimmy Bonson had a lot of talking to do. So from the comfort of his own hospital bed, with his voice box on standby and his throat moistened by a headset humidifier, Jimmy Bonson responded to her questions via Pilot *Precise* and 3×5 cards.

Hewitt had a decent-sized stack in her hand already. All pertaining to the events that had gone down the night his voice had gone quiet.

His information was succinct, edifying, not without humor.

Misha Sharapov had surprised him in the parking lot, put him under with chloroform, and that was the last he remembered until he woke up unconscious at the old house.

He was so drugged when he was pushed out of the kitchen, he only vaguely remembered Hewitt sitting on the sofa. He did, however, have a more vivid memory of the stockings around his neck.

He penned another note, asking Hewitt about the house where they'd all ended up almost dead together.

"It belonged to Misha Sharapov's aunt. One of the people who brought him over here originally. Apparently she died in her sleep several months ago. Coroner's office is deciding whether or not to exhume her and run toxicology."

Another card. *What the hell does it matter now?*

"I'm not sure it does. I'm not even sure her nephew would've been the one to juice her. Spheeris probably had plans for the house early on. To use it for staging."

With the subject of Bradley Spheeris broached, it was time for some additional Q&A. About the real reason Jimmy Bonson had fired him. About whatever the hell it was that made him want Jay Boniface dead.

Jimmy B still needed to take it easy with his humidified breathing. So once the questions had been voiced, he actually took his pen and wrote the words: *Deep breath. Pregnant pause.*

After a gestation period of half-a-minute or so, he began to write.

Hewitt's mom had always kept her recipes on 3×5s she warehoused in a little dime-store treasure box. She could see her mother's handwriting, the neat quasi-Victorian script in blue Bic, could see, in particular, her recipe for Chicken & Wild Rice Casserole. She could smell the dish too, with some serious olfactory imagination added to the prelunch smell of Chicken *Something* coming from the hospital's food service.

Jimmy B had completed three more cards. He sucked in some humidified mist, handed her the first one.

This is between us, right?

"Until I write my memoirs," Hewitt responded. "And that isn't exactly a priority in my life. So I wouldn't sweat it."

He nodded, said *okay* with his eyes, with the released muscles of his face, said he trusted her. Why the hell not? If she hadn't destroyed the monster, he would've still been lying on that living room floor.

She reached out over the bed, took the next card from his extended hand.

I fired him because he wanted my radio station. Spheeris and Mary Eau Claire, with backing from some other Queens Club members, were trying to buy me out. They threatened to pull their support if I didn't sell. It was all a power trip for Spheeris.

"Okay, that I get," Hewitt said. "A power grab by an egomaniac.

Where have I seen that in human history before? Obviously his power trip didn't end there."

He nodded yes, wrote fast without scribbling, handed her the next card.

It went beyond pressure to coercion. I had a thing with a violinist from the Chicago Symphony. She liked the Liquid Decadence too. She also liked Las Vegas. Spheeris knew about the affair, threatened to tell my wife. I refused to let him intimidate me. So he told her.

He stopped there as if that were all there was to tell on the subject. Hewitt sensed otherwise. "I won't be able to accurately write my memoirs unless you tell the whole story."

Jimmy Bonson got that, nodded, gave her a half-wink, a fractional smile as he began to write.

My wife left me. And after some kind of weekend binge in heaven, God decided it would be her fate to hook up with Spheeris.

"When's the last time you talked to her?" Hewitt offered, concerned the body count might rise even more.

Jimmy Bonson wrote his answer, not exactly overjoyed about it.

She came to visit me this morning. Apparently she and Spheeris have broken up.

"She's a lucky woman," Hewitt said.

He nodded. Looked away. Looked away as if he wished he never had to look back at any of the sordid shit that had come to orchestrate itself in his quiet little radio station.

"And now I've got a few little revelations for you," Hewitt said. "For *your* memoirs."

He lifted his hands to his ears, cupped them forward.

"It's pretty clear to me your buddy still had designs on WCLS."

Jimmy Bonson moved his hands away from his head, but his ears didn't quite return entirely to their originally position.

"We found a gun on him at the house in Berwyn. The same one he used to shoot my colleague. He also had a bottle of unscented cleanser. So he could wipe away his own prints and leave Misha Sharapov's. *Plant* them. After Misha had made the decision to shoot himself, of course."

Jimmy B inhaled. Carefully. Deeply. He opened his mouth to speak. *"Game. Set. Match."*

The rasp of his voice was as harsh as the look in his eyes. His pen started moving over another note card.

Would he have gotten away with it?

"Hard to say. There would've been strong suspicion. Whether a case could've ever been brought, who the hell knows? But I've got to give him credit. He was a damn good planner. I guess that's why he was so good at programming all those lovely nighttime selections for you."

Jimmy B had composed one last card.

I'll have to hire a new person.

"Suggestion," Hewitt said. "Let me do the background check."

CHAPTER 107

T HE young blond woman in the long black dress takes the stage to polite applause that seems to surprise her, embarrass her. As she approaches the piano bench, the handheld camera wobbles. Almost as if to anticipate a stumble from her, the result of equal parts self-consciousness and unfamiliar high heels.

But there is no stumble. Just a pause to adjust the left strap of her black dress as she sits down. She takes a preparatory breath, pauses to adjust the right side strap.

Allowing her hands to rest, palms down, against her thighs, she composes herself. She doesn't lift her hands to the piano then as much as the hands lift her.

The piece begins. And it begins as if it has never ended. As if it has never *not* been playing.

The camera wobbles again, but there is no waver in the music.

Hewitt turns away from the TV monitor to look at the eyes of the pianist's son. Not yet born when this performance was filmed. But all grown up now. All grown up and dressed in his Cook County jumpsuit, shackled at the feet and hands. But judging from the look in his eyes, totally unbound in his mind.

"It is beautiful," he says.

"Yes," Hewitt agrees.

"*We* are beautiful."

"We?"

"She is pregnant with me here," he tells her. "Even though I cannot see, I have a front row seat."

He smiles as he says this.

Hewitt, in the absence of candlelight and Ketamine, was under no pressure to return his smile. But her face started going there, and it took a concerted effort of muscle and skin to pull it back.

Misha Sharapov also had a front row seat for his mother's final performance as an earthbound soul. This he had been willing to share with Pete Megna in the hours after his apprehension and his recovery from Hewitt's attempt to permanently anesthetize him.

As the playing of his mother, Ekaterina, continued to cascade from the television speakers, Hewitt let her imagination run the movie from that final performance. Not a musical performance, but a dance. A dance choreographed by his mother's second husband. A dance involving just two performers. And a single prop. A pair of nylon stockings.

All of it played out to a mesmerized audience. An audience of one. A five-year-old boy with beautiful, some said perfect, hands.

"She plays wonderfully, does she not?"

His eyes were fused to the TV screen, to this video ghost. It had been Hewitt's job to deliver the tape from the garage apartment, from the drawer of the rolltop desk. This was the arrangement Hewitt had negotiated with him.

Tape for talk.

So far, the talk had been one-sided. The creator of ghosts had been more than willing to offer his story. As long as the ghost of his mother continued to play. And he'd offered it in an almost fully Americanized voice, with only an occasional vestige of a Russian accent.

"She was the winner of this competition. As you listen, she is winning. From her playing, there is no possibility the judges could decide otherwise."

Hewitt was watching the way his misshapen hands were responding to certain passages in the music. With a lift, a twitch, even though they were confined by the big institutional bracelets.

"Was this a Chopin competition?" Hewitt posed.

"Yes," he said slowly, gauzily. "She was a student of Chopin. More accurately, she was a daughter. She had two fathers in this way. Her birth father, Alexander. And her musical father, Frédéric."

For the first time since the tape began running, his eyes released a little from their pursuit of the images. His head dipped slightly, his eyes finding his hands. Hands that became motionless. Hands that seemed to die.

"I, as well, had two fathers."

Everything in the room shuddered. Even the air. Hewitt felt it reverberate in her own spine, knowing ground zero was a fault line somewhere inside the harmless-looking young man in the chair beside her.

"My birth father was a professor of languages at Moscow State University. An intellectual. An anticommunist. He was one of the last wave taken to the gulags before Gorbachev and glasnost. He died in the gulag of pneumonia within a year. That was the story. I was two. My mother had little means. Piano not being a viable source of income. She married out of desperation. To my second father."

Hewitt checked her notes from Megna.

"His name was Leonenko."

Misha Sharapov looked at her from the far side of hell.

"No. His name was *Suh-tahn-ah*."

Hewitt heard it that way, wrote the phonetics in her notebook. Around her, the air was shuddering again, caused, this time, by her own intake of breath.

"What did he do to them?" she asked, nodding at his hands.

He tried to smile, but his face rejected it. On the TV monitor, his mother had just completed Chopin's "Nocturne in G." After smiling uneasily in acknowledgment of the applause, she began her signature piece.

Misha watched his mother, listened to her, dreamed a brief but pleasant dream.

"I was going to be all the things she could not. I was going to come to the West. To America. I knew this. She told me this. I was going to play for her. To be her heart. To be her hands. For the world."

There was no shudder of the room this time. Just one great sigh of resignation.

"What did he do to your hands?" Hewitt said softly.

"I will give one clue," he offered, a painful curl at the corners of his lips. "The most popular ballet of Tchaikovsky is the one Tchaikovsky most hated."

Hewitt didn't know the hate. But she did know the popular.

"The Nutcracker."

He nodded, receded into a shadow of his own conjuring.

"After she was gone, I was the only thing left of her."

Hewitt started to see the pictures.

"Each knuckle of each hand. And both thumbs."

"He broke them?"

"Yes."

"With a . . ."

"Yes."

His mother continued to bathe them in Chopin. But it wasn't enough to keep Hewitt's ears from going to her own sound effects library. To the sound of small bones cracking in the laughing mouth of a Christmas toy.

"I'm sorry," Hewitt said. "I'm very sorry."

He gave her a fractured look of acknowledgment. Hewitt understood.

"And why did he kill her, Misha?"

For several measures, the "Nocturne in E flat" played brilliantly.

"She was pregnant with my half-brother," he said. "My half-brother. But not his full son."

Hewitt watched him, listened to his mother. She put her pen away, gently closed her notebook. Someday some shrink could finish the notes, could write the damn book. *MSNBC* could do an all-time great "Dark Heart–Iron Hand." They could fill in all the details. How Father Two, Vladimir Leonenko, had put a gun to his own head moments after strangling his wife and maiming his stepson's hands. How the stepson had felt cheated by that act of cowardice, cheated of the chance to one day make the stepfather pay for the worst thing a human being had ever done.

From there, the chronicle would tell how Mikhail "Misha" Sharapov had emigrated to America, to Chicago, within a year of the tragedy, with an aunt and uncle on his mother's side. The Americanization, the school years, including three semesters at a technical college at the behest of his aunt, studying as a pharmacy technician. How, a few years later, lying awake at night, with his radio on, he had been mesmerized, moved, motivated to contact the person at the station who understood what it felt like to be him at three o'clock in the morning. How, from that contact, evil chance, antiserendipity, had allied him with a man who harbored the latent genes of serial murder but was only able to experience it vicariously. The result, the perfect Molotov cocktail of Spheeris's sociopathy blending with Misha's post-traumatic psychosis. From there, anything was possible. Anything.

Hewitt knew her royal musings about kings and princesses, executioner and mystic, had been close. But the true dynamic had been simpler. Classically so. It was Beauty and the Beast. Beauty in all its variations. Beast in all its forms. With one mad, masked avenger trying to put the world back in order.

"I have only one more question," Hewitt said. "And then we can enjoy the rest of the performance."

He waited. Hewitt waited too. The music played. Chopin and his descendents lived once more.

"The table," Hewitt said. "The picnic tables."

Four, eight, twelve measures of the nocturne pleasured him as he thought.

"You know the American film *Citizen Kane?*"

Hewitt nodded.

"The table . . . The table is my *Rosebud.*"

Hewitt left it there, joined him in the audience for the rest of the Chopin recital, let the picnic scenes of mother and child from her own memories play against the backs of her eyes.

CHAPTER 108

T HE twentieth reunion of Hewitt's Wheaton West High School
class was held on the first Saturday after the Fourth of July. Hewitt
struggled with her decision of whether or not to attend. If she went,
there would be a lot of questions, a lot of staring, and no shortage of
under-the-breath comments from people who made a pastime of such
commentary. Not that she couldn't handle it.

If there was one thing she'd learned in the two decades since her
naked-under-the-robe graduation, it was how to take a hit, how to survive.

She was a celebrity. But not exactly for reasons to celebrate. That,
however, wasn't enough to keep her away from this one. She had sent
in the form. She had committed to the chicken.

She had even contacted Jimmy Bonson to find out what he was
thinking. But he had his own celebrity to deal with now, which was no
cause for celebration either. Hewitt had visions of the two of them driving up together in a classic white Camaro. They could find one to rent
from somewhere. Maybe even get the dubious-celebrity discount.

But Jimmy B wasn't ready. He was still on the mend. His head more
than his throat. Although he did get off one good line concerning the
type of thing he hoped to avoid by sitting it out.

"I could just hear Ricky Carlisle, giving me the once-over. Saying:
Hey, Jimmy. Nice sport coat. And nice *neckwear*."

That was where they left it. Because it felt right. They were two
people, in the great back-and-forth. Never wanting to exit a conversation, a situation, a life, without some tacitly agreed upon and mutually
acceptable ender, sound bite, sign-off. To leave a little something that
was somehow less than meaningless at the end of the day.

Something, well, something hopeful.

She had heard that same tone, that sense of hopefulness, odd as it was, from Jen Spangler's voice when she called the morning of the reunion.

It hadn't been there when she led off by telling Hewitt about the surgery that had been scheduled for her father the next week. The doctor's suspicion that one of the bypasses was leaking in a way imperceptible to the imaging equipment.

Hewitt, of course, pledged everything she had to pledge in the way of support at that point. So when the optimism level of Jen Spangler's voice rose, Hewitt had no choice but to bag the idea of going solo to the reunion, no other option than to release the damn chicken.

"I don't know if he ever mentioned this, but he started going to church again," Jen Spangler told her. "After the first operation. For the first time since my mom died."

THE whole thing would have looked better from the Ferris wheel. That perspective. The bird's-eye view. But she wasn't on the Ferris wheel. And all she could do was look at the big, light-bejeweled, double-spinning wheel from her crazy seat on the Tilt-A-Whirl.

Who would have ever guessed that a couple of weeks after her experiments in pharmacology with Misha Sharapov, she would be sharing a G-force-gyrating love seat with Jen Spangler at a church festival of the Catholic persuasion?

But Ed Spangler had been baptized, confirmed, married and had sent his beloved wife back to God at St. Eugene's Catholic Church.

And now here he was, making some kind of last stand at the St. Eugene's festival. No, it wasn't a last stand. He would survive the surgery. Not only that, he would get better. Right? The cardiac surgeons with all their little cameras and robotic assistance and miracle utensils would finally fix him up, make him all better. Right? Please?

It was hard to pray on a Tilt-A-Whirl. Praying would have been a hell of a lot easier on the Ferris wheel. From that place. Way up high.

Even if she was still paired with Jen Spangler up there, at least Jen wouldn't have been shrieking and laughing her ass off like she was now. At least Jen's pelvis wouldn't be fusing with hers with every damn tilt and whirl.

But that was just it. Tilt-A-Whirls were made to make you goofy. And that seemed like the totally appropriate place for her to be. In the centrifugal lunacy of that. With her thoughts speeding, shifting, spinning.

Translated to English, *Suh-tahn-ah* was Satan. And obviously an argument could be made that only the Prince of Darkness himself could have visited little Misha and his mother.

Thoughts of the case—whirling, tilting . . .

The irony that with the end of the death penalty in Illinois, Misha Sharapov couldn't be subjected to a lethal injection of his own.

How Brad Spheeris had unwittingly played *both* fathers to Misha. Intellectual birth father. And the substitute father from hell.

The fuzzy, *hairy* line between life and death. If Jimmy Bonson hadn't been such a stickler for personal grooming. If Brad Spheeris had just kept up with his trimming.

With the death penalty off the table, the thought that the inmates at Misha's final lockup point would be well advised to keep their own eyebrows under control.

The image from the photo album they'd found in the rolltop desk drawer. The wedding picture of mother and second father. Petite, tragic Madonna. And Rasputin-eyed, Brezhnev-browed monster.

The reciprocal nature of Misha Sharapov's inability to punish his murderous stepfather and society's inability to punish Brad Spheeris for aiding and abetting the murder-crazed stepson.

But punishment would come, wouldn't it? If not in this world, then in the next. And peace and joy would come in that same next world to those whose lives had been lost. Hewitt wanted to believe that. Surely the hundreds of Saturday night revelers on the St. Eugene's playground believed that.

At the Tilt-A-Whirl exit, Captain Ed Spangler was trying again to believe. Not just for himself and whatever life he had left on this earth. But for the granddaughter he held in his arms, as he watched his real daughter and his almost-daughter come whirling into view for the last time before the ride slowed and, with a series of metallic screeches and groans, came to a stop.

Hewitt wanted to ride the Ferris wheel. But the line for that mystical experience was still long. And there were just a few Christian thrill-seekers waiting for the next run of the Tilt-A-Whirl.

"That was fun," Jen Spangler giggled.

Her father heard that and, in one smooth motion, shifted the baby to his left arm while his right hand reached for his wallet.

"Stay on," he called from a distance that made it impossible to tell which of the girls he was looking at. "Take one more ride. Daddy's buying."